REMNANTS

Raegan of Ruin Book Four

A. L. Rook

PLAYLIST

Right Here - Ashes Remain

Rush - The Score

Can't Stop Me Now - The Score

White Flag - Bishop Briggs

The Fear - The Score

Angel with a Shotgun - The Cab

Another Level - Oh The Larceny

Born Ready - Dove Cameron

Slow Hands - Niall Horan

Body - Rosenfeld

Taste of You - REZZ

Higher - The Score

Born Ready - Zayde Wolf

Follow You - Bring Me The Horizon

Demons - Imagine Dragons

Gladiator - Zayde Wolf

Unstoppable - Sia

Take It All - Valley of Wolves

Next Level - Mountains vs Machines

Made for This - Carrollton

Raise Hell - Dorothy

Bones - Saint Phnx

Fire Up the Night - New Medicine

All This Power - WAR*HALL

Wild Things - Alessia Cara

Middle of the Night - Our Last Night

Never Be The Same - Camila Cabello

Strip That Down - Liam Payne

Moon - The Cab

I Think I'm In Love - Kat Dahlia

Lights Down Low - Max

I'm Dangerous - The Everlove

Burn - 2WEI

Spotify

TABLE OF CONTENTS

Chapter One

RAEGAN

Darkness engulfs the elevator.

Dane curses, drawing back from our embrace to check his phone. He strides to the panel, tapping each button as if one of them might work while the others do nothing.

The moment he walks away, Gordon's voice whispers to me, rising unbidden from memories in the pitch-black water tank.

"You're worthless."

No. Not now.

"No one cares about you other than me." His twisted voice fills my head, leaving no room for anything but him and the fear that always slipped past my defenses when it came to him. It spreads through my veins like poison, binding me in place.

My heart gallops, and my breathing shallows. Even though I can't see anything, it feels like the world spins in tight circles around me. I clutch at my chest, dragging in air that seems empty of the oxygen I desperately need.

"Fuck, everything's down. There's no power running to anything, and I can't get any calls out. Someone must be blocking our communications."

"You're a monster."

I grab my head with shaking hands, my eyes screwed shut.

Stop! Get out of my head! You're not here.

"It would be better for you to be alone."

You're dead. Thorne stabbed you in the back.

"You'll never be rid of me. Just accept it and give yourself to me, my pet."

"Rae?"

A wave of dizziness rolls through me, and I drop to my knees, gasping.

"Rae! Hey. Look at me."

"You're useless without me."

"You're safe. I'm right here."

Something strokes my cheek. It's warm and gentle, and I try to focus on it.

"Come back to me, Rae."

Slow, comforting words. This time, when I breathe in, it feels like a full intake of oxygen. The panic eases.

"What can I do to help?"

I listen to his voice. His words. The care in his touch. Gordon's voice begins to fade, and I lower my hands to latch on to his arm. As I open my eyes, a soft white glow illuminates the small space, fighting back the dark.

It's the light from Dane's gift, but even with his touch, I can feel my own power stirring, alive and ready, deep in my gut. I'm grateful he isn't muting it, or that may have triggered a whole new spiral.

His forehead touches mine, his eyes closed. "Take whatever time you need. I'm not going anywhere."

I nod once against him, taking another long breath, while my heart rate eventually slows to its normal pace. I keep my eyes open. It helps to see the elevator walls, the floor, and especially Dane to remind myself that I'm not back with Gordon. I'm not in solitary or the water pod alone.

Frustration swells and burns in my chest. What a shitty time for me to have a freak out, although I can't say if there's ever a *good* time for it. Maybe when no one else is around to see me. But definitely not when we may be under attack, and there are other things I should be doing.

Another breath.

Moisture gathers in my eyes, but I grit my teeth.

I'm fine.

Safe.

Gordon isn't here. He may even be dead, though I won't trust it until I see him for myself.

The Guild is in trouble. Aiden and Jack aren't here to help while they're fighting Thorne at the butcher shop. It's up to Kellan, Dane, and me to keep everyone safe.

"I'm okay," I mumble, and his eyes snap open.

"Rae!" He crushes me in a tight embrace. "Thank fuck. I wasn't sure what to do or if I'd make anything worse."

I grip his back like it's my lifeline to sanity. My voice is muffled against his hoodie. "Sorry you had to see that."

He pulls back just enough to capture my face with his thumb and forefinger. "Don't do that."

"Do what?"

"Apologize for something like that." His thumb grazes over my lower lip. "If you ever want to talk about it or need to get something off your chest, I'll listen."

I nod, too embarrassed to voice a reply.

Dane smiles. It's the sweet one that induces butterflies to run rampant in my stomach, making me feel like a sixteen-year-old girl with a crush again.

"Good. Now, we need to get to our room so we aren't sitting ducks here. Any chance you can make a hole in the doors without getting the rest of the elevator?" He lowers his hand from my face, though his other arm is still curled around my back, and the light from his gift fades.

I snatch his wrist without thinking as soon as I see the glow weakening. "Wait. I...I need that." To keep Gordon away and for my next task, but I'll keep the former detail to myself.

He brings it back without question, holding his palm up in front of me to give me the most light without blinding me.

"Thanks. Shine it on the doors so I can see what I'm doing." We both stand, and I shift to the side so I'm not blocking the light. I press my hands against the cool metal, drawing my gift out, slow and steady. The heat of my gift burns away any remaining doubt, returning my strength to me as I lock down the memories of my time with Gordon again.

The metal groans, *cracks*, as I stretch my gift outward. Once I have the size I'm looking for, I stop my gift from spreading and send a burst through the existing cracks.

The door disintegrates to ash.

Frowning, I stare at the elevator shaft wall.

Dane steps up to the edge, his hand fisting and bumping against the concrete wall. There's maybe a handful of inches between the elevator and the wall, which isn't enough for us to squeeze between.

I grip the edge of the opening, peeking out as far as I can fit to look up and down. There's a shadow of concrete jutting out far above us. "Could that be one of the floors?" I point, and Dane's gaze follows it, his brows pinched.

"I fucking hope so, or else we're trapped."

"I could always break one of the cables, and we could try jumping onto one of the floors while we fall."

Dane stares at me. "I hope you're joking."

Shrugging, I turn my attention to the square panel in the ceiling for emergency exits. "Unless you have a better idea…"

"I do," he counters, moving around me. "Living. That's a better idea." He bends a knee and interlocks his hands to make a stirrup above it. "Here."

I grasp his shoulder, place my foot in his hands, then push myself up with his help. I hit the panel and it knocks open without resistance. Gripping the edge, I work to pull myself up as he lifts me underneath until I can hold myself up by my forearms.

"Yes! There's a floor a few feet up."

He curses in relief. "Scoot back, and I'll help you down. Then you can help me, and I can pull you up."

I do as he asks, shifting and then dropping down with his guidance. We switch spots, with me offering him a lift instead this time and he pulls himself up all the way. He lies on his front and reaches for me through the opening.

"Ready?"

I answer with my hand in his. He pulls up, surprising me with his strength when he hauls me up and against him before falling back. We lie there panting, his heart pounding against my ear and my body suddenly aware of the firm muscle beneath me. I wouldn't have expected him to stay so fit while he'd been cooped up in the Tower all those years, but he clearly didn't waste that time sitting in front of a computer all day.

He slides his arms around me, tightening his grip and holding me securely to his chest as he catches his breath. My pulse quickens, as he strokes down my back.

"Dane…"

"I know. Just a few seconds…please."

He draws a deep breath, then releases me.

Standing, I help him up with a small smile and then palm the closed elevator doors of the nearest floor. My gift eats away at the doors as it had done the last time, leaving nothing but ash in its wake when I'm finished. Dane and I repeat our last steps, boosting him and then pulling me onto the open floor.

Groaning, I roll onto my side and then stand. I take Dane's hand between both of mine. "Do you trust me?"

He blinks at our hands, then raises his gaze to mine. "Yes," he answers without hesitation.

Now it's my turn to stare as I'm thrown by his immediate response. Even though I hoped he would say that, I had at least expected a bigger delay. "Oh. Uh, good," I mutter, gathering my scattered wits back and lowering our hands. "Then come with me."

His lips press to a thin line. "Where?"

"To check on the Guild members first, then find Kellan. The power cutting out like that wasn't a coincidence. And most of the Guild doesn't know how to fight, right?"

Dane watches me quietly, his amber gaze intense as he considers what I'm asking. I know why Kellan wanted us to go hide, but that was when he only thought Harvey was up to no good. But the power outage means that it's a much larger attack.

We never should have left Kellan.

"Alright." He squeezes my hand. "But promise you won't leave my side. If we're going out there to fight, we stick together."

"Promise. And same to you."

We share a smile, then release each other and break out into a run to search the floor.

Chapter Two

KELLAN

There were days, not long ago, where I would have given anything to feel the swift rush of adrenaline through my veins. To feel the firm, if eager, beat of my heart at the prospect of something out of my control.

To feel *alive*.

Back then, nothing and no one could hurt me. Not even myself.

But now I realize that my fear doesn't come from myself. It comes from the others; from her.

From the fear of losing the people precious to me.

This time, the thrill of danger doesn't make my pulse race with anticipation.

It makes my muscles tighten and temper sharpen in preparation for a fight.

"The door to the quarantine area opened on its own. Is that something? Or maybe we have a ghost?"

There's no reason for Harvey to be on that floor. Even though he'd been on the island team to rescue the people who are staying in quarantine, he doesn't have clearance to enter that area on his own. For him to open the door unaccompanied—and while invisible—it can only mean he's up to no good.

Raegan's worried gaze seeks mine as the elevator doors close between us. Every fiber of my being screams at me to go to her, to wrap her in my arms and act as her shield and armor.

But if there's even an ounce of truth in what Gordon said to Aiden and Jack at the butcher shop, if Harvey is somehow involved with GE, then it's my responsibility to protect the Guild. And to keep Dane and Raegan as far away from them as possible.

The smile plastered on my face is stiff from the effort of it, but I keep it in place until the elevator doors shut. Raegan has enough on her mind with Gordon's possible death and keeping Dane safe. If there's anyone she should feel the least amount of worry over, it's me.

My gift should put her at ease, and yet, she was watching me like she was preparing to dive out of the elevator to get to me.

I throw open the stairwell door and leap down the flights of stairs, bursting through the door once I've reached the quarantine floor. The double doors, which are locked by a security code only a handful of members have, are wide open.

A hand is visible behind one of the doors on the floor, its palm upward and unmoving.

The need for violence coils in my chest.

Harvey. What did you do?

Running, I yank the door open the rest of the way to reveal Claudia's still form on the ground. I drop to my knees and curse at the mess of blood on her neck. I carefully draw her eyes to a close. She'd been the one to help the rescues through their trauma, to reverse any brainwashing and ease them back to some sort of normalcy. Claudia had no gift. Just the desire to help people like us with her medical training.

She didn't deserve to die like this.

She didn't deserve to die at all.

I grind my teeth, fisting my hands and gazing furiously at the carnage of the room beyond her: overturned and broken tables. Chairs scattered around the room on their sides and backs. Whatever happened here, there'd been a fight. But now, there's not a single soul in sight after Claudia.

There's no way they could have fought and disappeared in the time it took me to come downstairs after Harvey arrived. After getting the call from security, he'd *just* arrived at the entrance, and I'd come down as soon as Raegan and Dane left in the elevator. That was a few minutes at most...hardly enough time to cause this level of damage. How much earlier did it begin? And by who?

A sniffing noise brings my attention to Claudia's desk. Standing, I stalk around it and find Harvey quivering in a ball and covered in blood. I snap, grabbing him roughly by the shirt and hauling him into the air to slam him into the wall.

"What did you do?!" I snarl viciously. "Where is everyone?"

His face is a mess of tears and snot. Rather than looking at me, his pale blue eyes swing over my shoulder and go round with fear.

Sharp pain stabs between my shoulders in a breath-wrenching surprise attack. Fluid rushes up my throat, and I hack the blood from my lungs. Every instinct in me screams to remove the blade from my back as soon as possible. Pushing through the pain, I throw my elbow back between coughs, dropping Harvey in the hope of striking the spineless attacker behind me.

The knife yanks free before I can land a hit, but that's all I need. I lean on my knees to finish coughing the fluid out, then gasp for air. The deep wound tingles, then buzzes stronger as my flesh reunites and hardens to scales.

"Fascinating," a voice muses, sounding pleased.

Shifting to face my attacker while keeping Harvey in my peripheral view, I rise, then freeze when I see who it is.

Charles Whitmore.

Raegan's father.

The older man smiles, then licks my blood off his knife like a goddamn psycho.

"What the hell is wrong with you?" I demand, my voice still rough. "Are you behind all this?"

Charles wipes the rest of the blood from the blade on his pants. "You know," he starts conversationally, "the more I'm out in the field lately, the more I see the failures of those in my employ." He inspects the knife like he's checking his reflection on both sides, smiling all the while. "Gordon, for example. Now, he had great promise. Fantastic control over his gift. He could see the potential in others' gifts as well. Or so I once believed."

"Fuck the storytelling bullshit," I growl.

"Ah, well. You'll want to hear the rest of this, I think. I know that patience is a learned skill, but this *is* about you in the end."

I could give two shits what this man has to say about me. The rest of the gifted rescues here are gone. Claudia is dead. Is the rest of the Guild under attack right now? Did Raegan and Dane make it to the room and lock it down? "What did you do to the others? Where are they?"

"Since you all brought me here to your lovely...shelter, I've witnessed many amazing gifts. Ones which would greatly benefit GE, if only Gordon hadn't been so...*focused* on a lost cause."

He tosses the knife aside, then reaches behind his back and pulls out a gun. "Now *your* gift, I like. I only saw it one time, so I'm still trying to understand the mechanics of it. If you get shot in the head, would that kill you? Or would you just lose your memory? Would you mind testing it for me? It's for science, you see. Nothing personal."

This man's insane.

I can't let him near Raegan or Dane.

I'm killing the bastard right here and now.

With a loud roar, I launch myself at him, swinging a fist strong enough to break bone. He dodges my attack faster than any normal human, easily jumping back with that stupid smile still lighting up his face.

The pain hits before I hear the sound of a gunshot.

Again.

And again.

And again.

Four bullets lodge in my chest in seconds. They should have gone right through, but my gift doesn't activate. This fucker shot me with hollow-point rounds.

I hunch over instinctively, grunting as I work to dig my fingers into the first hole. Charles studies me with a furrowed brow.

"Do you still feel pain? Of course, you must. You look uncomfortable, but any ordinary human wouldn't take four bullets to the chest without a single scream. And here you are, calmly making your wounds bigger to get to the bullet. Have you always had a high pain tolerance, or is this some aspect of your gift?"

"Are you actually asking, or do you just like to hear yourself talk?" I manage through gritted teeth.

He laughs—fucking *laughs*—like I've just told him a joke.

"You'd have been a much better choice for Gordon. But, no matter. The end result is the same." Charles bends to retrieve the knife in his free hand, then holds up his other arm and slashes the blade across it. Crimson flows freely down his arm.

Then the bleeding stops.

And his skin fills in with burnt bronze scales.

I freeze, staring at my gift he's somehow using.

"See? My questions are sincere. I needed to test this for myself, and I'm very pleased with it. But there are still too many unknowns I'd like answers to."

Did he steal my gift? Was it when he drank my blood?

My fingers pinch around the first bullet, nails digging into the groove at the end and then roughly jerking it out. The effort and type of bullet do a number on me internally, but as soon as it's free, my gift takes over to fix it.

Charles's eyebrows rise. "Ah, so you have to take them out first?"

Ignoring him, I force my fingers into the next bullet hole.

A gunshot fires, and the bullet hits the back of my hand. I clench my teeth, straining through the pain to lift my hand again when another bullet hits my arm.

Another shot to my kneecap, and I fall on that side just before the other knee goes down with it. I crash to the floor, my knees screaming from the wounds and impact all at once. The amount of pain singing through me is almost enough to make me black out. My vision darkens.

Raegan and Dane aren't safe. The rest of the Guild members are in danger. I can't let this man leave this room alive.

It's those thoughts that keep me awake. That fight off the sweet promise of falling unconscious that tries to drag me under.

"Alright, now sit still so I can see how this works. I'll bring you back with me, of course, so that I can monitor the results. Anything that happens to you is what will happen to me now. So, again, this is all in the name of science. A good cause."

Cold metal presses into my forehead.

I open my eyes, glaring at him.

My heart hammers wildly, blood roaring in my ears so I couldn't hear him even if he bothered to say anything.

But he doesn't speak.

He smiles at my boldness, then squeezes the trigger.

It clicks empty.

My heart ricochets, and I close my eyes and draw a breath. That was too fucking close.

Charles sighs, clearly disappointed, then tosses the gun away.

"Well, then. Let's see if you'll die by not taking out the bullets in time."

His hand covers my face, and then there's nothing.

Chapter Three

JACKSON

Gifted Enterprise agents swarm through the portal as a coordinated unit, circling around us and blocking any chance for an exit. They're armed with guns, aimed at either Aiden or me, but I wouldn't be surprised if any of them had gifts as well. I think we've at least earned that minimum requirement for anyone they send against us.

If not, and they still underestimate us, I'll make that correction now.

Thorne chuckles as the circle closes in front of him, separating us. "I guess that's all the time I have with you today, Jack."

I mimic his smile, unimpressed. "Running because you know you'll lose?"

"Jack," Aiden urges me again, reminding me that we need to leave. But with Reid unconscious and severely injured and us halfway across the city, it's not looking good for our timing.

Resting my arms behind my back, I send as many knives from the ground as I can over to Aiden.

My ex-mentor waves his thumbless hands at me, the result of Gordon freeing him from the power-blocking cuffs we'd had him in. "I'm at a bit of a disadvantage now, don't you think? You can't call it a fair fight when I'm handicapped like this."

"I've killed you enough times by now to say I'm stronger. I don't need to prove myself in a fair fight anymore." My smile ratchets up my face, a borderline crazed look in my eyes based on the visible shivers some of the agents have when they see it. "All I need is for you to stay dead, even if that means cutting you to pieces too small to be put back together again."

Thorne's expression sours. His pride doesn't like hearing that very much. Good. I'd like him to stay so I can end this once and for all. I'll cut him to pieces so small, there won't be anything left for Royce to resurrect.

But I have to be fast.

Hold on, little one.

"—ir. Sir. THORNE!" one of the agents yells.

"What?!" he shouts, finally looking away from me.

"He's doing something!" The agent points at the knives making their way to Aiden inches from the floor, piling up beside him.

Aiden places his hand on the pile before they can do anything, melding and morphing the pure metal into a shield. I keep sending the knives to him. As soon as the blade touches his shield, it immediately joins the rest. The shield widens, growing around Reid and Gordon on the floor and him as well, until he has enough to cover them from all sides.

Perfect.

There are only a few knives remaining, but that's more than enough.

There's a popping noise, and then something warm and tacky consumes my hands. I stare at the thick, gooey substance, and try to move my fingers. It's too thick and heavy. Pulling my hands apart doesn't work either.

"Ready!" the present leader of the GE agents calls out.

I glance at Thorne, who shifts his gaze between Aiden's metal barrier and my hands, then meets my stare.

"Until next time, Jack," he says mildly, and I smile. He knows how this fight is going to end, so he's leaving while he can.

I'd bait him again to stay, but I really have lost too much time.

"Aim!"

Time to go.

"Fire!"

I jump into a handstand, then swivel and kick my feet around, sending a forceful gust of wind throughout the room.

Their mistake was thinking I could only control my gift with my hands.

The burst of air throws the agents crashing into the wall.

Bringing my feet back to the ground, I step on the substance between my hands and pull myself up. It takes a solid few seconds of effort before it starts to move. To stretch and thin as I keep the momentum going.

"Jack." Aiden has a small opening in his wall where he's half-way through, his whip sword out.

He doesn't need to say anything else. I shift my body away from the goo as much as I can, holding my arms out and apart, and his sword slices through it with ease.

I doubt a regular knife could have done it, but Aiden's sword is made of pure titanium and sharpened perfectly to his will.

Gunshots fire behind me. I spin, waving an arm with a sludge-covered hand, and send the bullets back to their owners. It takes out five of the thirty agents. A couple are still knocked out or struggling to get up from hitting the wall, but the rest look like they're readying their own gifts.

Ordinarily, I would enjoy taking them down one at a time. But I've taken too long already.

Holding out my arms, I begin to draw in the surrounding air toward me, sucking it in with me at its center. It doesn't matter that my hands are blocked. My arms direct it just the same, until a wind vortex spirals around me. A few agents drop to their knees and grab their throats as the air around them thins.

Once I have what I need, I lash out with the accumulated air in a loop. Slashes of wind strike at the agents indiscriminately, cutting them with one or more deep lacerations like the one given to Reid.

All the agents fall at once, ruby red coloring the circling breeze. Whether an agent was struck multiple times or only once makes no difference.

They're dead.

My chest heaves as I catch my breath, the strength needed to pull off that attack draining more from me than I'd prefer, but it would be better to make it to Raegan faster than worry about conserving energy. The goo on my hands thins and drops in a heap of sludge now that its user is dead.

I turn before I'm ready, my foot catching on the ground as I stumble, but my other foot steadies me. I keep moving to Aiden, who has taken down the shield and is tending to Reid.

"Wake him up," I murmur. "I blocked some of Thorne's attack, so it shouldn't be fatal."

"How long would it take you to fly to the bunker first?" Aiden asks as he tries to wake Reid.

"Too long. Either he teleports us, or we're too late."

Aiden frowns, jostling Reid a bit harder while trying not to further injure the deep laceration crossing his back from Thorne. "Reid. *Reid*. If you want to save Tinsley, get up!"

I squat by Gordon lying on his front, eyes closed. His skin is pale, and blood drools past his lips. I press two fingers to his neck, seeking out his pulse.

Nothing.

I check again at his wrist.

He's dead.

I close my eyes and take a deep breath. It doesn't settle my anger and frustration at the situation one bit. We may have Gordon like I promised her, and I'll still bring him to her, but this wasn't what she wanted.

I yank the blade from him and kick him onto his back, pointing the weapon at him even though he's long gone. "You may be dead, but I'll make sure you get no second chances," I promise him. "She gets what she wants first, and then you're mine."

Reid groans.

"Reid!" Aiden shouts. "No one is answering at the bunker. Can you move?"

"Can you teleport?" I add, prioritizing that need over anything else.

He curses and struggles to push himself upright. "Ah! What—" He reaches back and winces when he touches the open wound on his back. I may have blocked the worst of it, but that just kept him alive. I'm sure every movement, every drawn breath, is painful for him right now.

I step up in front of him, flipping his two-point dagger in the air and catching it by the blade, then offer the handle to him.

He looks at it. Looks at me. Then takes it. "Yeah. I can teleport."

I nod, my respect for him increasing. It's going to hurt like hell, but he'll do it for the others because we need him.

"Good. We need to make a stop first with him"—Aiden gestures at Gordon— "so GE doesn't get their hands on him. Then to the bunker. We'll get Cassandra to heal you as soon as we can once we know what's happening there."

Reid doesn't waste any time, even though his face is pinched with pain. "Someone grab him and hold on."

Aiden swivels his head to where Thorne had been held captive by the cuffs and chains. "Wait." He runs to grab the gift-blocking cuffs, using his gift to drop the metal chains from them, then returns to our sides. "Now."

I grip Gordon since I'm closest, and then Reid with my other hand.

And then we're gone.

CHAPTER FOUR

RAEGAN

THE HALLWAY OPENS TO a massive room. It's the main area that's two stories tall and overlooks the hangout area, filled with tables surrounded by trees and vines.

Screaming from below sends my heart catapulting from my chest. Children's screams.

The kids we'd saved from GE. They wouldn't...

Dane takes the stairs at the railing three at a time, jumping to the short landings when he's near enough. I'm right behind him like a shadow, keeping pace and sticking close. We hit the bottom where the stairs end in the middle of the lower floor and race toward the two groups facing off.

Bright red curls stand out in front of the children, a knife in one hand and a gun in the other. Cassandra's body shakes, but she doesn't back down. One of the people standing opposite her slips a foot forward, and she immediately points the gun at him.

"Don't move!" she shouts, her arm quivering with fear. "I'll shoot."

The children are huddled and clutching each other, crying or shaking with fear.

"Don't let them take us!" a little girl wails.

"I want to go home!"

"Miss Claudia! Miss Claudia!"

"I'm scared!"

The woman who'd stepped forward hesitates, but I can see some of the others readying to test Cassandra as they creep forward. It's one against four, and she looks like she may collapse after firing her first bullet.

"Cassandra!" I call out, letting that group know she's got reinforcements before they get too confident. She spins, her arm with the gun swinging at me. I catch it and ease the gun from her grip. "It's okay. We'll take it from here," I offer reassuringly.

That's when I see the knife sticking out where her shoulder and collarbone meet.

She wasn't shaking from fear.

It was pain. Maybe blood loss.

"Don't remove it," she mumbles, then pitches forward, taking us both to the ground.

Dane curses, then carefully rolls Cassandra to her back in his lap, freeing me.

I sit up with a soft grunt of pain from my head and shoulder, but freeze when I notice her eyes are closed. "Shit!"

"She's just passed out. But we're fucked about getting the kids out of here and help for her."

"Can't she heal it?" I ask.

"She can't heal herself. She needs to go to a hospital."

The scuff of a shoe snaps my attention back to the group, and my arm with the gun jumps up automatically. "Move that foot forward one more time, and I'll put a bullet through your skull. I don't have enough ammo to bother with warning shots."

They whisper amongst themselves. Probably talking about their odds against only Dane and I while we're protecting a handful of kids and a wounded and unconscious Cassandra.

But the gun is the least of their worries.

None of them are in the usual black attire worn by GE agents. If I let any of them go, they could slip undetected back into the group. I can't remember faces well enough to memorize half a dozen at once.

"Dane. Is there anything nearby we could tie them up with?" I whisper under my breath.

He pauses, considering. His lips flatten. "In the kitchens, but I'm not leaving you."

"It's just upstairs—"

Dane grabs my arm. "Their lives aren't more important to me than yours. Whatever we have to do here, we'll do it. But it'll be together."

My heart squeezes, his words filling me with an unfamiliar emotion that floods my chest. I bite my lip and nod.

We'll have to knock them out somehow, then. It's the only option with what we have, short of killing them. I'll do it if provoked, but I don't want that to be my first answer. I may be capable of being a monster, but *I choose* when that is. Not to mention the young audience we have who have been through enough.

"Get ready to rush them," I murmur. "We're aiming to knock them out, so back of the head or jaw hits." I wish we could do the neck pinch that Jackson did to Dane. He made it seem like an effortless tactic to drop him unconscious in seconds.

Guess I know what I'll be asking Jack to teach me if I win whatever his next challenge is.

"Got it." Dane carefully sets Cassandra on the floor. The kids huddle behind us, clinging to each other and crying. They're lost in the bunker with no idea of where to run to be safe or how many others are here to kidnap them. My gaze stops on Mallory in the back. Her blue eyes are round with fear but free from tears. She catches me watching her and quickly looks away.

It's better than her crying or screaming at the sight of me, I guess.

Vines whip seemingly out of nowhere, wrapping around the four GE agents and yanking them together. They jostle and pull against their bindings, then topple over as one.

"Dane! Raegan!"

Silas runs toward us, Fabian jogging and huffing behind him. They both look tired and disheveled. Fabian leans on his knees to catch his breath when they reach us.

"Where's Aiden?" Silas asks.

"Fighting GE elsewhere, above ground," Dane answers. "Have you seen Kellan?"

Silas shakes his head. "You're the only ones we've seen since we left Evie and Cibrina. How can we help?"

"Can you hide the kids somewhere safe?" I ask, motioning to them and then Cassandra. "And she needs a hospital as soon as it's safe to leave."

"I've got her," Fabian declares, bending and lifting her in his arms.

Voices of triumph sound behind us. When I turn, three things spin toward us as fog rolls in at our feet.

A flash of pink darts out toward one of the spinning objects, grabbing it and yanking it from the air. I follow its movement the second time, my eyes widening as Fabian swallows it whole. His tongue, quick like a frog's, snaps out and snatches the third and final weapon before he devours that one as well.

"Get going," Dane tells Silas and Fabian. "We'll hold them off."

Silas nods. "Let's go, kids!" He herds them together, then takes the lead with Fabian holding Cassandra at their rear.

One of the agents jumps at me and Dane with sparks of electricity zapping between his fingertips, and we dive apart. The fog is up to our knees now. If we don't stop whichever one is creating it, we'll be blind before too long.

Raising the gun, I fire at the one I think is making it. He ducks for cover, and the rush of fog lessens for a second.

Gotcha.

Dane appears at my side. "Give me the gun and use your gift."

Keeping the gun pointed at them, I cast Dane a sidelong look. "Are you telling me to kill them?"

His eyes lock onto mine. "The kids are gone now and they aren't giving us a choice. If I have to choose between us or them, I choose us."

I nod, relieved we're on the same page. I'd worried that Dane would be the one against killing anyone, especially if he thought of every agent as innocent and brainwashed like his sister.

But there's no way we would survive the fight against GE if we tried to save everyone who works for them. Not everyone was brainwashed, after all.

"After those kids, all of you. I'll handle this," a familiar voice intrudes. "Well, well. I suppose the chances of me seeing you were high if I left that prison floor, but I couldn't help my curiosity to explore."

I whip around, my eyes widening at who I see standing there.

Charles.

My...father.

The other agents chase after the direction Silas and Fabian went with the children, but I'm too stunned to stop them.

Dane takes a step in front of me. "What did you do to Kell?" he demands.

Kell?

I look past Charles. Kellan is floating on his back, his eyes closed, and blood stains on his shirt.

"Kellan!" I shout, taking a step toward him when the gun suddenly rips from my hand.

"No!"

Bang!

Dane slams into me, driving me to the floor and knocking the air from my lungs. He shifts his weight off me to one side, making a noise of pain behind clenched teeth. Pulling his hand away from his arm, he reveals a bright red stain on his palm. "Fuck," he mutters, then turns to scan me for injuries. "Are you okay?"

"Me? You're the one who just got shot!"

"It's just a graze. Hurts like a mother—shit!" He grabs me and rolls us both away a second before I hear another gunshot.

"Dane!"

Charles *tsks* and shakes his head. "Oh, dear. I've missed again. Raegan, please stand so these bullets don't go to waste. I'd rather not hit your friend if I can help it."

"Get fucked," Dane growls, straightening to position himself between me and my father.

Or...should I even call him that?

"Who are you and why are you doing this? Are you really my father?" I demand, standing and trying to move past Dane, but he blocks me with an arm.

"We do share DNA, unfortunately." My throat tightens at the callousness of his words. It was dumb for me to believe I might have any family left. I thought I'd kept my distance enough from the idea of him being there, but his words cut me, slicing at my soul. "But that is the full extent of our connection. You're no daughter of mine. Just a failed experiment that needs to be put down."

I swallow past the uncomfortable thickness in my throat. "The stories about my mother..."

"All lies," he admits easily with a shrug. "She was a means to an end, just like all the others."

The others?

Charles's gaze flicks beside me. "Did I hear correctly that you're Dane?"

Dane tenses, his expression growing dark. There's no use denying it, but we don't confirm it, either.

Charles smiles, appearing pleased. "I'll take you with me as well, then. Just give me a moment to dispose of my mistake and we'll be on our way."

To dispose of my mistake.

Yup. I'm done.

Rage burns the emotional pain away, flooding my senses until there's nothing else. My gift activates all on its own, ready to *dispose* of this man first.

Fuck him. And fuck his lies.

"Don't talk about her like that," Dane snaps. "And I'm not going anywhere with you, you piece of shit."

I duck around Dane and charge at Charles, closing the distance before he can raise the gun. I grab his wrist first, then snatch the gun with my other hand and turn it to ash. Charles cries out when my gift cracks and spreads up his arm.

His fist smashes into my face, and I involuntarily release him as I stumble to the side. Dane catches me from behind before I fall, pulling me against his chest. My face pounds from the impact, and I reach a hand up to let my cooler fingers soothe the building ache.

I had enough of him to destroy that one arm. It'll put us at an advantage against him, which I have a feeling we'll need. He's too confident for me to believe he's just a paperwork guy. And somehow, he managed to incapacitate Kellan. We can't take him lightly.

When I check on my handiwork on his arm, my lungs constrict. The sleeve of his shirt is destroyed, but instead of ravaged and cracked skin, I stare at burnt gold scales. They're a dark and dull comparison to Kellan's, but otherwise unmistakable.

"Fuck. He has the same gift as Kell?" Dane breathes incredulously.

Charles laughs, turning his arm before himself as if admiring his own gift. "Truly marvelous," he commends himself.

What the—?

I glance at Kellan, remembering the time Charles had watched Kell's gift activate.

His interest in it had been subtle, but it was there.

"He stole it..." I whisper, in shock.

Dane curses, his arms tightening around me. "Keep him talking. I'll sneak around behind him to mute his gift, and then you can use yours."

"Can I use my gift on him while you're touching him?"

"Guess we'll find out."

He slides his arms down, releasing me slowly to avoid drawing Charles's attention back to us. He's so excited about his new gift that it's like we no longer exist.

Or we're not a big enough threat for him to bother keeping tabs on.

It's that thought which makes me hesitate.

"Dane..." I start, pinching his hoodie before he's out of reach. "I don't like you getting close to him. He's after you."

He covers my hand with his, gently tugging the fabric free. "There's no portal around right now, so now's the time. We don't have much choice if he has Kellan's healing and invulnerability."

Still, my stomach twists into a knot.

Something appears in my periphery, and I nearly collapse with relief.

Aiden, Jackson, and Reid.

Aiden immediately scans the room, his hard stare gathering as much information as possible in seconds before he speaks. "Are you Gifted Enterprise's president?" he directs to Charles.

I grab Dane's hoodie to keep him from continuing with our plan now that the others are here. Surely, if we combine our strength, we can take him down without risking Dane. He frowns at me, but doesn't fight it.

Jackson is by my side before I see him move, his hand gently angling my face up as he inspects what's likely a blooming bruise on my cheek.

Charles lowers his arm and regards Aiden with mild interest. "I am."

Aiden draws his whip sword free. "Good. Then we can end this here with your death or surrender, your choice," he threatens, his voice smooth and matter-of-fact.

My DNA donor laughs freely. "You think too highly of yourselves. I didn't become president by batting my eyelashes, Mr. Guild Master. But I'll gladly show you the difference between you and me."

"Was it him?" Jack asks. His thumb strokes over the bruise, and I restrain a wince when it stings. His eyes flash with anger, telling me I didn't do as great a job at hiding it as I thought I had. I nod in response to his original question.

"Get Kell first." Charles's attention is firmly locked on Aiden, so this is the perfect time for Jackson to sweep in and out with Kellan. "He stole Kell's gift somehow, so he won't be easy to fight."

Aiden stares back at Charles, unimpressed. "Before we begin, what have you done to my Guild members?"

"Nothing but take back what was rightfully ours," he responds, and Aiden's jaw tightens.

"No person rightfully *belongs* to anyone else—"

Charles snaps his head around. "Is that you, son?" he interrupts, casually dismissing what Aiden's saying with his gaze now pinned on Reid, who had dropped to one knee when they arrived.

Reid's hands curl to fists, but still, he doesn't stand.

Is he injured?

And, also...son?!

Does that make him my brother?

"Don't call me that," Reid bites out, pain laced in his voice. "I've cut all ties with you. Where's Tinsley?"

Charles's smile is sickly sweet, like he's taking great pleasure in what he says next. "Don't worry. I'll take good care of your girl."

Reid struggles to his feet. His face contorts with pain at the action, but he keeps moving, taking one step after another toward Charles. "Give her back. Give. Her. BACK!" Drops of blood trail behind him from a bloody gash stretched diagonally across his back.

"You had such promise, Reid. I thought you'd be my right hand until you met that girl. I'm disappointed in you becoming infatuated with some cunt."

He roars, leaping at Charles with flying fists that the man easily evades with a chuckle. Reid collapses to the ground, his chest heaving and discomfort tightening his face.

"It's not the motivation I'd hoped for, but it'll do. You need to be punished for turning your back on me, and unfortunately for your girl, she's the price you'll pay. I'm sure when you see her again, you'll come around. We've made exceptional enhancements in our programming department since you left."

Aiden moves in front of Reid and swings his sword at Charles, who once again dodges, but Jackson strikes him from behind.

Charles falls a single step forward, then straightens to square off, facing them both at once. The wound on his back heals instantly, adding another area of impenetrable scales. "That should have been a single death blow if you were serious," he critiques. "Now, I know you're in the fight, too."

Dane nudges me. I drag my attention away from them to find Kellan at our feet. Gasping at the bullet holes still in his chest, I drop to my knees and reach for the nearest one. Dane squats to do the same with another one.

Charles frowns, his eyes searching the area where Kellan had been until he finds him with Dane and me. Aiden and Jack are both mid-attack when he makes a motion with his hands, and it almost looks like they hit an invisible shield as they're repelled back. He casts one more glance at Reid. "I'd love to stay and keep testing my new gift, but I'm already late for an appointment. I'm sure you all understand."

He disappears in the blink of an eye.

"Wasn't his gift—"

"Almost forgot something," Charles's voice appears on the other side of Dane.

No!

I reach for Dane on instinct, grabbing whatever I touch first, and then everything vanishes.

CHAPTER FIVE

RAEGAN

MY KNEES COLLIDE WITH hardwood floors before I fall on top of Dane, the world spinning violently around me. Nausea swirls in my gut. I squeeze my eyes closed until the dizziness subsides. This teleport is ten times worse than when Reid does it.

Just like the scales on Charles's arm were similar to Kellan's, but not quite right.

Is his gift a poor imitation of other gifts?

"What do we have here? A stowaway?" Charles speaks from above, reminding me this is no time to close my eyes.

Dane groans, lost to the nausea as I was, and hearing him just as miserable as me forces my eyes open. Someone needs to be aware of our surroundings in enemy territory.

Slowly, I turn to look at Charles. He's standing with no ounce of discomfort on his face as he looks down on us. "I hope you're prepared for what comes next as an uninvited guest. I don't tolerate trash in my office."

The room around us is too massive to be called an office. Behind him is an oversized, ugly metal desk before a wall of windows two stories high. There's a single side table with a decanter of alcohol and two glasses, and otherwise, the room is bare. Silver walls, grayish hardwood floors, and his desk.

"Rae?" Dane mumbles, his hand reaching for me.

"I'm here." He laces his fingers with mine, and I use our grip to help him sit upright. He moans again, grabbing at his head with eyes closed. The nausea is clearly riding him even harder. I squeeze his hand. "I've got you. He's not taking you anywhere. I promise."

His eyes slowly open, blinking to adjust until he can look at me clearly. He squeezes my hand in return. "You, either."

"Sorry to disappoint you both, but that's not possible. Dane is coming with me and you..." His blue eyes land on me, and it hits me how much mine look like them. And Reid's...

Not now, I chastise. I can think about Reid and our possible blood relation after we make it out of this predicament.

"...*you* are not leaving this room alive. You had been fortunate I was going to leave you alive at your underground hideout, but to follow me here means you have a death wish. I won't be so lax now that you're here."

Standing, I glare at him. "You can't have him."

"I already do."

I stand between him and Dane. "No. You'll never have him so long as I'm alive."

Charles smiles. "Ah, very well. I accept." He raises a hand, then snaps his wrist up.

My body lifts into the air, then speeds backward, crashing into the wall. I drop hard to the floor, crying out from the pain shooting through my back.

"Rae!" Dane yells, shoving to his feet and tripping over himself as he tries to run to me.

Groaning, I push up to my elbows. "I'm okay." At least, I think I am. Fuck, that hurt. It wasn't like Jackson using air to move things. Or the feeling of hooks and strings that Royce used. This was just picking me up with an invisible hand and throwing me at the fucking wall.

"So, to tally it up, he has Kellan's gift, Reid's gift, and now some other gift that lets him toss people around without touching them? Did I miss any?" I grumble, rubbing the back of my head.

Dane's lips tighten. So, yes. All of those.

"We just need to stall him as long as possible. The others will come for us."

"How? *We* don't even know where we are."

"Let's just say that Aiden made sure you could never be kidnapped and hidden from us again."

I stare at him, unamused. "Please tell me he didn't put a tracker in me while I was unconscious."

He smirks, completely unashamed by that admission. "If he gets us out of this, you can write him a thank you card."

Ha!

"Ready?"

"No, but when has that ever stopped me?" I smirk at him, then break out into a run.

Charles's smile hasn't faded since I last looked at him. If anything, he looks relaxed.

Fuck.

I just know we're underestimating him. No one is that confident without good reason.

I stop without warning, slapping my hand on his fancy office floor and sending my gift through it to him.

His eye twitches at the sight, and he moves away before it reaches him. I curve it at him, chasing him, and he disappears.

Charles reappears on the opposite wall, and Dane charges at him from behind. Just as Charles turns, Dane grabs his raised arm with glowing hands.

As soon as Charles was gone, I'd waited for his new position and then ran after him. I slip the knife from my boot and thrust the blade into Charles's chest while he's occupied looking at Dane on his other side.

"Ahhgh!" His smile shatters. He stomps on Dane's knee and swings his arm down on his elbow, breaking his hold and gift on him. I jump back, grabbing Dane and dragging us both toward the door.

I risk a glance over my shoulder. Charles pulls the knife free and waits for his wound to heal and strengthen. He tosses the knife to the floor. When he looks up at us, he's smiling again.

Psycho.

The door is close. I reach my hand out, my fingers sliding over the handle...

I'm yanked backward, the force of it throwing our hands apart as we both sail through the air back to Charles. The man flicks his wrist, and a blast of *something*, hits me. I slam to the floor, all the air expelling from my lungs as I gasp from the pain. Whatever he struck with, it pummeled my entire body, leaving nothing untouched.

Dane coughs, like he's choking to breathe, and I force my head up to seek him out. He's lying on the floor a few yards from me.

My muscles scream when I make myself stand. Make myself *move*.

We have to make it through the door before he attacks again.

But how? He dodges my gift. Heals from any attack we actually *do* land on him.

Somehow, I make it to Dane. "Can you stand?"

"What the fuck was that?" he wheezes but accepts my hand to help him up.

"I'm not sticking around to find out. Let's go!" Even though it hurts, even though all I want to do is lie on the ground to catch my breath, I run.

Dane stays with me, but we're hardly a few steps in before we're ripped off our feet again.

Smashed with an invisible force.

This time, we keep our hands on each other, holding tight even after we crash to the ground.

"How many more of these do you think you can take? Three? Less?" Charles questions seriously, like he's genuinely curious.

Once I can breathe again, I pant between breaths to Dane, "Can't run. Fight."

His head tilts in what I'm pretty sure is a nod of agreement.

The GE president stands at the head of his office like he could do this all day. Like this attack costs him nothing while we're struggling just to stay upright. Even if there is a limit to this gift, he could always teleport to the door to stop us.

All we can do now is try to fight and hope to find a weakness.

Charles waits for us to get back on our feet. He could easily attack us when we're down, but he smiles pleasantly and *allows us* the time to try again.

Wearing down our resolve just as much as our bodies.

Dane and I rush at him for another attack. I try my gift. Dane uses his fists.

We run into an invisible barrier a couple feet from him that instantly tosses us back.

Before we get up this time, Charles pulls us toward him, then blasts us with another invisible attack.

And then another with no time to recover.

Pain grips my body in an iron, spiked fist, immobilizing me. The ringing in my ears echoes along with the insistent throbbing of my muscles. There's a sharp piercing in my chest when I breathe, and I'm forced to take shorter, shallower breaths.

"Oh, you have guests," a droll male voice speaks. There's a pause, and then he continues, "Playing with your food, I see."

"Royce," Charles greets. "Have I missed the meeting?"

Black edges my vision, oblivion threatening to consume me.

To sleep, or death?

"I pushed it out for you. I knew you'd be busy having fun with my puppet's Guild."

"Ah, you're quite reliable."

"I strive to be so, sir. If I may," Royce drawls in his dreary, slow tone. "Do you have plans for your...her?"

His words give me a boost of willpower to hold on. To cling to consciousness even if it's only to hear about their plan for me.

"Only to put her down as she should have been after she killed Vera."

A pain deeper than any physical injury burrows into my chest.

"Of course, sir. I recall you advising Gordon of that and his desperate plea to use her in his pet project."

"Then take care with what you're about to request," Charles warns.

"I have no intention of interfering. However, I can make use of her after death, with her free will limited, of course."

It's quiet for a heartbeat. Two. Three.

I blink, and it takes concentrated effort to drag my eyelids open again.

Don't pass out. Keep fighting.

"I suppose so. Just keep her from my sight."

"Yes, sir."

"Stay close. I've had my fun and should return to work. You can have her then."

Fuck.

Time's up.

I'd hoped their conversation would last longer to give my body more time to recover, but I'm in no better shape now than a few minutes ago. Worse, actually.

Shadows creep further into my vision. So much so that I'm not sure if I'm losing my eyesight or my lids are closing on their own.

The soft sound of footsteps on the hardwood floor beat and echo against my ear.

He's coming.

"Rae," Dane gasps in a painful voice.

A hand covers one of mine, squeezing when I don't respond.

I try to, but my body refuses to listen.

"Stay with me. Don't close your eyes."

Dane's face appears before me. He's on his stomach, lying there like he crawled to me.

My eyes shutter, and I force them back open.

"That's it. Don't give in."

My throat is parched, and when I swallow, it's like sandpaper rubbing together. "Never," I croak.

"I hope you don't mind my borrowing of your knife," Charles says politely above us. "I'd love to stay and play a bit longer, but I'm overdue for my work today. I'll act as your father one last time by ending this quickly."

Dane drags himself over me, his body molding to mine. "Don't you fucking dare!" he snaps, his voice gravelly because of his own injuries. "Leave her alone, and I'll do whatever you want. *Heal her*, and you can have my gift or whatever it is you want from me."

Charles sighs. "You have me mistaken, Dane. I don't negotiate. I apologize for your poor experience with my employee, Gordon, but that isn't how Gifted Enterprise operates. She dies. You donate your gift to GE. That's the only way we all move forward. Now, kindly remove yourself so I can make this quick, or I cannot guarantee her death won't be messy."

"You're not going to fucking touch her!"

I can't see anything beneath Dane except for small glimpses of light.

But I feel the force of him being struck above me.

"Aahhh...nnngh!" Dane cries out. He shifts only for a second from the impact before he's right back on me.

"Dane!" I pant, and an agonizing sting swells in my chest.

Still, I try to move my hands. Even a twitch will do.

Move, dammit!

He's hit again.

And again.

"Determined, aren't you? If you won't go by physical force, I'll have to remove you another way. She's the only one meant to die today."

Dane!

The weight of his body lessens, but his hands cling desperately to mine.

"No!" he chokes, his voice a harsh mix of pain and gritted determination.

A loud slam echoes through the room.

Dane's body drops onto mine. I cry out involuntarily at the blinding pain and then pass out.

Chapter Six

AIDEN

The blink of an eye.

That's how fast she's gone. Dane's gone.

The diamond blades of my whip sword burrow into the floor following my last attack. An attack that began with Charles in front of me and ended with him, her, and Dane vanished.

"Take me there," Jackson murmurs in a soft, deadly command. I didn't even see him move from my side. He grips Reid's arm and plucks a knife from his hoodie.

Reid's jaw ticks, his teeth clenched together when he answers. "Why would you think I know where he went?"

Jack angles his head, regarding him with the slow creep of a smile. "Because you're his son."

"Ex-son, if you were listening."

"So?"

"So, I don't know where he took them. They open and close locations too fast to keep track."

"Guess. If you had to pick one place, where would it be?" Jackson pushes, his usually solid patience starting to crack.

Reid looks away, considering. He has a lot to answer for, but other than using this new information about his bloodline to get to Raegan and Dane, I'll put it aside until this absolute shit show of a night is back under some semblance of control.

While they're busy working that out, I move to Kellan and kneel beside him to assess his condition. He's riddled with bullets. Three in the chest, one in each knee, one in the arm, and one in his hand.

"I don't know. He has too many offices to pick one, or he could have taken them to a testing facility," Reid finally answers.

I pull out my phone and open the tracking app I had installed not long ago. It takes a couple of taps to zero in on Raegan's location before I toss the phone at Jack. He catches it mid-air with his gift, then grabs and looks at it. He turns the screen to Reid, holding it in front of him.

"Take us here." Jackson zooms out for Reid to gather where that location is. "Do you know it?"

Reid sighs. "I know it."

"Good. Let's go." Jack tosses my phone back, and I catch it with my free hand.

"Not yet," I warn. "Let me finish fixing up Kellan first."

Jackson's lips thin in what amounts to his version of visible frustration, but he doesn't argue.

"We can't follow him," Reid rasps, still not understanding that we're going no matter what he says. We aren't letting Raegan be taken again. And we won't let them have Dane. We could be walking into almost certain death, and we would still take that chance in order to rescue them.

"And why is that?" I ask, digging my finger into the last hole in Kell's chest. As soon as my skin touches the metal, it wraps around my finger so I can pull it clear.

"You can't beat him. He would destroy us all if we tried to fight him."

"Mm...you say it like that would stop us from trying to get them back," Jack remarks.

Reid makes a frustrated sound. "It should."

After extracting the third bullet from Kellan's chest, I move on to his knees. "What makes you say that? Tell me what we're up against since this man is the endgame for Gifted Enterprise."

"His gift is copying other gifts. I don't know how many he has at this point."

"Which ones *do* you know about?" I press, seeking out the next bullet.

"His original gift, which requires him to consume the blood of the gifted person whose gift he's copying. He has my gift—"

"—teleportation," I fill in.

"...spatial tethering," he corrects, and I put a pin in asking that question of him later as well. "Sleep inducement. Frequency manipulation. Telekinetic fields and bursts are his favorite. And he used Kellan's regeneration, which is the worst news we could have."

Well.

That makes at least six.

"Is that all?" I free the last bullet from Kellan's hand.

"We can't go," Reid repeats.

"Hurry up," Jack says to me, his gaze flipping from Kellan to me, back to Reid.

"I'm telling you—"

Jackson hauls Reid up by his hair, his knife pointed at Reid's neck. His voice is a deadly calm when he says, "I'm telling *you* that we're going. We should already be there."

Kellan groans as he comes to.

I turn to face Reid. "If your father is as dangerous as you say, then even more reason we can't leave Raegan and Dane alone with him this long. Are you okay leaving your sister with him?"

"Half-sister," Reid replies automatically, then hesitates. His eyes close, and he sighs heavily. "No. We'll get her." He opens his eyes and shoots a pointed look at Jack. "But we're only going to grab the two of them and then leave. We can't fight. I'm not even sure if I'll last for the second jump, so it has to be quick."

"Son of a—" Kellan pushes himself up and rubs at his chest. He sees me, then Jackson and Reid's standoff. He scans more of the room, and his expression darkens. "Where are they?"

"Gone. With Charles. But we're getting them back," I tell him, and he nods, standing.

"Let's fucking go, then," Kellan growls.

We join Jackson and hold Reid's other arm. He mutters something under his breath, and we're gone.

We land in a hallway before two large doors.

"Where the hell is she?" Kellan demands, fisting Reid's shirt.

Reid glares at him, tugging fruitlessly. "Just because the tracker showed her in this building doesn't mean I know which room she's in. Behind here is his office. But maybe we should check the rest of the building first—"

Jackson and I smash the doors open in unison.

We aren't wasting anymore time.

Dane's hovering over Raegan's still body on the floor. Charles looks up sharply at our entrance, and Dane falls on top of her.

"Now!" I yell, breaking into a run toward them before Charles can act. Kellan lifts and carries Reid with him while Jackson sends a burst of wind at Charles to knock him back. We all reach Dane and Raegan in seconds, grabbing them and then Reid.

"How unfortunate," Charles comments mildly, his voice echoing in my ears even after Reid teleports us away and we escape.

"...six fractured ribs, which have led to a chest infection. We've put him on antibiotics and pain medicine," the doctor reports. His eyes trail to Kellan, who's leaning back in the stiff chair beside Dane's bed, his legs thrown out for comfort while his tattooed muscular arms are tense where they cross his chest. He's glaring at the doctor, his jaw working in frustration to keep his mouth shut.

Obviously, none of this is the doctor's fault. He's merely the messenger delivering the news of what Dane went through with Charles. It's the worst news of the group, all of whom we'd been forced to bring to the hospital once we discovered Cassandra and her injury.

Raegan suffers similar injuries to Dane, although not as many broken ribs and without the infection or bullet graze. Reid and Cassandra are also here, getting the emergency treatment they need.

There is a long list of reasons why I actively avoid medical facilities: being in the public eye, cameras, potentially dangerous medical tests and gifted reactions, having a gifted person's blood in others' hands, law enforcement and investigations, stacks of medical bills we'll have to pay out of pocket for. And so on. But this time, we had no choice.

"How long until he's recovered?" I ask, standing at the foot of Dane's bed in what should be a comforting wall between Kellan and the doctor.

The doctor clears his throat, uneasiness still radiating from the man since he saw Jack in Raegan's room and only getting worse. He'd been better when we'd visited the others to review their statuses, but not completely free from it. I'm sure it has something to do with the group of people we brought in with such injuries. It won't be long before the police arrive after someone reports it.

"Once his chest infection is clear, he should be able to return home. He'll need to be on bedrest or very limited activity for six weeks while it heals. Broken ribs are a painful and slow thing to heal, but there's nothing more we can do for them other than trying to keep the patient comfortable."

My knuckles turn white on the footboard of the hospital bed.

Six weeks.

I'm certain that GE will act sooner than that. They've exposed us. Our one place of safety is gone, and now that they know where we are, it's too dangerous to stay in the bunker. We'd be worse off there, where Vera could trap us underground in a steel coffin.

"Thank you, Doctor," Cibrina chimes in from the doorway, and I realize I'd been silently fuming. One more stressor to add to the poor man.

I release the footboard and turn to face him, plastering on a stiff but polite smile. "Yes, thank you. Please contact me if there are any further developments."

He nods. "Of course. They're in good hands."

No, they're in danger here.

Once he leaves the room, Kellan shifts forward, holding his hands together as he watches Dane. "How is she? And the others?"

"Not so bad as Dane, although all have slow recovery prognoses," I answer honestly, and he nods.

"This never should have happened," he growls.

Sighing, I further loosen my tie. I'd love to wrap it around Charles's throat and squeeze the life out of him. For pretending to be her father. For what he did to Kellan. Raegan and Dane. For being the president of GE and the man behind all of our pain and struggle. "No, it shouldn't have. We'll get to the bottom of this once we get everyone here home."

Kellan gives a caustic laugh. "And where is that, exactly? What's home?"

"We're going back to the Tower." His gaze shifts to mine. "No more hiding." We'll have to put safeguards in place and train the members in preparation for an attack, but if we're too busy running and hiding, then we'll never win. It's time to stand our ground and fight back.

"Ah, speaking of the Tower, Aiden..." Cibrina politely interjects.

"Yes, I know." I need to get back to the others to announce our next steps and put them at ease. I can't say for certain if I'll be able to achieve that last piece after the disaster that happened at the bunker. The one place that should have been most secure, and I failed in upholding that promise. Not only had GE gotten in, but I'd been complicit in its occurrence. I'd *brought* that smiling, psychotic man directly to us.

"Keep them safe, Kellan. I don't plan to be long, but I need to make sure the Guild is settled."

"With my life," he says, his tone serious.

I cast a final look at Dane, promising him silently that we'll get him home soon, then walk out of his room. Cibrina follows a few steps back, giving me the space I need without me having to say a word. For me, business comes first. There are steps that must be taken for everyone's safety and peace of mind, and I will always prioritize the others under my protection first.

But once that's done...

When I don't have to stand tall as a leader or be an example of calm for the others...

When I'm finally alone...

That's when I'll let go. When I'll release this pent-up anger that's burning me from the inside.

And I'll plan the death of Charles Whitmore to the very last detail.

It's unplanned, but I pivot and open the door to Raegan's room without warning Cibrina. I'd already visited her room, but I can't leave without seeing her one more time. Jackson's sitting on the narrow footboard of the bed, his boots rudely planted on the blankets as he sharpens one of his blades.

"You didn't stop me from opening the door," I croon softly, the accusation clear.

Jack smirks and continues to run his blade through the sharpener. "I knew it was you."

I fist his hoodie. "How?" I demand. "We still don't know every single gift the enemy has at their disposal. Someone could copy how I look, how I sound. *No one* enters this room until you've vetted them, understand?"

His smirk widens, and his eyes look wild while they pin mine. I restrain the instinctual shudder that look gives me, holding fast against him. This isn't something I'll back down on. I won't let them touch her again. No matter what that might look like moving forward. "Cassandra's at the door," is how he replies, and I release him to stalk to the closed door.

I hear Cibrina behind it. "You should be in bed!"

"Please. I can help," Cassandra begs.

"Yes, you can. *After* you're better," Cibrina soothes.

"I can do some now," the healer argues. "I know we can't stay here long. Let me at least get them better enough that we can all leave tomorrow."

There's silence as if Cibrina's thinking it over. Cassandra leaps at that opening to push even more. "*This* is what I'm here for. It's the only thing I can help with. If anyone can understand, it's you. We can't fight like they can. But this...*please* let me do this. I need to be useful, or else...I just..."

"I'll ask Aiden. He'll make the final decision."

As soon as the first knock hits the door, I open it.

"Aiden," Cibrina begins, and I wave them inside, stopping Cassandra mid-rush to get to Raegan.

"Wait." I hold her back by her uninjured shoulder, only releasing her once I'm sure she'll stay still so I can look at her. Her shoulder is bandaged, and her arm is in a sling. The rest of her is unharmed, thankfully, but I'm not sure what kind of drain these healings will have on her and how it will affect her own healing.

"I'm fine. I know my body better than any of you," she says stubbornly while raising her chin with a sniff.

Shaking my head, I mutter beneath my breath about strong-willed, stubborn women and move aside.

She sidles up to Raegan's bedside. If not for her pallid complexion and some bruising, no one would realize how injured she is. There's an IV feeding her fluids and pain medication on the opposite side of the bed. She could technically wake up at any time, which is what makes it so difficult to leave.

I want to be here when she wakes up.

Cassandra gently tugs the blankets down to expose more of the hospital gown, then places her hand on Raegan's chest. Her eyes begin to glow just before she shuts them, concentrating on rooting out every injury.

The room is silent while she works. Jackson even stopped sharpening after she started her healing, his focus consumed entirely by watching Raegan for any sign of improvement. Only because we're watching her so intently do I think we're able to actually witness the color returning to her face. The smoother rise and fall of her chest that's no longer agitated.

I breathe a relieved exhale, then touch Cassandra's shoulder to remind her this was only meant to be a brief healing. Dane and Reid will need far more, and I don't know how much she has left before she's drained.

Cassandra blinks, coming to, then smiles at me. "There. She should be okay to leave after she gets the sleep she needs."

Frowning, I ask, "How much did you heal?"

She shrugs, and her smile curls a bit before she looks away. "Enough. Can someone show me where the others are?"

"I'll take you to them," Cibrina offers, slipping me a smile and a nod. She knows I wish to stay here with Raegan, and she's giving me that extra time now at least until Cassandra is finished.

I owe her more than I think I'll ever be able to repay.

She was the one who gathered most of the Guild members and locked them away where GE couldn't find them. GE stole the ones we'd rescued in quarantine, but outside of that? Tinsley and five others.

It could have been much worse. But Cibrina's quick thinking and action kept the others safe.

The ones she didn't reach were protected by the members who stepped up to fight back. Members like Evie. Silas. Fabian. Even Gabriel and Zedd. And Cassandra. With no fighting gift, she still found weapons to defend and protect the kids who had escaped the quarantine floor.

The sound of metal scraping on metal brings me back. I cut a look at Jackson, who smirks but keeps his gaze on his work, and then I turn my focus to Raegan.

I'm not sure how long Cassandra will be, but I drag the overstuffed chair to her bedside and sit anyway. Leaning my elbows on the bed so I can be close, I take her nearest hand in both of mine, bringing it to my lips.

No more, I promise her silently. Whether or not she heels to my demands to make her safe is a problem for later. It's easy to imagine her doing what I say when she's asleep like this, when her expression is soft and peaceful now that she's healed, and her pretty lips part as if asking for me to kiss them.

Her present state reminds me of Sleeping Beauty. A princess in bed, asleep and vulnerable as she waits for her true love's kiss from Prince Charming to wake her.

But I'm no Prince Charming.

I'd be the villain who locked her away.

To keep her safe.

To keep her for myself.

Chapter Seven

AIDEN

The spacious, three-story room with massive wooden beams and rich hardwood floors—or, the Guild Hall as we call it—is bustling with wild energy. There are over a hundred and fifty members who live in the Tower, or the bunker for a few months, and another fifty or so who live or travel elsewhere most of the time.

Every single member, save for those at the hospital or who were taken, is here.

Off to one side of the room, nearest to the many tables and benches, is a stage that we usually keep hidden behind a faux wall. It's open now, and the crowd gathers at its base.

Cibrina sits with me backstage, her Archive gift active as she works on my latest request. I flip the switch to turn on the lights and microphones hanging over the stage so everyone will be able to hear and see me, and then stride to centerstage.

Members quiet or shush others when they see me, some fighting a bit to get closer, while others hang back and separate themselves from the tight cluster. I scan the crowd, making eye contact with those who want it and taking in the mood of everyone before I begin.

"Last night, we were attacked by Gifted Enterprise. The same group who fought us here some months ago and the reason why we'd moved to the bunker. They infiltrated one of our rescue missions among actual victims and then waited to attack until our event." Murmurs rise in volume, but it quiets again when I bow my head. "I'm sorry for failing to keep my promise of your safety at the bunker."

Shouts burst from the crowd, swelling as one to a deafening roar.

"—not your fault!"

"—bastards used them—!"

"—don't stop—!"

The individual words are lost to the sea of noise, but the overall emotion is a tangible thing that fills my soul to the brim with gratitude and pride. I close my eyes, soaking it in and fortifying my resolve with their support.

I raise my head and hands, gesturing for quiet so I may continue. "Thank you, all. I stand by my apology, but I appreciate your words. While I am glad to see so many of your faces here, six of us were taken by GE. It is going to be my mission, and the mission of this Guild, to not only get them back but to take down Gifted Enterprise once and for all."

I give them a minute to let my words settle. We're not sneaking onto islands to save the prisoners and then slipping away again. We chipped away at their feet, nibbling at their resources like it would make a difference in this war.

And that's what this is now.

A war.

"Gifted Enterprise has been around for a long time. It is an organization that kidnaps gifted—particularly children—and murders any who stand in their way. Their goal is the brainwashing and corruption of gifted persons who they can control and use to gain more power and influence across the world."

The sense of fear spikes, but I also see faces of determination—those who are willing and prepared to join this fight.

"What if they attack us here again?" someone calls out.

"They will," I reply curtly and without hesitation. "Since we are a group of people who fit exactly what they're looking for, I have no doubt that we will be seeing them here again. And they are going to keep coming, keep searching for us if we were to hide, which is why we aren't hiding anymore. I already have preparations being put into place here should there be an attack to give us an advantage. But that is all it will be. It will be up to the rest of us to stop them from there."

"I can't fight!" another person cries, and I nod.

"I won't force anyone to join this war, but I will say this. You're already in it. Whether you choose to chart your course or let GE decide is up to you." I scan the group, giving them another moment to absorb my words. "If you wish to try hiding again, then there is a long-term hotel where you can stay until it's over. There will be no protections or safeguards there, but you should have the advantage of the enemy not knowing about it. For now, at least. But if you stay, then it's to fight."

My phone vibrates against my chest. "Whether it's fighting with your fists or your gift or finding another way to help us find and take this organization down. And there will be mandatory training sessions for everyone. You should know how to defend yourself. How to create an opening that gives you a chance to escape."

Another rush of murmuring follows. Cibrina motions at me from the side of the stage and then points to her phone. I take that moment to read the name of the missed call on my phone's screen.

Fabian.

He's one of the ones on guard at the hospital.

Goddammit.

"I'll let you all think it over. Get some rest, and tomorrow, you can give Cibrina, Evie, or me your answer. Training sessions will be posted on the board by the end of the week. Do not miss them. Thank you," I conclude, bowing my head one more time and exiting the stage. "What is it?" I ask Cibrina.

She clicks the stage sound and lights off, then shows me a text on her phone.

Fabian: Reid is gone.

Cursing, I check my phone and see the same message. "I'm going back."

"I'll go with you."

"Make sure Evie knows we'll be gone again, but we'll be sending Fabian here."

Cibrina nods. "I'll meet you at the car."

I pop my head into each of the rooms with one of us in it on my way to Reid's room at the end. Silas swears everything has been quiet since Cassandra returned from healing the others and is now asleep herself. Jack and Kellan have no news to report, which leaves me with the final room.

Fabian is sitting in the spare chair of the room, his feet up on the bed while he sucks Jell-O from his overturned spoon. He glances at the door when Cibrina and I walk in, then slowly drags his feet down to drop onto the floor. "Oh. Hey."

If it were anyone else to casually say that after losing a valuable resource on their watch, I might lose my temper. But this is Fabian, and expecting anything other than sloth-like relaxation and his compulsive need to constantly be eating something is a waste of energy. I follow his spoon back to the cup that he continues to eat, even after our arrival.

Again, nothing to lose my head over.

He follows my stare and lifts the cup. "What? This? He said I could have it. I wouldn't have taken it from him without his permission."

Patience, I remind myself like a mantra.

"Fabian," Cibrina says, her tone professional as always. "What happened?"

"He left."

My eye twitches involuntarily.

"Yes, you mentioned that." I'm grateful that Cibrina decided to come with me. I'm already riding the razor's edge of my temper since all of this began, starting with the sight of Gordon on my camera, and it hasn't had a chance to come down since. I doubt it will until at least Raegan and Dane wake up to tell me for themselves that they're okay. "Can you go back to when he woke up? At what time, and then what happened?" she continues, guiding him through the information we need.

Fabian scrapes the bottom of the plastic cup and sucks his spoon clean. He sets it on the tray that hangs over the bed, swapping it out for a wrapped chocolate chip cookie. "Sure. It wasn't too long ago, maybe an hour, when he woke up. I wasn't expecting him up so soon after Sondra healed him, so it startled me a bit, y'know?"

Plastic crinkles while he talks until he finally pulls the cookie free. "He was startled too, I think, because he started freaking out about where he was. I told him it was the hospital, but he didn't seem to believe me. I told him we really were, and I asked him if he was hungry. I asked if I could have his meal and snacks if he wasn't, and he said to have at it. So, I did. Then he disappeared."

Silence.

Or, as close to that as we can get while he chews his cookie.

I draw a long, deep breath, fixing my tie and tugging the wrinkles from my suit jacket to give myself more time to calm down. "Did he happen to mention where he was going?"

Fabian shakes his head. "No, I'm telling you. He just vanished without a word." He pauses, then angles his head in thought. "Did he think we were on one of the GE islands?"

That's a very good possibility. Although he knows Fabian, and Fabian wasn't concerned about them being there. Then again, Fabian *never* seems concerned about anything. So, that may not have meant as much.

"I don't think any of us know what's going on in his mind," I muse tiredly. Months, he's been with us, and none of us knew that he was the son of the head of GE. He's Raegan's half-brother. It explains his interest in her. Did he really think he'd been captured, or is there another reason he left? Does he think he's not safe with us anymore, either, now that we know the truth? Or did he go after Tinsley on his own? "Since he's gone and likely not coming back to this room, head back to the Guild to help Evie with its protections."

"Yes, sir," he says with a nod, rising and leaving the room to do as I asked without delay. At least in following instructions he can move faster.

Sighing, I turn to Cibrina. "We'll have to get him discharged somehow without him here for a final doctor's approval. As far as they're aware, he's still injured and in bed." I look up and frown at the camera in the corner. "And there's footage of him teleporting that needs to be removed."

Fucking hospitals.

Reasons again to avoid them at all costs when it comes to gifted.

"I'll take care of it. Go visit Raegan, and I'll let you know when it's done."

"Cibrina..."

She smiles with soft understanding. "It's my pleasure, as always,

Aiden."

The woman deserves…whatever she wants. I have no idea what that is because the only woman I've ever paid that much attention to is Raegan. Maybe I can ask her to find out what Cibrina wants most. I doubt she'd admit that to me.

Once she leaves to work miracles, I return to Raegan's room, knocking softly to let Jack know it's me and then entering.

I frown when I only see Raegan in bed with no sign of Jack. The door clicks shut behind me, and I slip my hand into my other sleeve to grasp my nearest metal to prepare for an attack.

"It's me," Jackson says coolly, and I drop my hand. "Guarding the door, like you asked."

I nod, suddenly bone-tired as the weight of the last day, no, *week* if I include the party's most recent preparations, finally sinks in. My eyes catch on movement in front of him, where he's folding together a paper animal.

"Go get yourself something to eat or take a bathroom break. I'd like a moment alone, if you don't mind."

Jack pauses, his stare penetrating mine. I hold it, unyielding, for seconds, maybe a minute, before he finally smiles. "I'll grab us some snacks."

"Sure." I could personally care less about snacks right now, but my stomach growls angrily at being forgotten and the promise of food.

I wait until he's gone, and then I turn to look at Raegan. She's still fast asleep like when I left her, but her position has changed. One arm is thrown over her head, and the other folded across her abdomen. The low beep and chugging of the IV is a steady background noise. More paper animals of every color litter the flat surfaces in the room, even over the keyboard of the nurses' computer. Raegan is surrounded by a mini paper zoo.

Taking a seat in the stiff, overstuffed chair by her bedside, I lean back and cross my ankle over my knee, clasping my hands together. Even in the odd position she's splayed in, she looks comfortable. Her face sinks into the pillow I brought from the Loft, and her body is wrapped and bundled in the sheets and blankets I pulled from my room as well. She may be in a paper zoo, but she's still surrounded, first and foremost, by me.

As she should be.

Everything about her in her sleep is soft. The curves of her body. Her hair. Her lips. Her expression. It invites me in, drawing me inadvertently closer until I'm leaning in. My lips hover over hers. My hands twitch with the need to touch her. It would take nothing to act on it, to close the distance between us.

But acting on what I *desire* to do rather than what I *should* do is a slippery slope from which I won't be able to come back.

I withdraw, dropping back into the chair with my mood souring. It's almost comical how I'd described how soft she looks while I'm the epitome of hard, immovable lines. Just like the metal I command, I'm meant to defend and protect. Cut and attack. I don't know *soft*.

And here I am, craving it like a fool who wishes for the moon.

Raegan shifts in her sleep, and her hand falls over the edge right in front of me.

This time, I take the offering—I stroke the back of her hand with my thumb. "You know I'm terrible with what to say when it comes to you. But I'll do my best." I slip my other hand under hers, capturing it before I continue. "I'm sorry for what happened with your father. I sought him out, and I brought the danger to you and the Guild in my obsession with proving something to you."

"Nnngh..." Her hand spasms. "Aiden?" she asks at the end of a low groan.

"Are you awake?" After Cassandra's healing, I thought it wouldn't be until tonight at the earliest that she'd wake.

Her lips stretch into a smile even though her eyes remain shut. "I think I'd wake from death if I heard *you* say sorry."

Huffing, I lightly tighten my grip on her hand. "Very funny."

She peeks an eye open, looking at me with that smile. "You look grumpy."

I frown at her assessment. "I'm not."

"He says grumpily."

"I think I'll call the nurse in to have her check your pain medication dosage. It may be too high."

She moans sleepily, the sound doing nothing good for me here, and snuggles her face deeper into the pillow. "Leave me alone." I think she's fallen asleep again when she startles and pops her head up. "Where's Dane?"

"He's here in another room. But he's safe."

"I want to see him," she demands, sleep still coating her throat so it comes out cute rather than intimidating.

"He's resting, and I don't want him to wake up until he's gotten enough of it. Cassandra healed him, but now he needs sleep to recover."

Raegan lowers her head, burrowing back in. "As long as he's okay."

"He is," I promise.

It's quiet again, but I'm in no rush to push for a conversation if she needs to go back to sleep. It makes me wonder where Jackson disappeared to and if he ran into any trouble.

I watch her like I have all the time in the world to do so. To be content to just sit and look upon her for whatever time it takes until she wakes again.

I'm growing to hate every second she's not within my sights. And even then, it isn't enough. Charles took her from me while we were in the same room.

She wasn't close enough to reach.

"Give me a reason I shouldn't leash you to my side from now on," I muse in a hushed tone, my thumb stroking the back of her hand possessively.

Raegan hums, surprising me. "As a kink, I might be into it. If you try it in front of others, I'll stab you."

I freeze, stunned. The idea takes root faster than I can grab it, and the image of her leashed and collared to me, *obeying* me, fills my mind's view.

That's...

Fuck.

I rub my hand over my mouth as a distraction for myself, then clear my throat.

The vixen smirks, clearly not asleep and fully aware of what she's done to me.

The desire to turn her ass cheeks pink races in my chest, but I fist my hand.

She's still recovering.

Her damned smirk widens the longer I say nothing, even though her eyes are closed.

"How are you feeling?" I ask instead, hoping to drive the conversation to something more serious to get my mind and dick back on task.

"Mm...tired as hell. My body still aches a bit.... but not too bad."

"Go back to sleep." I gently push hair from her face.

"Bossy..." she grumbles but does as I ask.

This time, even when I'm sure she's asleep again, I keep my mouth closed.

Three knocks at the door bring me to my feet in an instant. I ready a blade in my sleeve, something less conspicuous than my whip sword, then open the door far enough to see who's on the other side.

A police officer stands in the hallway. "Aiden Adams?"

I hate that name.

It's a stupid last name that Dane came up with while pissed at me and setting up our fake identities. And I've been stuck with it ever since.

The fact that Elias addresses me by that part of my name is one of the many reasons that man and I don't get along. It's as if he's sensed my animosity toward it and enjoys poking me with it every chance he gets.

"Yes?" I reluctantly answer.

"I need to ask you and the patient a few questions."

Glancing over my shoulder to confirm she's still asleep, I turn back to him. "I'm afraid that won't be possible. She's sleeping now and needs her rest."

"Well, then, we can start with you."

I draw a calming breath. I knew this was what would most likely happen by coming here. Now, we have to get through it.

"I'm sorry, but I don't understand. Has someone filed charges?"

The officer shifts on his feet. "No..."

"Has someone filed a report? Or requested there be an investigation?"

He frowns. "That's difficult to say until the patients wake up."

"Wouldn't it make more sense to wait for them to wake up and see if they ask for the police before you think to interrogate people?"

"That's—"

"Oh, hello, Officer!" Cibrina hurries down the hallway, her heels clicking on the linoleum floor and her legs moving as much as they can in a tight sheath dress. She looks out of breath when she offers her smile to the police officer. "Do you mind if you and I go somewhere private to talk for a minute?"

"Did you also bring in these patients?" he asks gruffly.

Jackson strolls down the other side of the hallway, his gaze locked on the officer. He drags a few throwing knives from his hoodie that he somehow smuggled into the hospital. His eyes slide to mine, and I give the barest shake of my head.

"I'm his attorney," Cibrina replies.

The policeman nods. "Very well, then." He gives me a look, and I have a feeling this won't be the last I'll see of him.

Biting back all the things I want to say, I tilt my head in acknowledgment and watch Cibrina lead him away.

Jackson stops at the doorway.

"You were gone longer than I thought you'd be."

He smiles and shrugs. "Cibrina asked for some assistance with cameras." He pulls a cake pop from his kangaroo pocket and bites the top half. "Got some snacks, too."

Good. Time to eat before I head back to the Tower.

Or the police station.

Chapter Eight

RAEGAN

I scrunch my nose at the smell of burning food. On the couch, I'm leaning into Jackson's side as we stare at the news playing on the TV in the Loft, the guys' primary residence and a full floor apartment in the Tower. I'm not actually watching it; that's what Aiden is occupied with from his seat at the dining table while simultaneously responding to messages on his phone. I'm not sure how he can respond to people and listen to the news at the same time, but apparently, he's able to do both.

"What's burning?" I mutter when the smell only gets worse, and I don't see Jackson or Aiden jumping up to do anything about it.

Kellan curses from the kitchen, and I crane my neck around to catch a glimpse of him popping the toaster and pinching blackened bread.

"The numbers on the dial are the number of minutes you want the bread toasted for," Aiden remarks, his gaze still trained on his phone.

"I know that," Kell grinds out. "I just forgot to check which numbers they were on. Who had them turned all the way to the right?"

The plate of burned toast suddenly floats in front of me, stopping in front of Jackson. He plucks the top piece off, holding it out to me, and I vehemently shake my head. "No, thanks."

He shrugs and takes a large bite, the crunch loud enough to hear. "Food's food," he says with a smile, then goes for another.

"Yeah, but I like to enjoy the taste of it when I eat." I'm mesmerized by Jack devouring the charred bread without making a face. I think I'm waiting for him to crack, to show some sign that he doesn't like the taste, but he just smirks wider at me for watching.

"Eggs are almost up," Kellan announces.

"Are these ones edible?" Aiden questions dryly, but I don't judge him for it. It's an honest question.

Kellan smacks the spatula against the counter. "No complaints! Unless you want to cook while Rapunzel sleeps the day away, this is what you get. Or you could wake him up and ask if he feels like cooking."

Turning, I prop one hand and my chin on the back of the couch. "I'll bring him a plate and check on him."

"Don't pamper him too much, beautiful, or he'll come to expect it." He looks at Aiden. "He's milking this injury a bit, don't you think? Cassandra healed him, just like Raegan, and she woke up at the usual time like the rest of us."

Aiden sets his phone on the table, flicking his dark brown gaze to Kellan. "He's not milking anything. His injuries were more severe, so Cassandra wasn't able to heal him as thoroughly as the others.

Compounding that, since the healing was more intensive, he requires more rest."

We'd left the hospital last night, not staying more than the initial night there, and returned with the rest of the Guild to the Tower. Aiden told me that Dane had woken a couple of times, but after relieving himself and being reassured everyone was fine, he went back to bed.

Aiden slept on the floor of Dane's room to keep an eye on him, while I slept with Jack in his bed, and Kellan took guard duty on the couch. I'm not sure how the sleeping arrangements will continue when there's no bedroom for me here, but I have a feeling I won't sleep alone for a while at least until we're no longer on high alert.

I pull myself up from Jackson's side, and even before I spin to look at him, I can feel his eyes on me. "You're not planning on following me into his room, are you?"

His dimple pierces his left cheek.

"We'll be fine. I'll be one wall away."

"One wall too many."

Sighing, I run my fingers through my hair. "What if I...want some alone time with him?"

"For sex?" Jackson clarifies calmly, not an ounce of embarrassment or judgment in his tone.

Fuck a duck. Of course, he would call me out just like that. And in front of the others, too. But I'm already halfway there; why not just dive in? "What if I do?"

Jackson shrugs. "I can turn away if you don't want me to watch."

I stare at him, aghast at his honesty and lack of hesitation.

No. Nope. Not doing this.

"I'm going into his room with a plate of food, and the *three* of you can leave us be." Kellan cackles in the kitchen, and Aiden's intense stare fixates on me. Fuck knows what *he's* thinking about, but I've had enough honesty right now than to ask for more.

Jack smirks and nods.

Why don't I believe him?

I take a step away, waiting for him to move, too. When he doesn't, I release a sigh and walk to the kitchen to make Dane's plate. The eggs are a dark yellow. Dry and overcooked. Opening the fridge, I scan for alternatives. It's bare except for condiments. It makes sense, considering this apartment has been empty for months, but I'd hoped to have something else to offer Dane.

I grab the ketchup in case he eats it that way—or maybe he will today—and then take the plate to his door. Knocking softly, I let myself in when there's no answer. Dane is fast asleep in bed, his thick, longer blond hair at the top of his head sticking every which way. His room is tidier than I expected. Even with the rushed packing job they did before moving, everything is in its place, nothing on the floor.

I set everything down on his gaming desk in the corner and then crouch by his head. "Hey," I whisper, brushing some of the blond tufts off his forehead. "I brought you breakfast."

Dane stirs, stretching on a low groan, then reaches for me with his eyes still closed. "Mmm....c'mere," he says sleepily. His arms wrap around my back, dragging me closer.

"Move over, then," I tease. He shifts, and I crawl into that space, lying beside him. His arms slip around me again, pulling me against his chest before he tosses the blankets over me, too.

We're quiet at first. His heart beats steadily in his chest, his breathing calm and warm above me. Aiden told me he'd had more broken ribs, one of which resulted in him developing a chest infection that made it even more difficult for him to breathe.

I remember the feel of his body on mine when he protected me. When he refused to let Charles kill me, even when he was just as injured as me. When he'd been kicked hard enough that his body almost flew off me if not for his firm grip and sheer stubbornness.

Clenching the back of his shirt, I turn my face into his chest, breathing him in. His citrusy scent, his warmth. "Dane..."

He nuzzles my hair, inhaling deeply. "I thought I was going to lose you," he breathes, his voice thick with emotion.

I nod against him. "You saved me."

"I've never been so scared in my life, Rae. I was terrified that my hand would slip. That he'd get to you before I could stop him."

"But you didn't let go."

He swallows so hard that I can feel the drop of his Adam's apple.

"I'm sorry I was useless," I whisper.

"Useless!" Gordon's voice echoes in my mind.

"Don't apologize. That guy's an overpowered freak." His breath catches, probably when he remembers that said freak is my father, then adds a mumbled, "Sorry."

"It's fine. He's no father of mine. And he *was* a psycho."

"Worthless pet..."

I squeeze my eyes shut.

Shut up.

Will I ever get rid of him? I haven't even asked Aiden or Jack about him yet. Did he escape somehow? Do I want him to be alive so I can kill him myself? Do I just want him dead so it's over? Will his death free me from him, or will he linger like this, forever haunting me?

"What's wrong?" Dane shifts back, his hand lifting my chin so he can see my face. His dark brows are pinched, his mouth tight. "Is it Charles?"

I latch on to his golden eyes, seeking out the flecks of green in them as an exercise to distract myself from my other thoughts. "No," I admit breathlessly. "It's...disappointing that we're related by blood. But I didn't get to know him well enough to care about him like that. I was caught off guard when he first revealed himself, but now...it doesn't matter."

"Then tell me why your body was shaking."

I suck in and gnaw on my lower lip. I don't want to confess it was Gordon. I don't want him, or the others, to know that I'm still affected by that man.

But Dane already knows.

I had that panic attack in the elevator because of Gordon, and Dane helped me through it.

He didn't know I was hearing Gordon's voice in my head, though.

He didn't ask what caused it; just left the offer to talk about it without expectation.

"Is it him?" Dane's voice lowers, his tone deepening with lethal intent. "Gordon?"

I pull my gaze from his, staring at his shoulder instead.

"Whatever you're remembering, fuck him."

My fingers fidget at the front of his shirt. "I wish it were that easy."

He circles my ear, pushing my hair from my face, then strokes his thumb along my jaw. "Then let's start with what I've missed while sleeping."

"I don't know much. Aiden wanted to wait until we were all together. I do know we were in the hospital at one point. And then Cassandra finished healing us so we could leave."

Dane's eyebrows rise. "Aiden took us to a hospital?" He exhales a curse. "He must have been pissed about that. Being there will probably come back to bite us."

"Yeah, but I don't think he had a choice with Cassandra down and us injured like we were."

He hums, then cranes his neck back for a few seconds and brings it back. "Damn. It's already afternoon."

"It's fine. You needed the rest. Oh, and Kellan made you scrambled eggs."

The last words hardly leave my mouth before he replies, "Hard pass."

"What? Why? You need to eat."

"Kellan made it. I'll be better off not eating."

"You haven't even seen it."

Dane laughs, his tone mocking. "Don't need to. I'll make something myself. What do you want? French toast? Seafood? Steak?"

"There's no food in the fridge."

"Tell me what you want," he insists.

I pause, considering. "Pasta?"

"Pasta," he repeats, blinking in surprise.

"What's wrong with that? It was one of the few things I learned to cook for myself. I could buy a cheap box and some sauce, then cook enough to last me all week. And it tasted good."

He stares in silence for a couple of heartbeats, then releases a breath, closing his eyes and pressing his forehead against mine. "Pasta, then."

What was that about? Frowning, I grab his wrist, tugging to remove his hand, but he resists, holding firm. "Don't pity me," I bite out.

He opens his eyes, locking them with mine as he leans back to see me better. "I don't." His hand slides from my jaw to my neck, to the collar of my shirt, tracing my skin along the edge of the fabric. "I'm just thinking of all the other things I want to make for you. I'm going to spoil you with food so that no one else's will ever be good enough. Then when you're hungry, you'll come running to me," he finishes with a cocky smirk.

Oh.

A small smile touches my lips. "I'll run to you for more than food."

"Oh, yeah?" Dane challenges, his smirk widening and raising a single brow.

I slip a hand under his shirt, stroking up the hard planes of his abdomen. "Mmhmm..."

Something sparks in his eyes before they turn molten. He cups my neck beneath my ear. His breath is suddenly warm as he leans in, lips parted, and eyes lidded. I tilt my face to meet him, our lips melting together when they touch.

I expect the inevitable snap between us, the break of control once we give in, but it doesn't happen. Dane's tongue sinks between my lips, his kiss unhurried and languorous. Like he has nowhere else he'd rather be than kissing me in this bed all day.

I relax into it, into him.

Eventually, I push him to roll onto his back so I straddle him, and his hard length strains against his gym shorts. We take the seconds of fresh air to refill our oxygen before we're kissing again. This time with my core gyrating against his cock and too many clothes between us.

Dane groans, his hands gripping my ass as I rock against him. "Fuuuuuck," he gasps, breathless. He moves a palm up my backside, sliding under my shirt until he finds the band of my bra. He pinches it firmly, taking only two tries before it jumps free, and his hand seeks out my breasts.

The next time I break for air, he drags my shirt up, pulling gently until I drop my head and allow him to free me from it. Next are my arms, and he directs my shirt and bra straps down either side. Slowly. So fucking slowly that goosebumps appear in his wake.

I've stopped moving against him, my heart fluttering as I see the way he watches me with so much awe and appreciation that breathing becomes difficult.

"Come closer," he directs huskily, his hand guiding a breast to his mouth. He holds it firmly in his grip, his pink tongue flicking out to wet my nipple. I feel it all the way down to my core.

He licks it again, circling its pert tip, then drags his teeth over it, stretching the nipple before releasing it.

I throw my head back, eyes closed, as a shudder runs through my body like an electric current.

"Do you like that?" He sucks my nipple into his mouth, then only frees it through ivory gates. "My teeth?"

I nod emphatically. "Yes."

He does it more, his tongue a searing swipe of heat. His teeth are a pinch of pain that fades to pleasure. The action shoots a livewire of need straight to my cunt, and I writhe above him.

Dane strips my pants down to my thighs, and I help him remove them until I'm naked. He sits up and takes off his shirt and shorts in seconds, then pulls me into his lap and returns to tease and taste my other breast.

I bury my fingers in his hair, closing and tightening them to a fierce grip that draws a guttural groan from him. My hips rock against him again of their own accord, seeking friction where we touch.

Dane jerks his hips forward, pushing his cock against me. My pussy is already slick, spreading my pleasure along his shaft so I glide easily from end to end.

"Jesus. Fuck," Dane breathes before he grabs the hair at the back of my head, and we lose ourselves in a passionate kiss. I dig my nails into his shoulders as I hang on tight, the feel of him under me and his kiss a devastating thing that has me grappling for more before I burst.

I slide too high, too far, and feel his tip prod at my entrance in an exhilarating rush. Dane holds his breath. I'm tempted to end the tease right there. To take away this building ache in my lower abdomen. The need that makes me feel flashes of heat; pleasure to pool and tighten at my core.

Not yet. I deny us both, shifting and gliding back down. I keep moving, biting at his lower lip until I taste blood and then chase it with my tongue.

Fuck, this feels too good to stop. And, also, not enough.

I keep going until I'm driven mindless by it. There's only the short, panted breaths between us, the sound of our bodies slapping and sliding together, until finally, I drive myself onto him so quickly that it takes my breath away.

Dane curses, his fingers creating indentations at my hips, and he expels a long breath. He palms the back of my head, bringing our foreheads together. "I don't want to rush this, Rae. You can fuck me if you want, but you'll take your time with it. Or else I'll take over."

Take my time.

Right.

His eyes find mine, and he nods as if encouraging me to give it a try. I raise my hips slow and steady, then drop almost all the way down before returning to the tip.

Dane smirks and grabs my hips, seating me fully on his cock. He guides me to move in a circle, forward and back, undulating so his dick moves within me, rubbing rather than stroking my inner walls. It feels fucking amazing, and the flame I'd stoked, which had been ready to explode moments ago, sinks down, growing once again, but from a bigger flame than before.

My hips take over from his direction once I know what he's

looking for, and he releases me. His finger lifts my chin, leading my face back to his, and his heated gaze expresses so much emotion that he's overflowing with it.

It's so...intimate. Personal.

I try to look away to focus on the pleasure instead, but he draws me back to him.

"No. Look at me. I want to see you, and I want you to see me. Feel me. In this moment, it's only you and me."

He doesn't rush me, and eventually, I drag my gaze back to his and start moving again, rebuilding that pleasure that has my body buzzing with need from all the edging.

Dane licks his lips, watching me like a man enthralled by a temptress. He kisses me again. Like he can't help himself but take another taste of a forbidden fruit. It's long and desperate, telling me through it that he's just as affected as I am, needing me more than ever but denying himself the instant gratification for something greater.

His thumb rubs where we meet, finding my slick and spreading it to my clit. I jolt against his kiss at the contact, the desire so strong that I grind greedily against him once he starts moving his thumb. It's a double-win because of where his cock rubs inside me, and a wanton moan breaks from my lips unbidden.

He keeps his pace steady, and it takes *every-fucking-thing* in me to match it with my hips. Pressure coils tighter and tighter in me, almost to an uncomfortable feeling that demands it snap and be released. "Dane," I pant, on the brink of begging.

"Okay," he concedes. "Just a little." Like before, he guides me where he wants me at the speed he expects. This time, I'm brought to his tip and then curve my hips on the way back down. But still at a torturous speed.

It doesn't matter, though, because each time I'm fully seated, and his dick hits me deep, a burst of pleasure sparks through me. Again. And again.

Dane's panting, letting me control my movements, while he watches me with such raw affection that it makes my chest burn. He doesn't let me hide behind the pleasure or actions. It's like he's stripped me bare to my soul, and for this time that we're together, our souls are exposed and joining together. This feeling, it's unlike anything I've felt before, and it warms and fills my body in a rush of heat.

And then the coil breaks, my orgasm rupturing through me, hard and ruthless. My muscles contract, freezing me in place where I can do nothing but let it consume me. I'm faintly aware of Dane moving, of him thrusting into my tightened pussy, and—*oh, fuck*—it's too much. His hips slam against mine one last time as he releases a long, low groan.

I collapse, boneless, into him. He guides us back to the bed, then holds me tight to turn us until he's on top. Dane kisses my collarbone. My chest. My shoulder. My neck. My lips.

I let him take what he wants because I still can't move. He somehow has the energy to pull himself out to his tip and then slowly push back in. Another shudder of pleasure rocks through me like an aftershock, and he smirks, lowering himself to press a kiss to my cheek before freeing himself and rolling to his side.

"Here," he says softly, opening his arm and shifting me onto it and his chest. He holds me close, catching his breath, while I bask in the post-coital afterglow that has me feeling whole and sated.

We stay like that for a while, neither of us needing to say or do anything. Finally, I speak up when I begin to feel guilty that there are still things to do. "The others are waiting," I murmur softly. "We should get out there."

He's quiet for a moment, and I wonder what he's thinking. Eventually, he speaks, "And I owe you pasta. I'll check with Aiden to see if he can add the things I need to the grocery order, assuming he hasn't already placed it." He kisses my head. "Stay here. I'll be right back."

He carefully slides his arm free and then makes his way to his en-suite bathroom. I'm not sure how anyone lives without those now. I can't imagine having to walk across the hall to a shared bathroom in front of everyone to go clean up. He returns with a washcloth and wipes away the mess between my thighs. When he leaves again with the used cloth, I dress in my clothes.

He returns in a fresh set of clothes, his hair fixed, wearing a dangerous smirk. "I'm surprised you waited."

Shrugging, I don't bother telling him that the others already knew this was a high likelihood. Hopefully, no one will say anything, and he'll be none the wiser.

Opening the door for us, I tell him over my shoulder, "Grab the plate and ketchup if you—Wah!" My foot kicks something hard, and I pitch forward. Something pushes me back to my feet, and I glare down at Jackson, casually sitting in front of the door. His face is slanted my way, a smirk curling his lips.

For fuck's sake.

CHAPTER NINE

RAEGAN

KELLAN LOUNGES AT THE dining table, his plate empty before him, and no one else.

"Where's Aiden?"

He grins, pulling his hand down his beard like he's wrangling any stragglers back to the group. "Once he heard your wake-up gift to Dane, he got up and stormed to his room. Muttered something about taking a shower, but I'll bet he's in there jerking off to the sounds you were making, beautiful."

Oh.

Shit.

Here I was, worried about Jackson overhearing everything from the door, when apparently the walls in this apartment are thin enough for the entire living area to hear us.

"You can wake me up that way anytime, too," he adds, his blue-green eyes glittering wickedly. "No invitation or permission needed."

Ah. He's assuming I woke Dane with morning head. Rather than correcting him, I smirk, matching his energy when I reply, "Right back at ya." I blow him a kiss between a backwards peace sign with a wink, and he slaps a hand over his heart, falling back into his chair.

"Fuck, beautiful. You still look sleepy. Go take a nap."

Dane walks to the kitchen, shaking his head. "The two of you..." he mutters, proceeding to open cabinets and the pantry door. "Did Aiden order groceries?"

Jackson, who still hasn't left the hallway, answers, "He did."

Dane pulls a pen and pad of paper out of a drawer, scribbling a few things on it before tearing it off and handing it to me. "Here. Ask Aiden to add these to the order. I'm not sure when he scheduled the delivery for, so it can't wait."

I accept the piece of paper automatically. It feels weird to be worrying about something as mundane as groceries after everything that happened the last couple of days.

Wait.

"You're asking me to interrupt his shower?"

He shrugs, smirking. "Better you than any of us."

Right.

Kellan snickers from his seat, and Jackson opens Aiden's door for me before I get the chance to consider what I'm about to get myself into. Why does it feel like all three of these guys are offering me up on a platter, and I'm the only one who has no idea what I'm walking into?

Because Aiden is still an enigma. I never know what's going on in his head.

Jack closes the door behind me, trapping me inside. The sound of the shower echoes from the cracked bathroom door, steam curling around its edges before dissipating into the rest of the room. Aiden's bedroom is just as organized as Dane's. The floor is bare, all surfaces clear. Aside from his bed, a reading chair, and a small table, there's not much to it.

Kellan's and Jack's, by comparison, are wild and haphazard.

Clenching the piece of paper in my hand, I stride to the bathroom as if I have every right to be in there, even though my heart pounds harder with every step I take. Even though my breathing shallows as I get close enough to breathe in the hot, moist air.

It's just Aiden.

I make it across the threshold before I pause and squint to see through the steam. Even though it's my first time in the Loft, I recognize it. They must have modeled the safehouse after the Loft because aside from being somewhat smaller, they're nearly identical.

I take another few steps inside until Aiden's shadow appears behind the shower glass. He's leaning a forearm against the wall, his head bent, and his hand somewhere lower. Curiosity drives me closer again, thinking the steam and his occupied attention will be enough to keep me hidden.

A tattoo covers his back with a sword down his spine and bent wings on either side. A bat wing and an angel wing. Ink chains loosely wrap both and tighten down the length of the blade. My gaze travels lower. His other hand strokes his cock, his movements harsh and bordering on violence.

Crap. He's pissed.

I should go.

"Get out," he demands, his voice rougher than usual and startling me. He's turned his head, and his dark, bottomless eyes draw me in like gravity. There's a coarseness to him now that I'm not used to. Like something scraped at his control, leaving behind jagged edges.

Leaving is exactly what I'd planned to do, but something about this man telling me what to do makes me lose my mind. Defiance swells in my chest, burning away fear or self-preservation when I respond, "No."

Aiden's jaw tightens. He has yet to release the hold on his dick. When my gaze trails back up his body to find his eyes again, he's breathing harder. Faster. He shoves off the wall, stalking to the opening of the shower that has no door. "Then come here." This time, his voice comes out as a purr, soft and dangerous, like something's switched in his mind to help smooth those edges. To put him back in control.

I must be a masochist because I do it. Everything about him right now radiates anger and frustration. And I'm not being a narcissist for thinking it's because of me. I'm just not stupid.

Or, am I, because I'm too curious to leave? Too stubborn to make what is probably the *right* decision when he tells me to get out. But I hated it when he said that. That he feels he has to kick me out so he can struggle with whatever he's going through because of me, without me.

He doesn't wait for me to get there. As soon as I'm within reach, he grabs my throat and yanks me into him, the soft spray of hot water speckling my face and clothes. I don't fight him. I'm not sure why. I let him hold me like that, my body acquiescing and pliant, even though I look at him without an ounce of submission in my gaze.

"Leave. I'm not myself right now."

I know I'm going to set him off. He's like a ticking time bomb, and I'm the idiot who cuts the fuse short and then lights it before I can get out of range. "No."

"No?" he repeats, his voice a deadly calm. "Is that all you have to say for yourself? No?"

"Say for myself?"

"Take off your clothes," he croons in my ear, his voice decadent like drizzled chocolate.

Again, I surprise myself when I do what he says without a word, shedding my clothes and tossing Dane's paper to the side. He's forced to release me so I can remove my shirt and bra, but otherwise, he remains still.

"Go to the second drawer on the right," he directs next, indicating the drawers under the sink. "Take out the first thing you see and bring it to me."

Curiosity is a dangerous thing. It, tangled with the heat of this room and the thick anticipation of what he's going to do wrapping me in a chokehold, has me following his instruction once more.

I open the drawer, and items of all shapes, sizes, and colors roll backward at the movement.

He has a fucking drawer of sex toys.

But which one?

"The first thing you see."

The purple bullet at the front. I wrap my fingers around the smooth silicone. I catch my reflection in the mirror before I turn back. My blonde hair is starting to frizz and expand in the wet heat, adding volume and unruliness. My eyes are dilated, my lips moist from licking them, and my nipples are pebbled, even in this warmth.

There's no doubt that I'm aroused by whatever's happening here.

"Don't make me wait…"

I return to him, releasing the toy into his open hand and waiting with bated breath.

He skates his palm up my side, following the curve of my body over my chest and up my neck, his fingers wrapping my nape with a more relaxed grip. He caresses my pulse with his thumb as it hammers erratically against his touch.

His other hand cups my sex, and he slides a finger into my wet heat. "What did I tell you about this pussy?" he asks, his voice chillingly calm.

There's no resistance when he slips his finger in and out, the mixture of mine and Dane's remaining cum still lingering. But I'm not hiding it. My stare hardens when I reply, "I never agreed to it."

His hand on my neck tightens, and he removes his finger. But not to stop, as I expected. He continues upward, finding and caressing my clit. "That's not what I asked."

Pleasure spikes through my limbs at the simple contact. "You told me it's yours," I answer, some defiance still coloring my breathy tone.

"Good girl," he praises on a satisfied sigh, his breath hot between us, and then steps back, bringing me into the shower. The water hits my thighs where he stops us, where everything stops for a second.

"Hands on the wall," is my only warning, and then he's pushing me down, bending me over. I reach out at his command, and on instinct, my hands slap against the slick tile.

"And what did I promise you about my pussy?" He palms my ass, rubbing it with clear intent. My thighs quiver and clench in response.

"You'd punish me if I touched it."

"Did you?"

Smirking, I answer, "No."

The first slap is loud and raw, weaving with my audible cry and echoing through the room before becoming lost in the steam. He buffs the pain away with his hand, spreading the remaining pleasure and warmth beneath my skin. "I also told you I didn't think I had it in me to share."

"That's a you-problem," I retort. "The others are fine with it."

Another smack. Rub.

His lips graze the shell of my ear. "And are the others fine when you end up choosing one in the end?" he croons.

"I'm not. I won't."

"How can I know that's true? How can you know you won't get tired of one or more of us? When having four of us to satisfy becomes too much?"

"I want all of you, Aiden. It won't be too much. I swear, if you give in to it, it'll be the best thing."

"What about now?" he challenges.

"What about it?"

His fingers push into me, and I groan, leaning heavily into the wall to support myself. "Is your cunt raw and sore from just having sex with Dane?"

I sink more onto his fingers, encouraging them deeper. "No. Fuck me, Aiden. That's what you want at the end of all this, isn't it? Then take me. I'm yours. Just remember that I'm theirs, too."

His fingers are gone, replaced by his cock as it notches at my entrance before he drives inside in a single stroke. My legs tremble and quake, but I force them to keep myself upright. Aiden grips my hips hard enough to bruise like he's trying to imprint his fingerprints on my skin to claim me as his. I throw my head back, eyes closed, and a long moan slides past my lips as that's exactly what he does. Claim me.

Aiden fucks me with abandon, finally losing his self-control and allowing himself to take what he'd been holding himself back on. I'm barely holding on, my hands slipping and straining to keep myself forward while I'm driven up on my tiptoes for him to reach me better.

His pace slows suddenly, and the sharp click followed by buzzing tells me what's coming. "Do you want this or my fingers?"

He holds the vibrator close, his fingers spreading me wide on either side so I can nearly feel it touching my clit, but not quite. It's *maddening*.

"That," I pant heavily.

"Say it," he croons, and my heart flutters.

"I want the vibrator."

His fingers twitch, and I get the tiniest taste of it before it disappears, and I inhale sharply.

"You want it...what?"

Fuck. What word is he looking for? My mind scrambles with

the English vocabulary, tripping over anything and everything until something seems right. "Please. I want the vibrator, *please*," I beg, my hips jerking forward, but all that does is pull me further off his dick as he easily moves the vibrator out of reach.

"Good girl," he breathes, his length thrusting into me once more while simultaneously the vibrator is pressed at my bundle of nerves.

"Oh, fuck!" I curse and moan, grinding against it and him.

"You're going to come for me until I'm satisfied, aren't you? As many times as I tell you to."

This man really wants to kill me. By orgasm.

But I did tell him that would be my favorite way to die, and I'm no quitter.

"Yes!"

He moves the vibrator against me, increasing its speed and holding it there as he slams into me from behind. "Then come for me now, Raegan."

His words are my undoing, the orgasm shredding through me in a violent storm. Aiden holds me tight, both keeping me upright and the vibrator in place until I'm screaming and my knees buckle. He doesn't let me fall, lifting me effortlessly and shifting me until my legs are wrapped around his waist, and then he's sinking into me again.

Aiden kisses me fiercely, and I rise to his provocation. Our lips mash together, kissing like we're feeding off one another. Water beats over his back, the reflecting spray catching us both. I collar his neck, then palm his shoulders and back, dragging my nails up his skin.

He grunts, dropping his mouth to the side of my neck. The

vibrator is back, pinned between us and his thrusts. "Did he come in you?" he breathes into my skin, his voice roughened by his movements.

I hold him close as I urge my hips up to meet his strokes, to feel the short press of the vibrator that makes my cunt throb with pleasure. "Yes."

His teeth nip at the crook of my neck, replaced quickly by a hot tongue and soothing lips. "You drive me mad, Raegan. Everything you do…it takes me to the brink of sanity in seconds. Makes me want to fuck the words right out of your mouth. Bend you over and spank your ass until it's the same pink shade as your pussy. And then make you beg for my cock to fix the ache. Make you come until you'll do anything I say, when I say it. Be a good girl, for me."

Holy fuck.

His pace is just right, the vibrator pulsating in time with every stroke, his dick hitting that deep place in me that has my toes curling and pleasure intensifying at the base of my spine.

"I can feel your pussy quivering. You're close. But not yet. Not until I tell you. Understand?"

Fuck. Fuck. Fuck.

I don't think I can hold it back. I'm so close. So *fucking* close. And without him saying a single word, I just know that he'll punish me with the worst and longest edging and orgasm denial if I don't do as he says.

"Answer me," he commands, and I somehow manage a breathless, "Yes."

My entire body trembles with the need to come, only holding

back out of sheer force of will and desperation. I grip between his neck and shoulders, digging my nails in and hardly breathing.

Please, please, please.

Our hips collide again and again, and I can feel my control slipping. It's coming. I'm going to come.

Fuck.

"Now." At his husky command, I let go, my breath leaving me in a rush as my cunt clamps down on him, and I cry out in pleasure, triumph—I don't fucking know. He comes with me, his cock swelling and bursting with his seed. Aiden's expression is like a release of all the tension and problems in his life at once. It's filled with pure pleasure and contentment, things I never see on him, and then it's gone.

And now I've discovered my new obsession with seeing it again.

Just...maybe not this second.

I realize then that he may not be done with me. *"Until I'm satisfied,"* he said. I swallow, my arms tightening around him while he's preoccupied, catching his breath against my shoulder. He licks the beads of water there, groaning and looking almost pained as he pulls away.

"It's never enough," he mutters, and my chest squeezes uncomfortably. Aiden pins me with his dark stare, sucking me into that void as his prisoner. "I don't think I'll ever have enough of you. If not for the mountain of things we have to do, eating being high on that list, I'd be indulging in petting that greedy pussy of yours with my tongue."

Said pussy clenches at the dark promise—or threat—and I'm

convinced it's just pretending to be a good girl for him because there is no fucking way it can take anymore right now.

"That's the way I feel about all of you," I tell him, my voice still winded. Then, remembering everything he said, I add, "Minus the pussy part." He watches me with rapt attention while I continue, "I will never get tired of any of you. I'm in this for...life. However long that is for us."

His brows knit with concern at my outlook. "Long. I promise we'll be old and gray one day." I nod with a tight smile, and he pinches my chin. "I don't give platitudes."

"I know."

Aiden holds our stare a bit longer until he's sure I understand. Then, he withdraws and helps me to my feet. "Can you stand?" His hands never let me go, making sure I have my balance as he leans down to guide and check my Jell-O legs.

"Yeah, I'm okay," I tell him once I believe I can stand without falling over. But he doesn't right himself with that confirmation. Instead, he's eyeing a dribble of cum leaking down my inner thigh.

Aiden's frozen there, staring at it until a sliding trail of water threatens to touch it. He drags two fingers up my thigh, scooping it up, and pushes it back into me. I gasp, grabbing his shoulder for stability when he does it. He curses, muttering something about insanity, then looks me dead in the face. "Don't waste it, or I'll be forced to fill you with more."

I stare, open-mouthed, in disbelief. Is he fucking serious?

Without batting an eye, he pulls his body wash from the shelf and lathers it on a washcloth, proceeding to clean me without another word. I'm surrounded by the smell of cinnamon as the cloth works the scent into my skin. It feels like another claim of his. One more way he's marking me, between the bruises, his cum, and now this.

It makes me wonder if we made any progress at all, but I'm too tired and content to argue.

That's exactly how he wanted me, isn't it?

Well, fuck.

He wins this round.

Chapter Ten

RAEGAN

Aiden shuts the water off once we're both clean, then takes the towel he'd laid aside for himself to wrap around me. It's massive and could probably fit two people in it, and I hug it tightly around myself as I step out of the shower. Without the hot water running to produce more steam, the cooler air of his bedroom slips in, adding a slight chill that induces a full-body shiver.

"Dry off and get dressed before you catch a cold." Aiden wraps his new towel around his waist, then strides to his bedroom.

When I grab my clothes from the floor, a piece of paper tumbles free.

Oh.

Whoops.

I pinch the paper and hurry to the door, only for Aiden to walk through it first with a bag in hand. "Here are your things from the bunker. Make me a list of anything else you need: clothes, bathroom supplies, shoes, anything. I'll order and have them delivered here for you."

I nod, accepting the bag in my arms, though I don't need much more than what's already in there. Maybe a few restocks of bathroom supplies, but which bathroom will I keep that in? There's the shared powder room right off the living area, but the only full bathrooms in this apartment are in each of their rooms.

Hopefully that discussion will be part of the one we're about to have as a group. My living and sleeping arrangements.

"And one more thing," he adds, his hand closed around something and waiting for mine.

Freeing a hand, he drops a purple butterfly clip onto my palm.

Portia's clip.

"You grabbed this?"

"You said it was important to you."

I close my hand around it and swallow thickly. He remembered this tiny little thing, searched the bunker for it to make sure I was reunited with it, and that does more to me than I know what to do with. "Thank you." Clearing my throat, I wave Dane's piece of paper at him. "Dane asked if you could add some things to the grocery list. Is it too late?"

He checks his phone, which he apparently picked up at some point, tapping something with his thumb a couple of times, then brings it to his ear. "This is Aiden, the one who placed the order you're on your way to deliver. Yes. I have other items that need to be added. I understand. I'll add an extra hundred-dollar tip for the inconvenience. Great. I'll text them over to you now."

He takes the paper and holds it in front of him, then snaps a picture with his phone and taps away again. "There. The store is around the corner, so it'll still be delivered shortly." He returns to his bedroom, leaving me in the bathroom to get dressed.

I pull out something comfortable for today: a crew neck shirt and some jeans, for a change. Peeking into the bedroom, I spy Aiden working on his tie with only his dress jacket remaining. No time to blow-dry my hair, then. I stick to finger-combing the wet locks to avoid future tangles and make sure it dries somewhat nicely. Add a touch of eyeliner, and I'm done.

The sound of a door opening has me kicking my bag to the corner and tossing everything else on top so I can rush out at the same time as Aiden. We'd been waiting for Dane to wake up first, but now it's on me that we haven't all caught up yet because I'd been busy having sex with half of them.

Fuck. Don't think of it like that.

I round the corner after Aiden to the dining table. He takes a seat at the head nearest to us, while Kellan is seated at the opposite end, and Dane on the right between them. I'm assuming the last chair on the other side of Dane is Jack's, even though it's empty.

"You can have my seat," Jackson murmurs behind me, coming from fuck-knows where. But I don't react, having expected him to be somewhere close.

"Thanks." I offer him a small smile over my shoulder, which he returns, but there's still something off about it. About him. There has been since I woke up in his bed this morning, which means it has nothing to do with me and Dane or Aiden. I just need a chance to be alone with him to find out what it is.

"You feel better after getting your dick wet?" Kellan drawls toward Aiden, his grin sharp. Dane shoots him a glare. "What? He took a shower, didn't he?"

"That's not what you fucking meant, and you know it," Dane snarks.

I sit, and Jackson leans against the wall in the corner.

"Enough. We need to go over everything that happened and the next steps." Aiden's dark brown gaze pauses on each of us to make sure he has our attention before he continues, "I'm not sure how much you watched from the cameras, but when Jack, Reid, and I arrived at the butcher shop, Gordon had freed Thorne from the cuffs by removing his thumbs."

I grip my knees and concentrate on my lap. This is it. I'm going to find out what happened to him. Shit, am I shaking? I fist my hands, attempting to clamp down on whatever tremors are involuntarily taking control of my body.

"Wait," Dane snaps. He lifts his chair and carries it around the table, dropping it next to mine and sitting down. He puts my hand in his, encouraging me to release my grip so he can slide his fingers between mine, then settles our hands back in my lap. "Okay."

I can feel all their eyes on me, but I don't look away from Aiden. He's watching me carefully, waiting for me to tell him I'm ready, and I nod for him to continue.

I'm listening to what he says, and yet not. As if his voice is background noise, talking behind a veil where only key words jump out at me. Thorne attacked Gordon. Gordon admitted the president of GE was at the bunker. And then...and then...

"...moved his body to an ice chest temporarily, which we locked from the outside, here in the Tower."

Dane squeezes my hand and leans in, whispering in my ear, "Are you okay?"

...his body...

Ice chest.

That means...

He's dead...right?

The panic doesn't ebb when that thought passes through. It's not...solid enough. It doesn't feel real.

Could he still come back?

Is this another trick?

Another lie?

"He's dead." Jackson's voice breaks through my internal spiral, and it's like I can draw air again.

I realize that's what I needed. Someone to outright say it.

My eyes find his. He's now crouching where Dane had been seated so his forearms are leaning on the table, and his face is level with mine. His deeper blue gaze is shadowed, something unpleasant lurking there, and I recall the wishes I'd given him. The one where I'd wanted to make Gordon pay.

"He's dead," he repeats, our eyes locked, so there's no questioning it. So I can try again to process it.

He's dead.

Dead.

Gone.

"I'm sorry we couldn't bring him to you alive," Aiden says softly. "But you can do with him as you please. Or allow us to."

The room grows quiet.

What...do I want to...do...with him?

It feels like my brain is sluggish, thoughts struggling through a quagmire or sinking into it before I can reach for them.

Dane squeezes my hand again, and I return the pressure on autopilot. "Rae..."

"You don't have to decide right now," Aiden offers. "Take your time to think about—"

"I need to see him," I blurt out. The last time I thought he was dead, I'd based it on a lab coat beneath the rubble. And while I do trust Aiden and Jackson, I don't think I'll be able to accept it completely until I see that truth with my own eyes.

Aiden nods slowly, his gaze sharpening as he watches me.

"And I want his body burned down to his bones." The words fly out of me unchecked, but after I hear them, it feels right. "When his bones are all that's left, I'll destroy the rest with my gift. There will be no chance for resurrection."

"Do you care what we do to him before you burn him?" Jackson asks coolly.

I pause, considering. "No. He won't feel any of it, so it doesn't matter."

He smiles.

"I'll make the time for us to take care of that in the next few days, then," Aiden confirms, checking in with me again for a nod of acceptance. "Kellan."

"We got a report of the quarantine doors opening on their own. I figured it was Harvey up to his usual pranks, but sent Raegan and

Dane up to the room just in case." His expression darkens, and he shifts forward to lean on the table. "I found Claudia first. She was already gone when I got there. The fight was over. I don't know when it started, but the rats in the group grabbed the others and ran through a portal, I'd bet. Since the kids made it out somehow, I'm sure Claudia had something to do with their escape."

I remember meeting Claudia at Portia's apartment. When she'd shown up to take and help Isabel, she'd been so proud to be a member of the Guild.

What's going to happen to the children without Claudia here to help them?

"Harvey was crying behind the desk, covered in blood. I don't know the extent of his involvement since it looked like the fighting began before he snuck in, but I couldn't get anything out of him before Charles stabbed me in the back."

Psycho dad.

"The freak licked my blood, then began shooting me while asking me questions about my gift. Next thing I know, he's showing me that he has my gift, too. Once he ran out of bullets, he touched my head, and I can't remember anything after that. Until you woke me up." He motions to Aiden, who nods.

"Reid informed us that Charles can copy others' gifts by consuming their blood."

"Gross," Dane mutters.

"If that's all, why not just cut Dane and drink his blood to get his gift?" I question, confused.

"Now he sounds like a vampire," Kellan drawls.

"It's so he's not the guinea pig," Jackson offers, twirling a throwing knife across his knuckles.

"That's a good point, but I think we're missing something else." Aiden taps his fingers on the table in thought. "He was surrounded by the gifted in quarantine, but there were no reports of him doing that. Now, he could have found blind spots to hide what he was doing, but I haven't seen or heard of him doing anything outside of the list Reid gave us. I think there's some other limitation we're not aware of."

"Like why he didn't copy Vera's gift if it was so important to what they were working on? They had to use Royce," I chime in.

"Yes. Exactly. It could be a limitation of the number of gifts he can have at a time. Or else a characteristic of who he's copying the gift from," Aiden adds.

Dane scoffs. "That could be anything. Can't Reid answer all this? He and Charles seemed familiar."

"Because he's Charles's son." Kellan pulls his hair back, tying it half-up and away from his face, though a few shorter strands still fall free. "Which makes him our girl's brother."

Dane slaps a hand on the table. "I know that! I mean...*familiar*. Rae's related to Charles by blood, but they just met. Reid and Charles *knew* each other. I'm sure he knows all that guy's secrets."

"Half-brother, according to Reid. And we can't ask him because he left," Aiden answers calmly.

Dane stares, blinking for a full breath before his face contorts. "He *left*?! What do you mean he left? Did he turn on us?"

Aiden sighs. "After Cassandra healed him, he teleported away.

No, he didn't say where he was going or if he was coming back, but I don't think it was to rejoin GE. The most likely option I can think of is that he's attempting to find and take Tinsley back on his own."

I'm still preoccupied trying to wrap my head around the fact that I have a half-brother. I'd forgotten that in the midst of...well, almost dying.

I may not have a father to get to know better anymore, but at least I have Reid, right?

Except I don't. Not until he comes back, if he does at all.

"—suicide mission," Dane is saying when I tune back into the conversation.

"There's nothing more I can do about Reid right now. We need to make sure the Guild members are taken care of, and we need to put security measures in place at the Tower for when they attack. We've been lucky that they haven't done so already, but I'm not counting on that lasting long," Aiden says, then shifts his attention to include the rest of us. "Everyone living in the Tower is going to be required to start training in three days. We'll have two groups. The ones who want to and can fight, and the ones who need to learn how to defend themselves to get away somewhere safe. Kellan, you'll lead the training. I'll help when I can. And Jack"—Aiden pins Jackson with a look— "you're going to train everyone on how to use their gifts. *Without* throwing knives at them or threatening to kill them."

Jack smirks. "It's good motivation."

"They have motivation enough from their fear of GE. You've mastered your gift better than any other gifted individual I've met. I know you have insights you can share with others."

He shrugs, the motion modest even though his smirk is dripping with arrogance.

Aiden turns to Dane. "And I need you to build a virus for the Tower."

Dane frowns. When it clicks why he'd ask for that, Dane sighs and scrubs his hand through his hair. "A virus won't stop Vera. She can override it."

"I'm not looking to stop her. I'm just looking to manufacture a warning and opportunity for us," Aiden explains. "The virus should cause an instant system reboot. That gives us...five to ten minutes with everything shut down, correct?"

Dane nods warily.

"As soon as she accesses the system, it needs to trigger the virus and system reboot. That becomes our warning and gives us time to put ourselves in a better position. We'll work out the details of setting a trap for them from there, but that's the first step I need completed as soon as possible."

"Alright. I'll start working on that tonight."

Aiden's phone pings. He glances at the screen, then looks between Kellan and Jackson. "Groceries are here."

Kell stands, and they both leave without a word.

"Where are they going?" I ask.

"They have to pick up the food from one of the lower business floors. Non-Guild members can't access the floors higher than that," Dane answers first, his foot tapping beneath the table. "Since I can't be seen, and Aiden's usually busy, the other two are the ones who bring it up."

Hopefully, Aiden didn't order too much for them to bring up. At least there's an elevator.

Shifting topics, I turn to Aiden. "How's Cassandra doing?" I'd heard from Jack this morning how she'd stumbled into my room to heal me and the others. I need to find and thank her for it. For healing Dane's injuries, most of all.

His lips turn down at her name. "It's hard to say based on the face she's putting on for everyone. She should be resting in her apartment, but I've already heard from Cibrina that she's at the Guild Hall, helping where she can. The knife was small, thankfully, so it avoided major arteries, but it's going to take time for her muscles to heal for her to have full use of that arm again."

Damn. I really like her now. "She sounds dedicated to the Guild," I comment in her defense.

"Or desperate," Dane grumbles, and I smack his arm for it. "What?"

"Don't be a dick," I chide hotly. "She saved that group of kids in the bunker, and she healed your sorry ass while dealing with her own injury."

He scoffs, flicking a speck of something off the table. "I know all that. But she should do it because it's right, not just for the attention. She's been desperate since day one for a boyfriend."

"Who cares what her reason is? She's a great ally, and I'm glad she's on our side."

"Tell me that again if she switches teams and starts harassing you non-stop." Dane's gaze flicks to Aiden, whose face is carefully blank. "Aiden's had the worst of it."

My chest burns at the memory of her hands on them. At the easy way she'd flirted with them and even tried talking Aiden into a date. I only witnessed that one time. But what about all the times before I came around?

You weren't here then, so it doesn't matter.

"Well, she's backed off now," I try again, facing Aiden for the confirmation that I shouldn't need after what we'd just done, but I seek it out anyway.

Aiden looks between Dane and me, then sighs tiredly, as if he has absolutely no interest in this conversation. "Yes, she has."

"From us. Doesn't mean the other men of the Guild are exempt," Dane adds, not letting this go.

I know Dane can be an asshole, but she really must have pissed him off at one point. I shrug a shoulder. "You're all I care about. But if it's a problem, I could take her out for drinks and dancing. Maybe she'll find a good dance partner."

Once the words are out, my lungs squeeze as it hits me that I still haven't heard from Portia.

Something's wrong.

If Elias even got my message.

"No," both of them reply in unison, though I can't recall what question I'd asked.

The door opens, and a metal set of shelves on wheels rolls in, filled with bags. Kellan leaves it between the pantry and the fridge, returning to the table to plop back into his seat while Dane stands and starts putting the groceries away. Jack pinches an apple from one of the bags, then sits on the back of the couch facing us. There's an audible crunch when he takes his first bite.

It's so...natural.

Everyone has their role, their place, and they do it without a single word needed between them.

I'll need to figure out what my role will be in helping out.

But first...

"Have you heard from Elias?" I direct to Aiden, who shakes his head.

"No. It's been a few weeks since I've heard from him."

"Did he say anything about Portia? Or my voicemail?"

He doesn't answer right away, his dark eyes staring into mine as he deliberates over something before he finally replies, "He said she would call when she was ready."

When she was ready? What the hell does that mean?

Aiden's phone vibrates on the table.

It couldn't be. The timing is too perfect.

I hold my breath as he reads the screen. Then he stands and looks at us, his face serious. "Harvey's talking. And he told Cibrina there's going to be another attack."

Chapter Eleven

RAEGAN

THE ROOM THEY'RE KEEPING Harvey in looks like an unused office with the desk and chair shoved in a corner and metal bars running from floor to ceiling a few steps in. There's a space wide enough at the bottom for a tray of food to fit, as evidenced by the one on his side of the bars with a partially eaten sandwich and a bottle of water.

The five of us enter the room one at a time, and with Cibrina already standing as far to the right as she can against the desk, we fill whatever space remains.

Dane presses something smooth into my hand. "Here," he murmurs, turning his head to not draw attention to us. "Since my home-made pasta will have to wait, you at least need to eat something."

Nodding, I smile, bending my neck to see what treat he brought for me.

A protein bar.

It's probably the best option he could have grabbed on short notice, especially if we need to prepare for an attack. The last thing I want is to pass out from lack of food or energy. I tear it open as quietly as I can, but all of them eye me regardless.

Then Dane opens one for himself with a smirk, and I realize he'd let me go first on purpose.

"Asshole," I mouth to him with a smirk and bite through the thick bar.

"Harvey," Aiden begins when the blond-haired, blue-eyed Guild member stares intently at his sandwich, refusing to acknowledge us. "Tell me about the attack. How much time do we have, and where will it happen? Here, at the Tower?"

The corner of Harvey's lips twitch, and then he gradually disappears, like an invisible shroud unfurling over him from his head to his toes.

"Being invisible doesn't help you escape," Kellan growls, his hand wrapping around one of the bars.

The sandwich lifts before it, too, vanishes.

Aiden's brows are pinched as he concentrates on the now empty space of his makeshift cell. "Was everything a lie, then? You pretended to have trouble hiding yourself completely to, what? To trick me into underestimating you?"

I remember when I'd first met him, how Aiden had caught him "stealing" his phone. From the way Aiden's scanning the rest of the room, I can tell he has no idea where he is now.

"What are you going to do with me?" Harvey's voice sounds from the far right, near Cibrina.

"That depends on your willingness to cooperate," Aiden answers, his voice a soothing croon.

"And if I don't?"

Jackson twirls a knife. The motion on its own is benign, but knowing him and what he's capable of, it's a clear threat. I'm so focused on him, expecting him to act first, that I startle when Kellan's fist slams into the metal bar.

"Damn you!" he snarls viciously. "You killed Claudia. I could rip your spine from your body for that alone!"

The air in the back corner shudders.

Harvey's voice drops low, his tone grave. "I didn't kill her."

"Maybe you didn't hold the knife to her throat, but she died because of your betrayal," Kell rumbles. "Her blood is on your hands."

Harvey chuckles softly, and I stiffen at the callous response. The mood in the room immediately shifts, the taste of violence flavoring the air. He reappears in the center of his cage, his head thrown back and tears streaming down his face. "My betrayal, huh?" His voice is soft, if a little choked. "I wonder if it can be called that...if I came from the other side to begin with. If my talking to you isn't the betrayal that'll cost me more."

Aiden steps up to the bars. "Tell us everything, Harvey. I can't promise you what retribution the Guild will seek yet, but we will protect you from GE at the very least."

He laughs again, this one strangled, before he lowers his face and meets Aiden's gaze. "You can't protect me from him any more than you can protect the Guild. Or him." He points to Dane. "Or..." His crystal blue eyes find mine. "...her." He adds, "The one that got away."

I hold his stare. Something about it, about him, is tugging at my gut.

His blue eyes.

Not everyone with blue eyes is related to that man, but...what if...

"Are you his son?"

Harvey smirks, though it doesn't reach the sadness still clouding his gaze. He bows mockingly. "That's correct. I knew you were the smart one. But then, maybe we both get it from our father."

Dane curses. "I'm going to have a serious issue meeting anyone with blue eyes from now on."

"Well, there are many of us, so no one should fault you for it." Harvey bends to retrieve the bottled water. The cap snaps when it opens, and he takes several swallows. His expression evens out as if he's swallowing the turbulent emotions with every gulp. He clicks his tongue when he finishes, screwing the cap back on and tossing the empty bottle to the floor. "Screw it. I hate that bastard. I'll tell you everything on one condition."

"What is it?" Aiden asks.

"You have to save my siblings."

"Didn't you just say there were a lot of you?" Dane demands.

Harvey shrugs. "Not all my half-siblings. I don't even know how many of them there are. I'm only asking for my full-blooded siblings."

Dane scoffs. "Well, it sounds like you know about Raegan." He pauses. "Wait. Did you and Reid know about each other this whole fucking time?!"

"Who? Oh, the teleporting guy? He's another one?"

"Alright, you've gotta be fucking lying now," Dane growls. "You can't tell me you've been the Guild spy reporting to Daddy, and you didn't know about his other son he was so familiar with."

Harvey laughs softly and rubs the back of his neck. "Oh, that's exactly what I'm saying. Alright, story time." He sits cross-legged on the floor and stretches his hands over his head. "Ahhh, that's better. Please, sit. Sit." He waves at us to sit and join him, but none of us move. He shrugs. "Guess it's your choice to be uncomfortable."

"Harvey," Aiden warns. "Get on with it."

"Fine, fine." He shifts one last time and clears his throat. "A long time ago, a beautiful young girl—"

"—skip the details for now," Aiden cuts in, and Harvey frowns.

"But those tragic details are what you need to really feel for me and what I'm going through."

"I can listen to them later, Harvey," Cibrina offers reassuringly. "Just the cliff notes version for now."

He nods, accepting it and hopefully keeping his story short this time. "Mother was one of the first kids kidnapped and brainwashed by Dad back when he first started the company. Time jump until she's older, and he takes a liking to her gift of turning objects invisible. So, what does the pervert do? He buys an island just for her, filled with everything she could ever ask for and servants to attend to her, and he convinces her to have his kids. And not just a couple. But as many as she could."

My gut clenches, my stomach churning uneasily.

Was this what he tried with my mom?

No, she was still training to fight with GE.

"Anyway, about eight kids later, I was born. We were all raised on that island and isolated from the rest of the company. All fourteen of us were gifted, but only twelve had the ability to turn ourselves invisible. We were trained from childhood to become his personal spies. When not on that island, we were to be invisible unless specifically told not to be for an assignment."

"What sort of assignments were you given?" Aiden questions.

Harvey chuckles. "Mostly, spying on his allies." He rests an elbow on one knee and leans into his fist. "We would be assigned to monitor his Board. Or Board-elect members. Make sure there were no...ideas...floating about that he wouldn't approve of." He sighs. "Anyway, back to keeping this short. Somehow, he heard about the Guild when Thorne first created it. He sent me to infiltrate it and report back to him on it—more of a wait-and-see assignment. Thorne almost found me out near the end, but you guys actually saved me on that when you killed him. Something else must have happened around that time with Gifted Enterprise because Dad stopped contacting me after that."

He continues, "I didn't know what to do when he stopped reaching out, but I was too scared to remind him I was here. And, surprise, surprise, I actually liked what you did with the Guild. I think he forgot all about it for a couple years. That is until you messed it up by getting involved with the Board-elect Congressman."

"Joe?" I confirm, disgust coating my tone.

Harvey nods. "That's the one. Whatever interaction you had with him, I can guarantee one of my siblings was there. And that's how he found out about who you were and where to find you. Which brought him, and therefore my Dad, back to looking at the Guild."

Fuck. So, the night he'd been feeling me up and then Kellan and

Aiden showed up, someone else had been there?

"He reached out to me again, but we'd moved to the bunker, and I tried to play it off that service was bad, and we were being kept down there. I accidentally mentioned you were looking for him. That was when he came up with his great plan of luring you to an island full of agents in disguise so he could come to see it for himself. I just had to slip in the tip of where to find him."

"Why couldn't he teleport here if you told him where it was?" Dane asks.

"He can't teleport somewhere he hasn't been before, or he can't see from where he's standing. That's why I had to open the doors for them to get out to the rest of the bunker. But I swear...that's *all* I did."

"Tell that to the six kidnapped Guild members and Claudia," Kellan growls.

I rub my hand over my face. This is just...so much information to take in. "Why did you call me 'the one that got away'?"

Harvey smiles. "Because, dear sister. Of all my half-siblings, you're the only one I know about. Why? Because you got away from him. Somehow, your mother escaped with you, and after that, you were gone. Poof! And he was *furious*. I think he'd planned to try again with your mom, but then she...you know."

I nod, not needing him to say it.

"I was amazed to hear that one of his kids actually escaped him. And not once, but twice. I think it burned his pride a bit, but you were a hero to the rest of us."

"So then...all those times you offered to help me disappear...?"

His smile falls. "I meant it. Dad had his eye on the Guild again, so I knew you wouldn't be safe here."

Silence stretches through the room as I let that sink in.

Dane shoves his fingers through his hair, rubbing his hand back and forth. "So, you need us to save thirteen people?"

"Ten," Harvey corrects. "Dad killed Erik and Desmond for failure and Wyra because he suspected she was going to betray him."

Psycho bastard deserves the worst of deaths.

"And they're most likely spying on Board members?" Aiden confirms slowly.

Harvey nods and adds, "Or electees."

Aiden sighs, then looks to Cibrina, who's already documenting everything with her gift. "I'll stay with him to get as many details on each of them and the Board members as possible," she says.

"Good. We'll meet in a few days to discuss it and start working on a plan." Aiden swivels back to Harvey. "Now, what attack were you referring to when you let it slip to Cibrina?"

"Oh, right. Dad made a comment about the Pits when I saw him. Must've learned about it from someone, so I thought you should know. Since a lot of them are outsiders and might not know about GE, they're prime picks for him."

Shit.

That's the underground fighting ring Kellan took me to where people like us tested their gifts against others.

"Probably from Thorne by Royce," Jackson comments.

Kellan swears. "Tonight's a fight night. The fights will be starting soon, and it'll be crowded."

Jackson cocks his head. "If they're going to attack, they'll do it when they can grab the most people."

"We'll leave now, then. Invite them to join the Guild. We could use the fighters anyway," Aiden reasons.

Kellan pushes off the bar he'd been gripping. "Not everyone's going to want to pack up and move to the Tower."

"Either they move, or they stick around to possibly get kidnapped. They can make that choice after we warn them." Aiden turns to the rest of us. "We'll all go for this one. Hopefully, we can convince them to leave before the attack, but we'll be prepared for a fight if they do show up."

"If they haven't already," Dane murmurs, and I hope that's not the case.

The Pits beneath the Cactus Jacks bar is eight minutes away by car, but only two minutes as the bird flies. Or, in this case, Jackson.

While the others head for the underground garage to drive, Jackson and I take the elevator to the top of the Tower and then the stairs to reach the roof. The wind is strong tonight, or maybe just up here, because it pushes and pulls at me like it wants to send me over the edge.

I stand at the center of the roof, fighting to keep my balance as the breeze whips across it.

Jackson crouches with his back to me. "Climb on."

Grabbing his shoulders, I hop on. His arms wrap around my legs, cradling the backs of my knees before he stands. As we near the edge, I press more closely against him and grip the front of his hoodie tightly.

We're on one of the tallest buildings in the city. While I can see a few other buildings at or around this height, most are *many* stories below us. Jackson takes a step onto the small wall that perimeters the roof, and my stomach somersaults and spins at the height.

I bury my face into his hood, breathing in the comforting scent of dead leaves and wondering why I didn't go for the car ride. It fits four. I just didn't want Jack to have to travel alone.

"Don't be afraid," Jackson says, his voice calm and cool. "I would never let you fall."

He's right. I have nothing to fear when he's holding me, especially not from the wind. I *know* it. But knowing that truth doesn't stop the fear completely. Lessens it, maybe, but it's still there, crawling beneath my skin.

I force myself to look over his shoulder anyway.

"Let's fly, little one." He jumps off, and my heart catapults to my throat, lodging there as we fall. Because that's exactly what this is.

Falling.

The wind that tried to send me over the edge is now what slows our descent and carries us over buildings. The sun, which was already hidden from the street, is still sinking below the horizon from up here, its reddish-orange fingers never losing their brilliance even while the blanket of darkness encroaches. City lights begin to glow and shine as the day gives way to night, and it's like seeing the stars in reverse, below me rather than overhead.

The view takes my breath away.

Buildings rise on either side of us as we fall faster, descending rapidly without warning. I tighten my grip on his hoodie, but I don't look away.

We land in a closed-off alley. There's a single light above the door to the only building that barely illuminates the area, doing more to feed the shadows than anything. A man with long and shaggy black hair stands at the door, arms crossed. As soon as we land, he has a walkie talkie to his mouth and he mutters something into it.

"Evening, Gregor," Jackson greets, and the man shivers.

I slide from his back. I've barely stepped up next to Jack before he tucks me into his side, his fingerless-gloved hand holding my opposite hip.

The man—Gregor—looks at me, and Jack's arm around me tightens. He flips a blade out, toying with it in one hand and then pointing it at him. "Careful," he warns huskily. His voice is dark and threatening this time, and Gregor visibly swallows. He eyes the knife, then Jackson, purposefully keeping his gaze from mine now.

What the hell?

"I let York know you're here."

Jackson nods, then guides us to the door without another word. I wait until we're inside before whispering to him, "Do you not like that guy?" I'm used to Jack keeping back and quiet when we're around others, not actively threatening them. At least, not people who are potential allies.

He smirks, and it's a cold twist of his lips that I see only because he's angled his face my way. "I don't like anyone when it comes to you. Aside from the others," he adds about Aiden and the rest. "If you don't want me to murder everyone in the room, stay by my side. No more disappearing."

I frown. "If it comes to a fight, I'm not hiding behind you like some damsel on your arm. I thought you understood that."

"Fight whoever you want, little one. Just don't go far, or else I'll kill anyone standing between me and you. GE or not."

Oh. Well then.

We arrive at another guarded door, but this time, the guy there opens it for us without a word, his eyes staring holes into the floor. I don't comment on this one, just letting Jackson guide us down the stairs to the Pits. A fight is already in progress in the large cage, with people cheering on their side from the standing tables covered in drinks and cash. It's not nearly as crowded as when Kellan had taken me here, but it's still early. Do we wait until the peak of the night to tell everyone?

Jackson brings us to one of the tables in the back, grabbing a stool from the nearby wall and setting it next to me. I gratefully take the seat, then scan the crowd for familiar faces.

The kid I'd fought some months ago—Knight—is here. York is standing to the side of the cage where he usually is, collecting bets and emceeing the gifted melee.

Jack nudges me, and I follow his gaze to the other three of our group walking down the stairs.

"Kell!" I shout, waving my hand in the air and standing on the bar toward the base of the stool for added height.

He's already taller than most of the crowd and spots me easily, grinning and striding to our table with the others following behind.

"Any sign of GE?" Aiden asks, and Jack shakes his head. "Good. Kell, let's go chat with York to make our announcement." He casts a look at Jackson, who nods, then shares another look with me and Dane. "Stay here."

Fuck's sake.

Dane scoffs, rolling his eyes and folding his arms on the table.

Sighing, I lean on my hand and watch them leave. As annoyed as I want to be with them for their overprotectiveness, I recall what Jackson said to me. It's not about whether they think we can fight or not, which is how I originally took it.

They're still not over how fast Dane and I vanished on them. I'm not even sure how I made it in time to grab Dane, and I'm so fucking grateful my reaction time was quick enough. What might have happened if it had been only him?

Now you're thinking like them.

The worst part was not having a healer immediately available for our injuries. Cassandra's injury is a stark reminder that we can't rely on her for everything. We need another healer. Or a gifted person who's also some sort of medic or doctor, at least.

"Aaaand Crusher takes the win!" York booms in the speakers. "Everyone sit tight for a second. A good friend of mine has an announcement to make."

He passes the mic to Aiden, who surveys the room while it takes a minute for everyone to quiet. "I'll make this short and to the point...You're all in danger."

Murmurs spread through the crowd, raising in volume, while a few shout at him for interrupting their fun.

Dane turns on them, looking like he's ready to say something, and I put my hand over his fist on the table. "Let Aiden finish. If they don't want to come, then it's not on us to convince them."

He frowns but doesn't argue, flipping his hand around to capture mine and then nodding. "You're right."

"A group called Gifted Enterprise is searching for individuals with special abilities, like all of us, to kidnap and brainwash to follow their orders. It has come to my attention that they've discovered this location, and it's only a matter of time before they arrive. If you want to put your fighting skills to good use, then join us at the Guild. There will be a place to stay and onsite training. If you wish to hide or walk away from this place, then you're welcome to that as well. But you can't stay here."

A voice rises from the room. "And who says we can trust you?"

"Me." Kellan steps forward from the shadows of the stage. He widens his stance, crossing his arms and frowning at the crowd. "I'll be training anyone who joins us, but don't expect anything easy. You're going to fight to take down a group that's been hurting people like us for a long time. It's a fight worth having if you'll join us."

Seeing Kellan changes the mood of the room, and I can see more people nodding or with open expressions than those still disbelieving what's being said.

York accepts the microphone back from Aiden. "Unfortunately, folks, that means we're done for the night and all nights until further notice. I'll send a message out to anyone who's not here. If you're joining the fight, come to the stage for directions. Otherwise, have a good night and be safe!"

The room splits; those interested in fighting surging toward the stage while the rest linger behind at the tables.

"Hype is in danger, too," I say in a hushed tone to Jack and Dane. "GE may not know it's a hot-spot for gifted, but it's only a matter of time. We should at least warn them."

Jackson hums softly, so I know he's heard me, but he seems distracted by something. Before I can ask him about it, shouts echo through the room.

Chapter Twelve

RAEGAN

A portal appears at the foot of the stairs, blocking the one and only exit. GE agents run out of it, like wasps from their hive, immediately going on the offensive and grabbing people.

I swing my gaze across the room to Aiden on instinct. Our eyes connect for a solid beat before all hell breaks loose and something knocks our table over. Jackson catches it, aims, and then tosses it at an agent. I jump from the stool and knock it into the corner out of my way.

The gifted people here aren't afraid of fighting with their gifts, and they know how to use them. They fight back, gifts slinging through the air and hitting both friend and foe.

Calling on my gift, I fist my hands and search through the crowd for anyone I can grab. I can't send my gift through the floor without risking everyone else, which means I'm restricted to only the agents I can touch. But even then, people are shoving into one another or being thrown about. Can I take the risk of using it at all?

A Pits fighter falls into me, and I rush to release my gift and catch them, helping them upright again.

Nope. No gift.

I grab the knife from my boot instead. Time to put Kell's training to use with close combat fighting.

I dive into the fray, seeking out anyone with the GE logo. One of them swings a fist at me, and I dodge to the side, flipping the knife to my left hand and slashing his arm. The agent yells, grabbing the wound, and I switch my knife back and sink it into his chest to finish him.

The next agent comes at me from the side. I pivot, ducking down and then leaping at him from below with the knife. His blood hits my face, a warm and wet feeling that I brush aside.

A shoe squeaks behind me, and I spin in time to see a hand reaching toward me before the agent's forearm is cleaved from his body. His head follows, and the agent drops to the floor in a thud, revealing Aiden behind him retracting his whip sword.

That's when I realize the area around me is clear when I thought I'd run into the crowd. Dane grabs an agent attacking a Pits fighter, shutting his gift down and then punching him in the jaw for a quick lights-out.

Something bright catches my eye, and I turn to find Kellan ripping through agents, the golden scales covering the backs of his arms and reflecting even the dim lighting from above.

And in front of me, Jackson.

Most of the Pits fighters are now standing along the walls, watching him with fear as he decimates the remaining agents. His hood fell at some point, revealing his messy black hair and wicked smile as he effectively eliminates groups of agents at a time. Blood streaks his face, and I wonder how much is on his clothes that we can't see.

He looks like the God of Death, exacting his brutal vengeance on these agents who never had a chance.

The last one falls.

Silence fills the room as Jackson lands at my side. He looks at me, and my breath hitches. He's covered in blood and panting for air, but it's the look in his eyes that captures my full attention.

They shine with bloodlust. With the need to take more. Kill more.

The darkness emanating from him is a tangible feeling that evokes a sense of dread to be close to it—fear to snake down your spine.

His gaze darts to the people along the wall behind me.

I palm the side of his face to draw his attention back to me. "Jack."

His chest works double-time with his heavy breathing, and I can feel the fine tremble running through his body where my hand touches him.

"Look at me," I order, soft but firm. There's a second where I worry he won't listen, a heartbeat that I'm afraid he'll act on the murderous impulses driving him. But then his dark blue gaze lands on me, and its weight is staggering. My heart pounds relentlessly, my blood on fire. "It's over."

I wait for him to react, to show in some way that he heard me and understands what I'm telling him. There's no one left to kill. We're safe.

Jackson takes my wrist, his thumb pressing against my pulse. Finally, he takes a slow breath, closes his eyes, and releases it. When his eyes open again, they're calmer, if only a little. But I'll take it.

"Send them back through the portal," Aiden says from my other side. I didn't even notice when he'd gotten so close. "It'll save us the clean-up effort and show GE to think twice before trying this again."

Jack nods. He pulls my hand away from his face and looks over the mess we've made. He probably took out a majority of the agents, but it wasn't all him or us. The fighters here stood their ground. They may have hesitated to take the killing blow, but I don't blame them for it. It's still a huge improvement from most of the Guild members who are still learning how to fight.

We need these fighters, and they need us.

The agents are sent through the portal a few at a time, and after the last one disappears, the portal closes. I'd debated going through it to see if we could take the fight to them with this group, but we aren't ready. There must have been some setting on it that would close it automatically when all the agents returned, or else someone was waiting on the other side to do it. Regardless, the stairs have become accessible again, and some of the fighters here take to them immediately.

"I guess that didn't convince them that the threat is real," Dane mutters beside me.

"Knowing it's real doesn't mean they're prepared to fight. Some people may need time to come to terms with it. And others, they may not be fighters beyond the cage," Aiden reasons.

More people file out of the room, and I hope he's right. I hope a little bit of time is all they need to accept what's coming and to make the choice to fight with us.

"Are we going to see that blond guy again? The one you almost fucked?" Kellan drawls, his blue-green eyes glittering with mirth while his teeth are bared in a sharp grin. He knows exactly what he's done, stirring this shit up with the others right before we walk into Hype to warn them about GE's recent activity.

After last night's...event...at the Pits, we returned to the Loft to catch up on much-needed food and sleep. Anyone from the Pits who agrees to join us will show up in the next couple of days with their things, which sounds like a logistical nightmare to me, but Aiden assures me that Cibrina has it all under control. When I worried about her workload, he admitted that he'd already told her to hire two assistants to help her with all of her tasks.

He'd also asked me to try to find out from her what else she'd like as a thank you for everything.

Between her and Cassandra, I feel a girl's night coming up.

If only I knew how to plan one of those or what to do.

As always, my thoughts turn to Portia, wondering how she's doing and when I'll see her again.

Aiden clears his throat, and I blink from my thoughts to find the guys watching me intently, the mood ominous. "Well?" he prompts, and it feels like I've been caught daydreaming in class.

"Uh, what was the question again?"

His lips turn down disapprovingly. For not listening, or is it about the question? "We were discussing the guy you either had sex with or almost did."

The guy...Oh. Kellan's inflammatory statement about Ethan.

I roll my eyes and catch Aiden's hand twitching at his side. "First off, I never slept with him. But if I had, it was before I was with any of you, so it wouldn't have mattered." The threatening mood doesn't improve, and I sigh. "You know what? I think I'll be fine taking this on my own. You guys can guard outside the door, and I'll come out when I'm done."

"Out of the question."

"No fucking way."

"No."

"In your dreams, beautiful."

I put my hand on the doorknob, blocking it to make sure they don't try barging in first. "Let me do the talking, at least."

Aiden puts his hand on mine, his body a deep inhale away from pressing me against the door. "What do you think we're going to say? Are you afraid we'll embarrass you?" he croons, his velvety voice wrapping around me while all I can smell and taste is cinnamon.

Everything about this man is seductive, reeling me in and molding me to putty. His lips curve to a wicked smirk, my only warning, and he opens the door. I fall back, hitting the door that he stops short while his smirk grows.

Kellan laughs as I right myself. After shooting a glare at Aiden, I send it Kellan's way, too, with the added gift of my middle finger.

He winks back.

I'll get them both.

Pushing the door the rest of the way open, I stride toward the bar where I'm most likely to find Ethan. He looks up from where he's mopping the floor, his smile lighting up his face when he sees me. Then he notices the others, and it falls slightly. It's still there, still polite, but not as warm as it had been for me.

Probably because of Kellan's and Dane's attitudes the last time we were here.

I offer him a genuine smile, hoping to keep his attention away from them. I can pass along this message on my own to avoid any...unpleasant remarks the others might share with him. None of their attitude is his fault; it's mine. I'd rather keep the conversation we had outside between us for my own sake as well as Ethan's.

"Hi," I greet a bit awkwardly. Here I am, showing up again with an entourage that has doubled in size. I can only imagine what Ethan's thinking. "Sorry to show up without notice, but I need to talk to you about something. It's important."

He pulls his gaze from the others, his warm smile returning when he focuses back on me. "Yeah, of course. Do you want to go sit?" He motions to the booths in the back, then reaches for me.

I don't know how I know that Jackson's acted—call it instinct, intuition, whatever—but I see the knife out of the corner of my eye flying toward Ethan's extended hand, and I knock his hand aside right before it hits its mark. The knife strikes the floor with a *thunk*, burying halfway deep.

"What the—" Ethan starts, turning to look where it came from.

Aiden's frowning while Kellan and Dane smirk unapologetically.

"Excuse me." I turn and storm up to Jackson, grabbing his hand

and dragging him to the back hallway until we're in Elias's office. It's the only office I know, and he's not here, so hopefully he won't mind.

Closing the door behind us, I whirl on Jack. "What was that?! That wasn't even a warning shot. You were actually going to hit him. For what? For touching me? He's a *friend*, Jack. We don't stab friends."

Jackson smiles, but it's cold and sharp as ice. The bloodlust of last night is still there, lurking in the shadows of his eyes and cruelty in his smile. I'd held him back, but how long had I expected that to last? "I don't do warnings anymore." He steps closer, and I step back. The violent maelstrom of repressed energy falls off him in waves. My heart flutters wildly in my chest as he closes in on me. "People learn faster this way."

Another step.

My back hits the door.

His hands follow, slapping the door either side of me and caging me in. He lowers his face to my ear, his breath heating my neck and sending a thrill of danger through me. "Hold my leash, little one. Hold it tight," he warns softly, his voice coated in darkness. "There is no more patience, no more *wait and see* when it comes to you. I'm one breath away from lighting the world on fire. I don't need it. Everyone can burn if it means you'll be safe."

His words heat my blood, lighting a fire in me. I breathe in the cooler air around us, hoping to stay level-headed even as his monster calls to mine. "That'd be a dull world, with no one and nothing else in it," I tease on a low murmur.

"Not for me. You're all I want. All I need. Let them burn."

"Jack," I chastise on an exhale as if he's stolen the oxygen from my lungs.

I can feel the violence buzzing in him, vibrating beneath his skin and seeking an outlet. He'd lost himself in a killing frenzy last night, but there's more to it than that. He's been off since I woke up in the hospital; something not quite right about his silence. Something dark raging in the depths of his stare.

It could be any number of things, now that I think about it. My father getting the better of us by infiltrating the bunker. Him kidnapping and then hurting Dane and me. Gordon dying before I could get my retribution.

Last night probably opened the door to that rage, giving himself a taste of what he wanted without fully satiating that desire.

Now, it feels like something as small as a sneeze would unleash him on the world.

"Hold my leash."

I push him back enough that he raises his head to look at me, trapping me in his stare. His eyes are such a deep blue. Dark and dangerous like the unexplored depths of the ocean, dragging you down if you don't keep swimming for your life.

I reach for one of his hands, and without hesitation, he gives it to me, allowing me to guide it down my front. Down, down. Touching my abdomen and following the skin further beneath my clothes, down to my core. His fingers twitch, bumping against my cunt as I withdraw my own hand to shift my clothes and widen my legs to grant him more access.

He slides a finger in, then two when he feels how wet I am already. I groan when they sink deeper, clutching at his arm to both encourage him more and for my own sake. Our eyes stay locked, and it seems like he's hardly breathing until the moan bursts from my lips. Only then does he draw a visible, shaky breath, and it feels like I've made the first step to sating the monster in him.

I wrap my hand around his nape, drawing him closer until our foreheads press together and our noses touch. The air between us thickens. His fingers push in and out, stroking my inner walls with measured intensity that has me desperate for more. My hips jerk, thrusting against him to seek that friction as I cling to his neck and arm. Stroke. Stroke. Faster. Faster. More. *More.*

"Hold my leash."

Wait!

I snatch his hand, halting him before I find my release. I'm gasping for air, my body on absolute *fire*, but I move his hand to his lips in an unspoken request. Jackson takes his fingers into his mouth, sucking them clean with his eyes on mine, and my thighs clench.

Yes.

After shoving his hood back, I pull his face to mine, crashing our lips together. I swallow his groan, the taste of me that he'd savored like his favorite flavor. I kiss him without fear of what he might do but with unbridled desire for that dark part of him that does it all for me. Who willingly does whatever necessary for my sake. I want him, all of him.

I push away from him abruptly, stepping around him to back further into the room, my eyes returning to his as I do. His lips are swollen and wet, his eyes shimmering with obsession as they watch me retreat in slow, taunting movements. With each step, I lose an article of clothing.

My pants.

Shirt.

Socks.

Bra.

I strip my underwear last, dragging it down my legs in slow motion as I had with the others. A wicked smile stretches my lips as I continue walking backward around the desk to Elias's chair. If Jackson blinks at all, I miss it, his stare so intense that I feel an almost high from the attention.

The chair is wide and high-backed, stuffed patches on the arms for comfort and smooth fabric over a cushion that I sink into a bit as I sit on it. Naked. I throw a leg over one chair arm, spreading myself and then lifting my chin before I speak. "Kneel." My voice is low, but the command is unmistakable. I don't need to shout to get his attention; I always have it.

Jackson's nostrils flare, his hands clenching.

Still, I wait.

He stalks around the desk, stopping at the chair, then kneels before me.

Fuck, this is a heady feeling. Seeing him kneel for me, doing what I command without question...and knowing that I'm the only one he'd do this for. He may be a ruthless killer, a prince of darkness, but he's mine.

Jack shifts forward on his knees, his face moving between my thighs with a look that leaves me breathless. He drags his nose down the inside of my thigh, his breath tickling the sensitive flesh in his path. He flicks his blue eyes to mine, a slow smile spreading across his lips just before he yanks me to the edge of the chair.

He presses a kiss to the sunken space at the apex of my thigh, his lips skating down and leaving another. His tongue slips between my folds, finding my entrance, and then slides up my center in a devastatingly slow tease.

He groans, his tongue painting lines and circles in a way that has my inner walls trembling and clenching. His tongue slips inside, and my hips convulse.

My head falls back, hitting the chair hard enough to hurt, when a wanton moan scrambles up my throat and seizes my lungs. His tongue is relentless, leaving nothing untouched, no area left wanting. He swipes it between my pussy and clit, rubbing and sliding before moving around my clit, circling, circling. Tighter and tighter. Harder and harder. A finger rings my entrance, putting pressure there without fully breaching it, and I writhe with the desperate need for him to finish it.

"Oh, fuckkk," I pant, my nails digging into the armrests.

He presses his tongue harder, faster. Moving at a dizzying speed until it feels like my heart might burst from my chest. I thrust my hips against him, chasing the pleasure that's climbing higher and higher. "Ohhh, yeah. Yeah. Fuckkk. Jack!" His fingers drive into my pussy, and the pleasure hits me so hard that my back bows, and I grab his hair to hold on tight. My orgasm grabs me and throws me over the edge of a cliff, and I free-fall to the ground, shattering to pieces.

Jackson stands, his height making him tower over me, slumped in the chair. He licks his lips clean, then wipes whatever's left from his chin with the back of his hand.

I shudder at the hungry look in his eyes, his black hair wild from whatever I'd done to it. He paces around the chair, removing his hoodie and shirt as he goes until he's behind it and out of my periphery.

Click.

The back of the chair drops, and I let out a small scream when I fall with it. It's so far back that the chair is almost horizontal, and I'm staring up at Jackson's smirking face. He grabs my ankles, his gift assisting him in turning and flipping me in an instant. Gasping, I land chest-first against the back of the chair, my hips at the edge while my legs dangle over it. My feet kick the air, searching for the floor until Jack splits my legs and presses his cock against my core.

He sinks into me, his hands holding my hips steady while the rest of me scrambles to hold on to something. *Anything.* I grip the chair arms, but fuckkk. I'm trapped. Stuck partially in the air with no leverage, so all I can do is take whatever he's giving me without the ability to adjust or move myself.

Once he's fully seated, Jackson draws back to the tip, then slams back in. I cry out from the impact, my hands tightening as I expect to faceplant with the chair, but his hands on my hips keep me secure. He drives into me again and again, and I can feel the pent-up violence purging from him with every stroke.

I hook my feet around the back of his legs, needing something to support them, and then hang on for dear life.

My clit rubs into the chair, the softness of the fabric feeling rough there, but the dull pain builds to pleasure at the pressure. His unforgiving pace pushes my body to a crescendo, and I release a strangled cry of his name when it peaks, and I fall to ruin.

Jackson keeps going through it all, dragging out my orgasm until, at last, he thrusts one final time and holds himself there. He throws his head back, a pleasured gasp wrenching from his lips as his chest heaves from so much exertion.

He draws back, leaving me for a few seconds while I close my eyes and catch my breath. Then he's rolling me in his arms, cradling me to his chest. I look up at him, my fingers trailing the side of his face until he looks at me. His expression is relaxed. Calm. The shadows in his gaze aren't as prominent. They'll never be gone completely, but he's back in control.

Jack sits me on the chair after it's snapped upright and kneels between my legs. He holds his shirt and brings it to the apex of my thighs, and I put my hand on his. "I'll do it."

"Let me."

I hesitate, debating if this is a fight worth starting, then relent and drop my hand. He continues to wipe me down, his efforts slow and gentle. When he's done, he drops his shirt and helps me dress before pulling his own clothes on. He shoves the used shirt into his hoodie pocket, then looks at me.

There's no smirk or smile on his face. No hidden secret. Just pure, all-consuming focus that's concentrated completely on me. Jackson tugs me close, taking my hands and holding them to his chest. "I love you. If you want my heart, I'll carve it from my chest. Because it wouldn't beat without you."

My heart stutters out of rhythm, then burns and aches with emotion I have no idea what to do with. I try to put it into words, hoping it's enough and that he understands. "I love you too." More than anything else in the world, I love him and the others. I'd do anything for them, to keep them safe. To keep us together.

Jackson smiles, the dimple piercing his left cheek and giving me butterflies all over again.

I smile back, reveling in this moment.

Someone knocks at the door, and I curse, remembering we're still at Hype and the others are waiting for us.

"Either wrap it up and come out, or else invite me in," Kellan shouts from behind the door. "Aiden's running out of things to talk about to keep Ethan distracted from you two."

"We're coming!" I yell, taking Jack's hand and walking to the door.

"Again?" Kellan teases.

I shove the door open, hoping to smack him in the face with it, but the brute side-steps before my wish comes true. "Ha-ha," I reply, sarcasm dripping from my tone even though I'm fighting a smile.

We walk back to the bar and nightclub area, and Ethan looks past us as if he can see the office from there. "You know I'm going to have to de-con that entire office now, right?"

Oh, fuck. He's right. When I brought Jack to Elias's office, I didn't think that was going to happen. But what would happen if the clean-freak Elias came back and saw evidence of me and Jack?

Dane clenches his hands and moves toward Ethan, ready to defend me even though I'm clearly the one in the wrong. It's exactly how he was on the island. Vera and I could do no wrong in his eyes, and he would defend us to his last breath, either by being a complete dick to the other person or by getting in a fistfight.

I jump in front of him before either of those scenarios happens, placing my hands on his chest. "No, he's right. I don't know how well you know Elias, but...yeah. It needs to be cleaned." I turn to face Ethan, keeping my back close to Dane and my hand on his behind me so I know he won't jump down Ethan's throat. "I'm sorry. It was...necessary."

Ethan's stare slides to Jackson. "...Right."

"I'd offer to do the cleaning myself, but I don't think I'd do it well enough."

"We'll pay for it, whatever it costs," Aiden says, his eyes on me. "Just send the bill to the Tower."

Thank fuck for Aiden. His offer eases the knot of guilt in my chest that I'm not used to feeling. If it were nearly anyone else, I wouldn't have cared so much. But Elias?

Ethan nods to Aiden, then focuses back on me. "Thanks. I'll uh...pass along the message to the others and let you know if there's any interest."

Kellan crosses his arms and cocks his head, checking Ethan out from head to toe. "You a fighter, Ethan?"

"I can fight," he answers, almost defensively.

"What's your gift?" Kell asks casually.

Ethan hesitates, and I remember Portia telling me about it.

"Portia said you're a glow bug?" I guess, not quite sure if her description was accurate.

He sighs and chuckles, shaking his head. "Of course, she did. It's more than that."

"What do you do?" Kellan presses.

"I can emit light from my body."

I bite my lips, drawing them in to keep from smiling or saying anything, but Dane, of course, speaks up. "So, you...glow."

Ethan sighs again. "It's hard to explain. But I've had someone tell me it's a brilliant gift."

Dane snorts. Kellan laughs and says, "Marry them."

Ethan frowns, his brows pinching in annoyance, and thankfully, Aiden cuts in to save the day.

"You have my number now, so let me know if anyone here has any interest, and we can safely escort them to the Tower."

"Yeah. Will do," Ethan replies before looking at me. "It was good to see you again." I smile, and he looks ready to move closer, his body leaning forward when his gaze slants to Jackson, and he plants his heels. "Maybe I'll see you around again soon?"

Dane's hand squeezes mine behind my back, and I give him one in return before answering Ethan. "Yeah. As soon as this GE business is over with, I plan to be back here all the time."

That was apparently the *wrong* answer because the guys all practically snap their necks to look at me with varying levels of broodiness, but I ignore them and wave to Ethan before heading to the door.

Chapter Thirteen

RAEGAN

Aiden and Cibrina walk into the Loft as I wash the last dish from dinner. Jackson's gift lifts the plate from my hand, dries it, then passes it off to Kellan to put away.

"Cibrina's here with the information from Harvey," Aiden announces, immediately making himself a glass of bourbon before sitting at the head of the table. Those of us in the kitchen gather back at the dining table, taking a seat or—in Jackson's case—shifting around from his perch on the counter. Cibrina smooths her sheath dress and sits in the available chair.

Dane turns from the computer where he'd been working on Aiden's virus. "Was any of it useful?"

Cibrina nods, raising her hands as if poised over an invisible keyboard. Golden light shimmers above the center of the table, turning into words and then a paragraph of notes. "While he didn't realize it at the time, he had come into contact with two active Board members before his time at the Guild." Her fingers dip and rise, and the text expands to two lists of notes.

"We have a starting point for two of the sitting Board members," Aiden elaborates.

The rest of us are busy reading Cibrina's notes. In one column, it lists: male, dark brown hair cut short, brown eyes, at least six feet tall, fit, wore a white physician coat over dress clothes, looked crazy, medical director, manages hospital?, argued with Charles about blood for something, Charles shut him up with donations.

The second column has: older male, short silver hair, blue eyes, maybe around five foot nine, fit, wore business suit, talked lawyer-ey.

Dane scoffs. "Talked lawyer-ey?"

"You know Cibrina's gift records the information exactly as she hears it." Aiden's index finger taps the glass in his hand. "I understand this isn't a lot to go on, but can you make it work?"

Dane's amber gaze focuses back on the golden words, his jaw tight. "For the doctor in a management-type position at a hospital... maybe. But for the lawyer? There are thousands and thousands of those. Even if we're limiting our search to the States only. And who's to say these guys haven't retired or died since Harvey last saw them? He's been at the Guild for what...ten years?"

"Eight," Cibrina confirms.

"Right. Did he meet these guys while at the Guild, or before?"

Cibrina scrolls through more text and pauses over what appears to be a transcript of their conversation. "Before. One looks to be eleven years ago and the other...nine."

Kellan's foot bumps mine under the table as he stretches his legs and rests a tattooed forearm on the table. He shoots me a wink with a roguish grin when I give him a look for it. "I doubt GE Board membership is the sort you can just leave," he drawls. "Not with all the secrets they'd know."

"He could be dead, then. The notes show Harvey called him older with silver hair nine years ago," Dane presses.

Kellan opens his mouth with what I know is going to be bullshit aimed at poking Dane's temper. I lean forward and slap my hand on the table to cut in first. "I might have a lead," I blurt out, and all eyes fall on me. "I...back when we were at Old Red...I may have bumped into a lawyer with GE."

The sudden quiet as the others process that feels like a guillotine hanging over my head and I'm just waiting for it to drop. Aiden's completely still, his obsidian gaze locked on mine as his fingertips whiten where they grip his glass.

Shit.

Dane breaks the silence first. "What?! When the hell did that happen? How did we not hear about it?"

"Aside from the fact that you and I were hardly on speaking terms, I was still trying to find and fight GE on my own then."

Kellan joins in, his deep voice rough. "We were on more than speaking terms, beautiful, and this is the first I'm hearing of it."

Swallowing, I fist my hand on the table. "It was complicated back then. Let's focus on how this might help us now."

"What happened?" Aiden's voice is a low, dangerous croon. "Who is he? Where is he now? Tell us everything."

Cibrina clears her throat and stands. "I'll give you guys a minute to catch up while I visit the lady's room." She disappears into the powder room without looking back.

I slip a quick glance to Jackson. He's leaning into his fist, his smirk all-knowing as if he can see my soul flailing at how I'd just outed myself. When I turn back to Aiden, his dark stare is now pinned on Jackson, a disapproving crinkle appearing between his brows.

"His name was Ken—no, Steve. I met him when I'd been looking into Joe. He tried offering me an internship at his practice when he thought I was a law student. I didn't see him again until we bumped into one another after Joe died and we were all at Old Red. We exchanged numbers so we could meet up and talk about his internship offer and I could try to dig into his connection with GE." The three sets of stares feel like bricks weighing on my chest as I prepare for what comes next. A part of me hopes that Jackson sees my struggle and jumps in to finish it for me, but that smirk of his...I'd bet this is his form of punishment for what I'd gotten myself into.

The others don't chime in with questions or commentary, either, forcing me to continue. "He reached out when I was at the bar already feeling low. It was a public place and I thought—never mind, it doesn't matter. Anyway, he slipped me a sleeping pill at some point and I woke up tied to a chair in his apartment. Jackson showed up, asked him some questions, and I killed him," I rush through the worst of it. "He admitted to being a lawyer for GE, but it had been tied to helping Joe, a Board-electee. So, what if he worked for a practice that does all the legal work for GE? What if the head lawyer or CEO is the guy we're looking for?"

"He *drugged* you and *tied you up*?" Kellan growls through clenched teeth, the muscles in his arms tensing. "And why do I feel like you glossed over some more important details?"

"The only important takeaway is that he could have been an attorney at the firm where the Board member lawyer works. Or owns," I push, fighting to get the focus back on that rather than me.

The sound of a toilet flushing snaps Aiden out of whatever thoughts had caused his eyes to glaze over. He finishes his bourbon and it knocks sharply against the table. "This conversation isn't finished," he warns me in that smooth cadence that sends a shiver down my spine. "For the sake of Cibrina's time, we'll focus on the possible connection of this Steve with the potential Board member." Aiden turns to Dane. "Does that give you a good starting point? Steve, the attorney for the late congressman?"

Dane nods, working his jaw to restrain whatever he wants to say so we can keep moving forward with our plans.

Thank fuck for Cibrina.

"One of the hospitals in this city was tied to GE before I took down the corrupt doctors and administrators," Jack casually says. "See if the medical Board member was somehow tied to it."

Cibrina exits the bathroom and Aiden closes his eyes to regain his composure while Dane grits out, "Which one?"

"St. Marks."

Aiden draws a slow breath and releases it, directing his next words to Dane. "After you've finished the virus, this will be top priority. Find out as much as you can on them, particularly if you can confirm whether or not they are Board members of GE and if they have any gifts of their own. Then we'll put them on surveillance so we can learn their routines and anything else we might need for when we attack. We'll have to start combing through the data you've collected from each island we've visited to see if we can find any information on the eight remaining Board members."

He turns to the rest of us. "We're also going to adjust the training plan we've been putting together. While we'll continue to train in preparation of GE attacks on the Tower, we're also going to need to build additional strike teams."

"Strike teams?" I ask, confused. I assumed we would be hunting and taking them down while saving Harvey's siblings.

"When we go after the Board, it will have to be all of them at once," Aiden answers. "The second we attack one of them, the others could scatter or go into hiding. We have to hit them in the same night. Which means ten teams who work well together and against their assigned Board member or electee."

"And then we kill Charles and GE's done?" Kellan inquires.

"And Holt," I cut in.

His brows pinch. "Holt?"

"The lightning user. His death is mine."

Kellan drags himself upright in his seat as if readying to jump out of it to fight someone. "Aside from the obvious reason when Gordon took you, is there something else we should know, beautiful?"

Damn. I guess today's a big day of truths.

Taking a deep breath, I stare at my hands in my lap and explain slowly, "Gordon...he hurt me to punish me or...*coerce* me to do what he wanted. But Holt...he *enjoyed* hurting me...especially when I was at my worst. And when I panicked thinking Gordon shot Mallory...the bastard laughed." I look at Aiden. "He doesn't deserve to live."

"Is there anyone else we need to add to this kill list?" he croons.

"After Gordon and Charles, no one else has hurt me like that. But we should add the portal girl. I didn't see her once I got on the island, but she's used her gift to help GE ambush us enough that she's a problem. And then there's Royce. I don't think we'll get to Charles until we've dealt with him."

Aiden nods. "And through him, it may eliminate Thorne. And…"

We look at Dane, whose face is tight. "Yeah. And Vera," he mutters.

"We don't know if that will actually be the case, but we should be prepared either way," Aiden says.

Kellan huffs. "So much for the good news that we know the head of GE. There's still a line of people between us and him."

Jackson hums and flicks his finger, his gift knocking the salt shaker on the table over. "But the first piece has already fallen."

"Gordon," I whisper.

Dane shakes his head. "We can't take credit for that. They took out their own guy, which means everyone else in that line is probably a lot stronger or more important."

"Regardless," Aiden continues, "we need to learn the Board member names and everything about them so we can plan to take that group out."

"And the rest of the list?" Kell drawls.

"We'll need information on them, too, to find the right time and plan of attack," Aiden responds. The hope I'd felt with knowing the identity of the head of GE withers at the number of people still between us and him. If Thorne isn't taken out with Royce, then that adds another to the list.

Aiden finishes our discussion with, "Speaking of Raegan's kill list, we'll be leaving in a few hours to deal with Gordon's body. Make sure you're ready."

Chapter Fourteen

RAEGAN

The hum of the motor is the only sound on the long drive. The city lights disappeared a while ago, giving way to intermittent house or porch lights and our headlights to guide us.

I'm sitting sideways on Jackson's lap, my head tucked into his neck and chest while my ankles rest against Dane's inner thigh. His thumb idly strokes the inch of skin where my pant leg ends. He leans against his bent arm on the window, his hood down for once, gazing outside with a pensive expression. Now that we're not hiding from GE anymore, he doesn't have to care about being hidden or not. He's staying at the Tower, and they know it. If they want him, they'll attack him there.

Even though he's lost in his thoughts, his thumb never stops moving over my skin. Maybe he's thinking of me. Or maybe, even if his mind is elsewhere, I'm never far from his thoughts.

Jackson's heartbeat draws me back to him. To the slow, steady beat that encourages my own wild pulse to settle with his.

Kellan's four-seater car isn't the only reason I'm sitting on top of these two in the back.

I finger the thin, metal loop at the end of a knife within the hoodie I'm wearing. At first, I was fascinated by the smooth, protective material lining the inside. I keep finding myself playing with it, searching for another pocket for a knife to slip into, leaving only the smallest bit of handle exposed. Jackson left three flat throwing knives in his hoodie for me, but by my count, he could fit at least thirty of those between the front and sides. I can't reach the back to count the rest.

It's an easy distraction and one that I cling to for the beginning portion of the drive. Once that task loses its enjoyment, I burrow myself deeper into Jack, breathing him in on a drawn-out inhale that he mimics when his mouth presses against the top of my head. I've wrapped myself in his hoodie, in him, with the small hope that I can somehow soak in his calm confidence. That I can bolster my courage for what's coming next.

The guys didn't tell me where we're going to take care of my wishes, and I didn't ask.

We turn off the road into the woods, the car bumping and bouncing as the terrain shifts to dirt and rock. A thud in the trunk grabs my attention in a chokehold, and my breathing stops.

Dane curses when he hears it, too, snapping at Kellan in the driver's seat. "Turn something on the radio, for fuck's sake."

Jackson tightens his arms around me. He says nothing, knowing there's nothing to be done for me right now more than what he's already doing.

"What do you want to hear, beautiful?" Kell asks, his eyes reaching mine through the rearview mirror.

"We have another thirty minutes until we get there," Aiden answers my unspoken question from the passenger seat.

What do you listen to when you're on the verge of burning to ash the very man who ruined you? Is there a playlist for that?

"Anything. Whatever's on the radio."

Kellan pushes the button to turn the radio on, but it's Aiden who begins scanning the stations for a song. He stops on one, then casts a glance over his shoulder. It's an old song, one that brings up happy memories with them. I offer him a small nod and close my eyes.

The high-pitch sound of brakes and crunching tires on dirt wakes me.

"We're here," Jackson whispers.

Kellan drops his seat forward and helps me crawl out of the back, Jack following behind. It's darker than expected when I step out on shaking legs from sitting as I had for so long. I can hardly see my hand in front of me. The cover from the trees is thick enough to block most of the moon's glow, trapping us in its shadow. There's a low background hum of some bug that fills the area, while a sporadic *hoot* can be heard in the distance.

We're well and truly in the middle of nowhere.

It's perfect.

If we'd done this close to the city or Old Red, where I'd feared they'd bring me, then I wouldn't be able to pass by without thinking of Gordon. And what I want more than anything right now is to forget him. To make him so unworthy of my thoughts that I disintegrate them with his body tonight.

The doors slam, breaking the sound of the woods abruptly and taking away the small light that it had provided. Jackson's standing at my back, his hand on my hip to keep me grounded and with him. Someone walks up to me, and then a soft white glow illuminates between us, revealing Dane. He holds his other hand out to me. I take it, allowing his fingers to split mine.

"I've got her," he tells Jack, who nods and walks to the trunk. I turn away from it. I'll look at him when it's time, but not until then. We're on the side of a dirt road in the middle of the woods, the road rising and winding up ahead of us and a cliff on the opposite side.

Aiden moves in front of us and pivots so he can see everyone. His gaze falls on mine, and I hate how vulnerable I feel right now. This isn't me. I know I'm stronger than this. Better than this. But something about Gordon always breaks me down to the names he'd called me. His presence gives strength to the whispers, the self-doubt.

I look away, hating that he's seeing me like this, but not having the strength to muster any snark or challenge his way.

Not tonight.

I miss his expression after that, but it's probably for the best. I just need to get through this night, and then I hope to seal away this weakness forever.

"It's a bit of a hike to the spot. Are you ready?" Aiden asks.

Ready to be rid of Gordon, once and for all?

"I'm ready."

The walk is just as quiet as the first hour of the car ride. Aiden leads us, his flashlight turned on and the GPS open on his phone to guide us to whatever spot he'd picked out.

Finally, he stops, and Kellan drives a shovel into the dirt where Aiden's indicated.

I let go of Dane's hand and grab the only free shovel since Kellan's already started digging with his.

"Put the shovel down," Aiden starts.

"You don't need to do that," Dane adds, moving up to my side.

I stab the shovel into the ground again, burying it deeper with one foot, then angling it back. "No, and yes. I do," I say without stopping. "I can't just stand around waiting. I need to do something."

Dane makes a frustrated noise and moves out of my way.

"Why are there only two shovels?" he demands of Aiden.

"We're only making a hole wide enough for the body. Any more than two people, and we'd be bumping into each other or causing unnecessary injuries."

I don't know where Jackson's gone, although I assume it has something to do with the body. Kellan and I keep digging, and the physical labor helps take the edge off for a little bit.

Until it doesn't.

Until I keep losing myself to memories of my time with Gordon.

Memories when he'd threatened me.

Threatened the others.

Called me worthless. Useless. Dangerous. A monster.

How he'd always drag me back up after I'd collapsed, demanding more from me than I ever thought I could give. And somehow, I'd do it. I'd manage to accomplish what he wanted, and he'd let me sleep.

The words he'd slip into my head like venom, seeping into my mind and taking root. Words that cut me down. Words that offered me hope with him. Words of backhanded praise. Words and words and words. Over and over again.

Who needs a weapon or a gift when words can be so powerful to destroy a person?

"That's enough." The shovel jerks to a stop as my chest heaves gasping breaths. Now that it's still, I feel my arms tremble. It's from digging, I'm sure, until I feel something tickle my jaw. A drop of water falls to the dirt. The hole is four feet wide and probably three feet deep. There's still more to be done.

Kellan has paused his efforts to watch our exchange. I look up at Aiden, who has taken my shovel captive. "I can keep going."

"Maybe you can, but we can't." He tugs one of my hands free and scrutinizes it in the dim light of a fire someone built while I'd been working. His thumb trails over my palm, and a sharp pinch of pain makes me flinch. He frowns. "None of us can stand still and watch you hurt yourself any longer. I've let it go on long enough, if not too long. It looks like that will blister."

I yank my hand back, then scrub any weakness from my face with the back of my arm. "Good. It'll be proof that I was here. That this happened, and it wasn't just a dream."

His dark eyes soften. *Soften.* "Give me the shovel, Raegan." I hesitate, unwilling to give up the work to have one of the others take over for me. I can finish this. I can. "Now."

"Rae..." Dane chimes in softly, and I know I'm outnumbered. Rather than fight them when I'm already feeling brittle, I release the shovel.

Dane helps me step out of the small hole, and then we sit on the ground.

Aiden sticks the shovel into the dirt, then strips off his suit jacket and tosses it to the side. He removes his tie next, then rolls up his white sleeves to his elbows. Here we are, digging holes in dirt and preparing to burn a body, and he's still dressed to the nines like this is any ordinary business task.

He and Kellan get to work, focusing on depth and only a bit more width when they keep bumping into one another despite their best efforts. Finally, when all I can see are the tops of their heads—and Kellan's forehead—they emerge, tossing their shovels out of the hole and then climbing out.

Jackson appears from the darkness, the firelight casting a soft glow to one side of his face while the rest is dressed in shadow. He lifts a hand, and several dark shapes fall into the hole too fast for me to see.

Dane helps me to my feet, then moves to peek over the hole first, using his gift to bring light to it so he can see. His face twists with disgust, and he swears. "Fuck, that's ripe." He looks over his shoulder at me. "You don't have to look."

"I do." I may not want to, but I *need* to. To see with absolute certainty that it's him down there. That there was no mistake. It's him. And he's dead.

The others are standing at the edge, peering down.

"The freezer kept him from decaying too much, but it appears that rapidly changed during the drive," Aiden comments.

"What's in his mouth?" Kellan asks Jack, who smirks wickedly.

"His tiny dick."

Fuck. I don't want to see that.

Bile rises in my throat, and I force it down with a thick swallow.

I take a step. And another. Each step feels heavier than the last. As if the weight of the world is sinking down on me the closer I am. At last, I reach the hole, standing in the space equally between Dane and Jackson.

I look down.

I'm not sure what I'm looking at initially. It takes a few moments for my brain to register that I'm staring at *pieces* of Gordon at the bottom of the hole. The skin is sloughing from the muscle, making each part look...*wrong*. Nearly unrecognizable. The only thing in one whole piece is his head, which stares up with a haunting pale gaze and something wrapped between his lips and around his head.

I don't focus on that, now that I know what's there, and instead force myself to acknowledge the face that I'd still know, even though the decay has started.

It's him.

Gordon.

I'm free.

That should be it, right?

There's no magical change in me. No shift in my mood. No internal assurance or relief.

I stare at the pieces of the man who broke me, and I feel no more whole than I had an hour ago. A day ago.

"What the fuck are you doing?" Dane snaps. "Why do you always have your dick out?"

I blink back to myself, looking at the guys around me to see what's going on. Kellan has his dick in hand, pointed downward. He looks to me. "Do you mind, beautiful?"

"Uh...sure."

Grinning, he pisses all over Gordon, wagging his hips around to make sure he gets all of him.

"You're disgusting," Dane gripes, then checks in with me.

I shrug. He's dead already, so what happens to him doesn't matter now. Whether he's cut to pieces or peed on, he doesn't feel any of it. But I can agree with that level of contempt for him. I'd probably join him if I could aim as well as they can.

More liquid pours down the hole, and I turn to Jackson. He squeezes a bottle of lighter fluid over it. The bottle squirts empty, and he drops it in the hole, too. Jack pulls a box of matches from his pocket, makes eye contact with me, then tosses it.

I catch it on reflex.

"Light him up, little one."

Right.

Thumbing the box, I pick a match from the pile and strike it along the edge. The spark instantly catches, changing to a bright and then steady flame. Its heat warms my fingertips as the tiny blaze flickers and dances in the mild nighttime air. I take a deep breath, and the smell of sulfur fills my nose.

I drop the match over the hole.

The tiny light falls down the dark pit, then bursts into a full flame the second it meets the lighter fluid. It gobbles Gordon up, hungrily spreading over his remains and flaring brighter, higher, until I can see nothing but the fire.

I stare at it, mesmerized. Hoping it will melt and seal the cracks in my soul if I stand close enough.

"We're going to defeat Gifted Enterprise." Aiden's voice draws my gaze to him. His eyes are locked on mine, his expression serious. Dirt powders his white dress shirt, streaks smeared across his face and exposed forearms from sweat. "No matter what happens, the five of us will prevail. I swear this to you, Raegan, on Gordon's corpse. He's the first of many. We'll do the same with Thorne. Royce. Holt. Charles. And anyone else from GE who tries to stop us."

His words hang in the night with so much power that I can almost feel it resonate in my chest. Maybe it's these woods, or the time of night, or the ritualistic burning of our enemy at our feet. But it feels like his words hold weight that fills the air around us, suspended in time like the air in my lungs.

The others are watching me with a similar intensity, and I wonder if there was something to the calls for witchcraft hundreds of years ago. If there isn't some truth to what was said about what happened, if magical oaths like this are possible, or if it had been a single gifted user with that ability, and people assumed all others with *magic* could do the same.

My body heats beneath their stares, and I'm suddenly filled with the urge to touch each of them. To feel their skin on mine. My clothing feels tight and restrictive, and I want to rip it off. I want to stand at their center and offer myself to them, give in to them while they equally give in to me. My heart hammers in my chest, and electricity buzzes under my skin as I'm consumed by those thoughts. By the nagging need to press myself against each and every one of them. I crave their hands on me more than oxygen, my body pulsating with that insatiable ache.

I lick my parted lips, staring at each of them and all of them at once, ready to make that demand, when a loud *POP* from the fire behind us makes my heart stutter out of rhythm and my breath expels in a rush.

Fuck. What was I about to do?

I take another draw of air, realizing then that they're all waiting for me to say something. Focusing back on the fiery pit, I steel myself to speak to Gordon one last time.

"You are nothing to me. When the last flame leaves you with nothing but bones, I'm going to destroy those, too. There will be no remnants left of you in this world or the next. Because one day, I'm going to forget you completely. It may not be today or tomorrow, but I promise that day will come when I'll be free of you."

Kellan tosses another log on the fire—the one without the body in it—and the fire crackles and spurts a slew of sparks into the air.

I'm cuddled against Dane, his arm around my back as we lean against the boulder Jackson dropped by the fire for us.

"We need more wood," Kellan murmurs to Aiden, who stands from one of the logs he'd cut to make bench seats around the fire. He draws out an axe made completely of metal and follows Kellan out of the small clearing into the denser woods to pick out another small tree to fell for firewood.

I didn't expect burning a body to its bones to take so long.

Then again, I don't think I did a whole lot of thinking about what would come after seeing his body. That pretty much occupied all my thoughts.

Jackson has been keeping the fire in the hole well-oxygenated and burning, but it's been hours since it began.

I close my eyes, trying to let the quiet sounds of nature lull me to sleep, but it never comes. I can't sleep here, knowing what's happening a few yards behind me.

"How are you feeling?" Dane asks.

"I don't know," I answer honestly. "I feel...nothing...right now. Just...blank. No anger, no sadness, no relief. No sense of closure like I'd hoped."

He hums softly. "I'm probably the last person to give advice on closure," he teases gently. "When you told me Vera was dead...I don't think I ever accepted it. I never *saw* her after that, so it didn't feel real. I tried writing to her in my notebook to see if that would help, but I think it just made my denial worse."

My chest squeezes tightly at the memory of when I'd told him she was dead. That I had done it. And how he must have felt, day after day, as he wrangled with whether or not to believe me. And then what it was like when each day passed, and he never saw her. Years later, when I saw him for the first time in that auto repair shop, he was still drowning in the pain of her loss, as fresh as if it had just happened.

"What I'm trying to say is...I don't think there's some perfect moment that gives us closure. I think it's something we have to work on, on our own terms, about what that means to us. Whether that's accepting it's over, deep in our hearts, letting time create the distance we need to be able to leave it behind—and actually choosing to do it—or some other way."

He pauses. Swallows. "It's you who helped me move forward, Rae. As long as I'm with you, I've been able to live again. I can breathe again. Enjoy the little moments and have hope for the future. You mean everything to me."

My eyes and throat burn with emotion, and I grip his hoodie, needing to feel the beat of his heart and his warmth.

"Whatever it takes for you to get closure on him, on this, I'm here for you." He draws my face up to look at his, his eyes capturing mine in their golden depths that flicker and burn just as strongly as the fire reflected in them. "And I want you to know that I've forgiven you for what happened in the past. I'm not just saying it this time. I mean it with everything I am."

Fuck.

I hook my hand around the back of his head, bringing us together in a crash of lips that taste like salt and sorrow. Of sweet solace that feels like a balm on my soul.

I don't know if I'll ever completely heal from my past, but I know that I'll find happiness so long as I'm with these four men. They'll fill in the cracks left behind and make me stronger.

I can feel Jackson's presence before I hear the purposeful scuff of his boot on the dirt behind me. Dane and I break away slowly, not wanting the kiss to end but knowing the night isn't over yet.

"It's time." Jack's cool voice runs down my spine, inducing a shiver of desire. It's ungodly how much I want all of them, all the time. Maybe it makes no sense to others in this world how my heart can want them all the same, but I can feel it in the very marrow of my bones that the five of us are meant to be together. I glance over my shoulder at him, and Jack's smirk deepens at my expression, like he knows exactly what I'm thinking.

I know he would be on board with what I want, as well as Kellan. Maybe even Dane. But Aiden...

My gaze moves across the fire, finding Aiden and Kell standing at the edge of the fire ring and watching us. There's a hardness to Aiden's stare that tells me he watched enough of Dane and me to have triggered his jealous and possessive instincts. Only his care for his brothers and his role as leader is holding him back for now.

"Let's finish this, then," I reply nonchalantly. Like we're taking care of a simple house chore rather than completing the murder and annihilation of Gordon. Dane and Jackson help me to my feet, and they keep me between them as we walk to the pile of bones lying in front of the pit, stopping as one.

Kellan and Aiden join us a second later while I ready my gift. It responds at once, snaking up from my gut to my hand, giving it a dark reddish glow. Kneeling, I don't bother with words or promises this time. I touch the nearest piece of burned ivory, pushing my gift into it and every bone it touches. Bone cracks and shifts from the spiderweb of power that runs through it until, finally, I have them all, and I send a strong burst of my gift through it.

The bones instantly turn to ash, small piles lined along the ground at my feet. The particles lift as one, rising from the earth until they're high enough to be caught on the small breeze. Jackson buffers it, strengthening the air moving around us so the dust scatters in the wind.

And just like that, he's gone.

Chapter Fifteen

RAEGAN

An annoying, out-of-the-box ringtone interrupts my dreamless sleep. There's a huff, and then something slides under my neck and pulls me against heated skin. The familiar smell of cinnamon body wash promises me I'm safe, and I keep my eyes closed to cling to sleep and a worry-free existence for a bit longer.

The phone keeps ringing, even as lips plant at the top of my head and his abdomen concaves with how deeply he breathes me in.

Aiden clears his throat. "What is it?" he finally answers, his voice hushed and his head turned away from me.

Nosey as I am, I strain to listen. It should be easy with how close I am to him, but he must keep his phone volume low because I can only catch a female voice and a word here or there that makes no sense out of context.

"Yes." A pause. "A couple hours ago...No. Tell them tomorrow." A frustrated sigh. "No. No, it's alright...I appreciate it. Tell them we'll be there in an hour. That's the soonest we can do. Yes. Give us ten minutes."

I crane my neck to look at him. The back of his hand holding the phone is resting over his closed eyes. As if he can sense my gaze on him, his eyes open.

"Did I wake you?" He lightly chuffs, then sets his phone on the nightstand. "Never mind. I already know the answer."

"Was that Cibrina?" I guess, my hand sliding up his smooth and firm chest to get more comfortable. The last thing I remember is driving away from the woods at the cusp of dawn, curled in Jackson's lap. I assumed I'd be waking up to him this morning, considering where I'd been. His bed is also the one I've slept in the past few nights.

Which means Aiden took it upon himself to put me in his bed this time.

I wouldn't mind waking up in any of their beds, though I'm still holding out for my own. It's just the small issue of Aiden's inability to share that has me wondering what the others thought about him stealing me away to his room while I'd been unconscious.

His long fingers trail along the back of my hand before dwarfing it in his. "It was."

"And?"

"You, me, and Dane need to go to the police station to give our statements."

My nose crinkles in both confusion and displeasure. "Statements about what? When did the police get involved?"

"When we arrived at the hospital with four severely injured victims. Cibrina held them off as long as she could, but if we don't show in an hour, they'll issue warrants for our arrest."

Fuck a duck.

As if we don't have enough problems. The last thing we need are the cops sniffing around the Guild.

"What are we supposed to say? Hi, sorry! My psycho dad tried to kidnap two of us and kill me, but we made it out of there before he could. Don't try to find and arrest him or he'll probably kill you, too."

The corner of Aiden's lips tugs up in amusement, and I take that compliment and tuck it away in my memories for a rainy day.

Then his expression falls, and I can almost see the wheels turning through his focused stare at the ceiling. "We'll get the others up and discuss our cover story to make sure it all matches. I need to call Cassandra over as well since she'll need to be present for her own interview. Cibrina is already on her way. She'll be representing each of us as our attorney."

"What else?"

"Reid. Him not showing up for the interview means he'll be wanted by the police when he returns." There's conviction in his tone when he says Reid will be back. Like he can imagine no other path than Reid returning once he's gotten whatever he's trying to accomplish done or he realizes he can't continue without help. "That aside, it's going to make our story less convincing if one of the victims has gone missing."

Wonderful.

"I'll call Fabian to come in, too, just in case since he was in the hospital room with Reid." He reaches for his phone again. One of these days, when we're not fighting GE or dealing with the cops, I'm going to hide his phone for a day. I'll tell Cibrina he's unavailable, and I'm going to make sure he relaxes and has fun, whatever that looks like for him.

Maybe something involving a collar. And me.

I curl over him, slipping my leg between his and running my hand up to smooth the crinkle between his brows. His hand pauses over the phone.

"What are you doing?" he inquires in a smooth-as-melted chocolate voice when I slip my fingers through his soft bedhead. He's usually so put together. Suit and tie. Hair styled back with some product. A stern expression on his face that he wears like a mask he puts on for the day.

I'm seeing the man beneath that armor. The mess of his hair. The sleep still clinging to his voice. The suit gone, revealing his athletic build that you wouldn't expect of a businessman. And tight muscular arms that could probably pop a man's head off if he squeezed hard enough.

Even though he's wearing boxers, his cock is erect and firm at my hip, pushing at the fabric to be free the more I touch him. It reminds me that I'm only in a shirt and underwear, meaning it would be so easy to shift it aside...

He grabs my throat before I can act, bringing my face to his. "Don't tempt me," he purrs. "Besides the fact that Cibrina will be here in five minutes, and we have yet to wake the others, we also have an audience."

An audience?

His eyes slant to my right, and I follow them to find Jackson lying on his back on the floor, both arms behind his head as a makeshift pillow.

Jack's lips curve to a wicked smile. "Don't mind me."

Ah. That explains how he'd taken me from Jackson. As long as he could stay in the room, too.

I really need to get my own room.

Aiden is entirely unamused at the suggestion. "Get dressed," he orders, releasing me to roll off him.

He grabs his phone and walks into the bathroom to get ready himself.

Tilting my head, I peer down to Jackson with a teasing smirk. "He wouldn't let you in the bed?"

Jackson chuckles and sits upright. "Not yet." Then he's on his feet in one effortless motion, touching his forehead against mine and threading his fingers into the hair at my nape. "Morning, little one."

My heart does a little pitter-patter. My voice is soft and breathy when I reply, "Morning."

His smirk stretches to a smile, dimple piercing his left cheek as he pulls back. "I'll go wake the others," he says before leaving the room and closing the door.

Seeking out my bag of clothes in the corner of the room, I hurriedly change and tie my hair back, then leave the room.

By the time I'm out, Dane's already in the kitchen at the stove working on eggs. He glances up, and a boyish smile—that makes my heart throb and chest ache—lights up his face.

"Hey," he greets softly.

"Hey."

He holds an arm out expectantly. Butterflies scatter in my chest and my cheeks flame.

What the hell is this feeling?

I take my time getting there, hoping I'll pin a name to whatever unfamiliar emotion is flooding my system in a rush of heat and jittering nerves, but I am still clueless by the time his arm falls over my shoulders. He tucks me into his side, holding me there as his other hand guides the spatula to test the crisping edges of his eggs. They sizzle in the pan, and steam rises with the smell of cooking butter.

"How'd you sleep?"

I blow out a breath, mostly in an attempt to expel the nerves from my body but also to express my frustration with the lack of sleep. "Great...until the wake-up call."

He snorts. "No kidding. After this shit show interrogation, I'd say we've earned ourselves an afternoon of a movie marathon and a nap."

"Have you finished building that virus Aiden wants?"

"Yeah. I'm working on the first two potential Board member research now. Think the cops will let me bring my laptop in the room while I wait?"

Now it's my turn to snort. "Even if they did, I wouldn't. They'll probably spy on what you're doing and then ask even more questions."

"Mmm. Yeah. Guess I'll have to wait until we get back." He flips the eggs, giving them a few seconds to cook on that side before he lifts the pan and slides them onto a plate. "Do you want bacon or sausage with your breakfast sandwich?"

My mouth waters at the offer. "Is it greedy to want both?"

"You can have whatever the fuck you want, babe. Just tell me, and I'll make it for you."

Babe.

It's like a shot of pleasure strikes me in the chest, swelling and rolling through me in a wave of heat and throwing my heart out of rhythm.

"Um..." I start, too distracted by that one word to remember what I'm supposed to be telling him anymore.

Dane cracks an egg on the counter and splits it one-handed over the pan for the next round of eggs.

Eggs. Sandwiches. Bacon and sausage. Right.

"I want both. With cheese."

"Done. Go sit at the table, and I'll bring it to you when it's ready." He kisses my head and releases me to do as he instructed. I'm still too dumbfounded by that entire interaction to think twice about it. I move on autopilot, my brain still glitching and rebooting, until I find myself in Jackson's chair at an empty table.

"Ahhhhrrrrnngh!" Kellan's raucous voice followed by a yawn echo in the living area seconds before him. "I need at least eight hours of sleep to look as beautiful as I do. Two is shit to work with." He shoots me a sharp grin.

Jackson trails behind him, hands in his kangaroo pocket and hood up. He leaves the Loft, and I give Kellan a questioning look as he leans against the back of the couch with arms folded.

"To let the others in." He lifts his arm and the sleeve of tattoos there. "No one comes in or out of here without the key."

That's right. I'd seen one of them raising their arms or wrists in the elevator each time we'd reached the Loft floor but had been too distracted to realize why.

"Shouldn't I have a key?"

"You going somewhere without one of us?" he drawls with a cocky smirk.

Frowning, I cross my arms and lean back in my chair. "You don't have to worry about me running after GE on my own anymore. But yeah. I'd like the freedom to come and go alone if I wanted to. I'm done feeling like a prisoner."

"I'll arrange an appointment for your tattoo," Aiden calmly states as he emerges from the hallway. "Decide where you want them to put it and make sure it's somewhere you can easily get to for scanning it." He drapes his suit jacket over the back of his chair, then draws it back and sits.

The tension between my shoulders recedes in a rush of relief. I slide my fingers along the curve of my shirt's neckline, tugging it enough to reveal the top of one breast. A small smirk creeps onto my face when I open my mouth. "Ri—"

"Somewhere on your arm or wrist will do," Aiden immediately cuts in. "Though, I'd strongly advise you keep it somewhere between your forearm and wrist in case you're wearing long sleeves or a jacket." His dark gaze pins mine. "You wouldn't want to be forced to strip an article of clothing off just to gain entry each time."

I mean, it would be funny the first few times. But long term, he has a point.

Dane sets a plate in front of me and another before Aiden. The smell is mouthwatering. "Thanks," I murmur as he strides back to the kitchen. He smiles at me over his shoulder and nods, then gets to work on assembling the next sandwich.

I dig in, groaning a little at how delicious it tastes. Dane's expression is hopeful and nervous when he places a mug of coffee down for me next. "Is it good?"

Nodding emphatically, I manage around a mouthful, "So good."

His smile widens.

The door to the Loft opens, and a line of people enter, followed by Jack.

"Good morning, everyone. I'm so sorry for the timing. I tried to hold him off—" Aiden raises his hand, and Cibrina stops.

"There's no need to apologize, Cibrina. Have any of you eaten?" He indicates the counter where Dane's already prepared breakfast sandwiches for everyone.

Cassandra's looking around the Loft like this is her first time here; a small, selfish part of me is pleased to see that.

Fabian rushes to the counter, tossing the rest of whatever else he'd been eating in his mouth at once to free his hands and reach for a sandwich. He releases an unrestrained moan after a single bite. "Marry me," he directs to Dane, who scoffs.

"I'm taken. Besides, you're not my type."

Fabian shrugs. "My type is whoever can cook the best."

"Odd priority," Dane mutters, taking a sandwich for himself and standing by my side.

Jack grabs one and then leans against the sliding glass doors to the balcony behind me while Cassandra and Cibrina each take a sandwich and sit in the remaining two seats.

"Now that we're all here, let's discuss what we are—or, more importantly, are *not*—going to say to the detective," Aiden begins.

"Are we going to talk about how illegal this is?" Kellan speaks up.

Cibrina nods. "Technically, yes. It would be against the law for them to issue warrants for our arrest. Going to the station to answer questions when no report has been filed is our choice. Ordinarily, I would advise against going to avoid possible self-incrimination. However, with this particular detective..." She glances at Aiden.

"It would be in our best interest to comply enough that he drops it. Avoiding him seems to have only made his curiosity in us grow," he adds.

"Can we file a complaint against him for threatening us?" Dane demands.

"We could," Cibrina responds. "But, at most, he may receive a few days' suspension, and then his ire would be aimed at us, making matters worse."

Dane curses under his breath.

"Which brings us back to how we're going to answer his questions. Dane and Raegan, you'll both have been drunk and fallen down the stairs to sustain your injuries. And you won't remember anything from that night," Aiden says.

"What about my bullet graze?" Dane asks.

"Something that you fell on caused that wound, but seeing as you don't remember the night and only Raegan was with you at the time, you're unsure what it was." Aiden looks to the rest of the room. "He's going to try to get the victims to mention a name or some possible offender he can go after. We aren't going to give him one. And this was a private party, unaffiliated with the Guild."

Aiden and Cibrina continue their coaching as uneasiness swirls in my gut. If this detective already has it out for us, I have a bad feeling he's not going to be satisfied after these interviews.

I only hope we leave him with enough of a dead end that he drops it.

"Is that all you have to say?" The detective grinds out, his temper clearly frazzling. "You don't remember anything?"

I shrug one shoulder, relaxing back in my seat with arms folded over my chest. "I'm not sure what you're looking for, Officer. It was a hell of a party that went too far. I'm sorry if that's not the answer you want, but there's nothing more to it."

His frown lines deepen, his bushy dark brows drawing in. "It's Detective Unger."

"Huh?"

"Not officer. Detective," he corrects me.

Scoffing, I focus my gaze on the corner of the table in the interview room to keep my eyes from rolling. This guy definitely has a superiority complex. "Sure," I reply instead, doing my damnedest to be on my best behavior like I'd promised Aiden.

"Your hospital record says you'd broken several ribs and had some pretty severe bruising," he muses, flipping open the file he'd slapped down on the table when he first entered the room.

I cast a short glance at Cibrina sitting next to me and see her mouth turn down while staring at the file that I'm pretty sure he had no right to obtain.

Fantastic.

"Good for you," I reply, sarcasm drowning my words. "You can read."

Cibrina places her hand on my arm, and I force myself to take a deep breath. Right. This is almost over. I need to keep my head.

Detective Unger's lips twitch to an almost smile from my response. "And it was Aiden Adams who signed you in. What's his relation to you?"

Heat flares in my chest. I drop my hands to my lap, fisting them beneath the table. "He's my...boyfriend," I finish lamely. That word doesn't feel right. That little word isn't enough to encompass what we have, what me and the others have between us.

But it's none of this guy's business what word would fit us best, so I leave him with that.

"Ah, your boyfriend," he drags out slowly, then closes the file and laces his hands together over it. "The way I see it, Miss LaRoux, you're innocent. Maybe even a victim. Now, I don't know if this was some sort of domestic or company-based harassment or what...but I'm here to let you know that you can trust me. If you're covering for someone, you don't need to do that. We can bring them in and hold them, so you have nothing to fear from intimidation or repercussions if you were to give me a name."

Anger rushes through my veins, boiling my blood as I clench my teeth. This asshole is trying to get me to point a finger at Aiden. My gift burns in my gut, aching to slip free at the threat to Aiden. Leaning forward, I lower my voice when I answer him. "You wanna know how I see it?" His brows knit, and I know I have his attention. "I see a pathetic, wannabe detective grasping at straws, trying to make something out of nothing in the hopes someone will notice him. I think if you were a real detective, you'd have actual bad guys to catch, but instead, you're here harassing us because you have nothing better to do. Get a life because I have nothing more to say to you."

The detective smiles, then mirrors my position on the opposite side of the table. "One thing you should know about me is that I have great instincts. Some might even call it a *gift*." My stomach drops. "Thank you for your time today, Miss LaRoux. I have what I need for now, and I'll let you know when I have further questions." He stands, taking the file with him. "Don't leave town."

He exits the room, the soft click of the door behind him striking me with a bolt of fear.

Cibrina sighs. When I look at her to speak, she shakes her head. Another officer opens the door for us, leading us back to the entrance of the police station where the others are waiting. I'd been the last one, so we walk outside to the two parked cars before anyone says a word.

"How did everyone do?" Aiden asks Cibrina, who'd been present with each of us.

I'm half expecting her to look at me after the shitshow that was my interview, but she doesn't. "We've given him nothing further to investigate with this incident." Aiden nods, but she continues, "But he's not going to drop it from what I can tell. He seems to already have an interest in us, so since he doesn't have an angle from using the victims' statements, I have no doubt he'll be searching for another one."

"What other angle could he possibly have?" Dane questions, his arms crossed and one foot up against the tire of Kellan's car.

"The Guild, for one," Cibrina responds. "He may look deeper into the company, and Aiden as the one who runs it. That and he made a comment about having a natural gift with his instincts. It could be a coincidence, but..."

Dane swears and hits a fist against Kell's car.

"Watch it," Kellan growls.

Cassandra chews on her lip but stays quiet while Fabian tosses peanuts into his mouth and looks unperturbed.

"The cops aren't a problem. It's just him," Jackson comments.

Aiden turns to him. "Did you hear something?"

Jack nods once. "His superior. Demanded to know what we were all doing there." He cocks his head. "I can make him and all of this disappear," he offers chillingly, and Cassandra shivers next to me.

"Not yet," Aiden commands, and I frown. I know it's probably not the *right* thing to do, but I agree with Jackson. We have enough problems right now to add this guy to it, especially with that *gift* remark. Does he have a gift himself, or was he insinuating he knows about people with gifts? "We'll have someone keep an eye on him for now to make sure he doesn't get too close. If he does, then we'll address him. Until then, we keep our focus on GE."

I reach behind me to pinch Jackson's hoodie, which draws him immediately to press into my back without a word. I've barely had him back from watching Thorne. Is he going to be off stalking this guy now?

Aiden catches the movement, his eyes then finding mine. "Others can watch the detective. Thorne was a special case." He looks to the rest of the group. "Hopefully, this is the last we hear of this detective, but tell Cibrina or me immediately if he tries to reach out to you directly."

Somehow, I doubt we've heard the last word from Detective Unger.

Chapter Sixteen

JACKSON

Childish shouts and laughter pass unrestrained through the apartment door, bringing a small smile to my lips as I tap my knuckles against it.

"Be right there!" Briar calls out, sounding breathless. I tuck my hand back in my pocket, and it's only a minute before I hear the slide of the peephole. "Oh, Jackson! Is it that day already?"

The door opens, revealing a young blonde with her hair tied back. There's gaudy beads and jewels dangling around her neck and wrists, and a construction paper crown covered in glitter and dried macaroni on her head. She smiles when she sees me, one of a handful of Guild members who don't seem as fearful of me as the rest.

When I'd asked her about it, she claimed she trusted the kids' instinct over everyone else's opinions.

A silly reason. The kids have nothing to fear from me. Adults who know better do.

But she's new, having joined while the Guild was living in the bunker as Claudia's helper with the kids. After Claudia's death, she's taken over living with and handling the children full-time until they can be sent safely into witness protection with their families.

"Sorry things are a mess. We're playing knights and dragons." There's a long pause where I suspect she thinks I'll say something nice in return. When I remain silent, she blinks and calls over her shoulder, "Mallory! It's time for your lessons." She finally steps back, opening the door wide for me to enter.

The living room is overtaken by forts made from colorful sheets and string lights, draped over whatever furniture had been in the apartment. The six kids are running and jumping on everything, a whirlwind of energy as they play-fight with their foam swords and shields.

I move inside, my eyes latching on to the blonde-haired girl in a puffy pink princess dress.

Mallory gasps when she sees me, ditching her sword and flouncing toward me with wide blue eyes and a bright smile. "Jack!" She tackles my arm, wrapping hers around it and then tugging excitedly. "I've gotten so much better! Come see! Come see!"

I follow her to the fourth bedroom, now converted to a learning room, and she hops in front of the whiteboard, fluffing her hair. The blonde strands darken to black, then shorten to a bob framing her face. She wrinkles her nose, and the tip narrows and points further out. Her eyes are brown when she looks at me and throws her hands out. "Ta-da!"

"Better." Smiling, I push off the wall and retrieve a small mirror from the cabinet to hand her. Then, a book from the shelf with real-life people and images in it. Flipping to a page with a girl around her age, I place it on the table and tap on it. "Match her."

"Okay!" She kneels in front of the table, the book on her left and the mirror on her right, as she looks between the two.

I return to my spot on the opposite wall, leaning back with a leg bent as I withdraw a square of paper from my pocket and work on some origami while I wait.

Her work isn't quiet. If she isn't huffing, muttering to herself, or groaning when something doesn't look right, she's gasping sharply or releasing tiny squeals when something she tries works.

It's when she grows quiet that I look up.

She's staring at my hands—at the twelfth paper animal I've made—with ripe curiosity. "Why are you always making those?"

"They keep my hands busy."

"Why?"

Rather than explain, I tilt my head and regard her unchanged appearance. "Did you get stuck?"

"No!" she replies indignantly. "I just...I just...can I have one?"

"No."

"Why not? You have so many!"

"They're not for you."

She folds her arms and pouts. "Who are they for?"

"Raegan."

Her face falls. Even though we've talked about her before, we talked about what the bad guys said and did, she's still scared of her. I'm not expecting a change overnight. Logic and reasoning only go so far with children before emotions win. And unfortunately for Raegan, she's tangled up in a web of bad feelings that Mallory's still trying to work through.

It was the main reason I started visiting her. I want to learn more about what Raegan went through the last time with Gordon and to see if I might sway Mallory's opinion of Raegan.

I have a feeling Mallory's acceptance of her might help fix how she sees herself.

She stays quiet, and I don't push her to speak. I give her time to sort through her feelings and continue folding the paper as if I could do this all day.

By the time I've completed two more animals, tossing them into the air to join the others, she's found her words. "I think..." She tugs on her hair, rolling her lip between her teeth. "Um...maybe I might...do you think I could...or would she..." Her blue eyes plead at me to understand.

"Hm?"

Mallory hides behind her hands, groaning with frustration. "Why is this so hard?!"

Smiling, I squat and tap the table. She splits her fingers to watch me through them. "Maybe because it means something to you."

"Is...is that good? Or bad?"

I shrug one shoulder. "I don't know. You tell me."

She stares at me, unblinking as she tries to figure it out, then snaps her fingers closed again. "Ugh! I don't know!" she wails.

Chuckling softly, I return to my position against the wall. "Then you don't know yet. Don't force it."

"Okay."

Her voice is soft and sad, but she doesn't realize how much improvement she's already made. That she might ask to see or talk to Raegan when only a month ago she'd been terrified of her. Even if she'd found the courage to ask, I wouldn't let that meeting happen yet. I can't risk hurting Raegan if Mallory isn't ready. When it does happen, it'll be when I know Mallory won't run at the sight of her.

"Why do you make those for her?"

Back to the origami, then.

"She likes them."

"Oh." Mallory pauses. Thinks. "I like them, too."

"Mm. Something you two have in common."

Her mouth pops open, and her lips slide into a shy smile. "Yeah." She side-eyes the floating paper. "I want one."

"Then make one."

"I want one of *those*."

"No."

She huffs. "Why *not*?"

"These are something special between me and her. It would be wrong of me to share it with anyone else."

Her face scrunches with confusion. "It's just paper. What's so special about it?"

"It's the meaning behind it. Just for the two of us." Lifting the latest creature with the others, I drop my gaze to the book and mirror still in front of her. "Are we done for today?"

Mallory slaps her hand over the page. "No! I'm still trying!"

Her focus intensifies on the image and her reflection, her hair and eyes shifting first and easiest. She's been working on perfecting the rest of the facial features the last few weeks, particularly changing shape and structure.

It'll be a handy gift once she's gotten a better handle on it. Once she has the head right, we'll move on to the body—enough to pass with clothes on—then test if her gift can affect her voice and clothes as well.

I've been meeting with her almost weekly since we rescued her to help her with her gift; with Raegan. Of all the children we rescued, she's the only one we won't have a place for. There is no witness protection for her because we won't return her to the family that got rid of her like something defective. It reminds me of my own childhood before the island. How I'd been unwanted by my own parents and given up to the system. Then passed from one foster home to another until the last one sold me to GE, like I was a circus animal.

Unless Aiden can find a family that will happily adopt her with her special talent, it's more likely Mallory will grow up here. With Briar. With the Guild.

"Yes!" She smiles at me with her borrowed face, blissfully ignorant of the power she'll have when she's older.

"Good."

CHAPTER SEVENTEEN

RAEGAN

The mandatory Guild training begins in the fitness center on the first floor of the Tower. There's a full-sized gymnasium with a temporary wall splitting a third of it, followed by showers and locker rooms on one side and a fully-equipped weight room on the other. And a snack and shake bar. Can't forget that.

Jackson's sitting on the edge of the desk Aiden had brought in, one leg folded up on his knee and leaning into his fist as Aiden talks to him. Behind the desk are rolling corkboards with schedules and lists pinned to them.

Since we arrived early, I'm first in line to start scanning the lists to find my name and scheduled time in each session. There's offensive gift training, defensive gift training, weight training, self-defense training, and physical combat training. Each person is signed up for three sessions based on their skills or desire to be an active fighter or a background supporter.

But this initial gift training is apparently for everyone.

My finger stops on Kell's name. I glance over my shoulder at him.

"I thought you were a trainer."

He scratches his beard and shrugs. "I still need to work on my gift. I'm just the combat and self-defense trainer. Jack's the offensive gift trainer. Dane and Aiden are splitting the weight training. Cibrina is leading the defensive gift session."

Dane scowls at the list. "What the fuck? Why am I in the defensive gift group?"

Kellan cackles and leans forward to look at the list for the first time as Dane storms over to the desk, yanking out drawers and grabbing something before coming back. "He's not wrong. Your gift isn't really an offensive—"

"—it is when I shoot them after muting their gift," Dane snaps, scribbling his name off the defensive list. He adds his name to the offensive group and Kellan snickers behind him.

"What are you doing?"

Dane jumps at Aiden's voice, who had followed him after he'd stolen the pen. He turns around, crossing his arms and widening his stance, his lips turned down in annoyance. "I'm putting my name where it belongs."

"Are you saying you disagree with where Cibrina and I put you?"

"I'm saying I'm not staying behind while you guys go and fight GE, so why the fuck wouldn't I learn everything I can to be useful in the field?"

Aiden frowns. "Learning to use your gift defensively isn't useless…"

I tune out when I catch Jackson beckoning me to him with two curved fingers, slipping around the others to get to him. He drops his leg and tugs me between his thighs.

Sliding my hands up his collarbone to his neck, I smile at him. "Are you nervous?"

He tilts his head, a smirk curling his lips. "Nervous?"

I hum softly. "To talk to so many people." All the Guild members chose to stay and fight. None of them ran away to hide like they could have. And then there's the Pits fighters who are joining in as well.

Jackson's smirk intensifies. "No."

Well. I guess I shouldn't be surprised. I'm not sure if I've ever seen Jack nervous before. I trail my hands up to his hood. "You should take this down, you know. So they can see you."

He takes my hands and holds them between us. "They just need to hear me." He presses his lips to my hands, his deep blue eyes catching mine under dark lashes and spiking my heart rate.

I nod slowly, at a loss for anything else to say when he's looking at me like this.

An arm falls over my shoulders and pops the bubble I'd been in with Jack, the background noise of so many people chatting in the gym now a dull and constant echo. "Flirting with the teacher to get better marks, beautiful?" Kellan's wild grin claims half his face as he leans in between us. "Don't leave me hanging this time, yeah? Just tell me where we're sneaking off to. The locker room? The showers? I can't fit under the desk, but maybe if we got a table and tablecloth—"

I smack his chest just as Aiden walks over.

"Problem?" he asks, his gaze flicking between the three of us.

I do my best to smile sweetly at him. "No." Either I fail, or maybe my smiling like that to him is a red flag on its own because his eyes narrow. "We're just excited for the lesson. Come on, Kell. Let's grab Dane and make sure we find a good spot." Grabbing his hand, I drag him away to seek out Dane, then plant us front and center so we don't miss a thing. If it were anyone else teaching something, I'd be content somewhere off to the side. But if Jackson is teaching a lesson, you can be damn sure he'll have my full attention.

It's only another few minutes before the doors close to the gym, signaling that everyone is here. Aiden raises his hands to gather the crowd's attention, and within seconds, it's quiet. "Thank you everyone for being here. I know these sessions seem like a lot, but I promise they'll only take up the first few hours of your day, starting at six in the morning. You'll still be able to work and continue as you were after that. Today, Jackson is going to give a brief lecture on gifts before we break into different groups. Please give him your undivided attention."

He steps back and to the side, giving the proverbial floor to Jack.

Jackson uses his gift to lift himself to stand on the desk. His gaze sweeps over the people in the room, taking them in for a second with a small smile. He pulls a few throwing knives free and tosses them up. Aiden's face tightens, and I can feel Kellan and Dane tense on either side of me. What had he said about his training with Thorne? The wind master had tried to kill him as his training?

The knives flip and twirl in the air above his palm. It's like the room's holding its breath, waiting to see what he's going to do next.

"If I've learned anything about gifts in general, it's that there's probably more to it than you think," he muses, his voice carrying and echoing through the room even though he's speaking as he normally does.

Murmuring ripples through a small group to the side. I'd bet they're Pits fighters. Guild members wouldn't interrupt him.

Jackson smiles and directs his attention to them. "Mm...how did you know you have a gift?" he prompts the group as if he'd heard what they said. "Did something happen one day? And did you practice that one skill, accepting it as the end-all, be-all, of your gift?" He waits a beat before he continues, "Or did you try different things? Did you test your limits so you know exactly what you can do and how much? And then find ways to break past them?"

Kellan shifts at my side, his face drawn and serious for a change as he watches and listens.

"No one can tell you what your gift is. It's up to you to figure that out." Jackson flips his hand down, and the knives burrow into the desk at his feet. He waves his hand, and a strong breeze whips around us and then dies out.

"How are we supposed to break past its limit?" someone calls out.

"Mine only works for so long," another person adds.

Jackson nods, stuffing his hands back into his kangaroo pocket. "Keep your gift active every day. Get creative. Stop overthinking steps and feel it. But first"—he bends and tugs a knife from the desk, flipping it between the fingers of one hand— "you need to work on your physical stamina." He points the tip of the blade at the crowd. "Gifts don't run out. Your body does. Your body will shut your gift down to protect itself and give it time to recover. Exercise your body, your gift, and use it regularly and without thought—like breathing—and you'll be able to do more."

His eyes fall on me, and my breathing thins.

"Raegan."

Ah, crap. Please don't call me to the front of the room. It's school all over again.

Jack's lips quirk at the corners. He hops off the desk and motions me forward.

Frowning, I walk the few steps to him before he can use his gift to get me there anyway.

He holds the knife out to me. "Destroy it."

I call my gift to the surface, sending it to my right hand in seconds with only the mild burn it induces now. Before I can reach for the knife, Jackson tosses it to his other hand.

"Too slow," he remarks coolly.

I grab for it, stretching my arm and taking a step, but he steps with me. I shift my gift to my other hand that's in reach, snatching at it, but he's already thrown it back to his other hand.

"You wasted time accessing your gift." Jackson tucks the knife away in his hoodie. He stalks slowly around me. "And moving it."

"It was seconds—"

"—seconds too long." He's at my back now, his heated breath fanning over my neck.

"Jack," I whisper, a flush creeping along my skin at his proximity. "There's a room full of people."

He chuckles, his nose brushing the back of my ear. Goosebumps cascade down my neck, a shiver of pleasure rippling through me.

"You think I care about them, little one?" he murmurs huskily, thankfully quiet enough to keep it between us. "This lesson is all for you. They're only here to witness it."

His lips are twisted to a smirk when he moves back into my view. "Activate your gift," he instructs, his voice carried once again through the room. "Your whole body this time." He snags another knife from the desk while I do what he says, drawing my gift through every limb, every inch of me. Jackson lifts the knife between us in an unspoken command.

I reach for it. He moves it again, as expected, but my other hand is out and swiping it, turning it to dust the second I connect with it.

Jackson smiles. "When you're in a fight, your gift should already be active. If you have to stop and think about your gift"—he snaps his fingers— "dead. Practice with your gift constantly until it's second nature to use it, even when not in a fight. And then, when you know exactly what your gift can do, attacks will come naturally and on instinct—not planning."

His words hit me as I remember all the times I've seen Jackson using his gift. It's constant. Even when he's relaxing, he's using it to float paper creatures. To jump somewhere high. To listen to something far away. And it'll be more than one thing at a time.

"You make it sound so easy," a voice complains, and Jack shrugs.

"It is. With practice. Stamina first." He flips a finger up to start a count. "Gift active at all times, second." Another finger. "Test your limits. Know what it can do and how until it's second nature." One more finger. "Pass those limits." His fourth finger raises.

He turns back to me. "Last lesson." Jack holds up his hand.

"Touch me." I start reeling my gift in from one hand, and he shakes his head. "With your gift."

Fear grips my chest. "What? No. Jack—"

Even Aiden steps forward, ready to jump in, but Jackson cuts him a look over his shoulder to stop him, then brings his gaze back to me. His eyes are locked on mine, a small, relaxed smile perched on his lips as he keeps his hand raised and waiting for mine.

"You won't hurt me."

I want to believe him. I do believe in him. But the risk...I can't lose him if he's wrong.

I hold my hand to my chest, shaking my head slowly. "...don't ask me to do that, Jack," I whisper. "If I fuck this up..."

Jackson doesn't move. His gaze is so intense, so confident that I'll do what he asked.

Fuck.

I stare at his hand.

At him.

I don't know if I can bring myself to do it.

"You're the master of your gift, little one. It's yours. Not the other way around. Don't treat it as separate from yourself."

Isn't it? Doesn't it do what it wants sometimes? Spreading too far. Killing people when I didn't mean to...

He cocks his head the slightest amount. "Are you naked right now?"

The strangeness of the question startles me out of my thoughts. I blink at him, confused. "No..." I reply slowly with the obvious answer.

"Is the floor crumbling to pieces beneath your feet?"

I look down, trying to figure out where he's going with this, and see the reddish glow on my pants. On my boots.

My clothes. Shoes. The floor that I'm standing on. All of it is connected to my gift right now.

His smile is still there when I look back to him with that realization.

"Sometimes, the difference is simply intent. *Your* will, whether you're aware of it or not." Jackson turns his palm up, reminding me of my original instruction.

I look at my hand, at the reddish glow from my gift like a light beneath my skin spread to my fingertips.

I take a deep breath, though it does little to settle the fine tremble that's taken over me.

And I place my hand on his.

The room is silent around us. No one breathes the moment we touch.

Jackson's fingers wrap around the back of my hand, and he tugs me forward. His mouth crashes into mine, his other hand gripping the back of my head as panic *screams* through me, and I rush to gather and shove my gift away. His hand may be okay, but I am *not* ready to jump headfirst into testing everything at once.

His tongue pierces past my lips and buries deep as his other hand finds the small of my back and pulls me in tight. I sink into the kiss. Into him. My body buzzes with adrenaline, tingling and hot. Desire mixes with it in a fiery combination, pooling between my thighs as I press myself into Jackson as much as I can, my hands clawing at the back of his hoodie when it isn't enough.

Hands tug me back at the same time as Jackson's pulled away. I gasp at the loss, almost reaching for him when oxygen floods back into my lungs, and I remember where we are. Jack licks his lips; his blue eyes still pinned on me even though Dane and Aiden have grasped each of his arms. Kellan's at my back, his body blocking mine from the rest of the room.

I stay there for a moment to catch my breath, panting like I'd forgotten to breathe in that kiss; it was so intense.

I touched him with my gift. And I didn't kill him. My gaze drops to his hand. I didn't hurt him. There's nothing there.

Relief swells in my chest like a balloon...until it hits me.

If it acts on my innermost wishes...

If it doesn't hurt what I don't want it to...

Pain implodes in my chest, then squeezes my lungs in a chokehold.

Then I really did kill Vera.

Her death wasn't an accident.

My knees give out.

"Woah!" Kellan catches me before I hit the floor, instantly looping an arm beneath my legs to carry me. "You alright, beautiful? Was it the training? I'll be damned if you tell me his kiss made you weak in the knees."

"I'm alright," I gasp, even though it feels like I've lost all my strength at once. "I just need a minute." My eyes instinctually seek out Aiden, who nods.

"Take her to the snack bar," he tells Kellan, then moves around us to address the room.

I don't hear anything he's saying as Kell brings me to the other side of the massive room, putting plenty of distance between me and the others. We walk through the door to the smaller room. The outer wall is lined with windows in a curve that exposes the sidewalk just outside. There are small square tables and chairs in the middle of the room and then a bar with stools on the interior wall. It feels like an old diner that sells ice cream shakes.

Someone walks by the window, and I freeze in Kellan's arms. "Can they see us?"

He sets me down in a chair. "No. It's tinted glass. We can see out, but no one can see in."

One of the other chairs squeals as it's pulled back across from me. Dane plops into it, then leans his forearms halfway across the table. "Are you okay?" He reaches for my hand.

I hesitate, and his expression falls.

Drawing a slow breath, I take his hand. I notice Jackson sitting up on the bar, one foot up on it, as he leans into his knee and watches us. Watches me. Kellan's sitting on the next table over, arms crossed.

I try to block them out and focus on Dane. "Sorry. It's just..." His amber eyes are so open, so *warm* while they look at me. My heart aches, and I pull my gaze from his. Maybe that makes me a coward, but I don't think I'll be able to say it while looking him in the eye. "If what Jack said is true about my gift, then...when I...*killed* Vera..."

Dane squeezes my hand. "Stop."

He stands and shifts next to me, his hand never letting go of mine. Dane kneels and cups my face with his other hand, drawing me to look at him. "I'm done wallowing in the past. You keep saving my life over and over again. You owe me *nothing*. You got that?" He waits for my small nod before he continues, "It doesn't matter. None of that matters anymore. I'm not thinking about it, and you shouldn't either. We're focusing on the future now."

I breathe in shakily, and when I release it, it's like a weight falls from my chest, expelling with the used air.

If he's moving forward, then so am I.

Dane smiles, rising and pulling me up with him in his arms. I breathe in his warm, citrusy scent, soaking him in as my heart calms to its normal pace.

Once I know I'm okay, I pull back and find Aiden has joined us in the room. "The others?" I ask him.

"A group started in the weight room. Cibrina took another group, and Evie and Silas are working with the last group for now," he replies smoothly, with no sense of urgency or rush to get us back out there.

"Should we—" Movement through the windows catches in my periphery, and I turn toward it. A dark shape drops on the concrete. I run to the window, then gasp when I recognize who it is.

Chapter Eighteen

RAEGAN

"It's Reid!" I shout over my shoulder, and the others are around me in an instant.

"I'll grab Cassandra," Aiden says first, then leaves the room. Thankfully, she's only in the next room over, so the rest of us meet them outside over Reid's body.

A trail of dark red blood spreads over the concrete from underneath him, his body still and quiet.

"Reid!" I yell, hoping for a reaction and getting none.

Cassandra kneels awkwardly with one arm still in a sling, then places her free hand on the side of his face and closes her eyes. Her brows pinch, lips pressed together. "He's alive. Barely. I'll do as much as I can to get him stable."

"I'll bring him to the infirmary when you're done." Aiden's gaze circles to everyone else. "The rest of you, get back to training. It'll be at least a day before he recovers enough to give us some answers."

"Are we sure he shouldn't be locked up next to Harvey?" Dane questions, his expression serious. "This guy lied to us from the beginning. He said that he and Tinsley joined GE a while back. And he had no information to give us about locations because he'd been portaled everywhere." He jabs a finger at Reid. "*He* is the closest connection we have with the CEO of Gifted Enterprise."

"He's the reason we're here right now," I remind him. "If not for his gift, Charles would have killed me and locked you away in a lab where no one could find you."

Dane releases a frustrated sigh and runs a hand through his hair. "I get that, but what if he disappears on us again? What if he gets healed like he wants, and then teleports away without another word?"

"You volunteering to hold his hand until we can talk to him?" Kellan drawls, a grin stretching his lips.

"He's not going anywhere," Aiden smoothly counters. "He tried on his own, and this is where it got him. Back to us. We'll let him recover first and then we'll get answers. For now, all you need to worry about is training."

Cassandra withdraws her hand, the glow fading from her eyes as she peers up to Aiden and nods.

I exchange a look with Dane, who still looks nervous that Reid will run the second he has a chance to. I hope Aiden's right, and he'll stay. He's been the reason the guys have been able to save me as many times as they did. I owe him for that.

Two days pass before Aiden calls us to the Guild infirmary to talk to

Reid. He's sitting up in the twin bed at the far end of the room right next to the window. He's wearing a plain navy shirt, his legs hidden beneath the white sheet and blanket, as he stares out the window. Aiden sits in a folding chair on one side, his suit jacket off on the bed behind him and his tie hanging loose.

Reid's head spins toward us at the sound of our footsteps. His blue gaze stops on me, and the small crease in his forehead clears.

Aiden unfolds another chair next to his and looks at me, silently but clearly indicating I should sit in it. Once I do, Jackson perches on the bed behind us, lying on his side with his head resting in his hand. Dane leans against the footboard of the bed across from Reid while Kellan takes up a spot in front of the window.

Aiden stashes his phone away in his pocket and laces his fingers together. "We're all here now, so you can begin."

Reid pulls his stare from me to Aiden. "What do you want to know?"

"Everything," Dane replies.

Aiden doesn't look away from Reid. "The truth."

The teleporter nods solemnly. His eyes return to me. "I'm assuming they told you already that I'm your half-brother." I give him a small nod. "My mother died in childbirth, so I was raised by a nanny and Charles. He had me go with him nearly everywhere since I was five years old so I could learn the business."

"You daddy's heir, then?" Kellan asks.

Reid blinks, glancing his way to answer. "If his first plans failed, then that was probably his last resort."

"What do you mean?" I speak up, confused.

"If things go his way, and they usually do, he'll find a way to become immortal. To never die. There would be no need for an heir, then. Just a right-hand man to carry out the work he gets tired of."

Dane rolls his eyes and scoffs. I agree. What big bad doesn't go seeking immortality to keep everything they've spent a lifetime to build? I haven't heard of a gifted person with that ability yet, but it's a big world. And Charles's annoying ability to steal gifts makes something like that even more possible.

"We should find anyone with a gift like that and keep them hidden before he finds them," Dane remarks.

"No," Jackson immediately responds, and Dane frowns at him, but it's Aiden who elaborates.

"We could lead Charles right to them if we go looking too. It's better to take him out as quickly as possible before that person is found."

"Hopefully there's not more than one of them out there," Kell says.

"Hopefully there's *no one* out there with that gift right now," I add.

"What else can you tell us about him? About Gifted Enterprise?" Aiden steers the questions back to Reid.

"He's ruthless. And calculating. He's always one step ahead of you, no matter what you try. He maps out every possible scenario and comes up with plans for each of them. When one plan doesn't work out, he moves to the next one. And so on. His contingency plans have contingency plans. Even if his plan doesn't take the original direct route to get there, he'll still have enough backups in place to get him to his end goal regardless."

Well, fuck.

Superpowered *and* smart.

"What else?" Aiden presses on as if that last piece of information wasn't already terrible news for us.

"He's charming. He can win people over with a single conversation. It's how so many in the government are in his pocket. How all those children can disappear without a paper trail, or murders become accidents or tragedies instead." Reid rubs the back of his neck. "Not to mention, he's a master manipulator with control over his emotions. You won't be able to get him by making him angry to trip him up. The guy's only modes are relaxed and smiling or disappointed and straight-faced. He'll kill you without hesitation in either."

"You sound afraid of him," Jackson muses.

Reid's jaw tightens. "Of course, I am. You'd be a fool not to be."

Jack smiles chillingly. "I can acknowledge his strengths without being afraid of them. Everyone still has a weakness."

"He doesn't. There's no one he cares about other than himself. He's not impulsive or emotional. And he has six gifts at his disposal, which he masters as quickly as if he'd been born with them. He's a goddamn prodigy."

"He wants Dane," Jackson throws out, and Dane glares at him.

"Thanks," he snarks.

Jack shrugs.

"To a point," Reid answers. "He'd never risk himself or GE over anyone. If he feels cornered when it comes to Dane, he'd rather kill him for the emotional blow it will have on Raegan than allow someone to threaten him."

"He sounds like a real peach," I grumble.

Dane's frowning hard at his palm as if he can see and mentally curse his own gift. I can see the anger and frustration in him building through his tensed arms, tight jaw, and the look in his eyes. They're like windows straight to his heart, overflowing with emotion that's impossible to contain.

I get up and take the hand he's glaring at, holding it in mine. He smiles tightly, trying to pretend he's fine but failing miserably. "It's alright," I murmur just for him. "He's never getting close enough to reach you again," I promise. "I'll break the world to pieces if he tries."

A genuine smirk tugs at the corner of his lips. "You're such a badass. I fucking love you." He kisses my cheek, but my heart's too occupied skipping and then performing somersaults in my chest for me to react.

Did he just—

"I'm confused," Reid says, bringing me back to the infirmary. "I thought you were dating Aiden."

Kellan chuckles and opens his big mouth. I rush to cut in first before he says something mortifying. "I am. I'm with all of them."

Reid's expression hardens. "What?" He looks at each of the guys, his face darkening as that information sinks in. "No." He throws the blanket and sheet off him like he's preparing to grab me and leave.

Aiden stands to block him. Dane squeezes my hand, and Jackson sits up, a knife flipping between the fingers of one hand. Kell's grin sharpens to bared teeth, his eyes locked on Reid.

"Excuse me? What do you mean, no?" I demand sharply.

"I mean, no. I'm not letting these guys—"

"Don't finish that sentence," I interrupt, stepping forward and sticking a finger at him. "I *just* found out you're my half-brother last week. You have no say in anything in my life. This is *my* choice. You don't even know me."

"I did once. I was around when you were born. I played with you when you were little before your mother took you and ran. You're my baby sister I looked after for four years."

I don't remember any of that.

But I don't remember anything before my time with Grams, so I'm not surprised.

"That doesn't change anything. Look. I'm happy you think of me as a sister. I think I might like to have a brother. *If* you aren't a pain in the ass about it. So, are we going to have a problem, or can you respect my decision as a grown-ass adult?"

Reid's hands fist, his jaw working as he stares at the group of us with a new understanding.

I silently will him to let this go. I'm shocked he'd been upset about it at all, considering I didn't think I meant much to him. Harvey had said that he knew about me, but we'd never met. Knowing that Reid had been around me as a toddler, I guess, makes some things different. For him, at least, since I remember nothing of him. I feel a little bit guilty that I don't, considering his concern for me. If he'd played with me and looked out for me, I should have some memory of him buried somewhere.

Finally, he sits, and the room relaxes. "Alright."

"Glad we have your blessing, big brother," Kellan chortles, and I chuck a pillow at him.

"We got off track," Aiden says while returning to his seat. "Can you help us with GE locations? Maybe the homes or offices of the GE Board members?"

Reid shakes his head. "I went to the few recent ones I knew of to find Tins. They'll be shut down by now. GE rents spaces for a month at a time, then picks up and moves somewhere else if they feel their location has been compromised or if it's been ninety days. The islands are the only constant, but there are so many of them, and I don't know which ones GE owns or uses."

"What about Charles's office, where he brought Dane and me?"

"Already gone. I'd tried there first. As soon as we rescued you, I'm sure he had his things moved by the end of the day."

Aiden rubs his hand over the five o'clock shadow on his jaw and sighs. "Any other offices of his that you know of?"

"Aside from the ones I'd just tried, I haven't been around him in months. I have no idea where the others are. They could be anywhere in the country. He just teleports to the next one. As for the Board, they always come to him, not the other way around. So, I don't know that, either. I'm sorry, but when I told you before I don't really have any locations to give you, I was telling the truth."

"I'll have you mark all the previously known offices of his or GE, then, and see what we can get from that. Maybe we'll find a trend in the building or location that can lead us to potential sites," Aiden says, leaning into the small backrest of the folding chair. "Is he the one who injured you like that?"

Reid's lips tighten. "No. I never found him or Tinsley."

"Then who?"

"Royce and his puppets."

The memory of what it felt like to be under his control sends a cold shiver through me.

Aiden tugs his jacket free from under Jack and wraps it around my shoulders. "Here."

"I'm not actually cold," I murmur, even though my hands grasp the lapels and pull it tighter. His cinnamon body wash surrounds me, cocooning me in that safety like an invisible ward.

"I know," he practically purrs under his breath before he slowly withdraws to his seat.

A light burn creeps up my neck, and I bite my inner cheek to force myself under control.

"What can you tell us about Royce? He seems like a big player we'll need to address before Charles," Aiden continues the conversation as if there'd been no interruption.

Reid's gaze jumps between us before finally sticking to Aiden when he answers. "He's loyal to Charles. Would do anything he asked of him, just for a word of praise. And, unfortunately, GE has amassed a stockpile of dead people for him to...play with."

Kellan straightens. "So, wait. When I joked about a zombie army before..."

"He has one."

Aiden leans over his thighs, his dark brown eyes focused intently on Reid. "How does his gift work? What are his limits?"

"No one talked about it in detail, so take anything I say with a grain of salt. It's just based on what I've seen first-hand or overheard." He waits for Aiden's nod of understanding before he continues, "He can control souls to varying degrees based on whether they've been detached from their body at some point. For anyone alive, he can only manipulate a couple at a time, and he can't do it remotely. He has to be nearby. For anyone who's died, he can summon their soul back to their body, and then he has full control over them."

"By full control, do you mean their mind too? What they say?" Dane asks slowly, his fidgeting hands in his hoodie pocket giving away his uneasiness.

Reid frowns, considering. "I don't think he can make them say anything. Mostly, he keeps their mouths closed and manipulates their bodies. Especially the older souls, who've either lost their minds or gifts already."

"And the newer ones?" Aiden questions.

"If he gets the soul within twenty-four to forty-eight hours of leaving the body, then they'll be almost like new. They'll maintain their gift and their minds."

"Thorne died a few times. He looked like shit each time he came back," I comment, my nose scrunching in disgust at how he'd looked when Gordon had me. "It was why he wanted a new body. But Royce said something about using other souls to...freshen him up."

Reid nods. "The body can only be healed so many times after death. And the soul can't keep being stuffed into bodies before it also degrades. Usually, the mind goes first, followed by the gift. But he can do something with combining souls that reverses some of that, though it can mess with the original soul's mind and gift."

"I thought you didn't know much about it," Kellan drawls. "Sounds like you know a hell of a lot."

My half-brother's gaze cuts to him. "I'm observant. And he hangs around Charles pretty often."

"Why?" Aiden asks. "Who is Royce? How and why is he so close to Charles?"

Reid grimaces. "He's no one. Supposedly after his wife died, he learned about his gift but fucked up bringing her back. Then he went nuts testing his gift on entire graveyards of people to get it right, and he's been obsessed playing with his puppets ever since. Of course, he was arrested for grave robbing with some wild reports no one believed. Someone with connections to GE and involved in his case reached out to Charles about it. They faked his death, and now Charles helps supply and cover up bodies for Royce to play with. So long as Royce does as Charles says, he'll get to do what he loves without anyone trying to stop him."

"Creep," Dane mutters.

"There are a couple rumors I overheard about him, but I don't know if any are true. One is that he sleeps next to his dead wife and plans to figure out a way to find and bring her soul back. He's also been alive for over a hundred years and survives by eating souls."

I tighten Aiden's jacket around me to stave off another chill.

"Anything else?" Aiden prompts, and I chime in with a question of my own.

"Is there a way to break out of his control once he has you?"

Reid shakes his head, his face solemn. "Once he's got you, that's it. Unless someone picks you up and takes you far enough away from him, and he doesn't follow. And before he has you kill that person."

Swallowing that uncomfortable imagery, I nod.

"I think that's plenty for now." Aiden stands, and the rest of us shift to do the same. "You still need to rest. When Cassandra's given the green light, we'll take you to meet another half-sibling and see if there's anything more between the two of you we can use to help us win against GE."

Reid's brows knit in confusion. "Another half-sibling?"

"Harvey. He was spying on the Guild and sending information to Charles," Aiden replies, but there's no moment of recognition of his name. "The one who came on missions and could become invisible. He and fourteen other invisible siblings spied on Charles's Board members and electees, ten of whom we now need to rescue."

His gaze swings to mine. "Does he know about you?"

"Yeah. Apparently, he knew who I was the moment we met."

Reid's face tightens further. "Where is he?"

Aiden fixes his tie. "He's somewhere safe, for now, and he's not going anywhere. He's planning on helping us."

"If he was a spy for Charles, you can't trust anything he says," Reid argues, his eyes still on me.

"Well, you can hear him out yourself in a day or so. That is, if you're intending to stick around this time," Aiden adds.

Reid turns to Aiden. "I have to get Tinsley back. I can't wait for your big fight. She won't last there long on her own."

"You dropped everything to help us get Raegan back on multiple occasions," Aiden says, then tilts his head forward in affirmation. "Helping get Tinsley back is the least we can do."

Relief eases the tension in Reid's face as he blows out a breath. "I can—"

The lights cut out, and all the machines in the infirmary suddenly become still and quiet.

Jackson is the one to say what we're all thinking.

"They're here."

Chapter Nineteen

DANE

It takes a minute for my eyes to adjust, the city lights through the floor-to-ceiling windows offering a dim, but manageable glow for us to see by. The power outage is the signal given by my virus that Vera tried to touch something in the network, causing everything to reboot and power to turn off until it's back online. My heart thunders in my chest, racing at the knowledge that Vera is here.

It doesn't matter, I remind myself firmly. I'm not trying to win her over or keep her here this time. And after we take care of Royce, she might...

"Everyone to their positions, like we discussed," Aiden orders, fixing his jacket back on.

I scrub my face to get my head together. I can't get distracted.

"Where do you want me?" Reid questions, standing to join us.

Aiden tugs the sleeves of his dress shirt beneath his jacket down. "Here. No one should make it here, but if they do, then teleport somewhere else and come back. This shouldn't take long."

We don't have a lot of time before the power returns and systems come back online, so the rest of us are already running from the room and down the hallway to the main hall of the Guild. Jack, Rae, and Kellan split off in another direction, and I snap my teeth together to keep from joining them. This is the plan.

I catch Jackson taking Rae's hand in his and force myself to breathe through my nose. She'll be safe. Even if Charles or Royce do show up, she has Jack and Kellan with her.

Aiden appears next to me before we drop to the first table and flip it on its side for cover. Agents are already loose in the main hall, but the unexpected emptiness has slowed their steps, uneasiness clear in their expressions.

Other Guild members are spread throughout the room, hidden in their designated spots until it's time to use their gifts.

I don't see Vera when I sneak a glance around the table, but I know she's here somewhere. She triggered the virus that shut the Tower down, so by now, she's hacking the system to do what she'd originally planned.

Since I didn't have my laptop nearby when the power went out, I won't be able to complete my part to counter whatever cyberattack she's working on. We're stuck with plan B, which requires me to *stay put* for most of this.

I hate plan B.

"Remember..." Aiden begins, and I pull the gun from the back of my waistband and flick the safety off.

"Yeah, yeah. I'll stick to you like glue." My finger settles on the trigger, rubbing along it with the itching desire to end this all quickly. Patience isn't my strong suit.

Aiden slides his unamused gaze to me, but the first agents are getting close to the perimeter, to us, and he's forced to return his attention to them. "Get ready."

He places his hand on the floor, and I risk another peek at the portal. There are more agents coming through, but enough of them have filled the main open area for Aiden's plan to start. Aiden nods behind us to the bar, where another Guild member is crouched and waiting.

The hardwood floors split and crack in unison in a sound that snaps and echoes through the room. The agents all freeze, looking around to figure out what's happening, but it's already too late.

Metal spikes strike from the narrow openings in the floor, growing to needlepoints as tall as the agents and impaling anyone in their range. They fly up together in an instant until the main area of the hall is a maze of angled metal thorns as thick as a fist and bloody, screaming bodies.

"Fuck, that's brutal," I breathe, watching the metal retreat, sinking to the single thick sheet Aiden had added beneath the floorboards last week. Bodies thud to the floor one after another once the metal is no longer holding them up.

You'd think that would have gotten all of them, but Aiden only had a single area he could use that attack on without risking anyone from the Guild being injured. Some of the agents had already made it outside of the attack zone and are hurrying further away.

More agents rush out of the portal and skirt the center of the room, smartly running around the perimeter of bodies to avoid another attack. Aiden might be able to pick off another couple that stray too close, but he won't be able to use it to catch so many again.

Not that I'm fucking complaining. He took out at least two dozen at once, and the confidence the GE agents had when they first stormed in is gone. Shifting instead to wariness and anger for the ones who see their fellow agents on the ground.

Once the next wave of goons is through, the rest of the members trigger their own traps in their assigned areas of the room. Shouts of surprise and battle break out as everything descends into chaos. Agents are pushed back to the center of the room where there's more space, but Guild members are there as well, which officially ends Aiden's trump card. He grips his whip sword in his hand instead, checking over his shoulder that I haven't moved.

"Still here," I growl, aiming my gun at an agent who dodges another member's attack and lands a couple yards from me. He's down with a single headshot, and then I'm seeking out the next target. I try to find Raegan and the others in the chaos, but there's too much happening at once in a room full of people.

A table the size of a pontoon boat smashes down on a group of agents, flattening them in a single blow.

Vines dangling from the beams across the high ceiling are snatching agents up left and right, swinging and crashing them together or waiting for flying knives to catch them before they're dropped.

It's amazing the difference from a few months ago when we were the ones at a disadvantage against GE. And now?

Aiden's sword extends, the lethal diamonds splitting into a whip that he slashes at the three agents in his reach before his wrist snaps the metal back to him. "Dane."

"What?" I bark when my shot misses.

"Get ready to move."

I look over at him. Leaving this spot isn't part of our plan. He's too terrified of Rae or me being kidnapped again, so he wanted us to stay close to someone just in case. That's more difficult out in the middle of the fighting. I scan the room, searching for what could cause him to abandon his own plan so easily, then pausing when something moves in a blur, knocking Evie off her feet.

Well, fuck.

Tinsley.

"Don't tell me she's already on their side," I mutter irritably. That's going to make rescuing her for Reid twice as hard. I've already failed trying to get my sister back from them. *She'd been with them for most of her life, though. They've only had Tinsley for a couple of weeks.*

It just goes to show how fucking strong Raegan is for holding out against Gordon for as long as she did.

"Now!" Aiden shouts, and I jump to my feet at his command, racing after him.

He throws his arm out, his whip sword lengthening and rounding its sharp edges. Tinsley dives under it mid-run, picking back up on her feet without missing a beat. Aiden tries again, sending a shield of metal at the end of his sword to trap her against the wall. She scurries up the wall, her speed keeping her feet moving until she's standing on top of a beam high over the room.

She plants her hands on her hips and *tsks* at Aiden, her finger clocking back and forth. "Can't catch me!" Tinsley yells at him, her voice taunting and playful at the same time.

"I should get rubber bullets," I grumble while staring up at her. I don't think Aiden has enough metal to reach her up there. Not unless he pulls some from the floor.

Someone grabs my wrist that has the gun. I turn, yanking my hand back on instinct and then freezing when I see Vera there.

"Ver..." I breathe, my chest constricting. It doesn't matter that I've decided to stop chasing after her. Or that I've accepted she's the enemy. One of them.

"We have to go, Dane." She smiles at me. I follow the scar that runs from her eye to her lips, and then her words register.

I twist my wrist to break her hold, jerking myself free. "No."

Her face darkens, and she reaches for me again. "You never listen," Vera snaps.

I dodge her hand with a scowl. "If I go back, I'm dead. Do you get that? Or maybe you don't care. Maybe there's nothing left of my sister, and I'm just talking to a *puppet*."

Where the fuck is Aiden?

Taking a step back to put some distance between us, I look for Aiden and find a blur spinning around him, trapping him in the middle. Fuck. Tinsley was the bait to draw us out.

"Don't *call me that*!"

Sharp pain flares in my arm. "Aargh! What the fuck?!" Vera pulls something away from my arm, and I stare at the bleeding pricks there. "What was that?"

Before she can say anything, knives swerve in her direction, and I react before I realize what I'm doing, tackling her to the ground before they reach her. She yells beneath me, but mine are louder when pain in my side tells me I didn't get us out of the way in time and a knife buries into my side.

"Dane!"

Raegan's voice pierces through the agony. My eyes fly open as she runs toward me, and I throw a hand up, struggling to my knees and off Vera even as the pain in my side sharpens at the movement. "Stay back!" I can't risk Vera hurting her. Whatever she'd jammed into my skin could hurt her. Or she could have another one. I shift myself between them to make sure Vera can't get to her.

"Jack, don't!" she cries, grabbing his arm before he can attack Vera again.

Vera scrambles out from under me, but instead of glaring at Raegan like I'd expected, she's staring wide-eyed at me. "Why?" Her gaze drops to the knife buried in my side, then back to my face. "You picked her. Why would you take a knife for me? I thought...you saw me as your enemy."

I cringe when the movement of *breathing* causes the pain to intensify to white-hot levels, and I huff irritably. "You're still..." Fuuuuuuck, this hurts. "...my sister," I grit through clenched teeth. "Nothing will change that."

Her face draws together in a mix of emotion, like she can't figure out what she's feeling as she watches me in pain on my knees before her. She takes a step back. And another. Vera casts a fearful look at Jackson and Raegan as she backs away. She taps a finger to her ear.

"Enough. Pull back," she says, then touches her back pocket.

Water falls over us in a downpour, saturating the hall in seconds from the sprinklers. The remaining agents make their escape through the portal. I can't help but watch as Vera does the same, her unsure expression branded in my mind even after she's gone.

Chapter Twenty

RAEGAN

"Wait." Dane puts his hand between him and Cassandra before she can touch him. "What's in my arm? She did something." He holds it out to her, and I see two pinpricks of red there. "Is it poison? A tracker?"

Cassandra's face pinches, her eyes squeezed shut in concentration with her hands wrapping his arm.

"You can heal poison, right?" Dane continues.

"Enough, Dane. Let her focus," Aiden chides, his gaze locked on her expression.

I glance at Jackson on my left. "Did you see what she did?"

He shakes his head.

Frowning, I watch Cassandra finish healing Dane before she releases him and opens her eyes. "I don't know what it was. All I can heal are injuries, and aside from the broken skin there, I couldn't find anything else to fix. If it was poison, I can only heal the damage it causes, not remove it."

Dane curses and rubs his arm.

"I highly doubt Vera poisoned you. They still want you alive. And the punctures were too small to insert a tracking device," Aiden reasons.

"Then what the fuck—"

"I'll take you to the infirmary. You can sleep off the healing there while we have monitors on you, just in case."

"Did you get Tinsley?"

I whip my head around to Aiden. "Tinsley was here?"

"Yes. And no, I didn't get her," he replies.

Dane grimaces and stands. "So, she's already one of them?"

Aiden looks toward the hallway that leads to the infirmary and Reid. "No. When she was circling me, she told me she was putting on an act for the other agents. I tried to get her to stay for Reid's sake."

"Why the hell would she willingly go back with them?" Kellan demands.

"She said there was something she needed to do before she could come back. She just wanted me to pass a message on to Reid."

"What's the message?" I ask, and Aiden's gaze finds mine.

"She's safe. And to give her another week before he comes for her."

"That's it?" Dane mutters. "And we're supposed to trust that?"

"I'll let Reid be the judge since he knows her best. As we're going to the infirmary anyway, we'll give him the message and see what he says." Aiden scans the aftermath of the fight, his dark stare landing between Jackson and Kellan behind me. "Recruit any members who are willing to help clean up." He looks expectantly at me.

"I'm staying here to help," I answer his unspoken question. His forehead creases, his lips flattening, but he nods stiffly.

"I'll come back once Dane is situated."

I offer a short nod in return, then watch him, Dane, and Cassandra leave the room.

"You don't have to help, beautiful." Kellan crosses his arms over his chest as we look over the mess from the fight. Dead agents. Blood. Broken tables and benches. Glass. Bits of ripped plant life everywhere. And water covering all of it.

"I'm part of the team, Kell," I reply, suppressing a shiver as the cooler air clings to the water that soaked into my clothes, hair, and skin.

A soft breeze tickles my hair, and I look to Jack. "Don't dry me yet. I'm sure I'll get wet again while cleaning up."

He tilts his head. "Then I'll dry you again."

Smiling, I take his hand in mine. "No one else is getting dried off. I promise I'm fine. Now, how do you clean up so many...bodies?"

Jackson hums softly as if musing over the various options. "Too many to burn without drawing attention. Or to throw in the sea."

Kellan rubs his beard. "It'll be a hell of a hole to dig if we're burying 'em."

"A vat of acid..."

"Or me," I chime in, and they both turn their faces to mine. "Pile them up, and I'll...make them go away. No muss, no fuss."

Both men hold my stare as if waiting for me to crack.

Well, it's not that I *want* to do it. But what other choice do we have for so many? They're already dead and won't feel it, is how I reason with myself. If *this* is the way I can help, then this is what I'll do.

I cross my arms, returning their stares with a firm look of my own.

"You sure you want to do this?" Kellan checks with me anyway.

"Yes. Let's do it." I push my sleeves up past my elbow. "Start making a pile."

Jackson nods once and immediately uses his gift to do what I said. Kellan takes another second to watch me before he turns to do it. He stops to direct any Guild members standing around to either help him or work on the rest of the room.

Evie's pushing an oversized mop around one side of the room to soak up the water while a few others are mopping between tables or wiping them down. Fabian's abnormally long tongue zips out to snag some leaves, then whips it back. He swallows it. The next time, his tongue sticks to shards of glass, and then it disappears into his mouth again.

I cringe at the thought of eating glass, touching my hand to my throat and then looking away.

Kneeling beside the growing pile, I call my gift to my hands, the heat spilling free from my gut and warming my skin. It feels...good. I close my eyes and spread it to the rest of my body, letting its violent heat sizzle and scorch away the cold. I let it fill me up like that sweet burn of alcohol that warms you from the inside out.

I'm supposed to be practicing with my gift turned on like this all the time, but I've still been too worried about repercussions.

I'll start today, I tell myself, letting this moment be the beginning of my personal training.

"Whenever you're ready, beautiful," Kellan says from above.

I sneak a quick look at the pile, measuring the size and distance of it, then shut my eyes again. I don't want to watch it. I'll focus on my gift, on feeling that, instead of what I'm actually doing. It'll be just like the piles of concrete I'd worked tirelessly on. Just...a bit more than that. Using my gift on people has always been a greater drain, so I'm not sure how I'll do with this scale.

"You need to work on your physical stamina."

Right.

I lean forward until my hands land in the pile. I don't focus on the feeling beneath them or try to identify what I'm touching. Once I make contact, I pour my gift out in a steady stream, as I had before so many times. Stretching it out. Feeling the boundary with my gift rather than using my eyes, wrapping it around and over, through and under.

When I think I have it all, I trigger the rest of my gift.

It's not as simple as concrete, which would collapse to dust from a single burst.

This is a slower process. Apparently, bodies take more time and more of my gift to break down completely.

I keep going. On and on and on.

Until my arms shake and my body trembles from the effort.

More.

More.

Sweat clings to my brow and slides down my temple. The heat that had once warmed me is now sweltering. It burns beneath my skin like I'm being boiled from the inside.

I have to breathe through my mouth as the smell becomes unbearable, but even that can only help so much before it coats my throat. My lungs. I choke on it, pushing harder with my gift in a desperate attempt to finish it.

Just...a little...more...

I'm down to the last one before me. I don't let myself breathe until it's done, gritting my teeth and holding my breath until my hands finally meet the floor.

I draw a shuddering breath of air, the pain wracking my body like the world's worst flu. I fall back on my heels and slowly open my eyes.

They're gone. Red fills my vision. I raise my hands and stare at the deepest shade of crimson before a towel is suddenly there, covering my hands and forearms, and blocking them from view.

I lift my face slowly. Every movement right now makes me scream in my head with pain.

Aiden kneels in front of me so I don't have to keep craning my head back. He places a hand over the towel. "There's no need to look at that." His words sound like a distant echo. His dark chocolate gaze searches mine, looking for something. Then, his fingertips barely graze my face before they flinch away. His frown deepens when he studies his hand.

"Is her gift still active?" Kellan inquires from somewhere close, but I'm too tired, too immobilized by the ache and overwhelming heat to seek him out.

"No." Jack. He squats next to Aiden, his hand hovering close to my face without touching it. Cool air brushes along heated skin.

Yes!

Instinct drives me into his hand without thinking, desperate for that coolness to save me from burning alive from the inside.

"Jack!" Aiden looks concerned, though I'm not sure why. Jack's face pinches slightly, but he doesn't move away from me. The coolness keeps flowing, spreading down my neck and arms. I close my eyes and exhale, leaning more heavily into his hand as the rest of my body caves, and I collapse into him.

Kellan curses. "Shit, Jack. Your hand."

My stomach dips as I'm lifted from the ground.

So hot.

The cool breeze rolls down my body in waves. It's wonderful over my exposed skin, but it barely touches the feverish temperature beneath.

"She needs an ice bath," Jackson rumbles against my ear.

Other voices pick up around us, but I can't make them out. I can feel Jack's muscles tense, his hold on me tightening.

"We need to get her out of here," Kellan growls.

"I'll handle it," Aiden says after a pause. "Anyone who has a problem will answer to me or leave the Guild."

"It's not them. It's the fighters from the Pits," Jack murmurs.

"I'll get them to knock that shit off, then."

"Worry about them later. Jack, bring her to my room, and Kell, help me get ice from the kitchen."

We start moving, but all I can focus on is the air he's feeding me and clinging to that feeling like a lifeline. My face and head feel like they're going to implode from the temperature, and I wouldn't be surprised if steam passed through my lips in the short pants I'm managing.

Something cold presses against my backside, bringing me back to semi-consciousness before I'm laid on my back, and the chill of whatever I'm on elicits a pleasurable shiver. The air pets and strokes my skin from head to toe, sweeping over me. It takes the edge off but still doesn't reach the molten levels within.

I reach for it, desperate for relief in my head and face more than anything. My hand closes over something and drags it to my face, gasping when the coolness is concentrated on my temple and cheek. Without me having to do anything, the other side is given the same treatment.

"Take what you need, little one."

I slip in and out of consciousness, unsure if I'm awake or if I've slipped away into a fever dream. The sound of rushing water echoes around me, and then cold water drips over my scorched skin.

A groan slips from my throat, the feeling so good that my back arches, and the water slides down my side like chilled tears. There's a sharp intake of air above me before more water is painted across my skin, followed by a swift breeze. It feels so good. So *fucking* good that I writhe in my desperate hunt for more, my breaths coming in needy pants.

Something wet circles my nipple, winding it to a pert point, and then air chills it in place.

"Aahhnngghh!" I cry, my hips jerking as the next one is drawn into a warm mouth, teased and tugged and shooting a livewire of need to my cunt. My nipple is released and cooled before a tongue drags down my sternum, more water flicking over my flesh. My skin eats it up. Sucks the coolness from the water and air still dancing across my body and lets it sink a little deeper.

The tongue circles my belly button, and then water fills it, leaking down my sides in cold trails.

"More," I beg, though I don't know what exactly I'm asking for. More cold. More pleasure.

Air, like invisible hands, strokes my forehead and face. Tickles down my neck and every curve of my body. Cooling me. Teasing me. It blows at the heat between my thighs, offering me minor relief in more ways than one.

Slick fingers glide up my center, so wet and slippery that my body jerks when they touch my clit. I gasp and moan at once. Everything feels so good, happening all at once, that I don't know what's better.

I just don't want it to stop.

The smooth pressure around and over my clit builds, circling faster and harder with every lap. My body feels like it'll combust as the pleasure intensifies, gripping my muscles and straining for that release that's getting so close. I angle my hips deeper into it, frantically riding his hand rubbing me into a frenzy.

I claw around me and find only smooth tile. Nothing to ground me, to hold me here as I chase ecstasy.

Then, fingers breach my entrance, sinking inside and caressing my inner wall.

Oh, fuck! Yes! Yes!

"Jackkkk..." I moan, my voice thick and heavy with desire.

I'm right there, oxygen suspended in my lungs for the last few thrusts.

And then I erupt, pleasure and heat cascading through my limbs and core in a flood that overwhelms my senses. My screams echo around me in stereo, drowning out anything else until I collapse back to the floor.

"What happened?" a dangerous croon fills the room while I fight to catch my breath.

Another voice follows the first. "Goddammit, Jack. Look at you."

The sound of something being dumped into water blocks whatever's said next until the first voice is speaking again. "Go to the infirmary and have Cassandra heal you. But wash the blood off before anyone sees you," Aiden snaps.

I'm moving suddenly, held against something warm.

"She's still hot as hell," Kellan says.

Something touches my forehead for only a second, and then it's gone. "She's a little better than before, but not by much. Get her in the water."

The moment the freezing water touches my skin, I release a sigh of relief. It seeps into my skin, down to my bones and muscle, and quenches the fire that had been raging inside.

The warm body is still wrapped around me in the water, keeping me still as we lie and rest in the cold, and exhaustion settles over me. My arm is lifted from the water, and a washcloth runs over it even though I can feel two hands around my waist. Aiden. I should stay awake. Thank him and Kellan, but I can't find the strength to open my eyes or move.

Later...I'll thank them later...

Voices pierce through the fog of sleep, dragging me from what felt like a deep slumber. I feel heavy and tired as if I'd run my body into the ground. The memory of the attack on the Tower and then the clean-up returns to me, and I realize that maybe I had.

"—back in a few hours."

"You know she'd want to be there."

"She needs more rest. Jack told me what happened, and it's going to take her more than a single night to recover."

"How's Dane?"

"Fine, as far as we can tell. Whatever she stuck him with, it hasn't done anything. And there was nothing we could find on an X-ray or ultrasound. He and Reid are both in the infirmary."

"...go," I mumble, my voice scratchy and throat parched.

Footsteps. Then a large hand encompasses one side of my face. "Morning, beautiful. How do you feel?" His hand shifts to my forehead. "Can you open your eyes?"

That seems like an odd concern at first until I struggle to lift heavy eyelids. It's a fight to get them open, even after several blinks to convince them to stay that way. Kellan's face is close to mine, concern etched in his brow and pinching his dark eyebrows together.

"Help her sit up," Aiden directs, returning to the bedside with a full cup of water.

Kellan gets me upright, settling my back to his chest with his arms resting on either side of me so I'm supported on three sides. Aiden holds the cup out for me. I reach to take it, but he holds it in his grip.

"I'll do it. Just open your mouth for me like a good girl, and I'll give you what you need," he purrs, and I involuntarily clench my thighs.

The combination of praise and command freezes me in place, locking my muscles with indecision.

Aiden's thumb swipes my lips, then drags the lower one down. I slowly open for him, too tired for information processing in my head yet to do anything else. He perches the edge of the cup on my lower lip and angles it up. Water fills my mouth, and I greedily gulp it, feeling like I'd been lost in a desert for days with how dry everything feels. He tilts the cup the perfect amount, giving me the seconds I need to breathe before I take more and more until I've drained it all.

He pulls the cup away and then puts a hand to my forehead as Kellan had.

"What's going on?"

Aiden retracts his hand, then studies me. "How much do you remember from yesterday?"

I sink heavily against Kellan behind me unintentionally, the comfort of his body wrapped around mine something that calls to me. It feels nice being able to relax into him instead of trying to hold myself upright. Everything right now feels like a lot of work, even something as small as that.

"I remember the attack on the Tower. Tinsley. Vera and Dane. And then...cleaning up."

"And after that?"

I try to recall finishing the pile. Or anything that happened after. Had Kellan wished me a good morning? As if it's the next day already? I drop my head into my hand, trying to remember something.

"It's okay if you don't. Jack can explain it better, but the simplest way to put it is that you overdid it with your gift," Aiden says, his velvety voice something I could easily fall back asleep to.

I force my eyes open before I do exactly that. "Did I hurt anyone?" Kellan's arms tense, and I can feel his head shift up to look at Aiden behind me. My heart sinks like weights in my chest to the pit of my stomach. "I did?"

"Everyone is fine. I was just heading to the infirmary to meet Dane, Jackson, and Reid before we visit Harvey. Do you feel well enough to come or do you want to rest more?"

"Why is Jackson there?"

"He's just meeting us there."

I breathe a sigh of relief. "I want to go."

He nods, looking to Kellan over my head before holding a hand out for me. I'm still feeling pretty weak, so I take it without a word while Kellan keeps supporting me from behind until I'm standing on two feet. My legs quiver.

"Hold on to me, beautiful. I won't let you fall."

I shift my feet until the tremble begins to subside. "I've got it." I release his arm and Aiden's hand to test that claim. Even though exhaustion still weighs me down, I can stand. I can move.

There'll be time to sleep more later.

Aiden and Kellan keep close to me the entire elevator ride and walk to the infirmary, but I'm proud to say I make it walking on my own. Once we're in the infirmary, where the three we're meeting with are each sitting on top of beds due to lack of chairs, I pick a bed for myself to sit on and catch my breath.

Jackson moves next to me anyway, pushing my hair out of the way and touching his forehead to mine.

"What is everyone's fascination with my forehead this morning?" I mumble under my breath, and Jackson smirks.

"She's still a bit warm," Aiden comments from where he stands at the foot of the bed.

Jackson hums in what sounds like agreement.

"Mind filling me in on the details?" I ask him, still confused as fuck about what they're so concerned over. I've used my gift a lot before and drained myself to the point of passing out. Gordon pushed me to that point on several occasions. Maybe because this is the first time they're witnessing it, they're making it to be a bigger deal? Or am I missing something?

Jack nods, sliding his hand over mine and splitting my fingers with his. "Remember what I said about breaking past limits?"

I remember him mentioning it, so I nod.

"You did that beyond what your body could handle. You didn't build up the stamina first, and when your body tried to shut down your gift to protect itself, you overrode that instinct and pushed through it."

Oh.

"You sound like you're familiar with it," I murmur.

"I am." He's smiling at me when I turn to look at him. "I've done it a couple of times. It's a fast way to strengthen your gift, but it comes at a high cost. Thorne told me he'd seen a few gifted people kill themselves when pushing themselves too hard like that."

Dane curses from the bed across from us, his eyes wide and fearful when they look me over. "You mean she could have died?"

"Mm," Jack confirms, lifting my hand in his to press his lips to it. "You need to learn where your limit is, little one. Know when you need to pull back."

I frown at him. "But you just said you've done it. Twice."

"I wouldn't do it again or recommend it to anyone. It's not worth the risk. Since you did break your limit, I'm sure your gift has grown. But your body isn't ready for it. You'll need to focus in the weight room for some time before you try testing its full strength."

"Okay," I reply, trusting him implicitly. "I'll start today—"

"In two days," Aiden cuts in. "You still need to recover. Think of this as your one break from the Loft."

"Am I the only one confused about how hot she was?" Kellan asks the room. "I mean, I know we're all superpowered, but you caused second-degree burns, beautiful. And last I checked, that wasn't your gift."

I'm sorry, I did what?

"Because of her mom," Reid suddenly pipes in from a few beds away. I'd forgotten he was in here. "She could cause explosions from her body, which would then heat to extremely high temperatures. Anything that touched her would melt instantly."

That's right. She could walk out of an exploded and destroyed building without a scratch.

He leans his head against his fist, his tone almost bored. "Gifts typically follow the maternal genes, so it makes sense if Raegan has a higher resistance to heat. And the ability to produce it, too." His blue eyes slide to mine. "I'd bet it's a part of your gift you just didn't realize you had."

Frowning, I look at my available hand. Has there been a time when I could have noticed being resistant to heat? Nothing comes to mind except...the heat that always came with my gift. It had always burned me on the inside. I thought it was just the way my gift felt, but was there more to it? Would someone feel the heat when I touched them with it?

Then those times on the island with Gordon when I'd felt like lava flowed in my veins...I thought it was a combination of my gift and Holt's lightning. The water pod had always been there after rigorous training for his mind control, but had Gordon known I'd passed my limit and needed to cool down, too? It *had* felt much cooler on some days. How many times had I exceeded my limit in those two months with him without realizing it?

"How do you know all of that?" Aiden directs to Reid, who looks back at him.

"You think my dad doesn't have the smartest scientists researching gifts? That was why he would pick certain women to create his offspring. Manufactured gifts based on their mothers. And if they happened to be born with his blood type, even better."

"What would that matter?" Aiden follows up with another question while I'm still stuck on the new piece of information that he *manufactured gifts* by breeding women.

Can this guy get any worse?

Reid answers Aiden matter-of-factly, "Because he can only steal gifts from others who share his same blood type."

The room falls silent.

So...he used Harvey's mom to create a bunch of invisible spies.

He used Reid's mom and was able to copy Reid's gift because of his blood type? And Kellan's?

As for me...does this mean I lucked out on both accounts?

Dane, as expected, blows up at Reid first, jumping to his feet with a shaking fist. "Why are we just finding out about that now?! That's important fucking information! What else are you keeping from us?"

Reid's stoic expression doesn't falter. He just watches Dane and answers without missing a beat. "I've lived with the guy for my entire life. If you think I can tell you every detail of what I know about him in an hour, then you're the crazy one."

Aiden has his phone to his ear; his back slightly turned away from the two still talking. "Yes. A record of every member's blood type. And the Pits fighters, too." He glances to Reid. "What is Charles's blood type?"

"B."

Back to the phone, and most likely Cibrina, he adds, "Send me a list of everyone with the B blood type and their gift. As soon as possible. Thank you." He looks at the rest of us. "Aside from Reid and Kellan, does anyone else have the B blood type? Does positive or negative matter?"

"No."

"I have A," I answer, remembering that from my time on the island.

"A," Jackson says.

"O." Dane frowns. "This isn't like donating blood where O can be used for other types, is it?"

Kellan snorts. "If he could have, he would already have your gift. He had plenty of opportunities to get your blood when you'd been fighting him."

Jackson shrugs. "He might not want to be the lab rat."

We all look to Reid, who also shrugs. "It could be a few things. What Jackson said because he would always choose to have someone else suffer or the fact that his body can only handle five to seven gifts at a time depending on their strength. I doubt he wants to purge one of his current gifts for it. Or he may not trust his blood with the other gifts in there to work right." He pauses, pondering. "His copies are also mere imitations of the original gift. They aren't as strong as the original and have their own flaws. There'd be a high risk his gift might not be compatible or work right when synthesized. He would want the original."

"What happens if he gets the wrong blood type?" I wonder aloud.

"It makes him sick," Reid supplies. "I saw it once. The scientist got the paperwork mixed up, and when he tried the blood, he immediately retched it back up."

"That's a weakness," Jackson points out, but Reid is unconvinced.

"I'd hardly call a minute or two of him getting sick a weakness. You won't kill him in that time. Not with *his* gift," he points to Kell.

Jack shrugs. "It's something."

"I agree," Aiden adds. "You've listed a few limitations to his gift that we'll keep note of in case they can be of any use. If we're ready, let's get to Harvey. There's a text waiting for his response."

RAEGAN

Aiden slides a phone with a text conversation on the screen across the table that's pushed up against the bars. Harvey has a small table and chair on the other side where he sits and leans forward to read it. "What does it mean?" Aiden asks after a minute passes and he says nothing.

I eat another spoonful of the soup Aiden had picked up on our way here from the kitchens, apparently having requested it at some point after I'd woken up. I'm fucking grateful for it. By the time we'd walked to where Harvey's being held, a throbbing headache and body aches hit me all at once as an annoying reminder that I need to get back to bed. I'd shivered one time, and Jackson had stuffed me in his hoodie while Aiden laid his jacket over my lap, tucking me in.

Kellan had insisted on bringing me back to the Loft, but I'd argued I needed to eat my soup anyway.

I have until the bottom of this bowl to listen in before I think he'll drag me away whether I like it or not.

I'm sitting on Aiden's right, while Reid is across from me, glaring hard at the phone. I take another look at it, but it's just a running line of numbers.

Harvey stares at it like it's a death sentence.

"It's my new assignment," he says, fearful. He drops his head into his hands, scrubbing through his blond hair and then dragging them down his face.

"I take it that's a bad thing?" Kell quips while leaning an arm into the bars a couple feet behind Reid.

"That depends," Reid answers instead, his eyes finally rising to watch Harvey. "How many of you are there, again? Did I hear fourteen?"

"Ten left," Harvey replies, still focusing hard on the table.

"And he knows the Guild now knows about you?"

Harvey jerks his head in affirmation.

Reid leans back in his seat, turning his head to Aiden. "There's a small chance it's a new assignment. A bigger chance it's Harvey's grave."

"Can someone explain the numbers first? I feel like we're still twelve steps behind whatever conversation the two of you are having," Dane says.

Reid looks to Harvey, but when he still looks torn between terror and nausea, he answers instead, "It's a code. The first six digits are coordinates. Two more for the month. Two for the day. And four for the time."

"And the last five?" Aiden prompts while eyeing the screen.

This time, Harvey replies, "The last numbers are code for letters, spelling out the name of the assignment. It can be any number of digits, depending on the length of the person's name."

"So, who is it?" Dane asks.

"Royce." Harvey looks to Reid. "I hear you know the old man pretty well. You think it's a trap, too?"

Reid taps his fingers against the table. "Yeah. You've become a liability for him with the Guild. He could easily assign you to someone else but Royce is an odd choice."

Dane frowns. "Because he already trusts him so much?"

"Clearly Charles isn't above spying on anyone, particularly his allies. So, no, it's not because of that. Since Royce's gift is tied to souls, I wonder if that means he can see them," Reid speculates.

Harvey groans, his head knocking against the table between his arms.

"Meaning...he might be able to see Harvey even if he's invisible?" I guess, my headache growing stronger the more I learn about my father.

Reid nods. "It's just a thought, but knowing him, he'll believe you've been compromised and are no longer trustworthy enough to live. If there are still others who can be invisible spies for him, your value alive isn't as strong as it is with your death."

"Cold-hearted bastard," I mutter, having another spoonful but still trying to drag out my meal.

"The coordinates lead to a coffee shop downtown," Aiden tells us after plugging it into his phone.

Reid gives a curt nod. "Where a portal will be waiting to take him anywhere in the world."

"And the date is two weeks from now. 10:30 in the morning,"

Aiden finishes.

"But he's not going, right?" I look up from my soup to Aiden. "If we know it's a trap, then he should just stay here with us."

"What happens if you don't go?" Kellan directs to Harvey, who shifts his head to the side.

"Then he'll *know* I've betrayed him, and he'll hunt me down to kill me himself."

Dane cocks his head. "What's the difference between that and willingly walking into a trap?"

"At least with that, there's a chance he might believe I've stayed loyal to him, and he won't have me killed. A teeny-tiny one." Harvey holds his thumb and forefinger apart the barest amount as if to emphasize how small of a probability that is. He chuckles humorlessly. "So, I can take that chance and probably die by Royce, or I can go on the run until Dad finds and kills me."

The room's quiet.

"Don't all rush to tell me you'll miss me at once," Harvey says mockingly. He lifts his head to lean on his fist, looking at Reid. "I guess we can't all be daddy's favorite now, can we?" He grins at Reid's scowl before his gaze catches on Aiden's unamused frown. "What? Can't a dying man say what's on his mind?"

"You're not dying yet," Aiden chastises him.

Harvey grabs the bars between us and him. "What's the plan, Master? You always have one. I'll do anything, just please. Don't let this be the end for me. I still have to make it up to everyone at the Guild. To my friends."

"I didn't realize you had any friends," Dane mutters, and I shoot him a look.

"Don't be mean, Dane. He thinks he's going to die."

"Thank you, dear sister." Harvey holds his hands together, smiling at me. "I knew you were the best of us."

"Don't talk about her like you know her," Dane snaps.

Aiden sighs, pocketing his phone. "If the dramatics are finished, I'll tell you the plan."

Harvey leans over the table, his pale blue eyes focused solely on Aiden, and he nods eagerly.

"We're going to give Charles a reason to keep you alive and around the Guild. It's the best way for us to still keep an eye on you and avoid either of the death scenarios you mentioned."

"How?"

Jackson hums and then speaks up for the first time since we'd entered the room, immediately picking up on Aiden's plan. "Immortality."

Aiden nods. "You're going to message Charles that you have good intel to share. Ask if he'll be there at your next assignment so you can speak with him about it privately."

Harvey shares a confused look between Aiden and Jack. "And...what is that intel? What immortality?"

"You'll let him know that we're searching for someone with the gift of immortality. That we've found a lead, and you think we're getting close," Aiden explains. "He'll want you to stick around in case we do find that person so he can be the first to know about it."

Dane frowns, crossing his arms defensively. "I thought you said we shouldn't go looking—"

"We won't," Jackson answers instead. "It's a ruse."

"A red herring..." Reid murmurs thoughtfully.

The headache pounds more insistently in my head, beginning to drown out their words. I rest my head on my arm on the table, trying my best to keep following this conversation even as my body aches for sleep.

"You'll need to convince him that your cover is still secure for this to work," Aiden adds.

Harvey's voice is tight. "He saw Kellan confront me. It was pretty obvious I was discovered."

"You were discovered at the scene of the crime, but you could come up with a wild excuse for being at the wrong place at the wrong time," Aiden reasons. "Did you interact with your father in front of Kellan?" A short pause, then, "Did you ever say or do anything in front of Charles while he was here to admit you were with him?"

"No..."

"Good. And how are your acting skills?" Aiden asks. "When you meet with him, you're going to need to act like your life depends on it. Because it will."

That's the last thing I remember before exhaustion wins out, and I fall asleep.

While Dane and Kellan are occupied training Guild members and Aiden's downstairs working in his office, I decide I can't stay in the

Loft another whole day. I can't train yet, but I have enough energy to find Reid and learn more about my half-brother.

Popping my head out of the already-open door to the balcony, I tell Jack, "I'm going to visit Reid in the infirmary."

The words are ripped from my lips as a gust of wind whips around him and throws my hair in every direction. The planters are hovering off to the side while glass panes ripple and hum from the pressure. His dark blue gaze swings to me, and the wind stops abruptly, freeing my hair to fall haphazardly around me. I realize I'm panting as I claw my way free of the tangled hair in my face, the air now feeling fuller than it had a moment ago.

"What was that?" I gasp.

Jackson lowers the planters to where they belong, then closes the distance between us. He smirks at the rat's nest I'm sure my hair is, pinching a small clump sticking out to one side. "My new move."

I knock his hand away and try finger-combing the strands back to normalcy. "What's it do?"

"It gathers surrounding air, strengthens it, then sends it back as sharp cuts."

"How do you make it stronger?"

He cocks his head, his expression turning thoughtful as if trying to think of the right word. "I compress it." When I give him a look of confusion, he smiles and elaborates, "I take in all the air and force it to a thinner shape like blades. It's the same amount of force contained in a more precise attack."

I pause, wondering if I could apply that technique to my gift somehow and what it might do. Jackson gently untangles hair beneath my ear, the coolness of his fingertips and the leather on his fingerless gloves grazing my neck and inducing a heady shiver that breaks my train of thought.

"Reid's not in the infirmary anymore. I'll take you to his new apartment," he murmurs while still focused on his task. He trails his fingers through my hair as if to show it's been fixed, then pinches a section to bring to his lips while his eyes lock on mine.

The air catches in my lungs beneath his intense stare, my heart skipping as it picks up speed. Jack lowers his hand, leaning in, and my mouth parts automatically. His lips curve to a dangerous smirk. He stops a breath before mine and I feel the slow slide of his hand curving around my neck.

"Jack," I pant into his lips, my heart jumping again when they touch for the barest of seconds. I'm not sure if I'm admonishing him for the tease or because I told him I was leaving and he's distracting me.

"Just a taste, little one," he whispers darkly and then presses his mouth to mine, setting my heart on fire.

I throw my arms around his neck, clutching him closer as I kiss him back with everything I have, my body tingling and hot where we touch and aching where we don't. I could lose myself in his kiss, forgetting all our troubles as I give in to his dark demand. I almost do, bathing in his affection and letting it sink beneath my skin, filling me up with warmth.

Until he ends it far too quickly and pulls away, leaving me winded and bereft.

He slips his hand to the small of my back and directs me toward the door, his breath feathering the back of my ear. "I'll devour the rest of you later. Let's go talk to your half-brother."

Fuck.

Why was I in such a rush to leave earlier?

I huff, walking through the apartment to the door and then elevator before muttering under my breath, "Tease."

Jackson steps in after me, his dimple piercing his cheek. "Good things come to those who wait."

I sure fucking hope so.

Jackson halts before one of the many apartment doors on this floor, shifting to the side for me to knock. It's quiet on the other side of the door, no reply to acknowledge my knock or movement that I can hear. Could he be in the Guild Hall?

"He's here," Jack reassures me.

The door finally opens. Reid looks between the two of us, his gaze assessing. "Come in," he offers at last, stepping out of the way for us to enter. We're in a small hallway with two doors before it opens to a kitchenette. There's a small round table for four and a living area across from the kitchen and what looks like a sliding door to a balcony. Reid strides into the kitchen, pulling three glasses down. "I'm assuming you're here to ask me about our past?"

I nod, and he proceeds to fill the glasses with ice and water from the refrigerator, then passes them out. Reid sits in one of the upholstered chairs, setting his glass on the low table at the center of the couches and chairs. "I'll admit...I wasn't sure you'd come. Or care."

Am I overthinking things if I think he sounds a bit like Charles now that I know their relation? He'd been short and direct most times we'd interacted, but when he's been speaking more freely or explaining things...there's that formal tone. How much of how he talks and acts is because of that man?

Does it matter?

Jack and I sit on the couch, and once I've released my drink to the table, I weave my hands together and squeeze. Fuck. Why am I so nervous all of a sudden? My heart's pounding as I look at him, at his familiar blue eyes that regard me with a guarded stare that tell me nothing about what he thinks or feels.

Half-brother.

"Do you remember my mother?"

"I do, though I can't say much about her."

"Why not?"

"I was just a child, and we didn't talk much."

"Oh. Right." I tighten my hands.

A crinkling sound draws my gaze to Jackson, who unwraps a lollipop and sticks it in his mouth. After a firm suck, he pops it out. "How do you know Raegan? How did you meet?" His posture is relaxed and casual, but he eyes Reid with a dark and calculating look.

"It was right around the time when Charles started taking me along with him. I was five, so I didn't understand much of what I saw, but we would visit Merina when Raegan was maybe six or seven months old. He wanted me to play with you so he could talk to her,"

Reid explains to me, his eyes softening. "I didn't really know much about playing, so I tried anything to see what you'd do. What might make you laugh or smile. Merina and Charles were both happy when they saw us, and I was sent back regularly after that.

"I learned how to change your diaper, feed you, do everything you might need so Merina could go back to training. That went on for almost four years before she ran with you." He pauses, hesitating.

"What is it?" I press, now at the edge of the seat cushion as I hang on his every word.

His eyes flick to mine. "It was...hard...for me...when you were gone. I'd still followed Charles and learned his business while I'd been your playmate and babysitter. I attended meetings, negotiations, politics. Even the torture and killings he carried out himself. Or witnessed. We visited labs with dying or restrained gifted most often. And when I turned eight, Charles pressured me to participate in small ways with whatever he was doing or needed done.

"But when I was tasked to look after you...it was a breath of fresh air. You were so...sweet. And pure. You were the happiest thing in my life, and I wanted to protect you from whatever plan he had for you. I fought to stay in his good graces so I would be in a position to shelter you from the horrible things our father did. So, when you were gone without warning...I didn't take it well. I heard Merina died fighting off agents, and I thought you'd been with her." He stops to drink his water.

My heart breaks at how much he'd cared about me. How my disappearance had hurt him. And how guilty I now feel for not remembering any of it.

Jackson slips his hand in mine, tracing his thumb along the back of it.

"Reid, I..."

"There's nothing for you to be sorry for," he interjects matter-of-factly, his glass knocking against the table when he sets it down. Reid glances to Jackson. "So? What's your verdict?"

Verdict?

Jackson's smirk sharpens, the stick of his lollipop still trapped between his lips. "How many board members did you meet?"

Reid frowns, suddenly wary. "All of them."

I sit up straighter. "Wait. You know all of GE's Board members?" We could move on them as soon as everyone's trained. Dane wouldn't be stuck searching for them all day and night after training.

"Not all the current ones, no. I probably know more dead than alive."

"What about electees?" I prompt, undeterred from that minor setback.

Reid shakes his head. "I never met those. Just the ones who met regularly with Charles."

Swinging my hopeful gaze to Jackson, he adds one more question, "How many that you met are still alive?"

"Four."

Four. If they overlap with the two members we're already close to, then it's still two more and confirmation on the original ones. If not, we'd be halfway there.

Jackson nods. "You'll need to share everything about them with Dane and Aiden."

"Why?"

"Talk to Aiden," Jack reiterates, then looks at me with a single raised brow.

I snap my attention back to Reid. "Can you tell me more about Tinsley? You guys showed up together, and it's clear you care about her, but I'm not sure where she fits in if you were with Charles up until you left."

"She was one of the people in a special training program of older subjects I was assigned to monitor and report back to Charles on. The scientists still ran the program, but I was monitoring them as well as the gifted subjects." He sighs and rubs the back of his neck, a tiny smile threatening the corner of his mouth. "She was a fighter. No matter what they tried, they couldn't break her spirit. Her inner strength won against them time and again, and I don't think I even had a choice when I fell for her. I tried to hide it, but Charles found out. He tried to convince me to breed her for offspring, thinking I'd get over her as soon as I had her. I helped her escape instead, and he punished me for it. Tinsley returned and pleaded for my life, which started a year of torture for the both of us."

Reid clears his throat. "Anyway, that's the gist of it. I heard when you'd been found and when you'd escaped the island again, but I hadn't been able to find you. And then I saw you that night you fought the congressman, and I knew it was you. When Kellan offered us a way out with the Guild—where you were, and safe—I took Tinsley and ran. We stayed hidden for a while so Charles wouldn't suspect we'd gone to you. And then we filled out the application."

Wow. Everything he's been through...fuck. And I thought my life was crazy.

"I swear, we'll get her back," I promise, meaning every word. "Aiden told you what she said?"

He huffs irritably. "He did. I'm pissed about it but not surprised. If she says she's safe, I believe she is, but that doesn't mean her circumstances won't change. We still need to find her and get her back before that happens. And before Charles has produced enough gift-blocking accessories to control every gifted person in the world."

My stomach drops. "You mean the cuff? Are you saying there's more? It's not just a prototype?"

"A prototype? They've been making things like that by the thousands every year for the last five years. Collars, chokers, bracelets, cuffs, anklets, shackles, rings...bejeweled or plain and in various sizes. Then selling them off to the highest bidder. It's not just GE with those things now. There are tens or hundreds of thousands out in the world now with terrible people using them on people like us."

Wait. Collars. Like the ones in that business room with Thorne that captured me and Jack dodged. And the one I'd worn on the island with Gordon. How hadn't I realized there would be more of them?

"How? How do they have enough of Dane's blood for that many?" I demand.

"You were on the island for eight years, right? One blood draw a week? What do you think they did with that blood?"

"I don't know. Ran tests on it?"

Reid nods. "At first, maybe. But most gets stored away until they can find the best use for it. And once Vera learned how to put his gift into objects that can turn it on and off with specific frequencies programmed into it, they've been making them ever since."

"You mean the blood they'd taken from Dane on the island lasted them five years?"

"They still have some but it was starting to run low when I left. That means they're not in an immediate rush to get Dane, but there's a running clock. I expect that's why Charles hasn't shown up here to take him yet. He's biding his time. But you can be sure when they're down to their last batch, he won't waste time with sending agents out for his prize. He'll come for Dane and kill anyone who tries to stop him."

Chapter Twenty-Two

RAEGAN

Three short beeps jump the treadmill from walking to jogging, and I hurry to adjust to the speed.

"How's that?" Dane checks in with me, his amber gaze scrutinizing me for a sign that it's too much. It's been two days since I overdid it with my gift, and Aiden finally gave me the green light to get back to training. Dane and Kellan both argued for me to take another day off, but thankfully, Aiden and Jack sided with me. We don't have time to waste. Charles is coming for us whether we're ready or not.

"Slow," I tell him, even though my tied hair swings like a pendulum behind me with every step. "I can go faster."

Dane leans on his arms on the front of the equipment, releasing a small huff. "It's not a race, babe. Running the fastest on this thing isn't what's going to give you the endurance Jack's talking about. Slow and steady."

"I don't think he meant this slow, either. It's more work holding myself back right now than if I were to jog at a normal speed."

He laughs softly and shakes his head, shifting himself upright.

"*One* higher, then. Let's see how you do with that for some time before we make any more adjustments."

The machine beeps when he increases the speed for me, and I correct my pace to match. It's *just* past a relaxed jog for me, which is exactly what I want. If I'm not pushing myself at least a little, then I don't feel like I'm doing it right.

Dane waits for my quick nod that I'm okay before he pats the bar. "I'll be back. Everyone else is showing up now, so I need to get them set up."

I wave him off and focus back on my screen which shows how far I've gone and my current speed. I'm itching to increase it now that Dane's not here. According to Jackson, he thinks my gift has jumped in strength after what happened during the GE agent...cleanup. Before I try using my gift to that degree again, I'm under strict orders to build up my strength and stamina.

Dane's keeping track of my current baseline and will be sending the end-of-day and start-of-day numbers to Jackson for review. I'm not to test out the full strength of my gift until he says I'm ready.

With nothing else to do, my mind wanders to the news Aiden had shared with us over breakfast. He'd had cameras and motion sensors installed at Old Red to keep an eye on things since the last time we'd been there and were ambushed by Gordon and GE goons. Last night, he got an alert and found Vera snooping around. Considering the cuffs are with us, I can't imagine what else she might have returned there for. She didn't take anything we could see, but she disappeared into the room she'd stayed in where there wasn't a camera. Maybe she forgot something?

Her look of shock and confusion when Dane dove between her and the knives flashes to mind. Did she retreat because of it? Or had she already accomplished what she came here to do? Does that moment have anything to do with her returning to Old Red? She'd given me the cuffs back, too. Why?

I can't figure her out. First, she wants to kill me and get Dane. But then she helped us by giving me the cuffs, she's had multiple opportunities to kill me and didn't, and she called the GE agents back from the attack on the Guild. She could have grabbed Dane and tried to escape, but she poked him with something instead. Unless that was the attack and we have yet to see what it'll do.

I'm happy to report that I don't touch any settings before Dane returns to check on me. He drops me to a walk and sets a timer for fifteen minutes. "We'll bring you back to a jog when the timer goes off."

Frowning, I take a sip of water and screw the cap back on. "How do you know so much about all of this?"

He shrugs, his eyes scanning the room of people working at their assigned stations. "When you can't leave a building for two years, you'll do anything to get out of the apartment. I wound up here or the Guild Hall most days when I needed to get out. And one of the Guild members who was around in the beginning was a personal trainer. He taught me the right way to use each piece of equipment without causing more harm than good."

"What happened to him?" I ask, assuming it had to be something if Dane and Aiden were the ones running these sessions in the exercise room.

"Nothing bad. He just moved out of state." Dane checks the timer. "After your next jog, we'll switch you to weights and then finish out with the box."

He leaves to do another sweep through the room, adjusting members or switching up their exercise or equipment they're on. He gets me through the rest of my session at a steady pace. Each exercise gets my heart rate up and creates an almost pleasurable burn in my muscles without pushing me so hard that I'm ready to drop.

Until the box burpees.

Fuck. Those.

I lie frontward on the mat, one side of my face sticking to the plastic as I struggle for air in my lungs. Each breath is accompanied by a sharp pain, like a tiny needle jabbing me in the chest.

Dane crouches beside me, his smirk dripping with arrogance. "Was that too tame for you, too?"

I'd swipe at him, but everything hurts. I know I'd been making comments all morning about not being worked hard enough. Okay, maybe they were more like *complaints*, but still...no one deserves punishment like that. All I can manage back is a groan.

"Come on. Let's go for a walk." He offers me his hand, and I glare at it.

"You're joking," I manage, my tone flat.

He chuckles. "Nope. I'm not. You need to walk a bit and then stretch before you're done." Dane holds up a chilled bottle of water in his other hand. "You get to drink all of this a little bit at a time, too."

Oh, goodie.

By the time Dane releases me for Kellan's session in the main gym, I have a smidge of energy back. It's nowhere near where I started this morning, but at least I won't be lying on the floor.

Guild members and Pits fighters gather in the large space, a quarter of the numbers from the initial training day, but still a decent-sized group. I stay at the back, too tired from what I thought would be my easiest session to stand out at the front.

The whispers begin almost immediately.

I ignore them at first, assuming it's some circulating gossip within the Guild that I'd have no clue about until I make eye contact with a couple of the whisperers and realize it's about me.

Wonderful.

I have no idea what I did this time to be at the center of gossip, but based on the nervous and angry glances I get, it can't be for something good.

It never is.

It reminds me of the cafeteria on the island with Gordon. When everyone was too afraid to sit with or speak to me. I thought the Guild would be different, especially with Aiden in charge.

Two guys from the primary group break away, setting their sights on me as they walk closer so it's clear they plan to say something to me.

I'm too tired for this shit.

They stop out of arm's reach, which I notice because any normal person having a conversation wouldn't be so obviously distant while trying to talk to anyone. The one on the left with short brown hair crosses his arms, putting the myriad of scars riddling his arms on full display. But it's the curly blond on the right who sneers and speaks first.

"You the GE spy they found who flipped sides?"

Damn, word travels fast. It's probably for the best that Aiden hasn't let Harvey go if we did trust him more.

Even if that trust is still questionable, I don't like complete strangers going after him. Any potential for me trying to be nice vanishes, and I raise an unamused brow. "Who's asking?"

The one on the left's face twists like he bit into something sour, but it's the blond who talks again. "Like we'd give you our names, GE scum."

My gift is a flicker of heat in my gut, reacting to the subtle trip in my temper.

I smile at them, doing my best to channel Jackson into it. Their expressions falter when they see it, and I try not to admit that affecting them with a simple smile makes me cackle in my head. "What can I do for you, boys?"

It takes them a second to remember that they're trying to be intimidating and regain that composure. The one on the right answers, and I wonder if the other guy is just his hype man. Or emotional support buddy. "We're warning you to leave before things get messy. We came here to get rid of scum like you, not work with you."

"Mm...well, I don't think that's up to you," I counter.

"We saw you kill those GE guys the other day. If you could turn your back on them that easily, then we're not letting you stick around to stab any of us in the back when you change your mind again."

There are a few things wrong there, but one of them has my full attention.

"I'm sorry," I say, trying not to laugh. "Not *letting* me? Which of you thinks you're going to stop me if you saw my gift?"

"Spoken like a true villain," he spits out.

My chest squeezes at that word, hating it and the memories that come with it. But I'm not letting *that man* have any more control over me.

I'm finally accepting that I'm not a villain, and I never was.

But that doesn't make me a saint, either.

I fist my hands, readying a retort, when Kellan looms behind them, his dark fury freezing the words in my throat.

He yanks them to their heels by the backs of their necks, snarling, "Did you just threaten my girl?"

His usual grin is replaced by drawn brows and a sharp glare. His fingers tighten in their necks, creating visible indents. The muscles in his arms are tight and accentuated, pulsing with the strength of his grip.

A crowd circles us, eager to watch the show.

The one who'd done all the talking tries to pry Kellan's hand from his neck unsuccessfully. "Sh-she said she was the GE spy. She—kkkk." His words cut off, his eyes bulging.

"She's not. She's done more to fight GE than this entire building combined, so I'll stop that filthy lie right now. You're new here, so I'll give you my first and last warning. *She's mine.* Threaten her, or even disrespect her again, and I'll gut you from your shriveled dick to your throat." He releases them, and they both drop to their hands and knees. "If you can't accept that, then leave right now. We don't have room for spineless punks here." His hard gaze sweeps across the crowd. "The same goes for all of you. We're here to take down GE, not gang up on or threaten our own people. If I hear so much as a whisper of that happening, you're gone."

The two idiots on the ground make it to their feet and start to leave, one of them bumping into Fabian, who blocks the way. Silas stands next to him, a shit-eating grin on his face when he warns, "You forgot to apologize to her."

They freeze, then mumble a quick "sorry" before Fabian steps aside to let them pass.

"Partner up!" Kellan shouts, stalking to the front of the room and oozing violence. Well, this will be a fun training session.

I'm expecting everyone to steer clear of me after Kellan's threat, but Evie instantly joins my side. "Care to be my partner?"

I offer her a smile, reminding myself that there are good people here. "Sure."

She smiles. "Those were Pits fighters, by the way. No one at the Guild would have ever acted like that."

Kellan yells out the next set of instructions, so I nod to her and then get into position for our mock fight. "It's alright. I actually thought the whole thing was funny up until Kellan threatened everyone in the room with a gutting. I'm not sure if that's going to help or make things worse."

She chuckles and crouches into her own ready position. "Well, we'll quickly see who's fine and who needs to go then, won't we?"

Guess so.

CHAPTER TWENTY-THREE

RAEGAN

KELLAN'S MOOD DOESN'T IMPROVE by the end of his training. Within seconds of him calling it to an end, he grabs and throws me over his shoulder like a fucking brute, then slams the door open to the mini cafeteria that has the snack and shake bar.

"What the hell, Kellan?" I demand, punching and slapping his back. "I'm not a sack of po—Oh!" He flips me back on my feet, his hands slamming on the counter behind me.

"What else did Rafe say to you? I need to know if I'm killing him or ruining his goddamn life."

Rafe, huh? I realize now that I never did get their names. Cowards.

I release an annoyed huff, pushing against his chest for more room, then frowning when he refuses to budge. "It was just stupid words. I'm fine."

"He *threatened* you." There's a ripple of *something* along his arms, but it's so quick that I can't tell if I'd just imagined seeing it. The muscles in his arms jump, his damned shirt seeming to stretch tighter as he works his jaw like he's grinding words between his teeth. His blue-green eyes darken behind dilated pupils that nearly consume his eyes.

"Kell? What's gotten into you? What's going on?" I grab one of his arms, and it feels solid and smooth beneath my fingertips. Further inspection reveals golden scales, and my breath catches. Did he get injured during training? No, he didn't have any when we came in here.

"You're supposed to be safe here. I should have gutted him right there. Snapped a knee at least," he continues, his deep timbre darkening with more heat. More scales appear on his left arm, then the sides of his neck. I peek beneath his shirt and see them already there as well.

I hum distractedly, my mind marveling at his gift activating *without* an injury for once, while I also try to figure out what to say to calm him down without him losing it, either. "Mm...well, I'm not too worried about some fighters. They can say whatever they want, so long as they're still useful in fighting GE."

He growls, but it's even more animalistic than his usual sound. Wilder. Rougher. It reverberates in his chest and then settles in his throat. "We're not having people like that watch our backs."

"Then don't give them *that* particular job. But we can't be picky. We need fighters."

Kellan grabs my wrist when he realizes I'm touching his belt and was trying to sneak a peek down his pants...to check for his gift, of course. "What. Did. He. Say."

"Enough!" I shout, twisting my wrist to get it back from him, but it's like being in iron shackles. There's no breaking free from him when his gift is active. Well, fine then.

I fill my body with my gift, spreading it through every inch of me like a warm buzz of electricity coating my skin. I can feel it dance along Kellan's grip, pushing and testing the impenetrable skin there to find an opening it can crack apart.

He releases me, holding his hand in front of him while he rubs his thumb and fingers together.

Pressing my hand to his chest may not hurt him, but it grabs his attention, nonetheless. "Does it look like I can't handle some cage fighter with a bad attitude?"

His dark eyes flare, then heat with a feral-ness that sets my heart racing into overdrive. "No." He collars my nape and yanks me against him, gift be damned, then rumbles in my ear, "But that's my job, beautiful. To take out the trash for you."

He slams his mouth against mine, the prickle of our gifts interacting like tiny fireworks against our lips.

I moan into the kiss, the way his tongue ravishes mine and makes my core turn molten. Everywhere we touch erupts in tingles that are part-sting, part-pleasure, and have my toes curling with desire. Lust addles my brain in those first few seconds as I give in to the kiss, my body melting against his.

Then I remember what he said. Kellan would be one of the first to shove me behind him if we're in danger, but I'm not about that. I want to be right up front, protecting them or standing beside them at the very least.

I'm not some princess to be locked away or hidden from sight.

I shove away from him, putting a bit of my gift into it, and duck under his arm to step away. "I can handle myself, Kellan," I reiterate, a hand fisted at my chest as I catch my breath.

He turns, his teeth bared in a wild grin that looks more deadly than friendly. He's watching me like a wolf eyeing his next meal. I take an involuntary step back. "Are you running from me, beautiful?"

My breathing falters.

"No, I'm trying to have a serious—Fuck!"

He lunges for me, and I bolt, leaping around chairs and tables. Kell doesn't bother moving around anything and bulldozes straight through it to me. The furniture flies and crashes with a mere swipe of his hands, clearing his path in a second. His hand sinks into my hair, fisting it hard enough to make me cry out in alarm before he drags me back against him. Heat fizzles between us, and the front of his shirt disintegrates.

Whoops.

His teeth scrape over the hammering pulse in my neck. "Giving up so easily, beautiful?" he taunts on a cruel chuckle. "Is this how you handle yourself?"

Oh.

Game on.

I swing my foot up to nail him in the balls. It won't hurt him, but his gut reaction to block it is enough of a distraction that I dive out of his grasp and fall onto a table. It cracks and disappears beneath me. My body thuds to the ground unexpectedly, and I grunt, glaring at the table particles now dusting the floor.

Ow.

I could turn off my gift, but it's the only thing giving me the slightest chance against him while his gift is active.

He grabs my ankles and flips me onto my back, parting my legs. Kellan buries his face between my thighs, nibbling through the fabric of my workout pants and underwear to reach my clit.

Gasping, I grab his hair with the intention of pushing him away, but he switches to a hard suck, and my fingers clench automatically, holding him more firmly against my core with a soft groan riding my lips. "Ahhh, fuck!"

His teeth rake across my clit and entrance at once, snapping together at the middle. My pussy throbs with need, paralyzing me through a shudder of pleasure. I feel something at my waist and find his hands hooked in my workout pants and my shoes already removed.

Fuck.

I reach behind me and grab the legs of a chair, repeating to myself that I *don't* want to disintegrate it. When it remains solid in my grip, I swing it over my head and into his back.

One of the chair legs breaks off in my hand as the rest of the chair tumbles to the floor.

Or not.

I flip to my front, scrambling out from under him, even if that means I'm helping him remove my pants. As soon as I'm free from them, I rush to my feet and run, cursing at the tables and chairs that slow me down without having the same effect on him. I can feel him behind me by the hairs rising along the back of my neck. The sound of metal scraping on the floor or hard plastic crashing together.

Sorry, Aiden.

I stop trying to avoid the furniture and touch it instead, my gift obliterating it to clear my path.

A hand wraps around my neck from behind, then pushes me against the nearest wall. "Caught you, rabbit," Kellan mocks, his beard tickling the back of my ear. His hand dips inside my panties. He gives a hard tug, holding me in place by my neck, and then tears them off. "You won't be needing these," he growls.

He grips my ass, then kneads it in a slow circle. He smacks it once, short and sweet, and inhales sharply. My skin tingles and burns where he struck, the effect of our gifts entangling there in that instant, skyrocketing the intensity before fading to an insistent tingle that demands the area be touched again. I grind my ass against him, seeking that relief and finding the hard length of him bulging in his pants.

He chuckles, the jingle and slide of his belt so loud to me that it's all I can focus on. The hard clank when it falls to the floor. The soft *pop* of his jeans unbuttoning. "Should I take you like this? Fuck you against the wall?" I'm panting hard, the adrenaline pumping through my veins and drowning out anything but him and the wild beating of my heart. He rips the rest of his shirt free, dropping it to the pile of his clothes on the floor and kicking it aside.

He rocks his dick into my lower back, slowly grinding it against me as heat spreads and pools between my thighs. Kell curses, dropping his head and biting my shoulder. "I love the feel of your gift on my dick. I wonder how much more I'll feel when I'm inside you."

"Kell," I breathe, craning my head as far to the side as I can. I draw my lips in, wetting them and shooting him a heated look. *Kiss me*, it demands.

His lips close in on mine, no actual words needed between us as he drives his tongue against mine. He grips my chin, holding me in place as he takes my mouth with a savagery that makes my knees weak. I try to reach him, to touch him, but struggle against his unrelenting grip. Leaning into my gift, I strengthen it at my neck.

Kellan startles. I worry for a second that I somehow hurt him, but he only looks surprised when he checks his hand.

The moment his eyes and hands are off me, I escape. I run for the counter, diving over it and hoping I'll slide to the other side, when a hand clamps down on my thigh, stopping me while my upper half is dangling. He pulls me back a few inches, then pushes my thighs together around his dick. He thrusts between them, rubbing between my folds and gathering my arousal until the top of his cock is slick.

"That's right, beautiful. You're mine," he says fiercely, his breathing harsh. "I'm never letting you go."

My body clenches at his words, aching at the emptiness that's desperate to be filled and knowing how close the cure is. I moan loudly, unable to stop myself when it feels so fucking good. His dick glides more easily now down my center, making me wetter for him. Blood rushes to my head, making me dizzy and almost ready to give in.

He spreads my cheeks, his cock sliding back and notching against my entrance. "One of these days, I'll remember to put goddamn lube in my pocket so I can start training your sexy ass."

I squirm in his grip, but it's hard to say if I'm trying to get away or sink onto him. The rush is getting stronger now, filling my head and making it harder to think about anything other than the feel of him right where I want him. How close I am to the ecstasy I want. One tiny nudge to breach my core, and yet he holds there, letting the need grow and expand until I'm quivering with it.

"Tell me you're mine. Say it," he commands roughly. I almost do it. Almost give in to his demands because I'm on the verge of passing out and losing my mind from the tease, when he prods my core with the head of his cock, and I remember that he wants this as desperately as I do.

I still have some fight left in me.

"Bite me," I growl, reaching for anything on this side of the counter. I grip the handle of a blender and throw it back. I don't have time to see if I got him or what effect it had on him other than his hands releasing me. I fall to the floor, catching myself with my hands before I faceplant, and take a few gasping, blinking breaths while my blood begins to drain.

Kellan chuckles. "Whatever my girl wants, she gets."

Forcing my feet under me, I shakily rise and stumble through the mini kitchen for the snack and shake bar. I cast a quick glance back, where Kellan places a hand on the counter and clears it in a single jump.

Shit.

The small area ends with another counter and row of refrigerators along the back wall. I turn, my hands finding the edge of the narrow counter on instinct and then dropping when that collapses beneath my gift, the contents spilling to the floor.

Aiden's going to be pissed.

It's something I'll have to worry about later, though, because in a few short strides, Kellan is already closing in. I run around the other side of the center prep table, hoping to make it back to the front counter and bar, but he pivots and slides over it, blocking my exit.

His large frame towers over mine, gold scales catching and glinting in the overhead lights. Kellan's eyes are dark and wild, the flash of his teeth against his beard sharp. "Going somewhere?" he drawls.

Fisting my hands, I go for it. I swing at his jaw, hitting him with the strength of my gift and catching him off guard. His neck snaps to the side, but his body doesn't budge. I keep the punches flying, striking his torso, his head, a kick to his knee. Anything to bring him down long enough that I can slip past him.

None of it makes a difference.

Kellan bends and lifts me by my thighs, then plops me on the prep table. I focus on not destroying this one because the fall from it would hurt like a bitch. While I'm preoccupied, he flips my legs up, and I fall on my back with a hard thud. His teeth sink into my thigh, and I gasp.

I kick my legs and fight to pull away from him, but he laughs and drags me back to his mouth, his arms locked around my thighs where they're slung over his shoulders. He starts on one side, teasing the length of my inner thigh with kisses and love bites, branding the path to my cunt with marks that'll last for days.

I'm still wrestling for control, bucking and clawing at him after pushing myself upright as he suckles and claims my other thigh, biting me hard if I get too riled. I grab his hair, fighting to move his head and merely pulling out the tie that holds half his hair up.

He snatches one wrist and then the other, grinning wickedly at me from between my legs. "Remember, you asked for this, beautiful. If you're good, I may even let you come."

Kellan slips his tongue between my folds, finding my clit in a single slow stroke and then flicking it. My body convulses, pleasure wracking my limbs like an electric shock. The prickle of our gifts adds a whole new experience to his mouth on me there, and I'm fucking here for it. His lips suction around it, sucking and licking and eating me alive so thoroughly, so overwhelmingly, that I collapse like a rag doll on the table as I lose all control of my body. I'm nothing but need. A molten, desperate thing that aches. *Aches* for release.

Pleasure coils and tightens within me, building to an almost unbearable level. I tremble in his grip, straining to pull free from his hands while he only holds me closer. Harder. Forcing the pleasure that zings through me and threatens to detonate with only a little bit more. I grind my hips, seeking out that extra friction that will be my undoing as I push against him as hard as I can.

I'm right there, about to crest the hill, when his mouth shifts.

He *leaves that spot*, and I come tumbling down that hill instead of over it, my climax slipping from my grip.

No, no, no!

"Kell! Wait!"

He chuckles, adding another bite to my inner thigh, which makes my over-sensitized body jump. "Did you think it would be that easy?" He plants a kiss on my pelvis, his beard tickling and scratching my shaved skin. "Did you think I'd let you get away with that?" Kellan gives me a feral grin as he stands, pulling me upright and releasing my hands. He pumps his cock, then swipes the bead of pre-cum with his thumb and holds it out to me.

I open my mouth, leaning forward to wrap my lips around his thumb and suck it clean. I add circling tongue, trying to sweeten him to reconsidering.

His eyes shutter, and he groans. Kellan hooks his thumb down, grabbing my teeth and chin. "I think I know how you're going to make it up to me." His grip directs my face and eyes downward, where his other hand strokes his hard length. "What do you say, beautiful?"

I nod, his hold allowing me that much movement. He releases me, and I slide from the table and sink to my knees. He grabs the edge of the table with his hands like he needs something to hold on to.

I don't bother with light or slow teasing. I'm horny as fuck, and the sight of his dick has me salivating. I wrap my lips around his crown, tasting him with a swirl of my tongue and moaning at the salty taste. There's a crunch of metal and a curse, and I realize then he's using the table to keep himself from overdoing it if he were to touch me.

How much has he had to hold himself back to keep from hurting me while his gift is active? Just how strong is he?

I suck him down as far as I can, hollowing my cheeks and pulling myself down his shaft until he hits the back of my throat. Remembering to breathe through my nose, I grip the rest of him with my hand, twisting and giving him short pumps. I draw back, tongue working at the tip and then sucking him down again.

I work him over and over, sucking and licking, moaning and pumping, my head bobbing at a steady pace as drool begins to slide from the corner of my lips. I ignore the sound of metal groaning, snapping. His curses and praises rain down on me like fuel to encourage me faster. Harder. I even slip my teeth out at one point, raking them down his shaft while I tug and play with his balls, and Kellan's hips jerk forward, his hand holding the back of my head from moving. He slams his cock to the back of my throat so hard I choke.

"Fuck!" He tries to withdraw, but I grab his thighs and keep going. I'm ready to flip the tables on him. Bring him to the edge of ruination and then cut him off, just like he did to me. Even though my throat now has a bit of an ache, it's not too bad. I try to dig my nails into his thighs but meet the cold scales or thick protective layer wherever I go. He shudders as if feeling something still. I wonder if it's more than a tickle of my gift against his. If he feels the same pins and needles that both sting and feel good at once wherever we touch.

It's like my mouth is numb and electrified at the same time, and my body is throbbing with the need to feel it in my cunt.

Kellan's hips twitch, his balls tightening, and I pop my lips off him in a rush, nearly falling over myself to get to my feet and run again.

He snarls, and I have a second of sweet satisfaction at his frustration before I remember I still have to escape him to win. "Not so fast." He grabs me by the shirt that I'm still wearing, which I destroy with a thought and keep going. Kellan laughs and shackles my ankle, dragging me between his legs so he's straddling me. I scramble forward and kick at his face, but he grabs my foot and then flips me to my back, dragging my ass and hips off the floor so he can lock my legs against him.

Kellan uses his hips to line himself up as I try to twist or angle away, convinced I can still win this, but his hold is too secure, his determination greater than mine when he drives his cock inside me.

I come immediately, stars bursting behind my eyes at the tingling, hot slide of his dick as our gifts collide inside of me.

Holy fuck.

Kellan's moan is loud and long, his body hunched and shuddering as he absorbs so much at once. "Fuckkk, that's...fuck." He slowly drags himself out to the tip, then rolls his hips when he pushes back inside. My inner walls tremble at the feeling as I'm still coming down from my orgasm. He keeps doing it, agonizingly slow and steady, so the warm buzz liquefies my muscles.

He must sense that the fight's completely left me because he lowers my legs and leans forward, his hand finding my throat while his other arm still cradles one of my legs to keep me open for him. "I know you can fight and fuck and everything in between. But it's my goddamn pleasure to do some of it for you. Do you understand?"

His hips keep working their magic, like a wave that rolls in and out, my own hips working to meet his and ride that wave rather than fight it. Every stroke sends a burst of pleasure through me. Makes my body quiver and ache.

Kellan's grip on my throat tightens, and my pussy clenches deliciously on his cock, holding it in place at his slow pace. He pushes through it, picking up speed, and my eyes roll back in my head. "Answer me," he growls.

"Yes!" I groan, both answering him and in response to the faster pace that feels so fucking good.

He slams into me, fucking me in a frenzy. My core is on fire, burning and throbbing and gripping the air in my lungs. Or maybe his hand has cut off my air because I can't breathe, can't think as he pounds pure and devastating pleasure into me. I think my body is lifted from the ground, or he's fucking me so hard I'm going airborne, but I'm so blinded with the need to come that I can't focus on anything other than that spot he keeps hitting until my orgasm explodes through me.

Kellan roars as he comes too, my cunt clamping down on him and wringing him dry as my body locks and floods with ecstasy. I'd probably scream if I had any oxygen, but as it is, I can't see, can't breathe, can barely feel anything other than the lingering high that consumes me. I surrender completely to that bliss.

I wake up in Kellan's arms, his back against some cabinets and knees bent on either side of me. My ear is pressed to his chest, where I can feel the steady thump of his heart and hear the slow inhale and exhale of his breath. His arms are locked around my arm and leg as if he'd pulled me sideways against him with warm bands of steel.

I feel warm.

Safe.

I hum under my breath, content.

"You awake then, beautiful?"

"Mm."

It's quiet for a moment before he says, "You're not running away."

I open my eyes, a soft smile curling my lips at that realization—when I used to bolt the second I had a chance, too afraid to make that emotional connection with anyone. Too scared to let anyone in past my barriers. "Not anymore." I shift and his arms loosen enough that I can turn on my knees to face him.

His blue-green eyes are glued to me, open and waiting for whatever I'm about to say. I reach for the stiff bristles of his beard, stroking my hand over them and then grazing my thumb along his cheekbone. "I'm right where I'm supposed to be," I whisper, my chest ready to explode with the overwhelming emotions swirling and twisting there.

Kellan kisses me then. Raw and desperate. Languid, yet demanding. He kisses me like it's the first and the last time bundled as one, and my heart detonates as it's stripped bare, all the emotions releasing and flooding my veins at once.

I'd spent two years dreaming of a place I could call home. Then the three years after telling myself it was better not to have one, fooling myself into believing that a place like that didn't exist for someone like me. Now that I'm with them, I realize that home for me isn't a place.

It's them.

I was never going to feel whole or complete without them.

Kell tears himself away, his face pinched and serious for a change. "I'm sorry for everything that happened in the past. If I hadn't—"

I cover his lips with my fingers to stop him. "I don't blame you—any of you—for that. Not anymore," I add, because I had before. I'd blamed them for what Gordon did to me. For letting that man control me and do what he pleased. I thought it would help me to move on from them if I blamed Gordon's actions on them. If I hated Aiden, most of all, when I thought he had left me on the island. It wasn't until I was with Gordon the last time that I realized...none of us were responsible for Gordon's actions. *He* was the one to blame. For all of it. Not them. And not myself. "We were stupid kids then. How were any of us going to understand what Gordon was capable of?"

"We still should have fought for you," he argues.

"I killed one of us. Of course, you weren't going to jump to my rescue."

Kellan releases a frustrated growl. "You're giving us too much leeway that we don't deserve." He cups my face, and I lean into it. "But I'll take it anyway. Anything, if it means we get to keep you. Because I won't make the same mistake again. I won't let you go." He slips his hand into my hair, wrapping the back of my head and drawing me close.

He presses a featherlight kiss to my temple. "Let me be your armor." My cheek. "Your shield." Kell crooks a finger under my chin and lifts it, adding another kiss under my jaw. The side of my neck. "I was always meant to be that, for you." His lips find mine, coaxing them apart with excruciating slowness. His languorous tongue caresses mine, spreading warmth through my limbs. "I love you, Raegan LaRoux, or Laivins, or whatever last name you want."

"I love you, too," I confess. He looks surprised, either by my admission or how quickly I said it. "I'm not just saying it. I think...I always have. Even when I tried to forget you, or when you all hated me...I could never let you go. There's no one else for me but the four of you."

"Fuck, beautiful," he breathes, kissing me again like he can never get enough.

A voice clears above us.

I jerk back, suddenly remembering that I'm wearing nothing but a bra and socks, and Kellan's completely naked, where we're wrapped up in each other.

"I would ask if you were attacked based on the state of this room, but unless it was a clothing thief, I'm forced to assume you're the culprits behind this mess?" Aiden inquires smoothly, a single brow raised in a silent demand for an explanation.

He's standing on this side of the counter, deftly undoing the buttons on his suit jacket and sliding it free. Stepping closer, he fans it out behind me and settles it over my shoulders.

Fabric plops to the floor beside him. My pants and shoes. I glance up, finding Jackson smiling at me from where he's crouched on top of the counter. Kellan's pants, boxer briefs, and shoes drop next on the other side of him.

"When people heard crashing sounds coming from here, they thought we were under attack. You're lucky Jackson heard it first and blocked the door from anyone trying to come check it out." Dane's voice carries from behind the counter and out of my view. I hurriedly stand and tug my pants and shoes on, giving Kell room to do the same.

I look around the room and cringe at what I see. Half the tables and chairs are gone, mere piles of dust on the floor. The rest of them, well, the ones that aren't bent out of shape or missing legs, are strewn about. The mini kitchen has the worst of it. Missing chunks of counter. Food and supplies cover the floor. The prep table is warped and dented so far that it'll be a miracle if the cabinet doors on that side manage to open.

Tucking my arms into Aiden's jacket, I wrap it more tightly around my upper half so I'm covered. His thumb traces something on my neck, an angry crease furrowing his brow. Aiden glares at Kellan, who stands but hasn't bothered with his clothes. "Was it necessary for you to mar her whole body with your mouth?"

Kell laughs, his smile as wide and bright as can be. "Just marking what's mine," he responds, a challenge flashing in his eyes as he holds Aiden's stare.

Fucking shit stirrer.

I'm close enough to Aiden that I can feel his body tense.

Fuck.

I need to figure out how to deal with Aiden's possessive and jealous nature, and fast. Calling him out in an open challenge like Kellan's doing isn't the way to do it.

"Don't be a prick, Kell," I cut in, trying to stop that shit before it goes downhill.

"And get dressed already," Dane throws in. "That should be rule number one in this relationship. When you're not actively using it, put it away. I think I've seen your dick more in the last month than I've seen our girl naked. There's something wrong with those numbers."

Kellan howls with laughter, throwing his head back and slapping the countertop. His head drops down, and he looks prepared to say something else, but thankfully Aiden intervenes.

"Yes, get some clothes on. And then I expect an explanation for why you chose to destroy the Guild's snack and shake bar."

I duck my head, heat creeping up my neck.

Aiden turns to me, his dark gaze sweeping me from head to toe. "I'll call Cassandra to heal the bruising from Kellan. Are you injured anywhere else?"

"What? No, of course not. Why would you think he—" I stop short when Aiden's eyes trail to the disfigured metal. The destroyed cabinets and counters. "Oh. No, I'm fine. His gift was active, and mine, which is what caused the mess." Ah! Which reminds me…"Kell!" I grab his arm as he's buckling his pants. "Your gift. How did you turn it on without getting hurt?"

He lifts his arm and looks at it with a concentrated gaze. "I don't know. One minute, I was raging mad at Rafe, and the next, it was there. I didn't do it on purpose."

"Why were you mad at Rafe?" Aiden asks.

Kellan's expression darkens, his jaw tensing. "That piece of shit threatened her," he growls, hands fisting as his anger resurges.

I jump to the counter to grab Jackson's boot when he stands.

"Wait!" He looks at me, a cruel smile twisting his lips and a knife suddenly in his grip. "He already left. He thought I was the GE spy and was trying to get me to leave. He was a dick, sure, but he doesn't deserve to die for that."

"Where is he now?" Aiden demands, his attention on Kellan.

"He and Snyder took off after I threatened them. I don't know yet if they left the Tower for good or are just lying low."

"They sure as fuck aren't staying here anymore," Dane adds, fisting his hand.

But I'm still focused on Jack, who doesn't look the least bit dissuaded by my plea for their lives. I switch tactics. "Don't kill them," I say this time, my voice firm. "Being assholes isn't a death sentence."

"It is if it's to you," he counters, dipping back to a squat so he can reach me. He curls my hair behind my ear, then draws the ends of them to his lips.

I stand my ground even as pleasurable goosebumps break out where he touches me and spread down my neck and arms. "No killing them."

Jackson's smile sharpens, a light huff passing through his nose. "No killing," he finally promises, and I breathe a sigh of relief.

"Kell, come with me to check their temporary apartment and escort them out if they haven't left already. The rest of you, get to the Loft. We need to finish preparing for Harvey's meeting with Charles," Aiden directs, ending the conversation.

I take Jack's hand, wondering if he'll fight Aiden on wanting to be the one to handle Rafe and his buddy, but he jumps to the floor at my side.

Hm. I could pretend that means he's accepted whatever Aiden and Kell plan to do or accept that he'll likely go out overnight to deliver his own version of justice. I've already done my part to keep them alive. Whatever comes next is on them.

Chapter Twenty-Four

AIDEN

"She said not to kill them," Kellan growls, clearly displeased with the request she made of Jackson. "I don't trust spineless dicks like them to not come back and cause trouble."

I rub my thumb and finger over the smooth metal forearm gauntlet beneath my sleeve, molding it to a blade and combining it with its twin. The steel evens and sharpens to a point, its sides just as deadly up to the hand guard. "Then we'll make sure to give them enough reason to never come back."

"I'm taking Rafe. He was the talker."

Irritation stirs in my chest. As much as I'm playing calm and collected on the outside, I'm furious within. I'd given these Pits fighters a home. Safety. Training and food. And they *threatened my woman*.

I'm half-tempted to throw the rest out with them.

"Fine. They're both mine if we ever see them again."

"Only if you see them first."

Prick.

Stopping at their apartment door, I knock first, nudging Kellan to the side so I'm the one they'll see through the peephole. I withdraw my phone and prepare my first phone call, tapping Reid's name once the door opens.

"Yeah? What's—"

Kellan drives his fist into Rafe's face before he can finish, knocking him back into his apartment. He pushes forward, grabbing Rafe and shoving him through to the living room as I follow and kick the door shut behind me. The call rings while Kellan proceeds to beat the shit out of Rafe. The Pits fighter, to his credit, gets his own swings in and tries giving as good as he can. Unfortunately for him, it only fires Kellan up more.

The second fighter, Snyder, storms into the room just as Reid answers.

"Hello?"

"Hey! What the fuck's go—"

I hold my sword to his neck, stopping his words and momentum, then answer Reid, "Are you available? There's a small matter I need dealt with. The sooner the better."

Snyder steps back and to the side to maneuver around my blade. I spread the metal thinner, willing it to wrap his neck in a loose circle.

"Move again, and you'll behead yourself," I warn him.

"Where are you?" Reid asks, unperturbed by the threat he just overheard.

"Room 15401."

"Am I bringing anything or anyone?"

"No."

"I'll be there in a few."

The call ends, and I slip my phone away. A quick glance shows Kellan's already knocked Rafe out where he's lying bloody on the rug. We'll burn it with the rest of their things.

Snyder's shaking within the small circle of space his neck has, his nervous stare flicking from Rafe's body to Kellan and back to me. His forehead shimmers with sweat. "You're crazy," he spits.

"In future, before you begin harassing or threatening someone, make sure you know exactly who you're speaking to," I begin.

"We didn't know she was his—"

"—and *mine*. As the leader of the Guild, there are no lengths I wouldn't go for its members. I would—and already have—killed for them. I'd take on a shadow organization of thousands to eliminate that threat to them." I step closer, thickening the blade. "So, what do you think I'd do for the woman I love? To protect her from those who threaten her?"

Beads of sweat slide down his temple. "A-anything."

I nod. "If either of you had laid a single finger on her, you'd be dead right now. Since it was only words, we'll let this serve as a warning." A knock sounds at the door, but I ignore it to finish. "We're going to drop you off near a hospital where you can take Rafe. It will be far away from here. If anyone asks what happened, you tell them your friend got jumped in an alley and didn't see any faces. Do you understand?"

Snyder sniffs and slightly tilts his head to avoid the sword.

"If we see you in this city again, or we ever hear from or about you again, then you won't be dealing with Kellan next time. You'll be dealing with me." I lower my voice to a threatening whisper. "I'll bury you alive in a seamless steel coffin with your friend and you can spend your last hours fighting to have the last breath."

He shivers, and I use my gift to reshape and move the metal back to my forearm and then stretch it over my knuckles.

"Any questions?" I ask, and he quickly shakes his head.

Good.

I slam my metal-wrapped knuckles into his jaw, knocking him unconscious to the floor.

When I look up, Reid's taking in Rafe's beaten-up body and then Snyder while Kellan stands behind him, arms crossed. "What did they do?"

"Threaten Raegan," I reply.

Reid's stare returns to Rafe as if he's reassessing his injuries. "What do you need me to do with them?"

I pull up a map of the opposite coast, searching for a hospital and then switching to satellite view to find and expand on a nearby alley. I text him the coordinates. "Take them both and leave them at the location I just sent you. Snyder can help Rafe to the hospital once he wakes up."

"Anything else?"

"No. You can go back to what you were doing once you've done that. Thank you for coming on short notice."

He nods. "Next time something like that happens, invite me before the cleanup."

Kellan snorts, but I counter, "There won't be a next time."

After Reid teleports away with Rafe and Snyder, I call Evie. She answers on the first ring. "I've got a job for you and Silas when you're both free."

"Yes, sir. We're both free now. How can we help?"

"I have an apartment which needs to be cleared out. You can donate or burn the items. The rug will need to be disposed of, but the rest of the furniture will stay."

Evie's quiet, then asks, "Did the apartment belong to the two giving Raegan a hard time earlier?"

"It did."

"Then it doesn't need to be a job. We'd be happy to do it."

"Hey, wait—" Silas's voice sounds muffled in the background as if he or someone else is moving between him and the speaker. "—know I'd do it for free—" More shuffling sounds. "—if he's offering to pay—"

After a thud, Evie says, "Which room is it?" I give her the number. "Great. We'll be right up. Just leave the door cracked for us before you leave."

"I'll call Cibrina to reset the lock and give you a temporary key. Pick it up from her first."

I prepare to call Cibrina next, when an unknown number flashes on the screen and I pause my thumb. Almost all my contacts are in my phone. Even disagreeable, irritating contacts like Elias. Dane's put my number on every do not call list and registry possible so I've never had the issue of a salesperson calling me unless I'd initiated it.

Kell steps closer when he notices I haven't accepted the call right away. "Who is it?"

"We're about to find out."

"Guild Master," Charles greets formally with an edge of mockery when I answer. "I thought we could speak like civilized men, you and me. *Master* to CEO."

I grip the phone tighter, my blood heating in anger at the sound of his voice. All the ways I want to inflict the years of Raegan's pain and suffering on him cycle through my mind in an instant. Ways that I'll keep him within an inch of his life and then serve him to her on a platter.

"Civilized men don't treat other humans as animals to train or involuntary test subjects."

He chuckles. "I see. Your Guild is still new, still growing. You've yet to begin looking at the bigger picture. In business, in life, and for the future of our kind."

"I see it just fine for those under my protection."

"And what about the ones out there who aren't protected by you? The other gifted individuals in the world who are in hiding, ashamed of who they are or too afraid to be noticed? There's a world full of our kind finally ripening in strength. I've helped to keep any missteps out of the public eye for decades, you see. Keeping all our gifts secret and safe."

My breathing stills. Not just in our country. He's been covering up gifts *worldwide*. For decades. How deep does his influence run?

"Taking down my enterprise puts people like your Guild members at risk of exposure. I can't tell you how many slip-ups there are that almost make the news. The number of people we've had to pay off or color them as conspiracy theorists. I have an entire sub-division dedicated to this most important of tasks."

"Are you expecting a thank you?"

"Oh, no, of course not. It's my honor to look after our kind. And while I do dabble in experimentation, it's for the greater good of the gifted population. The more we know about it, the better we'll be."

Kellan huffs where he's leaning in to listen, circling his finger at his ear to silently call him crazy.

Charles continues, "I think, if you'd be agreeable, we could come to a compromise that may work out for the both of us. You and your friends have killed upwards of a hundred of my people, by my count."

"What's your point?"

"I'm owed those lives, Mr. Guild Master. And, according to your Guild records, your onsite membership closely matches that number."

I clench my teeth, anger spewing through my veins at the threat. And confirmation that Vera copied data from our servers during the last attack.

"I suggest a merger. You keep your Guild name and status but work under me. Under Gifted Enterprise. We'll supply you the jobs, the funds, and I'll buy out your Tower to eliminate the lease."

Kellan glares daggers at my phone, looking a second away from trying to reach through the phone to murder Charles. I take a step back before he loses his head.

"What about Dane?"

As expected, Kell's neck nearly snaps when he turns on me. It's impulsive anger clouding his judgment. Charles is feeling me out; there's no reason I can't do the same to him to understand his intention and goals.

"Dane will be handed over to me. He's unfortunately non-negotiable. But one life for the almost two hundred gifted you're currently harboring is a small sacrifice. And being a true leader is nothing if not sacrifice, as I'm sure you well know."

"And Raegan?"

Kellan snarls and seizes my shirt in his fist. I shoot him a look to calm the fuck down.

Charles is quiet on the other end for a minute before he finally responds, "I'll leave her up to you."

"Meaning what?"

"Either you keep her contained and controlled yourself—no efforts to attack myself or any aspect of Gifted Enterprise again—or else I'll be forced to kill her. I don't care how you do it. I'll even offer you a gift-blocking collar or cuff if you desire. So long as I hear no sight nor sound of her, she may live and stay with you."

Deep, calm breath. Don't overreact.

"And if I refuse?" I manage slowly and with every ounce of fortitude I possess.

"Then I'll destroy you and your Guild. Every skeleton, every missed penny...I'll find them all and leave you barren. Your members will be tossed to the streets, ripe for the picking."

Considering the resources I now know are at his disposal, it's no idle threat.

"Is that the end of your offer?"

"It is."

"Good," I purr. "Here's my counteroffer. You can save us all the time and effort by taking your own life while you're ahead now by your own preference, or you can live now knowing that we're coming for you. Your days are numbered, Charles, and I'll take immense pleasure in tearing you apart piece by piece before Raegan finishes you off."

He chuckles. "Very well. I think I'm going to enjoy this game. We'll see which straw makes you break, Guild Master. And then I'll take your life as you've promised to take mine, and you can die knowing that your precious Guild members will belong to me."

Chapter Twenty-Five

RAEGAN

"This is madness. He's going to know." Harvey paces the floor of the office he'd previously been detained in. The bars are gone, now that he's been moved to a locked-down apartment, and there's room for us to spread out. He tugs at his shirt, fanning himself as he mutters an endless stream of negativity. "He's going to look at me, and he'll know. He knows everything. He'll kill me, just like he did Wyra. I'm too young to die. I can't do this—"

"He needs to calm the fuck down or *I'll* kill him," Dane grumbles as he clicks and taps on his laptop at the desk still pushed in the corner.

"Hey," Reid interrupts Harvey. I'm not expecting Reid to slap him across the face. It happens so fast and unexpectedly that the room falls silent to watch on in surprise. "Get your act together. I'm not going anywhere with you if you've already given up."

Kellan snickers where he's leaning against the wall while Jack smirks next to him. I've paused my internet search on the laptop next to Dane to watch.

Harvey gapes at him, his hand pressed to his cheek before he seeks out Aiden.

"He has a point, Harvey," Aiden says before he can ask for sympathy. "There's no use continuing with this plan if you can't control your emotions." He strides closer, crossing his arms. "Do we need to go over what you're going to say again? How you convinced us that you were meeting with Claudia and were only a terrified witness. And that you heard us searching for someone with immortality to hide from him."

He nods, swallowing. "Yeah, I remember."

"Good." Aiden looks between him and Reid. "You'll have Reid with you to teleport back if anything goes wrong and we'll be listening through his earpiece. Just make sure he stays invisible, or else Charles will know you betrayed him."

Harvey shoots a sharp look at Reid. "Whatever you do, don't let go of my shoulder."

Reid stares at him, deadpan, not bothering to reply.

That's probably for the best.

Aiden sighs, checking the time on his phone and then running his gaze over Harvey. "Are you ready? Take a couple of deep breaths—no, don't make yourself hyperventilate. Slow, long breath—yes, like that."

Dane grimaces and rubs a hand down his face. "He's fucked," he whispers to me.

Harvey turns to look at us, but it doesn't seem like he heard what Dane said, thank fuck. I offer him an encouraging smile, then elbow Dane hard when he turns away.

Reid also looks unimpressed by Harvey even after he appears calmer and more put together. It'll have to do because the timer goes off on Aiden's phone. Reid gazes around the room, his blue eyes falling on me last. He places his hand on Harvey's shoulder and tilts his head forward. "I'll be back," he promises, and I wonder if he forgot to say 'we' or if that was on purpose.

They disappear before Harvey gets a chance to say goodbye.

Dane turns the comms on through a speaker on his desk. "I've got it on mute so we can make noise." On his laptop, he pulls up the tracker locked on Reid's phone so we can follow them wherever they go.

Harvey curses through the speaker. "Does your gift suck for you, too, or just everyone else?"

"Stop leaning on me and stand up straight," Reid replies.

"I'm just saying what everyone else thinks."

There's shuffling, then Reid reports to us, "Found the portal. I'm going quiet."

Aiden unmutes us. "If you think Charles is on to you, get out of there and we'll figure something else out."

"Thanks, Master," Harvey sniffles, and Dane rolls his eyes, re-muting our side.

"At this rate, I'm not sure they'll even make it in his office before Harvey fucks up," Dane mutters, his eyes locking onto his screen. "They're gone."

There's a three-second pause where I panic that we've somehow lost them before they reappear in the middle of the country. Dane zooms in on the building with their pin on it, grabbing the coordinates and then plugging them into a web search.

Aiden leans forward, eyes narrowing. "A shared office building...can you pull up its tenants?"

Dane clicks a few times, revealing a shortlist of company names. "Unless they're operating under a private lab, tutoring, or dentist office, none of these are GE."

"Uh...hi," Harvey greets someone, and our attention turns to the speaker.

"Hello. Do you have an appointment with someone?" a female responds.

"Yeah. I'm meeting Charles."

Distant keyboard taps fill the silence. "Harvey?"

"That's me."

"Wonderful. Please put your cell phone and anything in your pockets in this basket."

"Even gum?" he nervously jokes.

"Anything in your pockets," she repeats.

"Oh. Okay."

There's a brief pause, then, "Thank you. Have a seat and I'll let him know you're here."

"Uh, thanks."

Aiden points to Dane's screen. "Check public records for all active lease agreements at that address with a start date in the last ninety days. If there's nothing that new, we'll check in the last year."

Dane's fingers fly across the keys, pulling up window after window and performing whatever steps are needed to get the information Aiden wants. I watch, fascinated, though I should be continuing my notes on one of the board members Reid gave us.

The search pulls up no files in either date range.

"Keep going until something pops up," Aiden directs.

"The dentist office signed their lease almost eighteen months ago," Dane says once something comes back.

Aiden shakes his head. "That's not right. Are we sure they're in this building?"

Dane toggles to the tracker. "Unless they're in the hair salon next door, that's it."

"Check the owner of the building."

That search sends us down a forty-minute rabbit hole of investment firms owned by various capital management companies with no clear link to Gifted Enterprise. Dane now has a list of companies to dig into deeper to see which one, if any, is them.

"Bathroom," Reid whispers.

"Uh, excuse me," Harvey says.

"Yes?" The receptionist.

"Where's your bathroom?"

"Of course. Go down that hallway and take a left. It'll be the first door on your right."

"Thank you."

A few moments later, a door closes. "You've gotta hold it," Harvey snaps. "If someone comes in here, they'll see you. And I'm not letting you touch me while you're pissing."

"Calm down. He's making you wait on purpose to freak you out, and it's clearly working. I want to see what he's up to. Make yourself invisible too, and we'll sneak into his office."

"What?!"

"Shh!" Reid hisses. "Turn invisible, be quiet, and just stick with me. We won't be long."

"Master, tell him this isn't a good—mmf!"

"Your Guild Master isn't here right now, I am. Do it. Now."

Harvey whimpers.

I look at Aiden. He's focused intently on the speaker but doesn't intervene.

There's a muted scuffle followed by a light thump. Quiet. And then, Charles's voice.

I hold my breath at the sound of him, remembering how easily he'd beaten Dane and me down. If they're caught by him...

Be careful, Reid.

"—looking at them now. Most of them are acceptable, however a few are still too bulky to be considered jewelry." Pause. "I didn't ask how difficult it was to refine them. I've promised the buyers they'd look like any other accessory, and that's what we'll deliver. If I can tell the difference between them, then you've failed." Pause. "Good. Now, where are we at with the other thing? Yes, that." A long pause. "What do you mean, she's not there? Where is she?" Pause. "I'll handle it. Just be ready for her arrival. We'll be able to move on to our next phase if she's successful, so prioritize it. And Wes? If Vera disappears like that again, I want to know immediately, understood?"

My gaze flicks to Dane in time to see his eyes widen a fraction with the same surprise that's nipping at my insides for answers.

I stare harder at the speaker, waiting with bated breath for anything more, but when Charles speaks again, it's another call. "Good afternoon, Royce. Is everything well?" Pause. "Wonderful. Where are you now and I'll come have a look for myself." Pause. "Which beach house? Give me the address." Pause. "I'll be there after my next meeting. Is Vera with you?" Pause. "As much as I appreciate her wanting to assist with the little speed bitch's programming, tell her to return to the lab and get back to work. She can torture that girl after she's finished with my project."

Fuck. Tinsley.

He continues, "I'll see you soon."

Shit. Get out of there.

There's a short beep, and his voice sounds further away this time. "Lillian, please send in Harvey."

Soft shuffling noises fill the speaker, then finally the receptionist's voice. "Oh, there you are. He's ready for you, if you'll follow me."

"Oh. Yeah, sure."

"Harvey," Charles greets. "Have a seat, please, and let's hear about this vital information you have."

"Hi. I overheard Aiden and Cibrina talking about a search for a certain gifted person. He's having one of his teams start scouring the internet and putting the word out across the country to try and find them."

"And?"

"It's someone with the gift of immortality. One of their newer members mentioned meeting someone who'd claimed to have it."

There's a brief pause before Charles asks expectantly, "And?"

Fuck. Now *I'm* sweating for Harvey. I grip my hands in my lap to hide my sudden stress. Dane notices and slips his hand over mine, offering a gentle squeeze. "He'll be okay," he whispers.

Aiden's watching the speaker with a stern expression, and even Kellan and Jack have moved closer as we all zero in on the conversation happening hundreds of miles away.

"And…uh…Reid…he said you might be into that—*want* that, I mean. So, I wanted to report it to you in case he was telling the truth."

Charles chuckles. "He said that, did he? And I'm to believe that you're invited to these meetings after betraying them?"

"Oh. No, no. They don't invite me. I'm still spying on them using my gift…like you asked me to. And they think I was just a witness to what happened with Claudia. I told them we'd been seeing each other in secret, and we both got attacked but she protected me. Kellan showed up right after it happened and I was still in shock."

"Interesting you say that, considering the information from within the Guild has been lacking."

"I didn't think it was a good idea to text you while you were there in case they saw it. The immortal is the first big news I have to share since you left. And I told you about the others from that fight club who joined, too," he presses, a hint of desperation coloring his tone.

There's a long pause before Charles speaks again. "I see."

I squeeze Dane's hand and hold my breath, my eyes glued to the speaker.

"I have to say, Harvey, I'm impressed," Charles finally responds, and my breath expels in a whoosh. "I thought your cover had been blown, and they'd have locked you up. But not only were you able to convince them of your innocence, you've continued to gather valuable information from them in a time of particular importance."

Harvey's voice is paper thin. "Thank you, sir."

"I'll keep you at the Guild for the next couple of months. They won't be around much longer than that anyway, but you can keep me informed of any major developments with that immortal or any planned attacks on us until then."

"Yes, sir."

"Good work. Your siblings would be proud."

"Can I...see them?"

"They're all on assignment still, like you. Your mother is due with another in three months. If you help me with the Guild, then you'll be back home in time for their birth. I'll give you a few months break to be with them before your next assignment. Now, hurry back."

"Yes, sir." A door opens and closes.

Dane releases a loud sigh. "That nervous fucker made it."

"For now," Aiden remarks. "But it sounds like Charles is working on something big that we need to know about as soon as possible."

"He was talking about the cuffs and collars at first, right?" I chime in. "Reid said he's been making a ton of those, and now it sounds like he's trying to make them look pretty for people."

"If they're just being used on secluded islands or in secret labs, why would they need to look fancy?" Kellan drawls.

Aiden's expression is grave. "We'll know that answer when we find out who he's selling them to, as well as how widespread this is. My concern is his end goal with this. Is it for money, or an attempt to find and control every gifted person?"

There'd be no need for brainwashing and training, then. Or maybe this is the alternative for the ones who are strong enough to fight it.

A thud hits the middle of the office. Reid surveys the room, his brow furrowed and lips pressed in a flat line. Once he finds Dane, he strides over quickly, leaving Harvey groaning on the floor.

His hands slap on the desk. "I need you to pull up an address," he demands sharply. "382 Wisteria Circle."

Dane frowns at the command, but a nod from Aiden makes him complete the request in seconds.

"Is this Royce's beach house?" Aiden asks as the screen zooms over a beachfront property in a cape.

"You could have ruined everything!" Harvey cries, rising to his feet. He stumbles over to Reid, grabbing his shoulder and yanking him to look at him. "Are you insane?! The whole mission...just..." He makes an exploding sound and motion with his hands, then jabs Reid in the chest with his finger. "That was *my* life on the line!"

"Shut it," Reid snaps, shoving away from him to move around the desk. Kellan shifts back, giving him room to look at the screen. "You heard him, right? Tinsley's there."

"And Royce," Dane adds.

"And Charles," Aiden tacks on the heaviest reminder. He was heading there immediately after his meeting with Harvey.

"Then we go tonight," Reid counters, determined.

"Are you ignoring me after what I did for you?!" Harvey sputters. "What if he'd heard us?" He sniffs his armpit, and I crinkle my nose with disgust. "Or *smelled* us?"

"From the sound of your meeting with him, he didn't. Or do you have a reason to suspect otherwise?" Aiden inquires smoothly.

Harvey falters. "Well...no...but that doesn't mean he didn't."

Reid only has eyes for Aiden, though. "Are we going or not?" His tattooed arms pulse with tension. "I've never asked for anything since joining you and your Guild. I've done everything you've asked of me. But this...he said she was being *tortured*. What if they found out what she was up to? I'll go alone if I fucking have to, but there's a better chance of getting her back if I have your help."

Aiden's brows pinch, considering. I'm sure he hates the idea of acting so quickly without time to plan and prepare.

"It's a chance to take care of Royce at the same time," Kellan offers. "Get rid of someone off our girl's kill list. You said we'd handle them as we gathered information. Now we know where he is."

I chew my lip in thought, remembering what Reid told us about GE locations. "If they're always moving, we should get him now while we know where he is. We got lucky finding out about this place, but we might not be if he moves again and we have to start over. He would never expect us showing up now. It would be a surprise attack."

Aiden rubs his hand over the short bristles along his jaw. "We'll go tonight. Just us, so we can sneak in to assess the situation, fight Royce, and rescue Tinsley and hopefully the other Guild members if they're there. Cibrina and the others will keep a close eye on the Tower while we're gone." His finger traces a hard line between greenery and beach on the screen. "If this is a cliff, as I suspect, Reid will bring us to the beach below. Then he and Jack will scope out the house to make sure we're not rushing into an ambush. If it's just Royce, they can bring us in and we'll attack while his guard is down."

Harvey clears his throat. "When you said 'just us'..."

"Yes. You're coming as well," Aiden answers.

His face falls, and Kellan claps him on the back, his grin savage. "What good's a stealth mission without our invisible friend?"

Chapter Twenty-Six

RAEGAN

My boots crunch into the sand, the sound echoed by the others as we land on the beach at the bottom of the cliff. The night is eerily quiet, save for the soft crash of waves and the distant, muted roar of water. I scan the beach for the source of the sound, but a low, heavy fog blankets the area, obscuring my view. A shiver runs through me as the cool, damp air clings to my hair and clothes.

"I can't see shit," Dane mutters.

At least I can see the others within a few feet of me, but I can't see the cliffside from here. The sea crawls up the sand, spreading wider and faster until it meets my boots, then recedes just as quickly. The cliff must be in the opposite direction, then.

"It's good cover," Aiden muses, drawing his whip sword free, the sharp diamonds still latched together so it's shaped like any other sword.

Jackson angles his head back as if his eyes can penetrate the fog to see the top of the cliff. "Mm...even better if it reaches up there."

I keep going through the thick vapor until I can make out a rock.

And dirt. A whole wall of it appears, striped stone that reaches high above me before disappearing again into the fog. I press my hand against it, then check either side of me for another way up. The moisture in the air has leeched into my clothes, sucking away any of my warmth and making me shiver again.

Aiden plants himself behind me, so close I can feel the heat from his body teasing against my back, almost beckoning me to lean into him. "This cliff runs for over a mile down the coast. There's no way up...short of rock climbing or gifts."

On the flip side, that means no one should be able to come down here, either. We should be safe, hidden, and out of the way down here while the others do their recon above.

"You're up." Kellan's voice carries from further back on the beach.

"Wait. You want me to use my gift on *both* of them? And me?" Harvey whispers harshly. "I can only do one person after me. One!"

Aiden and I pivot to watch. The others must have followed us up the beach because I can see everyone a couple yards away.

"Well, time to figure out two," Dane snarks, his hood up and arms crossed like he's trying to keep out the chill in the air. "We're not waiting down here all night for you to find your courage."

"I'm a spyyy!" Harvey hisses, dragging the word out. "Spies don't need courage! We hide, we watch, we report back."

Dane grabs him by the collar of his shirt, yanking him close. "Then turn the other two invisible and go spy. But if I find out you abandon them for any reason or your gift fails us, I'll beat the shit out of you." He roughly tosses him back, and Kellan chuckles.

"Not a fan of the cold, Rapunzel?" he teases.

"Who the fuck is?" he snaps, his arms folding against himself again. "The sooner we get this over with, the better."

Harvey grasps for Reid and Jack, but my shadow shifts out of reach.

"I'll handle myself," he says coolly.

I close the distance between us. "Jack..."

He smiles at me, his icy fingers curling my hair behind my ear. "I don't need his gift to be invisible," he reminds me. I wonder if it's a lack of trust that Harvey can do it or that having the three of them stick together so close has him rejecting that plan.

Jackson faces Reid. "I'll stay on overwatch outside. Keep lookout."

Reid nods his agreement, then holds his elbow out to Harvey. "Do it."

Harvey grips Reid's upper arm, and an invisible curtain sinks over them. Kellan kicks sand where they'd been standing, and it falls back to the ground. They're gone.

Jackson strides to the cliff, eyeing it for a second before he leaps upward, his gift propelling him higher. His boot lands on a jutted-out rock, and then he jumps again, disappearing into the fog.

Once he's gone, Dane scoffs. "I wouldn't trust Harvey to keep me out of sight, either."

"He'll be fine," Aiden remarks, unbothered by any of it. I start walking along the cliffside, heading in the direction of the running water to see what it is. "His first instinct is always to hide, so I don't see his gift failing. I'm more worried about Reid leaving him behind at the first sign of Tinsley."

"Where are you off to, beautiful?" Kellan drawls, his long legs catching up to me even at a mild pace.

"Looking for the sound of rushing water."

I stop abruptly when I see it. A tall, narrow waterfall tumbles from the edge of the cliff, the fog opening around it so I can see all the way to the top. Trees of luscious green line the edge of the cliff, while moss and small bushes creep along the underside where it bumps out.

Following the water down, my eyes catch on something dark behind it. A cave?

Kellan presses his hand against my chest from over my shoulder, stopping me and pulling me against him when he sees I'm headed toward it. "Wait."

"What is it?" Aiden asks, him and Dane still catching up.

"Caves," Kellan replies, and I blink, dragging my gaze beyond the cave that captured my attention and finding a slew of others carved at the base of the cliff. Some are so narrow I can't tell if a body could even fit through them, whereas others are wide enough for two people to walk side by side.

Dane stops next to us, then looks at me. "You weren't about to walk into one of those alone, were you?"

I shrug. "I was just going to take a peek."

"What if GE uses those for something?" He shivers against the cold, tightening his arms.

"For what? Storage?" I counter. "It's all the way down here, exposed to the outdoors. I doubt they'd bother putting things in there.

And if they do, then better for us to take a look and find out, right?" Turning my head to Aiden, I send him a questioning look at what he thinks.

He rubs his jaw, his gaze focused on the caves. "There's a slim possibility that Guild members or others could be there as well. It's worth a look."

Dane's face tightens when he loses the discussion, but he doesn't argue. We all move to the closest cave, walking along the dip and curve of the cliff as the beach carves in, shrinking the closer we get to the caves.

Aiden pulls his phone out and turns the flashlight on, casting the light over the entrance. There's nothing but rocky sand, wet stone, a few crabs, and sea plants, as if the cave is partially filled with seawater at times. The light barely touches the shadows within, giving us only a couple yards of visibility before it's swallowed up.

"Kell, keep an eye out. We'll see if there's anything further in," Aiden directs, leading the way.

Dane lifts his hand, the soft white glow of his gift adding another source of light, then offers me the other one. "Hold my hand and stay close."

I huff, shaking my head even though a tiny smile tugs at my lips, and I take it. "I can't go far in a cave."

He smirks back. "Humor me, then."

We follow Aiden inside, careful with our steps around the slippery rock and fauna. The sound of waves is somehow louder in here, like an echo chamber of the ocean and dripping water. Its dull roar fills my head, making it difficult to listen for anything else that could be inside.

Darkness closes in at our backs once we're deep enough in, and I squeeze Dane's hand tighter. I may not be able to go far, but I'm still not a fan of pitch black. The two lights are small but bright enough to illuminate the immediate vicinity around us. It's enough to keep my demons at bay, to hold them back at arms-length even as they scrape and claw at my mind, fighting for a way in. Solitary. The water tank. That voice...

"If you need to leave, we will," Dane whispers. "But I'm right here, and I won't let go."

I nod, shifting so my whole arm is pressed to his as I breathe in slowly. He knew. He remembered what the dark does to me, and that's why he'd told me to stay close. I thought I'd grown enough in the last few weeks that I'd be better, but I guess there's no rushing it.

A foul smell slips through the salty air, making my nose scrunch. It comes and goes, sometimes smacking me in the face and then disappearing seconds later so my lungs are filled only with salt and brine.

Something shifts beneath my foot, my boot sliding over the ground until it catches a rock, and I fall forward. Dane bands an arm over my chest, and another hand—Aiden's—grasps my arm before I land face-first. "Shit," I curse under my breath, my heart ricocheting in my chest. They help me upright, and I glare over my shoulder at whatever made me lose my balance.

"I see something," Aiden murmurs, his voice distant as if he's continued ahead while I'm squinting in the light at the odd little thing on the ground. It's a few inches long and narrow from where I can see some of it sticking out beneath a rock. I squat down to get a closer look, but something about it is making me question what I'm seeing.

Is it the color? Or maybe the texture...

I'm sure it's just an odd sea plant, something that got swept in with the tide. When I pinch it between my fingers, I suppress the shudder of disgust at the squishy feel of it while raising it before me. The light from Dane's gift shifts away before I can really see it.

"Aiden, wait," he calls out. Dane tugs on my hand, encouraging me to stand. "Come on. He's gone too far ahead without us."

I let him pull me up, jogging a bit to catch up with Aiden, who throws his arm out to stop us when we get there.

"What—"

"Shh," Aiden demands, short and sharp to stop Dane. The flashlight sweeps over a massive pile of...bodies.

Oh.

Fuck.

I look at the thing still in my hand, using Dane's glow to see it clearly.

A finger.

I'm holding a fucking finger.

I drop it in a rush, cursing and scraping my hand down my pants as if I can wipe it clean.

The stench of death is unmistakable now, even as the smell of the ocean tries to overpower it. I cover my mouth with the back of my hand as my stomach rolls, bile burning my throat and nose.

"Fucking hell," Dane growls, stepping back and bringing me with him. "Have we seen enough?"

"—here!" Kell's deep voice echoes through the cave. "—up! Up! Up!" His voice bounces back and forth, his last words eclipsing the first part of whatever he's saying.

Aiden swings around. "Go!"

We turn, but movement behind Aiden makes me stumble. Dane tugs my arm, but I don't stop looking past Aiden. I don't let my eyes leave that one spot I *swear* I saw something move. Something among the dead.

Aiden follows my gaze. "What?"

"I..." Shit. Am I imagining things because I know Royce is nearby? Are my eyes just playing tricks on me? Fooling with me in the dim lighting while my heart gallops in my chest? "I thought I saw—" There! A twitch. The smallest jerk of a hand. My breathing stills. The hand slowly flexes, and then another begins to move. And another. "Aiden..." I gasp on an exhale, but his eyes are trained on the pile like mine.

He swallows. "Run."

Dane and I move in unison, throwing ourselves toward the entrance while still holding on to the other. The wet stone works against us the faster we try to run, the uneven and rocky terrain tripping our feet and scraping our shoes. Groaning and pain-filled cries rise behind us, echoing deep in the belly of the cave and flooding my ears, sending a flash of fear through my veins.

A stupid rock hits the tip of my boot, its sharp point snagging me back as my knees crash down, scraping against the rough surface.

I snap my teeth together to restrain the cry of pain that tried to fly from my throat. Dane yanks me back to my feet and pulls me forward, the light from his fist more of a blinking guide as he swings it forward and back.

I think I hear Kellan's voice shouting to us, but the cacophony of death is so loud behind us, growing louder with every breath, that it feels like it might swallow us up before we make it back. I gag on the putrid smell that clings to us, adhering to the bits of water particles hanging in the air or on us. It's as if the stench sharpened with the zombies' awakening.

A shadow moves in front of us, and my lungs seize.

"Is that you?!" Kellan booms, and I expel my breath in a rush. The entrance. He grunts, and I realize the moaning isn't just behind us, but in front of us, too. Kell roars. Something cracks, *snaps*, and then thumps against the cave wall.

The fucking fog is thickening again, but he finally comes into view, a smattering of blood on his arms and face, and small patches of golden scales where something had broken skin. His chest heaves like he's been doing this for some time, but another figure lunges at his arm, teeth biting down hard and drawing blood. Kellan grabs them by the hair, fighting to get them off but their teeth are too deep, too locked down that they don't budge.

Metal whips out, the curving blade slicing the body in two. The lower half thuds on the ground, but the top half...

"That doesn't work," Kellan snarls.

"Then take it with us," Aiden orders, pushing Dane and me forward. "There's more coming from behind, and we're not getting trapped in here. Move to more open ground."

I rush forward, drawing my gift to my hand as I shout, "I got it!" I grab the zombie and thrust my gift into it. The rest of it crumples in, disintegrating from the inside before the remainder of it follows. It doesn't even scream or make a sound. It doesn't struggle or stop its mission of hurting Kellan like it feels nothing.

As soon as its jaw slackens, it drops.

And we run.

Kellan takes point, throwing his arms to bulldoze through as many of them as he can to make a path for the rest of us. There are so many...more than what we'd found in the cave behind us. Did they come from the other caves? We pass the waterfall, racing to the beach on the other side and finding a break from the zombies.

And also, a dead end.

The cliff curves sharply into the ocean, blocking us from going any further. Kellan splashes into the water, fighting the waves as he gets waist deep and then switches to swimming. I bend over to catch my breath, hands on my knees as the chilled air pinches and stabs at my lungs. The water laps over our feet as we watch Kell. Aiden continuously checks behind us for signs of the zombies. I can still hear them in the distance, the sound carrying on the breeze as a cold reminder of what's coming.

Kellan reaches the end of the cliff, a wave shoving him roughly against it and then dragging him under.

"Kell!" I shout, perched to bolt after him until Aiden grasps my upper arm.

"He's okay. Look."

His head breaches the water, and he gasps for air, the next wave already bringing him back to the cliff face. He slams against it again, but this time, he gets a firm grip.

"We've got company," Dane warns.

The zombies are filling the beach, an entire hoard of them eating up every inch of sand in a violent mass with a single goal clearly driving them: us.

The forward procession is blown back, knocking the ones behind them to the ground. Jackson lands halfway between us and them.

"Where are Reid and Harvey?" Aiden asks, flicking his wrist to release the diamond-shaped pieces of metal on his sword. They separate along a smooth curve of silver and curl at his feet.

Jack knocks his hood back. "Still at the house. I smelled them." He jerks his chin at the swarm, then cocks his head, regarding them as they struggle to get back on their feet. "Where did they come from?"

Aiden answers, "Caves along the cliff. Who knows how many were lying dormant there, but we haven't seen an end to them yet."

Kellan jogs from the water. "The cliff stays in the water as far as I can see in the goddamn fog." He takes a few gulping breaths. "There's no way out."

"Jack can fly us to the top of the cliff. Or get Reid to grab us," Dane says, but Jackson doesn't budge.

Aiden frowns, looking from Jack to the danger getting closer, even as slow as they move. "What are you thinking?"

He takes a step back and to the side. "We take them out now so we don't find them at our backs when we're fighting Royce. Maybe it'll weaken him. Have any of them used any gifts?"

"None of the ones I dealt with did," Kellan replies, and Jack nods. "But they don't feel pain. And they sure as hell take forever to stop moving, even in pieces."

Gross.

"There are dozens, maybe even hundreds of them, against five of us," Dane argues. "Gift or not, they could probably bury and suffocate us by numbers alone."

Jackson's dark gaze finds mine, his stare igniting a fire in my chest. He smirks knowingly, turning his back on the oncoming zombies to stand in front of me. "They're nothing compared to you, little one." He traces the curve of my face with his knuckles, then captures my chin. "They should be the ones afraid. Show them who you are."

I nod slowly, my eyes locked with his, the cruelty reflecting back at me. I know what he's asking me to do. It's what I've been building my stamina for. What I've been training for.

He shifts back, his head bowed, as he gives me room to walk forward. My gift easily fills my body the second I think of it, slipping through my veins like an injection of warmth. It helps with the cold, burning away the chill until I'm toasty in my skin. I walk past the others, adding more space between us until the hoard closes in on me.

"Stay back," I warn them, wanting to make sure there'll be no one between me and the zombies. Even if I've gotten better at controlling when my gift triggers or not while it's active, I don't feel like testing that now. I build my gift up, drawing more of its strength from my gut until I'm scorching with it, and then I slap my hands to the ground and send it outward.

My gift flies free, racing through the sand and rocks under the dead men, reaching farther and farther as I continue to feel them there, even around the corner where more are still coming from the caves. The beach trembles. Quakes.

"Rae! On your left!" Dane shouts at the same time as I unleash my gift.

Anyone standing above my gift crumbles to the ground.

An arm drops in front of me, but I keep going, feeding more into my gift as it eats away at what's left. This time, I notice the strain for what it is when it happens.

"That's enough," Aiden says, crouched beside me but careful not to touch me just in case.

I reel in what's left, panting for oxygen as the cool air soothes my skin.

The beach is littered with bones and human tissue. Nothing moves.

Even the fog has lifted, as if the radiating heat of my gift burned it off, leaving a clear, star-filled sky above us.

And an entire stretch of beach showing just how many I'd destroyed.

They were far easier to use my gift on than the GE agents at the Guild, likely because their bodies were already partially decayed. Thank fuck for that.

I stand slowly, wary of the effect using my gift so much might have on me, when invisible hooks snare my limbs, my hands, my body...

Locking me in place.

Chapter Twenty-Seven

Kellan

The ground rumbles beneath my feet, a tremor slithering through the earth as Raegan spreads her gift hundreds of feet in three directions. I bend my knees automatically to keep my balance as the next one rolls through. The horde of death doesn't seem to notice the trap being laid before them. They shuffle forward, jerking and stumbling erratically, like their bodies aren't quite right, making their movements stilted and awkward.

Aiden eyes the cliff, scanning the reddish cracks through the sand and where it meets the hard rock, while the other two are laser-focused on Raegan. Dane's hands fidget and clench at his sides, a look of concern pinching his face like he's worried for her. Jack, on the other hand, is staring obsessively at her, his dark blue gaze flicking to the impending damage and then back to her with a wild, bloodthirsty look in his eyes.

Dane yells suddenly, snapping my attention to the zombie that's now within reaching distance of her. I lunge forward, but I'm not close enough. She demanded we keep our distance, and we obeyed, but now I won't make it before that monster grabs her…

The guttural moans shudder, and then one thud hits the sand after another. The zombie about to reach her is already on the ground, its wretched body twitching even after its insides are gone. Are their souls still trapped there without the shell to hold them? Is it tied to their bones, or whatever pieces of them are left?

The sand itself dusts to finer particles that easily lift in the breeze, sweeping over the long stretch of collapsed bodies.

She did it.

Hundreds of them.

Hell knows how many exactly, but she took them all out.

Dane rushes to her after Aiden commands her to stop. They're all down enough that none of them can move from where they've fallen.

Raegan rises halfway and then hesitates.

"What's wrong?" Aiden asks, his hand going for her arm to help her.

Her hand glows red.

A gust of wind knocks him and Dane back. "Something's off." Jackson strolls up next to them, his head tilted as Raegan slowly turns to face us.

Her face is blank. Empty.

Cold fingers trail up my spine, my breath hitching.

That fucker didn't…

"Rae?" Dane gets back to his feet, holding his own glowing hand out to her. "Say something."

She smiles, but it doesn't reach her eyes. It's a mockery of the one she wears, hollow and cold. A crack at our feet gives me the split second notice that she's sending her gift through the ground, aimed at the other three standing together. I dive at her, snatching her off the ground to break that contact. I growl through the sharp pain that burns my chest and arms while adding distance between us and the others.

"Come on, beautiful. Fight him," I grit out through the pain.

She palms my face and mind-melting, white-hot boiling erupts beneath my skin. Roaring with the blinding pain, I drop her and cradle my face. It's like a wildfire in my head. I can't think. Can't see. Can't feel anything but the intense pain flooding my senses.

Sizzling, molten agony drives into my sides, bringing me to my knees.

Piece by piece, my head heals, even as my torso and organs are simultaneously being brought to ruin.

At last, I open my eyes. My vision is sharper. Clearer. The reeking, rancid scent of death permeates my nostrils, coating my throat and twisting my stomach. Which—I touch my side where it had hurt the worst and run my fingers across the golden scales. Healed. I don't even remember when the pain stopped. Or why she stopped.

Damn it, the others.

Standing, I break into a run when I see them. Jackson's hand is fisted and shaking while Dane runs at Raegan from behind. She swings at him, even as I'm sure Jack has her oxygen suspended, and it reminds me of how Royce's puppets never seemed fazed by pain. Aiden jumps between them, a metal shield covering his forearm that splinters and drops to the ground in pieces when her hand brushes against it.

Aiden takes those seconds to move Dane out of reach.

"Are you sure it's working?" Dane asks Jack, panting. He doesn't get a chance to answer before streaks of red spider through the sand at them. "Oh, fuck!" He and Aiden run, but her gift moves without hesitation.

I have no fucking clue if she can still get to them if I pick them up off the ground, but it's the only thing I can think of at the moment to get them out of harm's way. I scoop up Dane first, throwing him over my shoulder even as he curses me out. Worst case, I'll see if I can outrun it.

Her gift pinches my heel, and then I'm airborne.

I pitch backward midair, Dane's weight throwing me off, so I'm hanging awkwardly. Jackson's hand is splayed toward us, his chest working as he keeps us and himself aloft. The fist he'd been using on Raegan is loose. I'd bet he had to stop in order to save us. He flies to us, Raegan chasing after him.

"Let him go." He points to Dane, then the top of the cliff. "I'll bring them up there to find Reid. Keep her away from it until I get back."

So she doesn't bring the entire cliffside down with her gift.

Right.

"Activate the rest of my gift," I bark at Dane, annoyed that I haven't mastered that skill yet on my own.

He slaps his hand against my back, and the rest of my scales and protective skin fills in the areas she hasn't touched. I release him and Jack drops me on my feet.

Raegan slams into me without warning, her entire body alight and causing a cascade of buzzing pins against my protected skin and scales. I lean into her heat, grabbing her arms and holding her tight. What scraps remained of my clothes are gone, hardly having made it through our first encounter and certainly not surviving the second.

"I've got you, beautiful," I tell her, my deep timbre strained as she struggles against me. "So give me all of it. Because I'm not letting you go. Not for a fucking second."

I crush her lips to mine, hoping…praying she's somewhere in there still and can break free. If I can somehow reach her…if I can make her *feel* something…

The kiss is like lava being poured down my lungs and burning through to my gut. I've never felt more human, more in pain, and more afraid than I do now. I need to get her back. It's the only thing that matters to me now.

Not my flesh and not the world around me.

Just her.

My tongue is a slash of heat against hers, challenging her, pushing her. I press her closer, holding the back of her head and spearing her with my mouth as my other hand grips her ass and grinds her against me. She doesn't stop moving, doesn't stop seeking an exposed or untouched bit of skin that she can attack.

I lift her legs around my waist, and she makes a choking noise that sends my heart plummeting. When I tear away from the kiss, there's a knife burrowed in her back. The reddish glow of her gift is gone, and she doesn't activate it to remove the knife either.

She stares at me, unaffected, as she reaches back for the hilt and yanks it free, then stabs at my throat. I catch her wrist, and something warm slides over my hand.

No.

Blood runs down the blade to my hand. Her blood. I chuck the knife away and sink to my knees, holding her struggling frame firmly to my chest as I check the wound.

A dozen knives fly at her, and a tidal wave of fury rises in my chest. I swipe them aside, my reflexes and speed hitting them one after another with a vicious snarl ripping from my throat before I find her attacker.

Jackson pulls three more blades from his hoodie, flinging them at her with the same apathetic expression on his face.

Rage swallows me whole, pulsing through my veins so viciously that my body aches with the need to *move*. To fight and wreak havoc on Royce and the threat to my family. First, Raegan is forced to attack and hurt us. Now, Jack is being forced after Raegan.

Cruel.

Filthy.

Coward.

For being too afraid to fight us himself. For trying to use us against each other.

I flip us around, shielding Raegan on the ground before the knives strike. The metal sings against scales. I whip my head around, baring my teeth in a snarl at him. Shoving off the ground, I race toward him while he tries reaching for more. I grab him by the throat, every fiber of my being *screaming* to punish him. For being a threat to her. For *hurting* her.

I throw him at the cliff wall, anger clogging my lungs until it's all I can breathe. All I can feel.

His gift cushions him before he hits, but I'm already there, my hand catching the side of his face and slamming him into the rock. Sanity checks my strength at the last second, pulling back so he doesn't end up with an injury too severe. Jackson crumples to the ground. My chest heaves, expelling some of the blind fury as I panic that I didn't restrain myself enough. I find his pulse with two fingers, and relief pushes the rest of the anger from my bones, filling in with exhaustion instead.

When I look back to where I left Raegan, she's gone.

I frantically search the beach. My heart stops when I find her. I run. As fast as I fucking can.

"NO!!!" I bellow, fear spiking my heart into a frenzy as she points the knife at herself and draws it back.

With all the strength in my legs, I leap the final distance between us, catching her arm and bringing her down with me. The knife snaps between my hardened chest and the ground.

Raegan tugs on her arm that's pinned beneath me, her hand still wrapped around the handle. I grab her wrist, then the broken blade, and throw it into the ocean.

I collapse on top of her, holding her down while I fight for air. She wriggles and pushes at me, but it's useless. She's not going anywhere.

A loud *pop*, like a heavy stone snapping in two, has my eyes flying open. Raegan's gift spreads through the ground under her. Under us.

"Rae!" Dane shouts. "Is she back yet?"

There's the sound of a struggle, and I glance over my shoulder. Dane's wrapped around Aiden's back, his gift glowing, while Reid looks between us and Jackson—who's already standing and stalking toward us.

"No. And he's got Jack, too."

"There's no time to waste," Reid says. "We have to get out of here before he controls any more of us. And once we're far enough, they'll be free of him. Get them both and get to me."

I growl in annoyance. "I hope you can teleport before they both try to kill you."

"I'm already ready. Just get close enough that I can grab you, and we'll be gone."

He fucking better be.

I heave Raegan up with me, wrapping an arm around her backside over my shoulder. Jackson jumps into the air, but I snatch the heel of his boot before he can get far and bee-line it to Reid. Aiden's still fighting to get Dane off, but Reid has Aiden's jacket clenched in his hand while his other is out waiting for me. I rush into it. The second my arm touches his hand, we're gone.

Metal crunches, the side of the infirmary bed hitting my knees and ramming into the next two beds in a harsh screech. Jackson crashes between two beds, splitting them apart and dropping to the floor. Raegan's cry of pain pierces the noise, my heart lodging in my throat as the world still spins around me, and I pitch forward. I catch myself on the nearest bed, my weight shoving it harder into the others until they're stopped by Jack's unmoving body.

"I've got you, beautiful," I rasp, struggling through the disorientation until I'm confident enough I can move without dropping her. I lay her on her front, and the world goes out of focus when I see the damage to her back. So much blood. So, so much. And I realize now I'm covered in it.

"Infirmary. Now." Aiden staggers to the foot of the bed, his free hand grasping it like he needs it to stay upright while he grunts into the phone.

Grabbing the sheet on the bed, I rip the bottom off and bunch it up, then press it against her wound. I tuck the hair out of her face behind her ear so I can see her. Her eyes are closed, her breathing still. So damn still. "Stay with me until Cassandra gets here," I tell her, my voice rough. "Let me know you can hear me."

A quiet, low groan barely escapes her lips. I hang my head, shuddering with relief.

"Is she okay?!" Dane scrambles toward us, trying to shift beds out of the way but unable to move them far enough for him to fit on the other side.

"Go check on Jack!" I bark before he causes him any more damage than I already have. He was moving before we left. That has to mean he's okay, right? Or was that only because he couldn't feel any pain?

Dane curses, searching the room for him and then pushing beds aside when he finds him. "What happened to his face?"

I grind my teeth. "Me."

Aiden moves beside me. "I'll hold that. Get Jack in one of the beds." His hand joins mine on the red sheet that was once white.

I almost argue for him to do it, but when I look at him, his face is bleached of color. Aiden's lips are pressed to a thin line, his brow furrowed as if it's taking all of his concentration and focus to stay upright and hold the sheet. An aftereffect of Royce?

Removing my hand, I knock the bed behind me back and stalk around Aiden to get to Jackson. I'm careful when I scoop him up, offering up an internal apology for what I had to do. I don't regret it. I'd do it again in a heartbeat if he threatened Raegan. I doubt he'd criticize me for it. In fact, I'm damn sure he'll be glad I stopped him before he could have done worse. He'll already be beating himself up over attacking her—and injuring her—after he wakes up.

Once he's on the bed, I see the full extent of the damage I'd inflicted when I crushed him into the cliff. That one side of his face is swollen like a balloon. Blues, blacks, and purples mottle the swelling, followed by cuts here or there and one big bleeding scrape. His eye is hidden behind the swelling, and his nose is crooked, fresh blood still draining from it.

I tear a strip of fabric from his bed and hold it to his nose. "Dane, take this." I check on Aiden, and he doesn't look good. "Aiden, sit or lie down." Dane takes my place at Jackson's side and I grab the sheet from Aiden, nudging him to the bed next to us.

Dane's worried gaze is pinned on Raegan. "How bad is it?"

"I don't know," I growl, frustrated that Cassandra isn't here yet. How much blood had she lost between when she was stabbed and now? She hadn't stayed still after it happened, making it worse.

Reid reappears with Cassandra, I guess having picked her up from her apartment upstairs, and for the first time I notice Harvey sitting on the floor holding his head. I completely forgot about him in the rush to leave, but I'm glad he's here, so we don't have to go back for him.

Cassandra trips on her way to Raegan's side, her eyes wide as they rove over me from top to bottom, then freeze between my legs.

Snarling viciously, I shout, "Heal her!" I don't give a shit that I'm butt-ass naked. Raegan doesn't have time for her to stop and stare.

She coughs and runs over, snapping back without looking at me, "Then give me some room."

Once Cassandra's hands are on her, I move back and to the side. Something soft hits me in the face. Growling, I find Dane glaring back at me. "Put it on."

I hold the thing up, but the hospital gown is tiny compared to me. "This isn't going to fit me."

"Then at least use it to cover your dick! As usual."

I don't have the capacity to joke or make fun of him at the moment as I normally would, so I tie it around my waist as best I can without a word and get back to watching Cassandra healing my girl.

She must have used the sheet to wipe away the blood enough that I can see the wound and watch it slowly shrinking in size. Tension sucks from my muscles like a riptide, leaving me drained and unbalanced. I lean into the bed Aiden's seated on and watch the scales of gold fade to my natural, golden-brown skin tone.

A bang snatches my attention to the other side of the room, where Reid's fist shakes against the cracked drywall. "She was there!" he grits out lowly, sounding more like he's saying it to himself than the rest of the room. "She was right there, and I couldn't do it."

Aiden rubs his face, trying to wipe away whatever he's still caught up in. "You saw her?"

"No, but..." He lifts a hair tie with two green leaf charms attached. "I found this."

Folding my arms, I quirk a single brow. "You're going to need to be a helluva lot clearer than that."

"It's hers."

With an exhausted huff, I counter, "Or any other girl's."

"No. This is hers."

Aiden chimes back in. "Even if that's true, that doesn't mean she's still there. If she had been. Who else did you see inside? Where was Royce?"

Reid's face tightens. "I didn't see him. But I did see Holt and Bea."

"Bea?" I ask.

"She's the one who can create portals. There were a few other agents inside but I didn't recognize them. They're the reason we couldn't check the basement or upstairs. We got stuck in the living room until Harvey saw Aiden and Dane fighting outside."

Harvey clears his throat, standing and brushing something from his clothes. "First of all, you're welcome for noticing you before the house full of GE personnel did. That could have been a cluster. And secondly—" Harvey pauses, sweeping the room to look at each of us in turn. "You knew I was invisible and with Reid when we left, right? You didn't all forget about me?"

"Excuse me," Cassandra mutters, trying to squeeze between me and Raegan's bed without touching me to get to Jack. I shift back, and she quickly makes it to him, freeing Dane to check on Raegan.

"She's okay?" he asks her.

Cassandra nods slowly, her hands cupping Jackson's face. "It was a nasty wound, but it's healed now. It was close, though. She almost didn't have enough strength." Her eyes close, signaling she's working through Jack's injuries and needs to focus.

I hadn't even considered that possibility. What if she'd overexerted herself with her gift taking down the zombies and didn't have the physical strength for her body to heal?

"I'm going to assume the answer to that is, yes, you knew I was staying invisible out of fear of being seen by Royce and ruining all our plans and that you do still care about me," Harvey cuts in.

Aiden sighs, long and hard. "Yes, Harvey. We do still care."

Maybe he does, but he was under Royce's influence. There's no way he noticed or cared if Harvey was there or would have said something if he wasn't.

It worked out that he was there, but I'm not gonna lie to the guy. All that mattered was freeing everyone from Royce, whether he was there or not.

"There." Cassandra straightens next to Jack, removing her hands as soon as she's finished, even though he's still unconscious. She frowns when she looks at Aiden. "You don't look well, Aiden. Let me take a look."

He doesn't immediately rebuke her offer, which speaks volumes to whatever's affecting him.

She puts a hand on his chest and another on his cheek, her face drawn with concentration and eyes shut. "Weird. I felt something like this on the other two as well."

"What is it?" Aiden inquires evenly.

Cassandra releases him, already finished. Color returns to his face, and he sits up taller. "It's hard to explain. Like something sticky." She shivers. "I didn't like the feel of it, but it's gone now."

"Thank you," he says, and she nods with a small smile.

"Is there anyone else before I get back to sleep?" She checks in with Dane, then Reid and Harvey, who each shake their heads. "Alright, well, goodnight, everyone."

We wave her off, waiting for her to leave before Aiden addresses the room. "The rest of us need to get some sleep. Reid...I'm sorry we weren't able to get to Tinsley. We'll need a better plan for Royce."

Reid nods solemnly, his lips tight. He grabs Harvey's arm. "I'll bring him back to his room." Harvey opens his mouth to speak, but Reid vanishes before we hear whatever he has to say.

Aiden stands, his fingertips brushing over the hole in Raegan's shirt where the injury had been. "Kell, grab Jack. I'll carry Raegan, and we can all sleep in the Loft."

"I'd put her with Jackson tonight. He'll sleep better and longer if she's there with him after what happened."

He doesn't look pleased about it, probably wanting her in his bed tonight, but if Jack remembers anything while he was under Royce's control, he's going to *need* that immediate comfort that she's alright.

Doesn't mean I can't join them, though.

Chapter Twenty-Eight

RAEGAN

"I don't know how you sleep with a footboard. Let me kick this annoying crap off, and you'll see how much more room you'll have," Kellan whispers, but it's so close that I'm instantly awake.

"No." Heated breath warms the top of my head as Jackson replies behind me.

My eyelids are heavy when I try to drag them open. I could probably sleep for several more hours, but the insistent need to pee is what forces me up. A golden brown and tattooed chest greets me when I finally manage to open my eyes. It shifts forward and back, the bed creaking beneath Kellan's weight as he tries to get comfortable with a frustrated growl.

His body is curved along the edge of the bed to fit lengthwise, one arm curled under his head and his other hand covering my bare thigh. Jackson is wrapped around me from behind, one leg tucked between mine and his arms holding me against his chest. I'm in only my bra and underwear.

"You woke her," Jack remarks softly. To anyone else, it might sound like a simple observation, but to me, I can feel the dark accusation in the coolness of his tone.

Kellan looks down, his roguish grin splitting his face when he sees me looking back. "Well, hello, beautiful," he drawls, blue-green eyes sparkling with mirth. His hand squeezes my thigh before his thumb lazily circles my skin, stirring heat at my core. "Sleep well?"

"Mm..." I hum, and I'm held so tightly to Jack that the vibrations in my chest echo in his. I turn my head as much as I can to see him, angling my body until I find he's just as undressed as Kellan is, wearing only boxer briefs. It's so rare to see him without clothes, to see the tattoos that are always hidden on his chest and arms.

I flick my eyes up to his, and my heart misses a beat.

Fuck, what did I miss?

I scramble to remember what happened before I fell asleep. What happened last that could have stirred his darkness, roused his anger to such a degree?

I remember going to rescue Tinsley. And then...and then...

Caves. Zombies.

Royce.

Whipping back to Kellan, I reach for his face as I recall what I'd done to it. All the pain I'd inflicted on him. "I'm so sorry."

He grabs my hand and kisses the palm. "You have nothing to be sorry for. It wasn't you." His gaze jumps over me to Jack. "Nothing you did under that dickhead's control is your fault." There's a long pause, like there's a silent battle of wills happening above me, before Kell continues. "I, on the other hand, can't claim that when I bashed Jack's head into the cliff."

A huff of air hits my hair. "I would've done the same."

Kell's grin sharpens. "I knew you wouldn't mind. Though I'm glad I didn't accidentally kill you. It was close."

Wait.

"What?!" I demand, yanking my hand from his to beat his chest. "What do you mean, it was close? Why would it ever be *close*?!"

Kellan has the humility to look embarrassed as he strokes his hand over his mouth and beard. "I almost lost it for a second. Thankfully, I caught myself in time when I remembered who I was attacking."

I jab him with a stiff finger in the kidney, then cringe when it hits nothing but pure muscle. "If I ever hear any of you getting *close* to killing one of us again, accident or not, I'll rip off your balls," I snarl at him, and the motherfucker laughs.

"I wouldn't expect anything less."

A knock rattles the door. "You guys up?" Dane calls behind it. "Food's almost ready. Come eat."

That simple reminder is all it takes for my body to reinforce everything it needs right now. Pee. Shower. Food.

As wonderful as it is being sandwiched between these two, and how much I'd like to start something else, those three necessities are calling my name more. I wiggle in Jackson's grip, and he easily frees me to slip from his arms and crawl off the side of the bed.

Kellan stands and stretches, groaning loud enough I'm sure the entire Loft can hear him. "Well, guess I'll go shower and then see what he cooked up." He rubs his hand over his stomach as he leaves the room.

I check in with Jack, whose eyes are latched on to mine as he sits upright. His sapphire stare drags down my body, setting my skin on fire beneath that look, even though I'm sure he's merely confirming I'm fully healed. I turn my back to him when he reaches my feet, still watching him over my shoulder as his gaze traces up my back, catching on the spot where he'd buried one of his knives.

I rub the spot to break his stare. "It's all healed, Jack. I promise." I move in front of him and capture his face in my hands. "It wasn't you. And I'm okay."

His hand hooks my nape, crushing our lips together in a torrent of need that I can feel all the way to my toes. His kiss is all-consuming. Deep. Demanding. And suddenly, I'm flipped back on the bed, Jackson's body covering mine as he pushes for more. Takes more. His hips pin me to the bed, the hardening length of his dick unmistakable. I wrap my legs around him automatically, my core grinding against him as I succumb to his unexpected avarice. To the obsession I can taste on his tongue, feel in the strength of his grip.

I want to give him everything and more. Remind him that I'm still here. Let him use my body until there's no doubt left in his mind that I'm here with him.

That's what I really, really want.

But my body has other priorities that break through the haze of lust, ringing like alarm bells.

I tear away from the kiss, gasping for air so I can tell him, but his lips move to my neck without stopping. Biting and sucking his way down and sending cascading waves of ecstasy rolling through me. I try to speak, but a wanton moan slips out instead when his teeth pinch the crook of my neck, his tongue licking away the small bite of pain. His mouth paints a trail of pleasure to the mound of one breast, his hand quickly freeing it over the cup of my bra. I slide my fingers through his raven-black hair—to stop him, of course—until he sucks my nipple into his hot mouth, lighting me on fire. I thrust my pelvis into him, gasping and tugging his head closer as desire ripples from my breast to pulse between my legs.

"Jack!" I pant, clawing at his hair to pull him away even as much as my body arches into him, seeking more. "I need...ahh!" His tongue swirls my nipple, then flicks it, and I can feel its pleasure echo in my cunt. The urgent need to pee threatens to break, and I hurriedly rush the words out. "Wait. Stop. I have to go!"

Jackson lifts his head, confusion bleeding into his expression, but it's enough space that I act, pushing and pulling myself free and then running to his ensuite bathroom, slamming the door behind me.

I'm part turned on, part horrified now, but he thankfully doesn't chase after me. Once I'm done, I emerge with embarrassment crawling up my neck. Jack is dressed, his strong body covered up in black and baggy clothes that give no indication of what lies underneath. His hands are tucked in his kangaroo pocket, a comforting smile on his lips that doesn't quite reach his eyes.

He's far from done with me, but he's giving me this time to sort out my own needs first.

"I'm going to shower quick, and then I'll meet you guys out there," I tell him, pointing to the door. Aiden's been keeping my clothes in his room, so I'll use his shower.

Jackson nods once, then opens the door for me.

Stopping in front of him, I slide my hand up his chest and lean into him. "We'll finish this later, I promise."

Not just because my body is still aching to continue what we started.

But because I know he needs me to soothe the chaos seething beneath the surface.

The Loft is on one of the highest floors of the Tower, giving it a view that reaches over most of the city. My favorite time to admire it is between night and day, like now. When I can see both the brilliant light of the sun burning the horizon and the deeper blues and purples of night higher in the sky until the colors blend between them. That moment when dark and light come together to form something beautiful.

It's just past dawn when I emerge, dressed and showered, and witness the unencumbered sight through the sliding glass doors. Aiden drags the door open before me, his hand fitting against the small of my back to guide me onto the balcony. We stop between potted trees and bushes against the chest-height glass panels.

I do my best not to look down or think about just how high up in the sky we are. I keep my focus outward, latching on to the colors painting the sky with hues so vibrant, no pictures or artwork could do it justice. A small part of me sees myself in dawn and dusk. Where light and dark can coexist. Where, maybe, one doesn't look as beautiful without the other, and it's seeing them together that makes them so special.

"I wish I could see the world through your eyes," Aiden croons, drawing my attention to him. He slides his hand beneath my ear, his thumb grazing my cheekbone. His brown eyes are obsidian in the mixed lighting, boring into mine with a fierce and unapologetic hold. "What wonder and appreciation you feel when you find something new. Something extraordinary."

My heart thunders beneath his intense stare, his soft touch. "What do you feel, then?"

"Nothing. I've never looked at something, even as stunning as I know it is, and felt anything for it." He crooks a finger beneath my chin, angling my face to his as he leans in close, our lips a breath away from touching. "Except you. You're the only one who can set my blood on fire. The only one who's ever made me breathless. Who makes me lose my head in emotions I can barely understand because I've never felt them so profoundly before."

The world around us stops. Narrows to the fraction of space between us, to his smooth-as-silk tone, and the words he's feeding me like the finest of sweets. Drizzling me with warmth and pleasure as I'm mesmerized by his fervent gaze.

"I've never seen anything, any*one*, and felt even a sliver of what I feel when I look at you, Raegan. Maybe I'm supposed to share those feelings with the rest of the beauty in this world, but we both know I'm a possessive man and to me, all that I am belongs to you. You are my everything."

"Aiden..."

His lips brush against mine, featherlight and slow. He does it again, and my chest feels like it's going to burst. It's like he's tasting me for the first time, measured and deliberate, so he doesn't miss a thing. Not the texture of our lips skimming together nor the heat of our breaths. I fist my hands into his button-down dress shirt, needing to feel the hard lines of his body against mine. His cinnamon body wash flavors the oxygen in the air until it's all I can smell; all I can taste.

I've kissed hundreds of times, but it's as if he's reduced me to a desperate teenager, trembling with desire at every soft touch of his lips.

I part my mouth at his silent direction, holding back a moan when his tongue strokes mine, and my core turns molten with pleasure. He sinks deeper, his hand on my head, holding us as close as can be, even though I want more, need more. Aiden keeps the kiss painstakingly unhurried, and I think I might lose my mind if he doesn't touch me. Ravish me on this balcony high above the city so my screams can echo to the world below. Take me against the glass...ruin its clarity with the press of my skin until it's imprinted forever.

A throat clears, and Aiden leisurely withdraws, banding an arm around my shoulders to tuck me into his chest. I'm grateful for it because I'm unexpectedly lightheaded. It's like the air's been sucked from my lungs, leaving me shaky and disoriented.

"Food's ready," Dane announces.

"We'll be in shortly."

The sliding door closes, and I will my heart to calm as I catch my breath.

He lifts my face, his thumb grazing my lips. "Are you alright?"

"Yeah. Let's go eat."

Nodding his agreement, he leads me inside to a chair at the table between him and Dane. There are two new chairs they've pulled out of somewhere, giving six available seats.

"I know it was dark when you started cooking, but you realize it's breakfast time, not dinner, right?" Kellan drawls across the table from me, stabbing his fork into a steak.

Aside from the cuts of steak, there's some sort of liver, spinach, oysters, and edamame.

"Be grateful I made you anything at all," Dane snarks, knife jabbing the air toward him. "I made this for Rae since she lost some blood. These are all high in iron."

Oh. That's...really fucking considerate. And sweet.

"Thank you."

He runs his hand through his hair and gives me a small, sheepish smile. "Sorry the food's so random. If you don't like anything, I can get you something else."

Impossible.

Everything is delicious, seasoned well, and satiates the hunger that had been carving into my stomach since I awoke.

No one talks while we eat, everyone so hungry from the last day and a half that no one even attempts to disrupt the meal until the last of us—me—is finished. I nudge my plate forward once I can't eat another bite, sinking into my chair with a hum of satisfaction.

"We need a better plan to take down Royce," Aiden begins.

"What did we miss?" Jackson asks from the other head of the table. I frown, noticing his hood still up even when it's just us, all but his lips shadowed from view.

Aiden fills us in on last night, on what Reid and Harvey accomplished—or didn't, rather—and how Royce had taken control of the three of us.

I chew on my lip, realizing how close it had been to him having us kill each other. "I thought Reid said he could only control two living souls at a time."

"He said he wasn't sure, so we can't take what he said as confirmed information. We know he can control at least three now without much limitation." Aiden taps his fingers on the table.

"And while hiding," Kellan adds. "I never saw the coward unless he was lurking in the bushes at the top of the cliff."

"We need to know where he is before we attack so this doesn't happen again. The fight with him is going to be a race to see who can strike first," Aiden surmises.

I push my hair behind my ear. "Did we already lose our opportunity with him? Is he going to leave now that we know about that location?"

"Considering the stockpile of bodies in the caves underneath, I think we've found more than a temporary location for him," Aiden replies. "But if we can get eyes on him, we can make sure he doesn't look like he's packing up and learn as much as we can about him and his routine to figure out the best time to attack." Turning his attention to Dane, he continues, "We need to get cameras in and around the house."

"How the hell are we supposed to plant the cameras without him noticing?"

"Harvey."

"That coward? I doubt he'd step foot in that house again, let alone go back after what just happened."

"He'll go. Leave that to me. But can you get cameras that can be easily hidden and give us access to watch from here?"

Dane frowns, falling back in his chair and folding his arms. "Yeah. I've already got some."

"Good. Get them set up today, and we'll go tomorrow night."

"All of us?" I chime in.

Aiden shakes his head. "The more people we bring, the more at risk we are of Royce's gift. It'll just be Dane, Harvey, Reid, and myself. The fewer people we have, the easier it will be for Harvey to hide us and Reid to get us out of there should we be caught. Otherwise, we'll plant the cameras and head right back."

I don't like the idea of them going back there without me. I want to see and know for myself that they're okay. But I also don't want to be used against them like I had last time. I don't argue only because of that, and I already know that I won't be able to sleep that night until they return.

CHAPTER TWENTY-NINE

RAEGAN

EVEN AS EARLY AS it is when Kell and I wander into the Guild Hall, it's still bustling with people and energy. Dane and Aiden went off to work out the details of their plan with Harvey and Reid and prepare what they need while Jackson disappeared without a word, leaving us with some time to relax on a training day off.

A large, round table in the middle of the massive room is particularly rowdy and filled with familiar faces. Kellan grins, spotting them and then directing us to them. "If you're ever alone with the Guild and in doubt, stick with Evie. Or Fabian."

"Why not the others?"

He snickers as we come up to them, not even trying to lower his voice. "They bring up the least amount of bullshit."

"What's that, *Dragon*?" Silas mocks, his eyes still glued to his hand of cards. He picks one and tosses it to the center of the table, then flicks his brown eyes to Kellan with a smirk. "You saying something about this table of upstanding, best-you-ever-had Guild members?"

Kell chuckles, dragging one of the open chairs back and offering it to me. "*He's* the bullshit you should avoid."

Silas snorts, whispering not-so-quietly to Evie beside him. "He's just salty he lost a hundred bucks in our last bet."

"Oh, you think I don't know how you won that bet?" Kellan smacks his hand on the table. The cards and drinks on it quiver, and Cassandra grabs her glass.

"Hey! Don't get me in trouble with Yaya or Cibrina over more broken glassware!" She turns sad eyes on Fabian. "I wasn't even the one to break them. How'd I get stuck with the bill?"

"Probably because you're the reason they broke it in the first place," Silas teases.

Evie smacks his arm. "Knock it off, or I'll shrink your dessert." She adds her selected card to the pile and smiles at me. "Do you want in on the next game?"

Kellan squeezes my shoulder. "I'm going to see what food's out and bring something back."

Giving him a short nod, I answer Evie, "I'll just watch if that's okay." I can't remember the last time I played a board or card game, if I ever did.

"Heyyy, Rae!" Gabe scoots his chair closer to mine. "You can be on my team!"

"There are no teams," Silas says, but Gabe makes a pfft noise and waves him off.

"They just taught me, but I'm no good at these."

"Uh, okay." He flashes me his cards, but it means nothing to me.

"Careful," Fabian warns, his mouth full of whatever snack he's binging this time. He's so big and broad he's almost on the open seat next to him. "Don't show the rest of us your cards."

"Oh!" Gabe slaps his cards to his chest, then points his finger at the others. "No peeking! Raegan rights only."

"Where's Zedd?" I ask, realizing his shadow isn't standing right behind him.

Gabriel smiles dreamily and indicates one of the long tables where Zedd's bent over a piece of paper and scribbling something on it. "He's working on a new song that hit him this early morning. Inspiration struck, and *bam*!"—he slaps his hands together—"he has to get it out before he loses it." He moans and drags one hand down his throat to his chest. "Uuungh, listening to that man sing is an eighth fucking wonder." Gabe chuckles and ruffles his brown hair. "I suppose it's a bit unfair for everyone else, though, when his gift is involved."

Did I know he had a gift? "What is it?"

"His singing voice can influence emotions. He can start anything from a mob to an orgy. Or help purge sadness from people who've locked it away." Gabriel pats his chest, his gaze distant. "It's beautiful."

"It's your turn," Evie reminds him.

"Oh!" Gabe holds his cards to me. "Pick one."

Silas laughs, shaking his head. "You're never gonna win like that."

He shrugs, still waiting for me to make my choice. "It's not about winning for me. I just like having fun with you guys."

I tug on a card and he takes it, adding it to the center pile.

Cassandra makes an 'aww' sound. "That's so sweet."

"That's a pretty cool gift," I comment. As I look around the table,

I think I have the gist of everyone else's gifts. Cassandra, healing. Evie can make things bigger or smaller. Fabian...eats things? "What exactly is your gift again?" I direct to him, but it's Silas who answers.

"He can eat anything. *Anything.* As long as it fits in his mouth, at least." Silas plays his card and then jerks a thumb at Fabian. "He ate an explosive once. Don't ask how or why we were dealing with one of those, but he swallowed that sucker down like it was cake."

I touch my throat involuntarily, grimacing. "How..."

Fabian shrugs. "My anatomy's a bit different. I've got a long tongue like a frog, and my throat can expand to consume anything."

"That's why my bud's always eating. If he goes even an hour without food, he'll get faint. He needs something in his stomach unless he's asleep," Silas adds. "My gift is the best in the Guild, though. Did you like the bunker? All me."

Evie chimes in. "That wasn't *all* you, Si."

He ignores her, pulling seeds from his pocket and spilling them on the table. "I control all plant-life. Trees, flowers, vines...and any properties the plant has too. Poison, sleep spores, medicinal stuff...the best, right?"

The others around the table make unconvinced sounds, and he frowns. "What? Come on! That's master-class shit right there. I'd bet on me any day of the week!"

"If we're betting, then my money's on Jackson," Evie comments, sweeping the center pile of cards in front of her and tossing a new card down.

Silas scowls, though it's hard to say if it's at her statement or his loss of the pile.

"I'd bet on Aiden," Cassandra puts in her two cents.

Fabian opens a bag of chips. "Can't exclude Kellan. He can out-last anyone."

Gabriel nudges me. "Speak up, girl. You're the strongest."

"I wouldn't consider it the *best* gift, though." I flick my gaze to Cassandra. "I wish I could heal others."

She beams at the compliment.

"Well, I could certainly use your help on some jobs if you're interested," Evie tells me. "Especially cleanup work."

Silas whips his head around. "Hey! I'm your partner on those!"

"Oh, uh, I'm not really sure how those work."

Evie explains, "One of the offices downstairs searches for odd jobs that would be a good fit. They do research on the requestor, vetting them to be sure they're safe, and we'll get paid, then print the request and post it for any of us to pick. The Guild is technically a temp agency, so there's a form on the website for requestors to directly submit requests as well. Especially repeat clients."

"Does everyone here have gifts?"

"Most of the ones working in the offices don't. They all know about us, though, because they're either family, friends, or spouses who want to help."

"I heard some jobs get pulled from the dark web," Silas inserts conspiratorially.

Evie waves him off. "That was when Thorne was in charge."

"Were you guys around when he was here?" I ask, curious what they thought of him.

"Just me and Fabian. Silas and Cassandra joined soon after Aiden took over."

"Si was causing so much trouble that Aiden had to recruit him directly," Cassandra narcs with a sly smile.

"Recruit him?"

"That's another office downstairs. The staff scour the internet—social media, online articles, police reports"—she gestures to Silas, who rolls his eyes— "for signs of gifted people. The second tier of recruiters goes out to offer an opportunity at the Guild. It gives them a non-destructive purpose with their gift and a place to live in a community of others like us," Evie answers.

"What happens if they accept? They get right in?"

She shakes her head. "Each recruiter has their own Guild business card with their name on it. They have to sign the back of it with the person's name they're inviting, and that has to be presented to the security desk on the first floor. That's their ticket to an interview with Aiden or Cibrina. They work out if the Guild is a good fit for them, and then there's a probationary period after that."

"Oh! That's what I'm in," Gabe says, extending his cards to me again for another pick.

"Anyway," she continues, "we do almost anything you can think of. Moving people is my specialty with Silas. I shrink the boxes and furniture, Silas moves them into a tub, and then we drive to their new home and do it all in reverse. Takes us less than an hour but we get paid by the job, not hourly."

"How do you avoid people seeing you use your gift?"

"It's in the contract that no one is present. Or we do the work when we know no one will be there, like at night." She taps a braided metal bracelet on her wrist. "These tell us if there are recording devices in range. If there are, or even just to make sure you're covered, you push a button on the side, and it sends a jamming signal until we're out of range." Evie smiles. "That's the gist of it."

"Don't forget you can't go on a job without approval first," Cassandra says. "You have to show Aiden or Cibrina and get their approval, and Cibrina logs it so she knows who's working which jobs."

When the hell does Aiden, or even Cibrina, have time for all that?

While we're squeezing in trainings, GE missions, and preparing for attacks?

No wonder his phone is always ringing or buzzing with messages.

"Oh. Wow," is all I can manage.

Evie gives me a reassuring smile. "Don't worry about an answer now. Just know that the offer is open if or whenever you want to give it a try to see what we're all about."

"Thanks. I've never thought of using my gift for anything...productive like that."

She shrugs. "There's something for everyone out there; you just have to get creative." She pinches a cookie from Silas and tosses it at him. "Catch."

"Shit, don't—!"

The cookie grows to the size of a large dog, knocking him and his chair to the ground.

Fabian ditches his chips and leverages the cookie on the ground, taking a bite out of it. "Thanks, Evie."

"My pleasure."

"Got you some fruit, beautiful," Kellan calls behind me. He sets a bowl of sliced fruit in front of me—predominantly filled with strawberries—and another at the empty seat on my right. "Cut it up myself."

I'm still stuck on Evie's example of playfully using her gift. How could I...?

Kell pulls out the chair next to me to sit in, and an idea strikes.

Right before his ass hits the seat, I shoot my gift through it. The chair disintegrates. Kellan lands hard on his ass, a look of complete surprise on his face that I can't help but laugh.

Silas snorts. Cassandra's hand is covering her mouth—to suppress a giggle?—while Evie, Gabriel, and even Fabian join my laughter.

Kellan grins. "You fit right in."

My eyes burn at the words I never realized I'd waited my whole life to hear.

Somehow, I'm suckered into playing the next game, which involves a whole lot of screaming at each other until I hear someone shouting the same thing as me to pair up our cards.

It's so loud, our voices echoing through the grand room, that I don't hear Aiden approach.

I'm tugged from my chair unexpectedly. I trip over myself to catch up with the direction I'm being pulled in, away from the table and chaos, but the hand on my arm keeps me upright.

"Can you hear me now?" Aiden purrs, his lips grazing the shell of my ear and triggering goosebumps.

Breathless from the adrenaline of the game and now him, I nod rather than attempt words.

"Good. I received a phone call you'll want to take. But it'll need to be in my office with the ruckus happening here."

My breath catches. A phone call? For me?

There's only one person—or maybe two—it could be.

Elias or...

Portia.

Aiden drops his hand to the small of my back, guiding me to his office. I run inside past Dane and snatch the corded phone from the receiver. "Portia?!" A dull ringtone echoes in my ear.

Fuck. Did I miss her?

A throat clears, and I whirl around. Aiden holds up his cell phone.

I lunge for it, swiping it from his hand and pressing it to my ear. "Hello?"

"RAE!!! OH MY GOD! I'VE MISSED YOU SO MUCH!" Portia partly screams, mostly gushes into my ear.

My knees shake as relief leaves me boneless. Dane pushes a chair to the back of my legs, and I collapse into it. "Porsh! Thank fuck! Where have you been?! I've been trying to call you."

I cling to the phone as if it's her I'm actually holding onto.

"I know. I'm so, so sorry! Please don't be mad."

"Of course, I'm not mad! I could never...I'm just so fucking glad to know you're okay."

There's a pause, which immediately raises a red flag when it comes to Portia. My tone drops. "You're okay...right? Where are you? Do you need me? I know someone who can get me there in seconds. Just tell me where you are, and I'll be there."

She sniffs. I tighten my grip on the phone and stand. "Portia, where—"

"I'm okay! I promise, I am. I wasn't for a bit, but...Oh, Rae. I have so much to tell you."

"Can you tell me now? Can I see you?"

A muffled, masculine voice comes through the speaker.

"Oh, right." Her voice sounds further away when she says that, before it comes back just as strong as before. "Sorry, this is supposed to be a quick call. I wanted to tell you as *soon* as I found out that we're all coming home!"

All?

But that is the least important part of that announcement right now.

"When?! Wait, GE's still around. It's not safe—"

"Don't worry, we're going to help!"

That male voice speaks again, and I strain to hear it.

She makes a noise of disagreement, her voice once again distant. "We *are* helping." Pause. "Fine, that's what *you're* doing. But *I'm* helping Rae when we go back tomorrow." Pause. "Oh, we're not leaving tomorrow?" Another long pause. A sigh. "Sorry, it sounds like we aren't coming home *right* away, but it'll be soon, okay? And then I'll tell you everything, and you can tell me everything, and we can lock ourselves away from men for a night."

I realize there are at least two different male voices on the other end talking to her, and frown. It's not just Elias?

"Deal. I'm at the Tower now where the Guild is, so come here as soon as you can, or I can go to Hype." Dane makes a sound in his throat, but I continue, "I'm just so glad to hear from you."

"Yes! I can't wait! I've really gotta go, though, but I'll be there before you know it! Love you! Bye!"

I drop into the chair and hold the phone to my chest, eyes closed with a smile.

Finally, some good fucking news.

Chapter Thirty

JACKSON

The Loft is dark and quiet when I return. Aiden's talking on the phone on the balcony in a pair of sweatpants like he'd been woken from sleep. The bedroom doors are all closed, which tells me where the others are. It's barely after dark, but considering how early we'd started our day and that most of us are still recovering, I'm not surprised.

It's what I would be doing, if I could.

Grasping the knob to Aiden's room, I silently ease the door open. Raegan's fast asleep in his bed, her hair wild behind her and the rest of her hidden beneath silk sheets.

I draw a steadying breath.

She's right there. Uninjured. Unbothered. Safe.

But what Royce made me do...

What I'd been *powerless* to stop...

The darkness I keep carefully contained is thrashing within, thirsty for blood. My body trembles from the adrenaline, the *need* to hunt him down for what he's done ever potent. I can't sit still while he's out there. Can't let his manipulation of *my* body, *my* gift, stand.

I've never felt helpless before.

The sight of my blade sinking into her back is a nightmare that haunts me even when I'm awake.

I fist my hand to cease its shaking, but it does nothing to deter the violent energy bursting at the seams for release. If an entire day of training, of pushing myself close to my limit, couldn't stem the bloodlust, then there's only one other option if I'm to keep my promise.

It doesn't matter that this is Aiden's room and his bed. It's about time he learned to share.

I leave the door open a crack as my warning to him that she's not alone once he's finished with his business, then work quickly to shed my clothes. Crawling over her on the bed, I drag the silk sheet down, slowly revealing her body. She doesn't stir at the silken caress nor the shifting of the mattress at my movements.

I'm amazed how anyone can sleep through something that I know would wake me in an instant. How blissful sleep must be for them. To not worry about the world around them while in such a vulnerable state.

I lick my lips, ready for a taste of her. We'd talked about this before, about pleasuring the other while they were asleep. It's always been a fantasy of mine, but when her eyes glowed with excitement at the idea, I knew it wouldn't be long before I made that dream come true.

I just didn't expect that moment to be because my control was slipping.

Unfurling my gift, the invisible hands of air whisper over her skin, painting long lines around her curves. Tickling her hair. After retrieving a knife from my clothes, I slice through her bra and underwear, flipping the fabric to the side until there's nothing between us.

She's stunning.

Perfect.

I squeeze my hard shaft as it throbs mercilessly, inhaling sharply at the burst of pleasure the action gives me.

Not yet.

Tucking some flyaway strands of hair behind her ear, I trace my thumb over her cheek, her jaw, her neck. "I need you, little one. Your monster needs you." Her pulse beats steadily, a constant drum that soothes a small part of me, helping to rein me in. I kiss her there, tasting it with a long swipe of my tongue before moving to her breasts. I play with them with my hands, my tongue, my mouth...all the while flicking brief glances to her face to see if this is the moment she wakes.

I scrape my teeth against her hip bone, and she jerks reflexively. Smirking, I continue my descent between her legs, shifting them open and bending at the knees for both of our comfort, then expose her core. I lick her entrance to her clit, dragging the pad of my tongue in a firm stroke that has her legs twitching. It's an effort to contain my groan as I taste her, breathe her in. She simultaneously soothes the fraying ends of my sanity and ignites them.

I'm both settled and more incensed than before.

She's mine.

My little one.

…and I'd hurt her.

I eat her pussy without holding back. Whether she wakes at this point or not is moot; because I have her. I'm not going to rest until I have my fill of her. Her cunt clenches when I tongue her entrance, trying to draw me deeper, trying to grasp for something more. My gift continues to play with the rest of her, fondling her breasts, caressing her skin until it's needy for more attention.

I take my time with her, sucking, nibbling, petting her pussy until she writhes above me, soft moans drawn from her throat though she doesn't wake. Her body is so responsive, so *reactive*, to me. A flick of her clit elicits the most visceral jolt. Latching my mouth over it, I suck and lick it while pressing a digit to her entrance. It slides right in, her body slick and welcoming.

"So good, little one. So wet for me, even asleep as you are."

My rage smooths a little bit more. We're so close to bringing it to heel.

I need more.

Slipping from the bed to the bathroom, I grab a bottle of lube from Aiden's toy drawer and lather it over my cock. Even though her body's aroused, it might not be enough. And the one thing I'll never do is hurt her.

I shift her to her side, lifting her leg over mine as I wrap around her back. The smell of her vanilla conditioner is mixed with Aiden's cinnamon body wash, creating a delicious combination that I breathe in deeply, shuddering when I release it. Guiding my dick to her center, I press the tip inside and suck the crook of her neck to block my groan.

I move so, so slowly. Her cunt is still tight, still fighting me, but the lube eases the painstakingly measured progress as her body begins opening for me. I rock my hips, the barest amount of my length rubbing in and out the single inch I'd earned, coaxing her body to grant me more. I can't restrain the groan this time, the grip of her warm embrace doing something for me that nothing else can. It's bliss. Ecstasy in its purest form. Inch by inch, I sink deeper until I'm finally seated, my pelvis flush with her pert ass.

Pausing, I pant at the level of control I'd needed to get us here, soaking in the relief of being sheathed inside her as the tension riding me slackens.

Footsteps warn me of his approach, but it doesn't stop me.

I roll my hips against her, my dick rubbing her inner walls and drawing a breathy moan from her lips right as a blade nicks my neck. Smirking, I pause to address him. "Before you lose your temper, she agreed to this."

Aiden is furious. The emotions he normally controls so well, the indifferent or stern mask he always wears, is gone. I'm not sure if words will be enough to pierce through the anger that's consumed him, but I keep talking to make him see that our girl isn't afraid of trying new things. She's not afraid to put herself at our mercy, to be vulnerable for us. I know he's afraid of doing the things he wants with her, but he shouldn't be. He only needs to ask her to be sure.

"See how she likes it?" I whisper huskily, grinding into her and teasing her clit with my slick thumb. Her body moves against mine, seeking more friction as her breathing quickens. "How she begs for more?" The blade moves with my Adam's apple when I swallow.

Raegan moans louder, pushing against my thumb as I circle her harder, faster. Her eyes slit open.

"Sorry, little one. I couldn't wait." I don't stop, moving my hips faster even if the side of Aiden's sword grazes and cuts my neck from the motion.

Raegan nods, her hips matching mine, before she notices Aiden and falters.

"Are you staying or leaving?" I ask.

He takes her in, watching her writhe with pleasure on my cock and without argument. He removes his sword.

Raegan reaches a hand to him. "Let me see."

His sweatpants do nothing to hide his fully erect cock that I realize she's referring to.

I don't know if he would have left if she hadn't said something, but Aiden closes the door and stays.

She moves her arm to the edge of the bed, directing him where she wants to see him better, and he pulls a chair up to sit in. Aiden frees his cock, stroking it with eyes only for her.

I chuckle into her nape. "You can't see him very well from here, can you?"

"No."

Shuffling us around, I put her on her hands and knees facing Aiden and then drive back into her sweet cunt from behind. "Put your hands on his thighs, little one. Get closer. But don't touch."

Aiden frowns when he hears me, but something on her face seems to stop him from countering.

I pull her hips up higher, pushing her shoulders down so her panting breath will hit his cock, and then I slam into her. "Do you want to taste him?"

"Yes!"

"He put a sword to my neck. I think he should be punished, don't you?"

Raegan hesitates. She wants him too, but it's further proof of how much she trusts me when she answers, "Yes."

That's all I needed to hear.

I fuck her with single-minded intensity after that, trusting that she'll keep herself from touching his dick even as close as she is. Even as much as she's probably drooling for a taste. As he pumps his cock in her face and wishes for her mouth.

"Oh, Jack! Fuck! Yes!" She releases a strangled cry, her body clamping down on my dick and almost making me come before I'm ready. I clench my jaw, forcefully holding it back until her pussy lets me go.

Retracting myself from her, I whisper in her ear, "Go sit in his lap for waiting patiently."

She nods, doing exactly as directed so she's straddling him. He watches her, completely enamored by our goddess, as she sinks over him. Aiden's eyes shutter. Close. That's about as much as he can handle restraining his control-freak tendencies because his eyes snap open, and he grabs her hips, driving his cock into her with unrelenting force. Raegan's head falls back, eyes closed, and mouth open on a voiceless moan.

Grabbing the lube, I squeeze the bottle over her lower back, guiding it to her other hole and circling the entrance. I add more. And more. Then, push the excess inside.

"Oh, fuck!"

I keep working the lube into her hole, spreading it around, pushing deeper once her body accepts it until I'm two fingers deep in her ass. I scissor my fingers, stretching her hole and then pushing them in and out. "I'm taking this next time," I breathe against the shell of her ear.

She convulses, her body stuttering out of rhythm, but Aiden holds her still as he keeps going until he drags her down his shaft one final time. Raegan collapses against him, panting for air.

I give her a short break, washing my hands before I return, bending where she's resting her face on Aiden's shoulder. "Can you handle one more, little one?"

She pushes herself up, nodding emphatically even as Aiden protests. "Yeah."

Smiling, I help her on the bed.

"Wait." Aiden fixes his sweatpants and goes to the bathroom, reappearing with lacy underwear.

I'm busy fixing the pillows and positioning her where I want her when he holds the tiny thing with more gaping holes than lace out to Raegan. "Give me your legs," he commands. It isn't until both feet are through and he's tugging it up for her that I see what it is.

Crotchless, vibrating underwear.

I test it out, dragging my dick through her folds as I hold her back to my front by her throat and hips. I'm pleased to find that it doesn't interfere, her and Aiden's cum coating my shaft. The buzz of the vibrator travels through her, tingling my dick when I get close.

I notch at her entrance, meeting Aiden's gaze before I take her. He grabs the back of her head and crashes his lips to hers at the same time as I push inside. He swallows her groan, locking it in her throat where I can still feel it.

My fingers twitch over her neck, tightening as I move mercilessly to purge the pent-up frustration, shame, and anger. Aiden's still kissing her, still toying with the varying pulses of the vibrator as her body quakes, trapped between the two of us.

It's a good look.

Her pussy quivers like a flickering of pressure to warn me she's close. I tell Aiden as much, and he breaks their kiss to hold her chin. "Look at me when you come on his cock."

Raegan screams, her body stiffening in an instant and choking my dick. It spurs my orgasm, ropes of cum spurting into her and leaking down my balls.

Before I can catch my breath, Aiden's peeling Raegan from me and cradling her. "Wash off before you get any of that on my sheets."

My laugh comes out as a huff, too tired for anything more before I follow them to the bathroom. I help him wash Raegan first, and then we take turns holding her and washing ourselves. She's in a daze, tired and dick-drunk, and curls into my chest while Aiden finishes.

We sandwich her under the sheets, each of us with an arm or hand on her while I bury my face in her hair, kissing her shoulder and falling asleep to her intoxicating scent.

Chapter Thirty-One

RAEGAN

Aiden's gone by the time I wake. The sheets and a blanket are tucked tightly around me where he'd been, and I hold them to my nose, breathing in the lingering cinnamon scent.

Jack chuckles against my hair, tracing his fingers in an intricate pattern on my thigh beneath the covers. "Miss him already?"

Humming softly, I lean further into him. "He's always so busy. We never get moments like this." He says nothing, so I continue, "I wish I knew how I could help. What to do so he can have a break."

"It'll settle after GE's gone."

"Unless we're going after them tomorrow, that doesn't help him now. What should I do?"

"Train. Stay here. Stay safe."

Releasing a short huff, I turn in his arms and frown at the knowing smile there. Even though he knows what I'm going to say, I say it anyway. "I was hoping for something more productive than that." He arches a brow, and I guess training with my gift *is* considered productive. "I feel like I've already come so far with my gift. It doesn't...hurt like it used to."

"You've stopped fighting it."

I pause, considering that thought and realizing he may be right. He usually is. Flipping my hand on his chest, I imagine my gift there and all it's done. All *I've* done.

"I always hated it. I thought it made me destined to be the bad guy. What hero destroys things?" I swallow past the lump in my throat. "But you, the others, the Guild...you've shown me it's not the gift that makes a villain. It's what you choose to do with it." My eyes search his, finding his full focus riveted to me. I never have to question if he's listening or if something else has stolen his concentration. When he's with me, I feel like the most important person in the world.

"I'm not really sure who I am now that I've accepted that. If I'm not a villain or a monster." I fist my hand, asking the question I've always wondered from him. "What do you see when you look at me?"

"A candle in the dark," he answers without hesitation, his voice a dark, husky sound that curls around my lungs. "My guiding light."

My heart ricochets, thrashing wildly while my stomach flutters, and I lose all sense of how to breathe. How? How does he always know the things to say that knock the air from my lungs and make me feel weightless? I don't even know how to respond. How does anyone respond to something like that? All I know is...

"I love you." I trail my hand up his chest, lingering on the paper crane tattoo, then slide my fingers to the back of his neck and into his messy black hair. "I love you so much that sometimes I'm afraid my heart is going to burst when I'm with you. Swear you'll never leave my side, Jack." I grip his hair as the demand falls from my lips.

His smile is sharp and wicked, his gaze shadowed in darkness. "Never," he promises, his hand gripping my thigh and pulling it over his leg. He runs his hand along the length of my thigh and over my hip, dipping to my waist and up my scarred back to hold my nape. Jack leans closer, his lips feathering over mine. My breath catches. "You will always have me. Until every star in the sky burns out. There will never be a me without you."

Fuck.

It's exactly what I needed to hear.

Jackson kisses me like I'm the oxygen he needs to breathe, and I fall into him like gravity. Pressure swells in my chest, overflowing to my limbs and head until I'm buzzing with warmth. He flips me onto my back, his kiss deepening until I think he'll devour me whole. I open to him completely, relaxing into the bed as he kisses me with dark possession. As his hands caress my skin until it burns. His mouth owning me like a brand.

He touches my slit, inserting a finger into my core, and my inner walls tighten, trying to hold him inside. Jack adds another finger, angling them to stroke my front wall as he pumps them in and out. Our lips smack apart, and I gasp for air.

"You'll never be rid of me, little one. Not unless you decide to kill me."

"Never."

He smirks, trading his fingers for his dick, then thrusting inside in a single strike. The sudden stretch makes me cry out until he collars my throat and squeezes. "Even if I use you to fuck my demons out?"

I grab his arm as my breath hitches, and he slams into my pussy like he owns it. I'm getting wetter with every slide of his dick, my cunt weeping for him as he uses my body and sends me into a euphoric state. I couldn't answer him even if I wanted to. The lack of air, the blankness that overtakes my brain as I'm reduced to nothing but sizzling nerve endings and tightening muscles. Reeling me around his finger like an overly-bound spring that's ready to pop.

Black dots my vision as he fucks me into oblivion, snapping the restraints on my orgasm. Ecstasy floods my body, sweeping me away in a riptide of pleasure.

Jackson groans above me, and I force my eyes to open. He drops onto his forearms on either side of me, panting steadily and eyes brimming with obsession as they stare into mine.

He's absolutely right.

I would have to kill him myself to get rid of him.

No one else could do it but me.

I cup the side of his face, brushing my fingertips through the streaks of sweat and finding myself addicted to the way he looks at me.

"You'd have to kill me, too," I admit breathlessly.

Frowning when I realize Jack hasn't left the elevator, I stop and spin around. "Aren't you coming with us?"

He presses a button for another floor, then shakes his head with a smile. "No."

The doors begin to close, and I slam my hand against one of them so they jerk back open. "Why not? Where are you going?"

Kellan chuckles, leaning over me to place his hand above mine. "He doesn't usually hang around the Guild members."

"Then we'll go back to the Loft."

"There's someone I need to see. Work on your gift being active, and I'll find you when I'm done."

"Who?"

"Mallory."

My chest tightens with unease, and I drop my arm from the elevator. It feels like I've been punched in the gut, all the air expelling from my lungs.

Jackson answers my unspoken question. "I've been helping her with her gift. And you."

"Me?"

He nods once, but I'm still too stunned to ask anything else. Kellan lowers his hand, and the doors begin to close. "I'll see you soon," my shadow promises before the doors shut.

What...is that about?

"Come on, beautiful. I'm sure he'll fill you in later if you ask."

I don't refute it because I know it's true. The bigger issue is figuring out where the fuck do I begin with all the questions now running rampant in my head. How long has this been going on? Why is he training her on her gift? What is he helping her with when it comes to me? Why is he doing this? What is he trying to accomplish? Is he hoping to use her gift against GE somehow? Or is this just about me?

Kellan prods me with a slap to the ass. I smack his chest in return and pivot out of his reach. "Smack my ass in front of the others, and I'll squeeze your balls," I quip, and he laughs.

"You'll have to get to them first."

Calling on my gift, I fill my entire body with it and wiggle my fingers. "Oh, I think I'll manage."

His grin sharpens. "You're proving to Jackson you have full control over your gift now, remember? What'll he say if he sees a hole in my jeans?"

I snort. "Probably that you deserved it."

He cackles and settles a hand on my back to get us moving toward the Guild Hall. "I think you may be right. Let's not start anything too reckless while Aiden and Dane are gone, though."

The reminder smothers my playful mood. He's right. Aiden, Dane, Harvey, and Reid went to install the cameras at the beach house. If all goes well, they should be back soon. If not...we need to be prepared to back them up. It's probably why Jack insisted on me testing my gift, so I'd be ready no matter what.

The hall is wild with energy and noise. Which is a silly thing to notice anymore because it's *always* like this. Morning, afternoon, and night, they're always rowdy and carefree.

So, when a hush suddenly falls over the area where we walk in, it's obvious.

I glance around, trying to figure out what caused the sudden silence and find the tables nearest us all staring at...me.

Kellan wraps his arm around my back protectively, ready to snap in their direction when a voice sing-shouts across the room.

"REGGIE! Over here, my dear! I've saved you a seat!"

All the eyes on me swivel to Gabe dancing on his chair as he waves me over in an exaggerated performance. I can't help but laugh at his outrageous moves and ignore the rest of the room to join him and the other familiar Guild members. He pounces on me, knocking into Kellan in his effort and ignoring the fact that my gift is active. "Oh, so glad you could come! They're kicking my butt again, I tell you. I need your wisdom."

"I'm not sure I'm much better, but I'll do my best," I offer him with a smile.

He fluffs my hair. "Wonderful." Gabe grabs my hand and drags me to the table, waiting until I've taken the seat he'd apparently saved for me before he plops into his and loudly scoots it next to mine.

Kellan scoff-laughs—muttering something about being forgotten so easily—and walks around the table to the other open seat next to Fabian.

Gabriel passes me his cards. "Here, take a looksee."

"Is this the usual game?" I ask, and the others nod. Not that it makes a big difference. I'm still figuring out a strategy for how to play to win this one, but at least I have a small idea of where to start. Lowering my voice, I whisper to Gabe, "Thanks for that."

"Don't worry about those coots. Half of 'em are from the Pits and the rest are just nervous."

I get it. I only just figured out how to use my gift without destroying everything I touch. Hopefully, I can earn their trust by showing them while I'm here with my gift active that I'm in full control.

The sound of plastic and something like beads rustling around and clicking draws my attention to Gabe.

"Ah, perfect." He pinches a tablet from a small bag and flicks it into his mouth. "Down the hatch!"

Zedd suddenly appears, snatching the bag from his hand. "You've had enough."

Enough?! How many has he had?

Silas chokes on his drink. Evie slaps his back until he swats her away. "That doesn't actually help choking victims, Eves."

She shrugs. "Well then, consider it my consoling back pat for you realizing you're only winning your bets because he's been high."

"You should give him his money back, Si," Fabian adds mildly, dropping a few peanuts into his mouth.

"What? That's *his choice*. He didn't have to take the bets!"

Gabriel and Zedd aren't listening, still focused on each other.

"Do you have any more?" Zedd presses, and Gabe smiles, a dreamy look on his face.

"Do you see how he takes care of me, Reggie?"

"Uh, yeah. I don't mean to pry, but...are you okay?"

Gabe pats my arm. "You're a sweetie, too. I promise I'm okay. The drugs just"—he twists his hands in the air by his head— "keep the memories at bay."

I frown. "Even when you're not using your gift?"

He chuckles. "Oh, there's no forgetting what I've remembered. And I've remembered...*so* so many horrid things. But these...and Zedd...I'd be lost without them."

Zedd huffs, striding away to sit at the next table over.

He may not talk to us much, but at least he cares about Gabriel.

"So, are we still playing or..." Silas trails off, his dark eyes flipping between me and Gabe, who sits forward in his seat.

"Still playing! I've got Raegan with me now, so I'm getting my money back!"

"Wait," I intervene. "We're playing with money?"

Gabriel wafts his hand. "Don't worry about that. I've got us covered."

Kellan leans back in his chair, arms crossed. "Oh, good. There's—"

Something hits Evie's back and then slaps to the ground. She whips around, glaring behind her. "Who threw that?"

Silas sighs, tossing his cards defeatedly to the middle of the table, and the others follow suit. Kellan grabs my arm and tugs me from my seat. "We need to get out of range—"

"Sorry, Evie! Jared dodged and—"

The girl doesn't have time to finish her explanation before Evie chucks it right back, nailing her in the face. The guy with her sends something at Evie's chair leg, then yanks it and sends her tumbling to the floor.

The room breaks out into chaos. Kellan drags me behind the bar as chairs, tables, shoes, and gifts fly around the room. Silas catches a table aimed at Evie with his vines, then tosses it to the side, where it cracks and splits. Evie throws baseball-sized peanuts at someone, who deflects them with a shield.

The broken table reminds me of the first time I'd seen the Guild.

When Aiden and Cibrina had watched a fight from the sidelines while casually discussing compensation. I'd almost forgotten the chaotic introduction.

Cassandra crawls behind the bar with us, peeking her head above the counter to watch. "Mind if I join you?" She ducks when something flies toward us, but Kellan bats it to the side.

"Get Cibrina so she can catalog who breaks what," he orders. She nods and races out of the hall.

"Why'd you pull me out? I can handle myself."

The floor shakes, and then the wood shifts to reveal a layer of metal. Nothing happens under us but under the tables and members? Metal bands creep from the floor and snatch members off their feet.

"That's enough." Aiden stands in the center of the room, his expression thunderous. "All of you to the training gym. *Now*."

Kellan snickers. "*That's* why."

The metal sets everyone back on their feet, then sinks to the floor. A guy with buzzed hair touches the floor, and the wooden boards move back in place. Aiden thanks him, then waits for the members to file out of the room to the elevators before he follows.

"What is he going to do?"

"Wanna watch?"

"Does a bear shit in the woods?"

He snorts. "So unladylike."

I jab him in the ribs, and he uses my elbow to tug me against him, then sucks on my ear. "Don't tease me, beautiful, or I'll fuck you in this now-empty hall." He rubs his hand into the fabric over my pussy, and my blood heats.

Fuck.

No, I want to see what Aiden's doing.

Tickling his elbow where I know he's sensitive, I twirl out of his reach the second it does the trick. "Bye!" I run, but it only gets me as far as the elevator because there is fuck-all chances of me taking the stairs down eleven floors.

Kellan laughs as he strolls to catch up with me, knowing there's no escape. I wait for the elevator to arrive after dropping off the last batch of members. Racing inside, I jab the door close button in the tiny chance it can beat him, but his hand slaps on the door, and he saunters inside.

Damn.

He stands behind me, his grin turning feral when he bends to whisper in my ear, "You know how I get when you try to run from me, beautiful." His hot breath tickles the wisps of hair around my ear, and my thighs clench.

"I want to see what Aiden's doing," I rasp.

He chuckles, the sound rumbling deep in his chest. "I'll let you watch." He slips his hand under my dress, grazing his fingers between my folds over my underwear. "Then maybe I'll bend you over the couch at the Loft and fuck you in this dress. You don't know how hard it's been to keep my hands to myself." His other hand dips into my bra to squeeze my breast. He thumbs my nipple, and my cunt throbs.

"Kell," I pant. "If the doors open..."

Kellan bites the crook of my neck, swirling his tongue over it and then sucking it hard. "Open where? You haven't pushed the button yet."

My eyes fly open.

"Shit! I'm going to miss it!" I poke the first-floor button and shove him off, and he laughs.

"There'll be plenty of time."

He doesn't touch me until the doors ding open, and then he leads me through a side door to the weight room.

"Kell, this isn't—"

"Shh..." he growls, pushing me against the small lip in front of the window that reveals the training gym. "You can watch him from here."

A crowd surrounds Aiden on the other side of the gym. He has his whip sword out—blunted where I see it strike the attacks down—and a single shield. Members attack him on their own or in units, trying to find an opening. He knocks them down one after another, sending some flying or off their feet.

Kellan circles my clit, dragging his fingers through my arousal and teasing me with it as Aiden takes on the Guild single-handedly. "I knew you'd like watching him." He laughs, his fingers getting more slick the more I witness. He yanks my underwear down to my thighs, then glides a digit into my wet heat. "Did you know he trains every day too? He's down here in the weight room every morning before anyone else wakes up?"

I can't restrain my groan any longer, letting it pass through parted lips as I rock into his fingers and watch Aiden.

One of the members gets around his sword, closing in on him, and my breath hitches with worry. Aiden slams his fist into them, and they fall to the ground. The others rush him in that moment, and instead of gathering his metal around him, he drops it.

Kellan's cock breaches my entrance, then pushes into me inch by inch, forcing the air from my lungs on another low groan. I'm not using them anyway, not while Aiden seems to be at a disadvantage. Until he dodges the first one, uses the momentum from the next one to shove them past him, trips the third one, and on and on, as he fights the ones who'd abandoned using their gifts in the hopes that hand-to-hand fighting might give them an edge.

Oh, fuck. I need Kellan to move. I need friction. I push my ass into him, grinding back and jerking forward, my hands gripping the window ledge. "Seen enough? This isn't one-way glass, so if you want me to fuck you, we'll have to leave."

I curse him, torn between the two options. Kellan undulates his hips, his dick pressing against my inner walls and making my knees weak.

Fuck.

Aiden keeps fighting, and my chest heaves as I struggle to stay and watch, but Kellan's teasing escalates when he lazily circles my clit.

"Let's go, you fucking prick," I snap.

He fixes himself and then me, offering me a savage grin before dragging me back to the elevator.

We don't even bother trying to make it to the Loft.

A few seconds after the elevator moves, Kellan smacks the stop button and shreds my underwear off, lifting me and impaling me against the wall. I cry out, my legs winding around his waist and my hands grabbing his hair and shoulder as he drives into me, his cock scouring against my inner walls and sending me into a climax that has me seeing stars. He continues to thrust through it, my body twitching and clenching over him, but he's not finished with me yet.

"One more time, beautiful. Your pussy's begging for more. I can feel it gushing around my dick. Tell me how much you liked me fucking you while you watched Aiden. Should we tell him about it? Do you think he'll get jealous and punish you for it?"

My core squeezes his shaft, and he groans, cursing. "Fuck, you filthy girl. You want him to punish you that badly? Should we get into some more trouble, then?"

His thumb circles and kneads my clit, winding my muscles tighter and tighter, his words fueling me until I break for him again, my body grabbing his in waves until he yanks me down his cock one last time, burying himself as he comes with me.

CHAPTER THIRTY-TWO

AIDEN

HURRIED KNOCKING AT MY office door snaps my head up. "Aiden?" Cibrina calls through the door, her voice pitched higher than usual. I brace myself for the worst, steeling against whatever news she's bringing this time.

"Come in."

She barely waits for me to finish before rushing in. "Wait here," she instructs over her shoulder to someone, then closes the door for privacy.

We've been plagued with bad news nearly every day since my call with Charles. Members are being attacked on the street by random thugs and thieves. Jobs have been drying up because of slander—from people who've never been clients of ours, I might add—spreading online about the Guild. Less income for the members means missed or late rent payments and therefore a smaller budget for food and maintenance after the Tower lease is paid. If that isn't enough, we received a letter from the IRS that the Guild is being audited for the last seven years of taxes.

The latest issue has been an investigation into our offshore account that stores money we'd obtained in less than legal methods being frozen.

At this rate, our available funds will be depleted within six weeks and we'll all be out on the street.

"I just got off the phone with Erik," she gasps as if she'd run here. Erik is one of the three members assigned to shadowing Detective Unger. "Someone sent a package to the detective anonymously with a note claiming that you murdered Thorne for ownership of the Guild."

I mentally curse the GE president. I don't know how much more we can take. If the police open a murder investigation into Thorne, that drags me and the Guild into it. We'll be under surveillance, limiting what we can do and where we can go without raising more questions.

Closing my eyes, I draw a deep breath. Clear my head. "If there's no missing person report and no body, he won't make it far," I reason.

"The package had Thorne's severed thumbs in it."

Fuck.

A DNA test will come back positive if Thorne's ever been to a doctor. Now I have to fucking hope that he'd been far enough removed from regular society that there won't be a match when they run the test.

Unger has already tried snooping around the Guild once, but we'd turned him away. He promised he'd come back with a warrant. I expect a positive result will give him exactly that.

Maybe threatening Charles had been ill-advised, but I've never been the sort of man to roll over or play dead. This means we need to speed up our timeline of taking them down. Once GE is gone, most of these problems will resolve on their own.

"Get the crisis PR team we have working on fixing the Guild reputation looped in on this investigation to get ahead of it. I want the best criminal defense lawyer who can't be bought. Make sure they have no ties to GE, either. We'll get them on retainer and start building our defense case now. Thorne's alive, as far as human legal terms go, so if we get proof of that, the case will drop."

"Getting anyone of high caliber on retainer will take almost half the money we have left."

"Sell my Aston Martin. We'll do a retainer fee, but we won't pay anything else until they win in court, if it gets to that."

Cibrina nods. "Understood." She hesitates, glancing to the door. "Should we reschedule the end of month review?"

Of course, it's that time again.

"No, let's do it now." I'm going to continue managing the Guild as if the world isn't on fire around us because when this fight with GE is over, we'll still be here and have a business to run.

She nods, then lets in the two she had waiting in the hall. I take that time to shove the issues from Charles out of my mind so I can focus on regular Guild maintenance. I won't let other things fall behind because of him.

Cibrina begins, "The fight last night resulted in twenty-two hundred in damages, which I've split by the responsible members and added to their rent. We'll have to source a new furniture store, I think, which sells higher quality, solid wood tables that won't break so easily."

Money many of them won't be able to afford next month, but I put that aside. I'm less concerned with the tables. I would rather have breakable furniture than broken and injured Guild members.

"I presume you've already researched alternatives?"

She smiles, and the younger woman, who is a step behind her and to the side, titters. Cibrina hands me a file. "They're sorted by least to most expensive options, with images and their qualities for comparison on each."

I flip it open and scan the first and second pages. "While I appreciate your thoroughness, how have you had time to compile this in only twenty-four hours?"

Cibrina motions to the girl beside her, encouraging her to step forward. "Penn, here, did most of the work."

Ah. One of her new assistants. Penn practically preens when Cibrina's attention is on her, smoothing her already tidy black hair and straightening her glasses with a proud smile. Which means the male on her other side...

"...And this is Quinn. He's been helping stay on top of member requests or issues, building maintenance, and working with Miranda on the kitchen and bar stock."

Quinn bows his head in greeting but appears far more serious than Penn. His black hair is styled back, his skin a deep olive shade and his eyes a dark brown. He's wearing a neat and pressed suit, while Penn is wearing a sheath dress that looks oddly like something Cibrina might wear...if she was a foot shorter.

"It's nice to meet you both," I reply, nodding to each of them in turn before returning my attention to Cibrina. "I'm glad you have help. I'll look these over and give you a decision tomorrow. Is there anything else?"

Cibrina looks to Quinn, who steps forward and offers a stack of files. "Here is the meal plan menu for the next month, as well as the required shopping list of items. There's also a report of the maintenance tasks completed this month for member apartments, as well as the Guild's main areas. We'll need to look at replacing or upgrading our water heaters in the next couple of months, so I have a list of options and what deals we could get if we order them by a specific date..."

Quinn continues to summarize each file, then steps back for Penn to add her stack and rundown. Cibrina finishes it off with some items I can answer immediately and then the ones that require review.

A glance at the clock on the wall reveals it's already after nine in the evening.

"Thank you for your hard work, as always," I say—my sign of dismissal. They leave the room, while I stare at the paperwork. Dane's tried convincing me to have all this done electronically, but I keep better track of these things in their designated folders and either signing off on or rejecting them there before returning them. I'm afraid I'd lose track of so much if they were all emails.

One day, I'll suck it up and convert.

But it won't be tonight.

I start by organizing the files by order of priority, which takes some time. The rest of my evening is spent working through one file at a time, adding my notes and decisions before sliding it into the growing pile of completed work.

By the time the words blur together, and my third cup of coffee is empty, I call it a night.

I've barely made it through ten percent.

Sighing, I pocket my phone and head for the Loft, trying not to fall asleep in the elevator on the way. It's just after three in the morning. I'll get a couple hours of sleep, then keep going.

The Loft is quiet when I enter and remove my shoes. The balcony door is cracked open, and Jack is sitting on the railing. He and I are alike when it comes to sleep. I don't have the time for it, and he has trouble sleeping at all. Not unless Raegan's with him. On his own, he's almost always moving around, thrashing in the sheets until either he or they wind up on the floor. But when Raegan's with him, he hardly moves. Like her presence calms whatever demons haunt his dreams.

He gives me a two-finger wave when he sees me, then returns to his watch over the city. I head straight for my room, showering and removing the stress from the day under a hot spray beating into my muscles. Once I've pulled on a pair of sweatpants, I seek *her* out.

I've passed the point of caring that it's selfish of me to do this.

They see her all day.

If I have to steal her from them to get my time in, then so be it.

She's sleeping in Kellan's bed tonight, so it's easy to scoop her sleeping form into my arms and bring her to my bed without his notice. Raegan doesn't stir, perfectly content to mold her body against mine once we're both under the sheets.

I wrap my arm around her, pulling her into my chest. She nuzzles her face closer, and my heart catches fire. I'm sure I feel plenty of things during the day, but I can't remember any of them when I'm with her. When the sight of her, the feel of her, puts my heart on steroids and pumps my veins with so many emotions that I can hardly pick one out to name it.

I've never felt so alive...so *exposed*...as I do with her.

It's simultaneously addicting and terrifying.

I push the hair in her face behind her ear, following her silky tendrils to their ends and then bringing them to my face. A long inhale gives me the vanilla conditioner scent that I crave and a hint of cinnamon that brings a small smile to my lips.

It gives me great pleasure that she now uses my body wash over any of the others. Physical proof on her skin that she still belongs to me even if I'm not with her as much as I'd like.

The two hours of sleep I'd planned for begin to disappear as I graze my thumb over her cheekbone. Down her jaw. Across her parted lips. My thumb stalls there, my heart ratcheting to galloping speed as I stare at her soft lips. As I remember what Jackson's been telling me about her. It's all based on trust, though, and have I earned hers? He's had her trust since almost the beginning, but me...I'm still trying to earn that back. All while I'm testing and exploring my own desires and what they entail.

I can't afford another misstep with her.

But I'm not sure how much longer I can hold myself back.

I drag my thumb down her lip, watching it catch and pull before it bounces back. My breathing hitches, the knuckle of my index finger angling her chin up as I lean in, as if drawn by an invisible force. Her breath hits my lips, warming them as I hold myself a hairsbreadth away.

I should wake her if this is what I want.

I shouldn't interrupt her sleep.

I know how hard she's been working with Kellan and Jackson on her gift. On fighting and building up her stamina. She's even been spending more time with the Guild, which is another thing that gives me a burst of pleasure. The Guild isn't my brothers, but they're the rest of the family I've been building the last two years. They mean more to me than I'd ever admit to them, and seeing her with them, seeing them accept her and give her another piece of her life that she's been missing...

Fuck it.

My lips sink into hers, and I pull her flush against me. She doesn't wake, doesn't fight me as my tongue dashes across her lips. As I slip it through her seam and stroke her tongue with mine. My cock jerks to attention, growing at my hip, but I ignore it—as I've learned to do so many times before with her. I may have caved to kissing her while she's asleep, but that's as far as I'll take it.

I slide my hand up her face, cradling it and pulling it to mine as I soak in the lushness of her lips. Memorize the feel of her mouth on mine. Drown in the taste of her, like sweet strawberries and a hint of mint toothpaste.

I kiss her until I'm breathless.

I kiss her until I think I'll burst.

Until that raging need for her lips finally quiets, and I press soft kisses to her lips, adamant that this one will be the last and finding my lips on hers again anyway.

If she only knew how much she affected me.

Finally, I withdraw and catch my breath. My gaze fixates on her swollen, shining lips that reflect the moonlight through the window.

It takes concentrated effort to drag my eyes away from them before I start this all over again.

I think I can say with certainty what obsession tastes like now.

For me, it's strawberry and mint.

One hour of sleep later, my alarm goes off.

It's not a typical alarm that would wake anyone, but I rouse at the slightest noise. This one is the soft chirp of a bird every few seconds. Even so, I hurriedly swipe the alarm before it can potentially wake Raegan.

She's wrapped around me, her head and arm over my chest and a leg splitting mine. My dick strains against my sweats, desperate for attention where her hip leans against it.

Five seconds.

Five seconds, I let myself linger with her. Run my hands over her back, her curves, her hair. Listen to her relaxed breathing. Imagine grabbing her pert ass and grinding my cock into her. Flipping her over and having her sweet pussy for breakfast before sheathing my dick in her heat.

Fuck.

I grip my dick, the throbbing need pulsing angrily when I don't move to do as I imagined immediately. My balls ache, and a quick probe sends a bolt of pain through me.

Carefully, I extract myself, tucking the covers tightly around her to keep her warm, and then wake myself up with a cold shower and rough hand job. It's nothing, absolutely *nothing* compared to the feel of her hands. Her mouth. Her tight pussy. I wonder what her ass will feel like next. Beyond my imagination, I'm sure.

As it usually does, the image of her collared and leashed to me appears unbidden in my thoughts. Ever since she somewhat agreed to it in private, that picture hasn't strayed far from my mind. She's on her knees, her hands bound behind her back while I have her dressed in some skimpy strips of lace. She's wearing vibrating underwear, completely at my mercy as I edge her to insanity while feeding her strawberries.

Only after she begs, sobs for release, will I fuck her.

Ropes of cum spurt from my dick, decorating the tile in streaks of milky white. Leaning a hand on the wall, I gasp to catch my breath and wait for the tension to drain, but it doesn't. My cock remains at half-mast, and I curse it, dropping the cool temperature to frigid, and finish washing myself like that.

I dress in workout clothes and bring my suit with me to the weight room. It's empty, as always, and I go through my routine for the current day of the week, focusing on strength training today.

Once I'm finished, I take a third shower in the locker room and don my suit.

The kitchen is just starting to work on breakfast, so I swing by to pick up my breakfast sandwich and carafe of coffee from Miranda, then return to the office.

Back to work.

At some point during the day, I take a break from the files and call Dane for a status check.

"How's the surveillance of the beach house and Royce going so far?" It's only been a day and a half since the cameras were installed, but we'd worried some of the angles might have blind spots.

The sound of typing fills the quiet as he wraps up whatever sentence or code he's in the middle of. "No issues with the cameras yet. I've been documenting everyone's schedule from what I can see, but I'm also trying to keep researching the Board members when things are slow."

"Who watched them the last two nights?"

"Reid's been taking the night shift."

Probably a good idea. Dane has no qualms about falling asleep in the middle of a task once the sun's gone down. "Have you found any new Board members?"

Our last count was four of the ten we still need to find, while we gather more information on the six we've identified. It's taking longer than I'd like to track and vet these people, but I see the advantage of taking them down before Charles. Once they're gone, we won't have to worry about someone going into hiding to restart GE after Charles is dead. It's better to strike now, all at once, to prevent GE from being reorganized under someone else.

"I'm looking into one right now that could be. But she's covered up her tracks really well on a surface search. If she tried deleting anything on the internet, I'll find it."

"Any change in your arm?" I ask, referring to where Vera had stuck him with something. I can't believe she would poke him with nothing just to break skin. Did she need a blood sample from whatever she stabbed him with? But the holes were too small to gather any useful amount. None of it makes sense, which worries me that we're missing something.

"Nope. I'd forget all about it if you didn't keep reminding me."

"That's what I'm worried about. Don't forget it. Tell me if even the slightest thing feels off."

"You sound like Rae."

"You and I both know it's the other way around. But good. Maybe between the two of us, you'll take it seriously."

He scoffs but doesn't argue. "Are you going to be here for dinner tonight? You've missed the last few nights."

I haven't told the others yet about the last couple of strikes from Charles. I've been so busy since the tax audit hit us the day after we'd fought Royce's zombies that I haven't gotten the chance to sit with all of them again to explain the frozen offshore account and the murder investigation.

"I'll try, but I can't make any promises. Things are busier than ever with the Guild. And we're still waiting on GE's next attack. I can't believe we've scared them off that easily."

"If they do attack again, we'll take care of them like last time."

I doubt they'd attempt the same attack again. If they do show up, I'm sure it'll be with a stronger team. Or worse, Charles himself.

The door to my office opens, and Raegan pops her head through.

"We'll talk more later," I say to Dane, and after his acknowledgment, I hang up.

"Hey," she murmurs once I put the phone down, slipping inside and shutting the door.

"Did you come here alone?" My first and last thought with her now is her safety. She needs to be within reach of one of us at all times. I thought I'd made that abundantly clear with the others, and I can feel myself getting riled up at the thought that she's been walking the Tower on her own.

"Jack's with me. He wanted to wait outside."

The anger cools, relief swirling in its stead. "Is something wrong?"

"I wanted to see what you were up to. If there's anything I can do to help."

She had been terrible with doing any sort of paperwork at school on the island. She and Kellan were frequently written up for not doing their homework or writing nonsensical things on it instead and turning that in.

I wave my hand at the desk, covered in stacks of files and strewn papers so there's no sign of the hardwood underneath. "As you can see, it's all just boring paperwork. Nothing exciting to help with."

She chews on her bottom lip. The same pouty lip that I devoured last night.

My cock stiffens, and I nonchalantly tug on my trousers beneath the desk to get more comfortable.

"What is it?" I demand on a low croon. She's worried about something, and I've made it my personal mission now to see to any of her concerns from here on out.

"I'm just trying to figure out how I fit in with…all of this." She waves at my office, but I take it as the Tower. The Guild. "With you and the others. Everyone seems to have their place and what they do best…except me."

"Aside from the fact that you're still helping us fight GE, you've already done more for the Guild and the gifted community than anyone." She frowns, but I continue, "You're training, like every Guild member, so you'll be ready for the big fight against Charles."

She cocks her head, considering. "Am I a Guild member now?"

"No." When her brow pinches, I continue, "Do you want to be? Do you want to pay me rent every month, pay for any damaged property you cause, go on jobs to bring in money for yourself and the Guild—"

A tiny smirk lifts the corner of her lips. "Call you Master?" She steps closer, her eyes hooded. "Would you like that?"

My dick throbs, and I restrain the urge to grip it. To so much as *touch it* while she's watching me so closely. I've lost control over my heart—it having taken off in a race the second she'd sunk her teeth into that bottom lip. Drawing a long, calming breath, I answer her honestly, "If you start calling me Master, I'll forbid everyone from doing it. I won't be able to hear it from anyone else." I never liked the members calling me that anyway.

She hums, moving around the desk and forcing me to turn my chair to follow her. Her ocean blue eyes drop to my pants, to the clear outline of my dick, then jump back to my face, her smirk curling wider. "You know...I've been meaning to tell you what Kell and I did the other day."

"And what might that be?"

"We saw you fighting everyone. Taking them all on in the gym."

"I didn't see you there."

"Mm...no. We were...*watching*...from the weight room."

I narrow my eyes. "Watching?"

She kneels, her hands sliding up my thighs while maintaining eye contact. "He fucked me while I enjoyed watching you," she admits, her tone challenging.

I lunge, gripping the hair at the back of her head and pulling her to me. "Are you telling me this to make me jealous?"

She rubs a hand along my length, and my fingers tighten, air sucking through gritted teeth. Her eyes light up, that taunting smirk bringing out the sharper, more controlling side of me. "Maybe. Maybe I've been a bad, bad girl."

The invisible thread on my self-control finally snaps. I undo my pants, freeing my cock while I hold her in place. "Yes, you have. And what do you think bad girls get?"

Raegan eyes my dick hungrily, licking her lips and making me so rigid it hurts. "Punishment?"

"Good girl. But first, you're going to suck me off and swallow every last drop of my cum, aren't you?"

"Yes, Master."

Fuck.

It's ruined. At least for every Guild member, because I only want to hear that word coming from her lips or not at all.

My cell phone rings, and I freeze. I realize then that I'm panting, my heart racing wildly while I'm knuckles deep at her scalp, her mouth held mere inches from the head of my cock. A quick glance shows Cibrina's name. She only calls me for timely things, then texts or meets me in person for the rest. With our recent luck, it could be yet another attack from Charles. "I have to take this."

A spark of something flashes in her gaze, but I grab the phone and answer it with a swipe. "Yes?"

Raegan doesn't wait. She grabs my dick and sucks so hard I go blind.

I slam my fist on my desk, clenching my teeth as if my life depends on it to keep any sound trapped while Cibrina talks in my ear.

Tightening my hand in Raegan's hair, I squeeze until she squirms, drawing her back with a silent snarl. She looks up at me through dark lashes, that challenging smile on her lips as she swirls her wicked tongue around my crown, over my slit.

It takes all the control I can muster to suppress the groan that sticks in my throat.

"...right now, but I let her know we usually schedule appointments for interviews..." Cibrina continues, completely oblivious to the war happening between Raegan and me over my dick.

I change tactics. Rather than fighting it, I lean into it, dragging her face over my cock until it strikes her throat. Her nails dig into my thighs, her eyes watering as I fuck her face. Just like she wanted. The pleasure is overwhelming, electrifying my body with so much ecstasy that every muscle tenses. I breathe through my nose, controlling my airflow as much as everything else while Cibrina continues to tell me about last-minute interviews that I sure as fuck am not attending to right now.

Raegan's hand disappears from my thigh. I switch to speaker-phone and drop it on the desk so I can snatch her hand when she tries to slide it between her thighs. I shake my head, *tsking* softly when I place it back on my thigh, then swipe my thumb through her tears and suck them off.

She moans, the sound escalating the pleasure but putting this moment at risk of discovery. I pinch her nose, cutting her off, then release it a second later before she chokes. Her eyes roll to the back of her head, and I just know she's getting off on this as much as I am. As long as she doesn't come. Not until I tell her to.

Holding her head still, I thrust into her mouth, bringing myself over the edge with the firm press of her lips and smooth glide of her tongue. My jaw nearly pops as I lock the groan of release in my chest, my hot cum emptying down her throat.

"...that brings us to two tomorrow, three on Friday, and then what do you want to do about the walk-in?"

Deep breath.

Raegan tries to pull off of me, but I hold her there while I answer. "I'm unavailable today, so schedule her with one of the others."

"Understood. And the matter with the referral?"

"Bring it to my desk in an hour. I want to think about it more before I make my decision."

"Of course. I'll see you then."

The call ends, and I free Raegan from my cock. Her blonde hair is a mess from where I'd held it, her lips red and swollen as I carve my thumb over it. "We'll consider that punishment for being impatient, but there's still the matter of you and Kell." Gripping her face, I kiss her, sweeping my tongue into her mouth like I'm claiming it as mine, demanding her submission as I own this, her, for the next hour.

"Yes...Sir..." she pants, her eyes blown with lust.

I lift her easily into my lap, maneuvering her to her front with her top half hanging over the arm of my chair and her ass seated perfectly over my leg. Tugging her pants and underwear down to her thighs, I slide a finger between her slit. She's soaked.

"Such a good girl," I purr, stroking her pussy. Brushing over her clit. Her body twitches at the contact. "Maybe I will let you come after your punishment. I should clean up the mess I made, shouldn't I?"

"Please," she rasps.

I'll need to make this quick before too much blood rushes to her head from this position. With that thought, I strike her ass, pink blooming over her skin where I struck in seconds. I rub it in firm strokes, then warm up her other cheek.

Slap! Caress. Spank! Rub.

Over and over again. She moans and cries out beneath me. She's leaking between her thighs, her arousal dripping to a wet patch on my slacks.

She takes two fingers in her cunt with ease. I pump them in and out, and she releases a garbled plea for more. I lick my fingers clean, groaning at her taste. I shove the papers on my desk to the floor, clearing that space and then laying her on it, length-wise.

Raegan moans, her hands going to her breasts as her hips grind on air and seek me out. I bring her to the edge of the desk, straight to my mouth. She's so wet. So drenched in arousal that I get to work on licking her clean. On taking her taste for myself, licking and sucking every bit of her. I love the way her body quivers and trembles when I hit a spot just right. How she writhes when it becomes too much, her thighs clamping around me as she rocks her needy pussy into my face. I stiffen my tongue, sinking it into her entrance, and she sobs, begging me to fuck her as her cunt clenches, trying to find something more.

I bring her to the brink again and again, waiting for the sign that she's about to break, then back off. Again. And again. Each time, I wonder if this punishment has been enough or if she can take one more.

At last, I stand without warning, driving my cock into her pussy hard and fast. It glides right in, and the second I strike the end of her, she detonates, screaming my name. Before her orgasm is finished, I slam into her in rough, wild strokes. Her body squeezes my dick, her inner walls fluttering already as I fuck her into my desk. I lift her thighs, her ass, giving myself a better angle as I thrust the full length of my cock into her repeatedly.

She feels like heaven. Like a drug I'll never get enough of. This is all I want, all I need. Her tight embrace on my dick, her screaming my name, and my name alone as I give us both the release we need.

Raegan shatters again, and this time, she brings me with her. I hilt myself one last time, groaning when I come, and her convulsing pussy sucks every last drop of cum from me. I fall over her, my forearms keeping myself from weighing on her as I catch my breath. I'm spent. Thoroughly and perfectly expended.

By the time she opens her eyes, I'm dressed and put back together again. I guide her underwear and pants back over her legs.

She looks to the papers and files littering the floor. "I'll help you clean up," she offers.

How I ever thought this woman could be anything other than the considerate, selfless person she is, is a fucking wonder. Denial in its truest form.

"No, I'll handle it."

Raegan's face falls as if that rejection was aimed at her rather than the task that I'd created for myself. If she asks, I'll admit that the clean-up effort will be worth every second I spent with her just now. "I guess I'll let you get back to work then," she remarks coolly, though I can see through it instantly. She stands from the desk, tugging on her shoes.

"I'm not going back to work yet." She frowns, giving me a questioning look. "We're returning to the Loft for a hot bath, where I'll massage the muscles that I worked up so much so you don't end up with muscle cramps." I pinch her face gently, drawing her lips to feather over mine. "I'm not finished with you, Raegan. Not in the slightest."

Work can wait another hour.

CHAPTER THIRTY-THREE

DANE

Watching the beach house every day is like watching paint dry. Nothing of interest happens here, at least on the first floor. We were only able to plant cameras outside and on the main level due to the creaking stairs that lead upstairs and to the basement.

If I didn't already suspect the Guild members being held in the basement for fuck-knows-why after hearing Charles make that comment about Vera hurting Tinsley here, I would now.

The only times I see Vera are when she comes and goes from the basement. Any time she's not down there, Holt remains within eyesight of the basement door as if he's waiting to shock the first person who tries escaping.

Sometimes, Tinsley is with her when she disappears through a portal, and I'm forced to wonder what the hell they're up to.

The one person I'm meant to watch the most is the worst of the bunch. He disappears at dusk before my shift ends and Reid's begins, and then returns before the sun is up. Reid says he goes straight upstairs, to sleep most likely, and so I spend most of my day waiting for the old geezer to wake up and come downstairs.

"Hey."

The sound of Raegan's voice snaps my head around on impulse to seek her out. She's wearing her workout pants, sports bra, and a loose tank top, with her hair tied back. She smiles at me, her eyes a clear ocean blue, and my heart somersaults in my chest.

"Morning," I respond with a smile, my hand finding hers and drawing her closer.

"How's your watch going so far?"

I started less than an hour ago, so Royce is still asleep on the second floor and Holt's preparing his breakfast within view of the basement door. "Dull, as usual." I tug her into my lap, wrap my arms around her waist, and bury my face into her neck to breathe in her warm vanilla and cinnamon scent.

She shivers when I trail my mouth along the arch of her shoulder, wiggling in my lap and inadvertently grinding against my excited dick. Slipping my thumb beneath her top, I stroke just above her hip, obsessed with the feel of her smooth skin and forever giddy when I get to touch her like this. When we're not wrapped up in the heat of the moment, but sitting together first thing in the morning.

"What can I make you for breakfast?" I ask, my lips tickling her flesh.

She grips my thigh in a failed attempt to restrain another shiver while leaning deeper into my touch. "Mm. Maybe after training."

"Coffee?"

"Please," she nearly begs on a breathless moan, and my dick throbs in response.

Fuck. I could probably come from that sound alone if she kept talking to me like that.

Lifting her in my arms, I stand and turn, sitting her in my computer chair and pressing my lips to hers in a brief kiss. "Coming right up." I spin the chair so she's facing the monitors. "Keep an eye on them for me?"

"Sure."

I already prepared a pot of coffee for the morning, so it only takes a couple minutes to prepare her a thermos of coffee to go.

"Awww," Kellan calls from the hallway before entering. "You make one for me, too?"

Scoffing, I shake my head and ignore him, handing the thermos to Raegan. "I put an ice cube in it, so it'll be easier to drink right away."

"Thank you." She waves at the screen while standing. "Nothing happening here other than Holt making a mess of the kitchen just to cook some eggs."

Jackson strolls from the hallway next as Kellan makes his coffee in the kitchen.

I plop back in my chair, checking the screen in a cursory glance before returning my gaze to Raegan. "I'll see you when you're back from training." I wave her and the others off, then focus back on the computer. I pull my Board member research up on another screen, getting to work on that as I wait.

Royce finally goes downstairs, alerting me easily by the sharp creak of the wood, making himself a slice of toast with jelly. His face twists as he takes in the result of Holt's cooking. "Clean this mess up. Now," he snaps, his usually droll voice sharpened with outrage.

The old man's anal about keeping the beach house clean and tidy.

A portal appears in the kitchen, and the girl controlling it steps through.

"I told you no portals in the house," Royce admonishes, stepping around it to leave the suddenly-tight kitchen.

The girl—Bea, Reid had called her—shrugs and smirks. "I forgot. I'm just here for a snack and then my portal and I will be gone." She rummages through the pantry, piling junk food into her arm. "See ya." She walks back through the portal, leaving the pantry door open wide with fallen goods on the floor, and it closes behind her.

"I'll be grateful to be rid of you both after our next assignment," Royce mutters drearily, walking slowly to his chair in the living space. "Clean up her mess as well."

This isn't the first time he's mentioned a "next assignment" as if they're all here waiting for Charles to give them the signal. They haven't said anything about *what* that assignment might be, though.

"I don't know why we're waiting. We should do it now," Holt grumbles, sweeping his arm over the counter to push everything on it into the waiting trash can.

"All of you are so impatient. The President would not have us wait unnecessarily. Besides, I have to curate more puppets after that feral girl destroyed everything I had. Do you understand how long it took me to gather so many? Decades, boy."

"I'm not waiting around here for decades, so hurry it up."

Royce clicks his tongue and eats his toast, not bothering with a reply.

Another hour passes. Royce's eyes are closed for most of that time, and I assume he's taking a nap.

At this rate, we'll just attack him when he's asleep. Morning seems to be the best time after he comes back from wherever he goes at night. Even mid-morning could work out while he's sleeping in the living room. Holt is the only obstacle we'd have to get through first, and somehow without waking Royce. As for Bea…she pops in and out at random times, but it almost *seems* like she's aware of the conversation that had been happening before she shows up as if on cue.

If she can see what's happening at the beach house, that'll be more difficult. She could send a swarm of GE agents at us if she finds us there.

While Royce is sleeping in his chair, Vera appears from a portal outside and stalks into the house.

"What's that?" Holt asks, eyes narrowed.

I follow his stare to an item in her hand. My lungs constrict.

It can't be.

"Are you an idiot? It's a notebook." She passes him to the basement door.

It's a black and white composition notebook. Just like the one I'd given her, filled with some of our old coded messages and then the letters I'd written her after she died. The one she'd left behind at Old Red.

"Why would you carry one of those around?" he asks suspiciously, and she pauses with her hand on the knob to glare over her shoulder at him.

"Why does anyone have a notebook? To take notes. Fuck, you're dumber than I gave you credit for." She opens the door and slams it closed behind her, and he scowls.

"Cunt." He whips out a cell phone and taps it a few times. A portal appears outside within a minute, and he storms from the beach house to leave through it.

I'm still reeling from the sight of my notebook in her hand. I know it's mine. Mine was filled to the brim, little colored papers sticking out of it, and worn or dried pages making them wrinkle and puff the notebook out.

Didn't Aiden say she was sneaking around Old Red the other day?

What if it was to get my notebook?

Why would she want it now? Because I'd saved her? She'd been *surprised* when I'd jumped in front of her.

As if I couldn't possibly care about her and Raegan simultaneously.

I thought she was lost to me.

She'd been twisted too much by GE, her morals skewed and her hate for Raegan giving me no other choice but to fight her as an enemy.

But what if she's changing? What if she's starting to break away from their influence? Why else would she have my notebook, unless she wants to try meeting me halfway?

Fuck.

Chapter Thirty-Four

RAEGAN

The next few days pass in a blur. I spend most of my time training with Kellan and Jackson, even after the mandatory Guild sessions have ended. I've never felt stronger or more confident in my gift as I do now. There are some limits to what I can test in the training gym, but I've handled the basic application of anything I try to do without difficulty.

I'm able to recognize when I'm stretching myself too thin, working my gift more than my body can handle, and I stop there. Kellan is the one who helps me in the weight room now that all of Dane's time is occupied with watching the beach house and investigating more Board members. When I'm not training, I usually try to help him with what he's doing. Watching the cameras is boring as hell, but I take note of every detail just in case.

After Reid takes over camera watch on his computer, Dane and I settle on the couch with a movie. We've fallen asleep every night this week without finishing a single one.

On the fourth night, Aiden joins us for dinner.

"I'm going in!"

"Wait! I'm not ready!"

"Rahhhh! Take that! Eat it!"

The door to Aiden's room slams open, and I startle on the couch. He's breathing heavily, his hair un-styled and wet, while his light gray shirt clings to his chest, dark spots appearing as it soaks up the water he didn't bother drying off. He immediately seeks me out, his unusually expressive concern fading to confusion. He takes in my shirt—his—and shorts, my hair tied up in a messy bun, as I sit cross-legged on the couch with a gaming controller in my hands.

"Watch out!" Kellan hollers.

There's a slew of zombies entering the room I'm in with no other exit. I start shooting wildly, sweeping my gun back and forth as they're seconds from grabbing me. "Shit! Shit! Shit!"

"I'm coming, beautiful."

"Use your grenade," Jack murmurs from his perch on the back of the couch.

"That's right!" Running to give myself a few seconds, I sift through my inventory, select the grenade, and chuck it at them. It explodes, body parts flinging in the air and splattering the screen in fake blood. Damn, this game is graphic.

"I don't know how you guys can play that game after the zombie attack we dealt with. Literally, *any* other game would have made more sense," Dane mutters from the kitchen. He convinced Reid to start earlier on his camera duties so he could finally make the homemade pasta he'd promised me what feels like forever ago.

When Aiden walked in, Kellan declared tonight a break for all of us. No GE. No Royce or beach house. No Board members or training.

Just the five of us relaxing together. We haven't done that in…a long time. Even with the Guild party, Jack and Aiden had been working and on guard. And any other times we've tried to relax, it's never been all five of us. Not since the island.

"Come on, Aiden. Grab a controller," Kellan shouts when he walks by the living area.

"I'll pass."

"Does Aiden play video games?" I ask distractedly, finishing off the last of the zombies with Kellan's help.

"Just strategic one-player types," Dane answers.

Kellan snorts. "He builds empires for fun."

"I've played other games with you before," Aiden remarks before he disappears down the hallway beyond the kitchen. There's nothing in that direction other than a storage closet and the armory. "Raegan," he calls, and I whip my head around.

Jackson chuckles. "Behind you."

What?

His gaze darts to the screen, and by the time I follow it, my avatar is already being devoured.

Damn.

Tossing the controller next to me, I hunt for Aiden. He stands in the doorway to the armory, his body blocking it from view. Footsteps thump behind me, and the other three guys all crowd at my back.

Okay…what?

"Uh...what's happening?"

"It's not finished yet, but I figured tonight was as good as any for you to see the progress we've made." Aiden steps back, the door falling open behind him and giving me room to look inside.

The lockers and cabinets that once covered the walls are gone, painted over in a dark, moody gray. One of the walls is gone, replaced by two glass doors surrounded by windows to overlook the city. A small, private balcony waits beyond the doors with a pergola strung with vines and fairy lights.

There's a small sitting area by the windows. A cozy circular chair that could fit multiple people sits in front of a small rectangular fireplace and television. The floor itself is covered in a plush, luxurious-looking carpet that begs to be touched.

The bed is...well, it's massive, taking up half of the room in its width. Four posts rise just shy of the ceiling, draped with creamy gauze sheets that fall like waves. Vines curl around the posts, intertwining with more fairy lights that hang like stars, surrounding a mountain of pillows.

There's a door to the far right that I don't remember being there before.

"That's where your private bathroom will be," Aiden says when he sees me looking at it. "It's still in the demolition and plumbing stages."

I scan the room again, stunned.

"It's beautiful," I breathe. Amazing. Stunning. Unbelievable. A simple room was somehow converted into a private oasis, unlike anything I could have ever imagined. "All this...is for me?"

"If you want it."

Scoffing, I shake my head. How could anyone *not* want something like this? "Can I go inside?"

Aiden steps further into the room, and I follow.

Bending to the floor, I run my hand through the carpet as I'd been itching to do. So, so soft.

"It's water-resistant and shouldn't stain easily," Aiden comments.

Kellan throws himself on the bed, arms and legs wide, and still, there's room on either side of him. "This is what I'm talking about for a bed. And it's hella comfortable."

Dane smacks his leg. "Get off before you break it."

Kell laughs, rolling to his side. "Didn't Aiden tell you? He custom-ordered this bad boy. For its size *and* durability. I could jump on it, and it wouldn't break. Isn't that right, Aiden?"

Aiden pins him with a look. "Don't jump on it."

I'd laugh if I wasn't so overwhelmed by everything. Running my hand along one of the posts, I dip over carved grooves. When I look at Aiden, his gaze is heated, and I swallow my question down, a flush of warmth crawling up my neck.

He shifts behind me, crooning in my ear, "There are more surprises in store for you here, but wait until it's finished before you start looking."

A shiver of pleasure rolls down my spine, goosebumps scattering along my skin.

"Fuck! The pasta!" Dane dashes from the room.

Jackson fingers a string of lights, smirking.

If I'm going to eat Dane's homemade pasta, I need to get out of this room. While it looks cozy and warm on the surface, it's equally sensual. And having Kellan, Jackson, and Aiden giving me individual licentious looks the longer I'm in here means I have seconds to escape while my mind's still clear.

I practically run from the room, and I don't stop until I'm in the kitchen.

Kellan cackles from the bedroom, but three sets of steps let me know they're leaving it.

"We scare you away, beautiful?" he taunts.

"Dinner's almost ready," I snark back, jabbing him in the chest. "I've been looking forward to this for a while."

Turning to Aiden, my nerves suddenly titter in my chest. I've never had anyone give me something so...*grand* as that. He could have thrown a bed in there and been done with it, and I would have been happy. But the *detail*, the *beauty* of it...

"Thank you," I whisper, my voice choking in my throat. "I...I don't even know what to say. It's amazing. More than perfect."

He smirks, crooking his finger beneath my chin. "Don't go painting me as some nice guy in your head. It's a bribe to convince you to stay with us. I'll give you whatever you want, whatever you need, if it means you'll stay."

"I'm not staying for the stuff."

"Then consider it a bonus."

A soft moan coaxes me from sleep. Dane's breath is hot on my ear, his arm a heavy weight over me. He grinds his hard dick against my ass, then tucks my body tighter against him, as if there might be any room to spare with how he's already curled around me like a second skin.

I'm expecting his hands to rove or him to say something, but he stills after that, his breathing deep and even.

A slow smile curves my lips.

He's sleep-humping me.

Another noise escapes his throat. His arms squeeze around me, and he rubs his cock into me again, moaning in my ear.

Fuck.

That sound is my undoing.

It sends a wildfire of heat through me, burning away any fragments of sleep. I don't need to touch my needy cunt to know it's already wet. Already throbbing with an ache to be filled. I return the favor, rolling my hips to brush against him when he's stopped.

I want to remove my stupid underwear. I want to reach behind me and free his cock from his briefs so I can feel its heat pressing against me. I want to rub my pussy all over his dick until I can't take it anymore.

But I can't.

Biting my lip, I withhold the tiny scream of frustration. I'm trapped. What was once enough to turn me on is now what's holding me back from any sort of relief.

This time, when he grinds against me, I meet him with greater desperation, shifting my hips and ass as much as I'm able to. That wicked, drawn-out groan pours through his lips again, driving me mad.

"Dane...*Dane*..."

His breathing pauses, then rushes out at once on a low chuckle. "You humping me in my sleep, babe?"

I don't stop moving against him, waiting for the moment he gives me room to shift. "You started it," I pant, growing impatient. When he doesn't *immediately* take his dick out, I groan. "Touch me already, dammit! Give me something."

Dane laughs again, his lips brushing the crook of my neck. Pleasure scatters over my skin like goosebumps. "Something? I can give you something."

Fuck, this isn't fair. He started it, and I'm the one begging now.

I strain against his arms, fighting for wiggle room. He moves behind me, and I freeze when I realize he's removing his underwear.

Yes!

He strips mine next, then tests two fingers at my core. "Fuck, you're so wet. What do you need, babe? My mouth? My fingers? My dick?"

All of it.

Everything.

I push on his fingers, on the closest thing to giving me relief. "Any of those. Just..." His dick glides between my folds, collecting my arousal as I hold my breath and grind against him. He doesn't need more than a few strokes before he's covered.

Dane hikes my leg further over his, positioning his tip at my entrance, and then pushes inside.

All the air releases from my lungs.

Yes. Finally.

…until I realize he hasn't moved from there.

He kisses the back of my shoulder, his hand unhurried as it finds my breast. Circles my nipple. Flicks it.

My cunt pulses in reaction. Clenches, when his fingers pinch and tug on the hardened point.

"Nngh…Dane. Please." I grab his thigh and rock into him, but his dick is fully seated in me, and the motion doesn't give me anything. I tighten my grip, trying again unsuccessfully, if only because at least I'm *trying* and might win a smidge of movement.

"I'll take care of you, I promise." He presses another kiss to my shoulder. And another. Moving in a slow trail toward my neck. The soft touches shoot tingles of pleasure in short bursts through me, collecting and pooling at my core. I writhe against him.

He finally reaches the back of my neck, where he's pulled my hair to the side to grant him that hidden bit of skin, and I think he'll finally give me what I need. But then his hand slides from my front. He traces a shape the length of my back and returns to the top.

My scars.

It's easier to forget them when I'm covered. When I can pretend they aren't there because no one else can see them.

I still as he continues to touch them, to outline their long, ugly shape until he's done all of them.

Dane kisses between my shoulder blades.

"I'll never be able to make up to you all you've done for me," he whispers so quietly I have to hold my breath to hear him. "I owe you my life, over and over again. I owe you for all the shit things I said and did to you. I owe you everything." He turns my face, leaning over me so our eyes lock together. "Whatever you want, Rae. Anything. If I can do it, I'll do it for you. If you want my life, you can have it. It's yours. I'd be dead already if not for you."

I open my mouth, but no words come out.

"I love you, Raegan. I may not be able to make it all up to you before I die, but I'm going to spend the rest of my life trying."

His lips find mine, warm and pressing, and the feeling behind it surges in my chest. We kiss until my neck burns from the angle. We kiss until we shift with him on top, our lips and bodies breaking apart for a breathless second before we're joined again.

And when his hips finally begin to move, it's the sweetest ecstasy.

I bury my hands in his hair, my hips syncing with his so we're moving as one. It feels so good, this mounting pleasure that curls in my spine. He thrusts in short, measured bursts that hit just right, like sparks from two objects struck together until they burst into a flame.

He sucks on my neck. My chest. Draws my nipple between his teeth, and an electric current of pleasure strikes my core. My hips stutter out of rhythm, the pleasure breaking my concentration.

Dane hooks my leg up and slams in deep, and I curse at the impact. Pleasure rolls through me in waves each time he buries himself in my cunt. He thrusts wildly, chasing my orgasm until it finally caves to him, bows and snaps from his voracity, then strips me bare.

Shuddering through the last of my climax, I catch my breath and slowly open my eyes. Dane tosses his phone to the floor.

"What was that?"

He grins, leaning in for a kiss that I warily relent to. "Something for you," he answers mysteriously. He tucks himself around me, then flips us around with me on top. "Ride me, babe." He grips my thighs and pushes his hands up, then drags them back down. "I know you want more. Take it."

Hm.

I close my eyes, getting back into it as I work my hips. He holds my calves down, giving me a firm anchor to push off from, and I lose myself to it.

Until something cold lands on my ass, flowing in a stream between my cheeks.

Dane's smirking when my eyes snap open on a gasp.

Aiden's behind me, smearing lube over my ass with his fingers. His dark eyes lock on to mine. "Are you ready for me to take your ass?" He rings my hole with a finger, and I inhale sharply, gripping the sheets as my entire body tenses. Aiden clicks his tongue. "You need to relax."

"Easy for you to say," I snark, and he spanks me.

"Oh, fuck!" Dane groans when I clench around his dick. I sink onto Dane's chest, my arms shaking from holding myself up while Aiden rubs at my other entrance again.

"Any other thoughts you'd like to share?" Aiden purrs.

Dane lifts my face to his. "I've got you, babe. Just focus on me." He kisses my jaw. The corner of my lips. Then grips the back of my head to pull me into a deep kiss that makes my chest ache. He gyrates his hips beneath me, teasing me slowly until I melt into his arms.

Something small breaches my ass, but it's slathered in lube and doesn't go further than my body allows it. My body tingles where my ass circles whatever's there—his finger, no doubt—and I breathe through the nerves. I've handled fingers before. This, I can do. It's what he's promised is coming that has me on high alert.

I'm snapped back to Dane when he teases my clit with slippery fingers. It's so smooth, so wet that my body instantly trembles from his touch, and I'm so focused on riding his fingers that I don't even notice Aiden's sunk another finger into me.

"Oh, yeah. Fuuuuuck," I moan, rocking into each of them.

"Good girl. That's what I like to hear."

"That's it, babe. Take what you need."

I push back against Aiden's fingers. Onto Dane's dick. Taking them as Dane's fingers swirl and rub my clit into a frenzy.

The fingers disappear, and something larger, wider breaches my core.

I falter, even though my body quivers with pleasure at the pressure there. I know what's coming. I know he's much larger than his fingers.

Dane flicks my clit, snapping my attention back to him. "Look at me. Feel me." He rolls his hips, his cock thrusting into me as he refreshes the lube on his fingers and soaks my pussy in it. "Focus on this. What does your body want?"

Ugh, *yes*. I moan so loud it vibrates through me. I undulate my hips, taking the pleasure he's offering me and losing myself to it. He keeps talking, encouraging me to take it. Take everything.

Even when I feel the crown of Aiden's dick pushing inside, I'm so turned on, so wet and in need of that orgasm, that I let him.

"Just like that. Good girl, taking me so well. You're going to take all of me, aren't you? This greedy body of yours wants all its holes filled, doesn't it? Who should we call to fuck your mouth next?"

Dane and I groan in unison, the feel of his dick slowly working its way inside, sending both of us to ecstasy.

"Is that what you want? All four of us around you, worshipping your body?" Aiden hisses as he slides in the last inch. "Mm, your ass feels so fucking good. I knew you could do it." He doesn't move once he's in, the three of us panting as we all adjust to the new sensations. "Fuck her, Dane." He dips his other hand through the excess lube and takes over, rubbing and circling my clit as Dane grips my hips and fucks me. Aiden barely grinds his hips, rubbing his dick against my inner walls, and it's over.

Pleasure explodes through me, every nerve-ending shattering as I scream and fall to pieces.

Dane catches me when I drop, wrung dry and stripped of anything but the racing beat of my heart and the warm cocoon of bliss surrounding me.

Chapter Thirty-Five

KELLAN

Throwing the door to Aiden's office open, I barge inside. "Lunch is ready. Let's go."

He glances at me for half a second, then returns to flipping through papers on his desk. "A phone call would have sufficed," he replies distractedly. "I won't be making lunch today."

I cross my arms, and a challenging grin splits my face. "I'm also here to make sure your stubborn ass gets upstairs by any means necessary."

Aiden ignores me, his mind too engrossed in whatever he's doing. That's the worrying part. He's been busy before. He told us what Charles has been up to with trying to tarnish the Guild's name and going after members to scare them from working at all anymore. Then there's the tax audit that's taken up so much of his and Cibrina's time. They'd both been digging for old returns and receipts and coordinating information between the Guild's current accountant and the one Thorne thankfully had when he'd been in charge.

But he'd turned that information over a few days ago. We thought he'd have a small reprieve after that, but we've still hardly seen him. It's been a week since he joined us for dinner. We're all worried about him and what else he's been dealing with that he hasn't told us about.

I slam my hands on his desk, catching and closing his current file. "Family meeting, Aiden. Upstairs. Now," I growl.

"Later, Kell. I don't have time—"

"Make time. This is us, Aiden. Drop the hero complex of carrying the goddamn world on your shoulders and tell us what the hell is going on. It's clearly more than what you've told us, and I'm sure Daddy Psycho is behind it."

"I'm not trying to keep it from you," Aiden snaps, which goes to show how frazzled he is for him to lose his composure. "I'm trying to get ahead of it all before it gets out of control. Once I have that, I can take a break and fill you in."

At this rate, Charles is going to break us before we've even raised another fist against them.

"I'm not here to argue or reason with you," I drawl, standing and taking the file with me. "That would have been Dane or Raegan. If you don't get up in two seconds, I'm going to throw you over my shoulder like I do Raegan and make sure the Guild Hall gets a good look before delivering you to the Loft."

Aiden glares at me. "You're a real prick in my ass, Kellan."

I bow mockingly. "At your service."

He stands and stalks around the desk, snatching the file from my hand but proceeding from the room to the elevator. I follow him like a guard on his heels to make sure he reaches his destination without interference. We don't say another word to each other the whole ride up and into the Loft.

The others look up from the table when we enter, Raegan and Dane both appearing relieved and Jackson looking like...well, Jackson.

Aiden drops the file on the table and sits in his seat where a sandwich is ready for him.

"Eat." I jab my finger at his lunch and then take my seat opposite his.

He sighs, caving to a single bite and swallowing before diving right in. "Our offshore bank account with most of our funds is frozen pending an investigation. With fewer jobs available and some members too freaked out to go on any, more than half of them have missed their last rent payment. We're running on whatever we have in our domestic account, but with the money we've needed to counter Charles's other attacks and no real income coming in for the Guild, it's quickly being eaten away. I'm going through our assets to sell what we can and don't need, but that's only a short-term fix."

Dane curses. "I can try to find money elsewhere. Go back to some of the high-paying jobs on the dark web."

"What happens if we run out of money?" Raegan asks.

"If we can't pay our utilities, then those will go first. No water, no heat, and no electricity or power. None of that means no cooking and no food for our members, who already can't afford food because they aren't making any money," Aiden answers after finishing another bite.

Raegan chews on her lip. "You told me Elias owns the Tower?"

She waits for his confirming nod. "He wouldn't kick us out if we don't make a lease payment or two. Maybe he can help us with the utilities, too, so we can focus on buying food."

Relying on Elias Thorton is the *last* thing Aiden would want to do. I'm surprised when he doesn't immediately dismiss it out of pride.

"That's something I've already considered if it gets down to that. The most recent mess is the criminal investigation that's been launched into the disappearance and possible murder of Thorne...with me as the prime suspect."

"What?!" I demand, hitting my fist into the table at the same time as Dane exclaims, "How?"

"Charles sent Thorne's thumbs to Detective Unger with an anonymous tip that I killed him for the Guild."

"Oh, fuck," Raegan breathes, her hand flying to her mouth.

Dane scrubs his hand through his hair. "That bastard...how the fuck are we supposed to fight him if we're too busy defending ourselves from everything else he's throwing at us?"

"That's the point," Aiden replies, leaning back in his chair and ignoring the rest of his sandwich. "He's trying to wear me down so we can't interfere with whatever he's working on."

"It's working," Jackson comments, head tilted as he regards Aiden, who frowns at him.

"Yes, I'm aware." Returning his gaze to the rest of us, Aiden continues, "I've been trying to put metaphorical tape on each issue as it arises, thinking there might be an end for us to make our move, but Charles clearly has no intention of slowing down these attacks."

I squeeze my fist, eager to aim it at GE. "So, we fight. Aiden gets a good night's sleep, and then we move on to Royce. We have the most intel on him."

"I know he's on the kill list, but does killing him help Aiden at all?" Raegan questions.

Aiden shakes his head. "No. But it's a step closer to defeating GE. We can use all the progress we can get."

"Holt and the portal girl have been around the necro's beach house pretty often," Dane muses. "We might be able to get those three out in one shot. Then it's just the Board members, elects, and Charles."

That doesn't seem so bad.

Aiden's phone rings, halting the conversation. His expression darkens when he stares at the screen. "Charles," he answers, tapping the speaker button so we can all hear.

"Ah, I'm glad I caught you during such a busy time. How are you holding up?"

I grind my teeth with the effort to keep my mouth shut, wishing for the second time I could wrap my hands around his throat to stop him from talking.

"I know you're calling for more than checking on the baseless accusations made against me and the Guild," Aiden states.

Charles chuckles. "Oh, how could I have forgotten about those. No, no. I figured you might be in mourning."

I freeze, my chest growing tight.

No...

"Maybe that's a bit presumptuous of me, expecting you to care about one of your precious members," he goes on, and the silence at the table is deafening.

"Who?" Aiden asks, his voice tight.

"You don't know?" The asshole feigns surprise and concern, then *tsks*. "In your own home, too. Didn't you realize you're not the only one with invisible allies?"

Jackson and I stand in unison, our chairs screeching back. A breeze sweeps through the room, and the scattered origami animals Jack leaves everywhere fly on it like invisible detectors. I instantly move to Raegan's side, helping her out of her seat and putting her behind me.

"Dane, take my hand," she says, reaching for him. He accepts it and stands beside her while I press a hand against her hip behind me.

We watch the paper animals sailing through the Loft, waiting to see if one of them will bump into something midair.

Aiden grabs the phone as Charles continues to talk. "Or, *were*, I should say."

"Harvey," Raegan gasps behind me.

"Loft's clear," Jackson reports after checking the other rooms.

"Dane," Aiden commands after tapping his phone to mute it.

Dane nods, rushing to his computer and pulling up the cameras we'd installed in Harvey's locked down apartment. Raegan follows him, moving her hand to his shoulder so she keeps contact with him and I do the same with her at her back. The apartment appears on the screen. Everything looks normal at first, and then the feed flips. I grip Raegan's hip when I feel her body tremble.

There's blood all over the living room as if there'd been a struggle. It's sprayed on one wall, then a bloody trail on the carpet leads to the kitchen. And a pool of blood.

But no body.

"Where is he?" Aiden demands.

"Dead, as all traitors should be, don't you agree? Harvey lied to me. He shared Royce's location after daring to eavesdrop on me. I gave him the opportunity to prove to me he could be trusted with that information; of course, I knew he and my other son were in the room. I've been around invisible gifted enough times to spot the signs. I prepared Royce just in case, and unfortunately, I was right not to trust him. Now, he'll be handed over to Royce for a second chance at redemption."

He pauses, but we're all too stunned to say anything. "Let this be a warning, Guild Master, of what I'm capable of. You'd do well to reconsider my offer before I lose my patience."

A television screen mounted to the wall in Aiden's office displays twenty-one boxes of different views and angles of the beach house from the area around it to various rooms on the first floor.

"When was the last time you saw Royce?" Aiden asks Dane.

"Just before I made lunch. The old geezer went upstairs to take a nap."

Which means we've lost any eyes on him. The stairs creak louder than a haunted house in winter. Aiden and the others hadn't been able to place any cameras up there.

"So, we're killing him in his sleep?" Reid inquires, his tone flat. As soon as Charles hung up, Aiden called Reid to tell him about Harvey, had us get ready for a fight, and we gathered in his office.

Jackson shrugs, flipping a throwing star between his knuckles. "I'll do it."

"What about the others?" Aiden prompts, his gaze glued to the screen.

Dane crosses his arms, his own stare skipping between the different camera angles. "Holt left on an errand just before we came down here. He's usually not gone long whenever he does leave. The portal girl—"

"Bea," Reid supplies as a reminder, and Dane nods in acknowledgment.

"She left this morning and hasn't been back since. A portal appeared for Holt outside when he left, but it vanished as soon as he walked through it."

"After Royce, she's our biggest problem." Aiden turns around to face us. "She can bring in other agents at will, shifting the numbers against us. Or she could disappear and force us to take time hunting her down. If you see her, take her out as quickly as possible."

"I'll do a fast sweep of the house and everyone's positions when we arrive," Reid offers. "If she's there somewhere, I'll fight her. Our gifts are similar, so it'll be better if it's me."

I check on Raegan, who's been quiet since finding out about Harvey. She stares resolutely at her palm, flexing her hand before dragging her gaze up and finding mine. I angle my body in front of hers to give us privacy from everyone except Jackson, who stands at her side. "You okay, beautiful?"

She nods, pressing her lips into a firm line. "Yeah. I'm ready to take down Royce. And Holt and Bea if they're there. But now I want to get Harvey's body back, too, before Royce fucks with it. He doesn't deserve being forced back under GE's control again. I won't let them do that to him."

"*We* won't," I agree, letting the anger at his death burn and pump in my chest. We were supposed to protect him from GE, and not only did Charles kill him anyway, but he did it right under our noses, sneaking into the Tower with one of Harvey's own siblings to murder him. It was a power move by Charles to prove that none of us are safe while he's alive.

We can't wait until the perfect opportunity to act anymore.

It's time to make our move.

Aiden has Cibrina putting the Tower on lockdown while we're gone; no one in or out until we've returned.

"Our focus is on Royce," Aiden reminds us as I face the group again. "No hesitation, no holding back. If you hit him, make it count."

Uncrossing my arms, I flex my hands in preparation.

Jackson whispers in Raegan's ear. She nods, and—as if she ignited some internal lantern—reddish light glows softly wherever her skin is exposed. Her hand grasps his hoodie, and he grabs Reid's arm. Aiden, Dane, and I follow suit, and then we're gone.

We appear outside of the beach house in the sandy grass...right as Holt joins us from a portal with Harvey's body in his arms. He halts, confusion tightening his face for a split second before he drops Harvey and raises his hand.

Reid vanishes.

Raegan's gift spiders through the ground.

Lightning flashes.

This is the man who stopped us from saving Raegan. The one who held us prisoner while Gordon took her from us. The one who *tortured* my girl while she was "training."

Whatever scraps of information she gave any one of us about her time with Gordon, we've worked to piece together between the four of us. Holt has been the easiest for her to talk about, so we know the most about him. About how he'd laugh at her pain. Smile at the threat to that little girl's life. Strike her down when she was already weak.

The moment I see him, my blood roars. My chest fills with heat, and red clouds my vision. I widen my stance, flex my arm, and feel the rolling shudder of scales over my skin.

Before Raegan's gift reaches his feet, lightning strikes. Her gift stops where it is but doesn't diminish.

The electric current skates over me, dancing along my scales and into the dirt without so much as a tickle.

But Holt isn't looking at me. He's watching her and her gift that creeps toward him. He fists his hand, another strike joining the first and slamming into her.

The last time he did that to me, it seized my heart and lungs.

Run.

I reach him in seconds, too fast for him to realize I'm not trapped by him or to do anything to stop me before my fist smashes into his face and sends him flying.

The others drop to their knees when the lightning clears, but I keep at him, stalking his fallen body and grabbing him by the throat. He grabs my arm, jabbing his elbow into it to break my hold and meeting hard scales instead. His feet kick out, unashamedly aiming between my legs like a coward. And I let him. I let him see how unaffected I am by all of it. I let him struggle and fight, and I watch the realization and dread sink in with a savage grin.

Lightning hits me. Scatters. Its brilliance is blinding against the gold, and Holt is forced to look away from me.

He tries again.

And again, his fist clenching, arm bulging and shaking with the strain as he throws everything he has at me.

Sweat slides like subconscious tears down his face.

"P-please. I did what he told me to. It wasn't me!"

My rage swells at the fucking lie. His eyes widen fearfully at whatever he sees on my face, and he chokes when my grip twitches involuntarily.

"This is going to be a fucking pleasure."

When I toss him to the ground, he cries, *begs* for mercy, and it only feeds the fury coursing through my veins. At the fucking *balls* he has to ask for compassion when he'd shown none of that to and for my girl. At his cowardice by hiding behind Gordon for his actions.

He *laughed* at her pain.

He didn't hesitate to make things worse for her.

I won't hesitate to do the same to him.

He fights me when I straddle his chest, swinging his fists and trying to twist and escape. All wasted effort. I reel the scales and my gift back from my fists.

To make this last.

My first strike knocks his head to the side.

He starts screaming, flailing beneath me, and I hit his other cheek. Back. And forth. Right. Left. All my anger gathers in my fists, and I let them fly. The rage in my chest pumps out in rhythmic pulses, sending it to my hands as I mete out justice. As I give him what he deserves for laying a *finger* on my girl.

I wipe any chance of a smug smile off his face when I break his jaw.

I make him *bleed* when his nose crunches beneath my knuckles.

My body is moving on its own, wrath piloting every punch, every jab. I can't see anything in front of me anymore. Just red. Blood. Her. The pain in her eyes that she tries to hide. The vibrant red of her gift. That beautiful, deadly gift that has the power to destroy the world if she wished it.

"That's enough."

Someone catches my wrist. Snarling, I rip my arm free and turn on them.

"Unless you're trying to take his death away from her, stop."

Those words make me pause. Make me blink back the red haze until the bloody mess of Holt's face appears. Chest heaving, I stare at the disfigured and broken face, worried I'd killed him too soon. His chest rises imperceptibly. It's enough.

Standing, I nod once in gratitude to Aiden for stopping me, then grab Holt by his short hair and drag him across the ground. He doesn't fight it. Doesn't move at all. Just releases a high-pitched noise of pain as his body scrapes over the rocky sand and intermittent tufts of grass.

I dump him at her feet.

Chapter Thirty-Six

RAEGAN

Holt lands in a hard *thud* before me. Sand clings to the blood on his face like an ugly mask. Spittle drools from the corner of his lips, his ragged breath stirring the dirt.

The others move around him like wolves forming a predatory circle. He wouldn't be able to escape even if he wasn't so injured. They watch him; watch me like they're bearing witness to my vengeance.

Sinking to my knees, I bend so he can see my face, poking his arm and sending a single thread of my gift into him. "Are you still alive, Sparky?"

He screams, and the pungent smell of electricity saturates the air.

Kellan snarls and presses his boot over Holt's neck. "Touch my girl again, and I'll rip your body apart while you're still breathing."

Holt whimpers. The impending lightning clears, and Kell withdraws. "I s-soh-ee," he cries pitifully, unable to form the words with how his jaw is now angled. "Do'n kill ee."

"No?" I arch a brow, amazed he thinks so highly of me to let him live after what he helped put me through. After he held a six-year-old girl, pleading with him to let her go while a gun was pointed at her.

"H-heese. I soh-ee," he continues to sob, his words becoming more difficult to understand.

I tap my finger against his arm again, but I keep my gift from spreading to him so he can hear me. "You know...I didn't get the satisfaction of killing Gordon myself. I have over a year of trauma I'd hoped to take out on him. It looks like I'll have to settle with you."

He begs more. Crying and pleading with me for mercy, but all I can see is Mallory doing the same to him. And the cruel smile he'd worn for her.

"When I was spent...or in pain...when I needed someone most...you were there to inflict more pain. To smirk down on me like you thought you were somehow better than me. But you were the fool for not seeing what I was capable of. For believing Gordon would always be around to protect you. And I'm sure you remember...Gordon taught me that I'm a monster. I'm *dangerous*."

I lick my suddenly dry lips. Take that moment to feel the adrenaline pumping through my veins, my heart galloping wildly. I continue, my voice cold and apathetic, "He was right. I'd have no problem attacking every individual muscle in your body one at a time and drawing out your pain. I could have you healed, like Gordon did for me, giving you relief and hope that it's over, only to start from the beginning and put you through it all again. You'd deserve nothing less."

Holt sobs uncontrollably.

It doesn't make me feel any better.

"Luckily for you, my demons don't control me. I control them.

And you're not worth bringing back for a long torture." My gift pierces his skin. He chokes, shrieks. I spread it everywhere, invading his body like webs of disaster until I've got it all in my grasp. "Goodbye, Holt."

His body ruptures in an instant, spraying me with his blood before collapsing in a broken heap.

It's faster than the deaths I'd given to the innocent victims Gordon brought me. I could have held back, could have drawn it out to imitate my inexperience and let him feel everything that the others had, but for all that I said to him, I'm not one for torture.

I'd rather be done with it and move on.

Reid hasn't returned.

It could mean he ran into trouble with Royce or Bea if she returned. Or he rushed to look for Tinsley without waiting for backup.

Dusting off my pants while standing, I survey the beach house. There's no noise, no sign of activity or a fight from here.

"What are we doing with him?" Dane kicks sand at what remains of Holt's body. It lifts a few inches from the ground.

"I'll toss him in the sea." Jackson's deep blue gaze captures mine as if waiting for my approval first.

Aiden rubs the light scruff on his jaw. "With any luck, Royce won't find him, or the water will destroy enough of him to make him useless."

I nod absently, no longer worried about Holt, zombie or not. "I'm going to check on Reid." Everything is quiet as we approach the door and my gut twists. Surely, we should hear *something* if Reid is inside.

The door is still locked when I try turning it. Aiden takes the knob next, metal clicking inside to shift at his silent command. He opens the door and takes the lead, Dane hot on my heels and Kellan behind him.

For a house belonging to a necromancer, it's creepily bright inside. White shiplap walls, kitschy beach décor, and painted wicker furniture in the sitting room just past the foyer.

Aiden stops, halting the rest of us as he points to Kellan and Dane and the basement. He looks at me and circles his finger. We'll be checking this floor. Once these floors are cleared, we'll all head upstairs to Royce. Nodding, I stay on his heels, watching his back and our sides as we move from room to room. There are muffled sounds coming from the basement but there's nothing on the main floor.

We pause at the entryway to the kitchen, Aiden peering in first before he goes in. Empty.

The larger living area is just as clean and tidy, just as empty, as the rest of the floor. I walk along the wall, inspecting the pictures of sand dollars and starfish. Maybe Royce killed the original owner of this home and didn't bother updating it to his tastes. I remember what Reid said about a dead wife. Maybe she decorated the home if this belonged to them. A line in the shiplap makes me pause, fingering the vertical separation that seems like a misstep in the design.

The wall swings inward, and a hand grabs the front of my shirt, yanking me inside.

I open my mouth to yell, but a hand slaps over it. "Shh!" a voice hisses. "I just want to talk." Blinking in the dim lighting of the tiny room I'm now in, I find Vera.

And Tinsley.

The latter makes me pause. Vera stands in front of me with her hands raised and empty. "See? No weapons." She turns her back to me so I can see her shorts and shirt appear clear, then faces me again.

"It's okay," Tinsley urges, her hands in a placating gesture. "Hear her out."

I look her over, searching for any sign of injury. "Are you okay? We heard she"—I indicate Vera— "was torturing you. Reid was freaking out."

"I'm fine. That was just her cover for us being together so much."

"Why? What have you been doing here?"

"Raegan? Raegan!" Aiden shouts.

The wall I'd come through is closed again; only the thin line of natural light outlines the panel I must have come through. "We can talk out there. I don't want them to worry something's happened to me."

Vera shakes her head. "What I have to say is just for you. Give me two minutes, and you can go on your merry way."

Aiden keeps calling my name, and my chest tightens. I don't want to make him or the others worry again. Pounding steps join Aiden, and I can hear Kellan and Dane looking for me now, too. Fuck.

"Hurry up."

"Royce and Charles made me program a machine that can synthesize Dane's blood with material objects and into serums without me. And before you say anything, I didn't have a choice. He's already had me make thousands of these things over the years, but with this machine, they'll be able to mass produce them at a crazy rate. Without me. I won't be able to stop it or slow it down."

"Why do you care? I thought this was what you wanted."

"Because of what it means for my brother!" she snaps. "The weekly blood draws had been enough to sustain what Charles wanted for the last five years. I thought—when they got him back—he'd just have to go through weekly draws again. But with this machine and what I've seen them starting to do..." She fists her hands. "The amount of blood that's going to be needed to keep up with that machine...he'll be tied to it for the rest of his life. They'd drain him and have to pump him with more blood, waiting for his cells to take over, and then drain him again on an endless cycle."

My blood chills, and a heavy weight sinks into the pit of my stomach.

No. I won't let that happen to him.

Vera's face looks pained as she grips at her chest. "When I was ordered to make that machine, I started getting nervous about what they were doing. I tried to stall for time, but Royce *made* me do it. I was afraid for Dane and got Tinsley to help be my alibi so I could make something for him."

"In exchange for her protection of the other captured Guild members," Tinsley adds with a smile.

Vera continues, "I wasn't able to test it, and I have no idea if it works, but if it does, it'll block Royce's gift from him."

"That thing you stuck him with?" I clarify, and she nods.

"It was hard enough getting what I needed for one with Tinsley's help, so there won't be another." She takes a shuddering breath, her eyes closing to compose herself for whatever she's planning to say next. "After Dane protected me from those knives—when I thought he'd already abandoned me like Charles said—and seeing what they're doing with that new machine, I started to question *everything*. I found his notebook and finally read it. I know..."

She swallows, slowing her words. "I know I messed up on the island. I didn't think Dane was in any danger. Gordon...he promised me he would be fine and I believed him. I loved him. I just wanted to impress him. I'd recently figured out how to synthesize gifts into objects, and he'd been so *happy* with me. I didn't want to disappoint him."

My stomach churns at the familiar words. Making him happy. Not disappointing him. Fuck...how long had he manipulated her? How young had she been when it started?

Softer, she continues, "I never fit in with you guys, you know? I wanted to. You and Dane wanted me to, but it just...it didn't work. I wanted to fit in somewhere. To have friends so close you called them family like Dane did. And I thought...I thought Gordon and GE were giving me that. They made me feel special, as if I was one of a kind. They *needed* me to better the world. Yes, some people got hurt along the way but it was for the greater good of our kind. But now I know they were just using me."

Vera pins me with her amber stare, her voice hardening. "They've been making more than collars and bands, Rae. They're weaponizing Dane's gift and others' gifts. They'll be able to overpower every gifted person in the world within a matter of months if you don't stop them."

"Why me?"

"Because I've spent the last couple of weeks studying your gift, and I know what it can do. Tinsley and I destroyed what we could find of your blood before GE fed it into my machine, but not before I analyzed it."

Tinsley chimes in, "I helped get rid of as many blood samples as I could before they locked away the rest."

Banging hits the panel. "Raegan?" Jack. He found me, which means we're out of time.

"I'm okay!" I yell so they don't panic.

"I don't want to hurt Dane anymore. I need to end this before they force me to build any more of those machines or weapons. I need *you* to do it," Vera urges.

I step back. "What? Is this some sick ruse to try and make Dane hate me? I'm not killing you again. I won't do that to him."

"You've done it before to protect him, and I know you can do it again. Kill Royce, and I'll finally be free of this miserable half-life I've been living. You're going to do it anyway. I'm just telling you that it has to be you."

"But you gave Dane that serum against Royce."

She nods. "Dane's the only one who can stop him, but I know he won't deal the final blow. He'll hesitate. Now that I know he still cares about me, I'm sure of it. There's no way he'll finish him. You have to. The second Dane gives you that opening, take it before Royce escapes."

A blade stabs through the center of the panel, then morphs into a grappling hook and slams back. The wood snaps and splinters as it breaks in half.

Vera grabs my arm to regain my attention. "The Guild is under attack. Royce is calling me there. Don't fuck this up." She turns to Tinsley. "Get me past them to the portal outside. Our deal's over after that."

Tinsley nods, offering her back for Vera to climb on.

"Raegan!" Kellan booms, bursting through the broken wood to make more room. As soon as he passes through and leaves a large enough hole, Tinsley and Vera speed off. Kell whips around when he sees it.

"Let them go," I say before he or the others try to chase after them.

Kellan yanks me into his arms, swallowing me within his beast form. "Are you hurt?" he demands.

I rest my hand on the back of his arm, feeling the smooth scales there and finding comfort in his embrace after all the information Vera shared. "No." I take a deep breath to calm the racing thoughts so I can focus on the most important and timely one. "We have to get back to the Guild. Was Royce upstairs?"

Kellan helps me through the wreckage to the living room and the others. "No. Upstairs was empty."

Before I'm completely clear of the hole in the wall, Aiden pulls me to his chest, his heart galloping frantically against my ear. "Leash," he mutters, reminding me of what he'd said in the hospital room.

Smiling, I withdraw and bump into another body directly behind mine. Jackson wraps his hand around the front of my neck, holding me tight against him while his thumb angles my chin up to look at him. His midnight blue gaze pierces mine, and a cool shiver snakes through me.

"I'm sorry," I breathlessly offer. To him. To all of them for making them worry.

Dane grabs my hand, stroking my wrist softly. "I'm glad you're okay."

Jack releases me, and I shift so I can see everyone.

"Reid found the five hostage Guild members in the basement. I guess Tinsley was with you," Aiden fills me in. "He's dropping them and Harvey's body off at the Guild and he'll be right back. What happened?"

"Vera was filling me in on what GE's been working on and what she and Tinsley have been doing. But we can talk about that later. She said that Royce is attacking the Guild and he was calling her there."

Reid appears suddenly behind Dane. "There's trouble at the Guild. I dropped them off in the infirmary, but there are zombies and agents flooding the Hall."

Tinsley zips into the room and crashes into him, taking them to the ground. "Reid!"

"Tinsley!"

He grabs the back of her head and pulls her into a kiss. She moans unashamedly, and Dane snaps, "Save the make-out session for after we defeat the zombies and Royce."

Tinsley pops back, beaming at Reid and then helping him to his feet. She latches on to his arm and whispers something in his ear, drawing a small smile to his lips.

"I thought I destroyed all his zombies." When I look at Jack, he nods once and strides outside. I follow him, the others doing the same, until we're standing on the edge of the cliff overlooking the beach where the zombie caves had been.

Three portals line the beach, and zombies pile into them. I bring my gift back, flexing my hand as it tingles beneath my skin. "Jack, get me down there. I'll take care of them." I have no idea how many already made it through, but I can cut them off here.

He kneels before me, and I climb on his back.

"Reid, bring us down, too," Aiden orders. "We're returning to the Guild together."

Reid frowns. "We should head back now to help."

"I'm not risking the two of them alone in case Royce is waiting around to turn them on each other. The Guild can hold their own until we get there. It's what we've been training for."

He's right. We need to trust that the Guild is fighting back.

Jackson jumps over open air, guiding our descent toward the caves and portals. "Where do you want to be?"

"Between two of the portals."

He swings his arm out before we land, a blast of air throwing the zombies back. As soon as his feet touch the ground, I drop and thrust my gift into the sand. I channel my gift, the beach fissuring and glowing red within those cracks as they spread beneath the mass of zombies before us. I latch it onto their feet, immobilizing them as I work further back. All the way to the caves and then spidering my gift along the cliffside.

"Don't overdo it," Aiden warns from the side.

I don't make a move to acknowledge him, but I hear him. There's still a fight happening at the Guild, and if I overexert myself here, I won't be able to help there.

Once I've outlined the framework of my attack, I trigger it, releasing the burst of my gift to flood the zombies and the rocky cliff.

The beach trembles. Stone snaps. Pops. The first opening in the cliff caves in, stone separating and falling inward. Then, the next one and the next, a domino effect of cave-ins that bury the dead and block their escape.

I pump one last burst through my gift, making sure the zombies on the beach are unable to move. Unless Royce returns to fill them with more souls and heal them, they won't be going anywhere.

The rockslide is over, and the cliffside on this cutout of the beach looks more like a steep, slanted slide of rocks now.

I keep my gift active and at the ready. Dane shifts to my side. "What else did Vera say?"

"That you're the only one who can stop Royce."

"How?"

"That thing she injected you with." I squeeze his hand and look at him. "She also read your notebook. I think...she's realized her mistakes with you. But—"

"Raegan. Dane," Aiden calls to us. "Let's go."

"Through the portal or teleporting?" Kell questions.

"All of us through the same portal to conserve Reid's strength." Aiden motions us to the one he's in front of, then takes my other hand. "Now."

CHAPTER THIRTY-SEVEN

DANE

I'M NOT GONNA LIE. I'm distracted when we walk through the portal. Hearing that my sister *did* read my notebook, that she's coming around...hope burrows involuntarily into my chest. What if she broke through the brainwashing? Is there a way to save her still? She gave me something to protect me from Royce, but what about herself? Did she figure out a way to separate herself so his death doesn't affect her, if it even would? What if she plans to join us after we deal with Royce?

A rush of exhilaration floods through me as my thoughts spiral. If she's switching sides now, why did she leave? Why did she tell Raegan and not me? Does she still have to play her part for Royce until we stop him?

Shouts and screams break my train of thought in time for me to realize a table is flying straight for us as we're exiting the portal. Raegan rips her hand from mine, jumping forward with her hand outstretched. It disintegrates at her touch, and its ashes float toward us instead.

Fuck me, this woman.

She crouches to the hardwood floor, aiming her gift beneath the swarm of zombies. Our members are fighting back, hacking away at them with their gifts or weapons, but the dead don't stop. Raegan curses when something flies across her view.

"What's wrong?" Pulling the gun from my holster, I flank her to guard her back and side. Aiden, Jackson, Reid, and Tinsley have joined the members in their fight, taking on the GE agents in the room while Raegan, Kellan, and I handle the puppets.

"There's too much movement. I'm trying to tag just the zombies, but I can't tell who's who with my gift. I have to see them."

"Cast a smaller net," Kellan suggests, and she nods, reeling her gift back to the area nearest us where she can clearly identify the ones to attack.

The zombies collapse to the ground while the Guild members look around with surprise.

"Go!" I bark, snapping them out of their stupor to get back to the fight.

Once Rae's incapacitated the current group enough that they won't be able to hurt anyone else, we move further in for her to repeat her steps with the next batch. As she's working, fog creeps over the floor from the other side of the hall.

"Kell..." I warn.

"I see it," he growls, searching over the chaos for its source.

"One of us has to take them out so she can see."

"We're not leaving her. We'll have to count on Aiden or Jackson handling it."

Fuck. What if they can't get away to do it?

The fog builds faster than any natural occurrence, thickening and expanding to our knees in seconds.

Rae finishes the batch of zombies and stares worriedly at the fog that's now reached our hips. "We'll go find the fog user together, then. I can't use my gift anymore without risking Guild members."

Kellan nods, and we head in that direction.

Only problem is, there's a mass of zombies and fights happening between us and the other side.

Kellan shoves the zombies away, and Rae uses her gift on any that are in her way one at a time. I shoot the ones that get close to me or her, then switch to trying to knock them down with my fist instead. My bullets are wasted on them when they don't feel pain, but knocking them away to give us time to keep moving is the best I can do right now.

Before we know it, the fog's everywhere, coating the main hall in a thick blanket of shit visibility.

We're sitting ducks now.

Shoving my gun away—I'm more at risk of shooting a friend by accident in this fog—I realize that I'm suddenly alone. "Kellan? Rae?"

Fuck. Where did they go?

A shadow grows in the fog. "Kell?"

There's a low groan as my only warning before a zombie slams into me, knocking me off my feet. "Fuck!" It gnashes wildly at my face, and I smash the heel of my hand into its chin. I push my other hand behind it for added strength when its crazed movements threaten my hold. One slip and those teeth are going to bite my face off.

Its bony, unwashed fingers scratch and claw at my skin and clothes, but I'm too fucked by his teeth to do anything about it. The smell curdles in my gut, acid crawling up my throat as I choke on the smell of death and brine.

And then it's gone.

Kellan tears the zombie's head off, dropping the disgusting thing at his feet and right-the-fuck next to me. I simultaneously roll away from it and to my feet, swallowing the bile back down.

"You couldn't have thrown that thing *anywhere* else?" I demand as Raegan runs to us. I made it out with mostly mild scratches and a deeper one that I pray won't wind up with an infection based on what caused it.

Kell eyes the fog like he's waiting for the next zombie to launch itself at us. "And possibly throw it at an ally?"

"Do you guys smell that?" Raegan asks, her face scrunching with distaste.

"You mean the dead guys?" I question, but she shakes her head.

"No, it's...something sweet."

Kellan slaps a hand over her mouth and nose. "Don't breathe it in, beautiful. Dane, use your shirt."

A breeze sweeps around us in a tight circle, clearing the fog momentarily as Aiden and Jackson join us. "Sleeping gas," Jack murmurs.

"Is it the fog?" Rae's muffled voice sounds from behind Kell's hand.

"No. It's coming from the air vents and hanging around our ankles."

"I haven't found the fog user. Jack's going to clear it from above while I block the vents. You three need to find and stop whoever's controlling it," Aiden commands, and I bite my tongue from adding the small detail where we're also dodging zombies and fighting other GE agents. He hands Jackson a thick piece of metal with a stubbed point.

Jack whips another vortex of wind around us before he leaves, and the wider dispersal of fog exposes GE agents lining the walls of the main hall. To avoid the fog and gas? I'm about to tell the others when my gaze catches.

Vera.

She, like the other agents, is shooting what looks like darts at Guild members. We're fucking fish in a barrel as they drop one member after another.

"Dane, let's go!" Raegan grabs my arm, pulling me back into the thick fog.

I yank my shirt over my nose and mouth for whatever fucking good it'll do and jog with her and Kellan as they push through the zombies in our path. "I didn't see any fog by the walls!" I shout, dodging a flying body part and then kicking a zombie. "We've gotta watch out for tranq darts, too. They're picking us off one by one."

Kellan curses. "Get between me and Raegan! Those won't affect us."

Shit. He has a point. With their gifts, *I'm* the weakest link.

Fuck.

Why couldn't I have a cool gift? Why'd I get stuck with something that I can't really use to help my friends, help *her*, and has only put us more in danger than anything?

Somehow, we make it to the bar on the other side of the hall just before the kitchens. The fog is thicker here. So thick it clogs my lungs, making me choke out of fear that the gas is in it. Where are those fucking vents in this room anyway?

"I think I see someone!" Rae whispers as we creep around the bar, using our hands as our guides.

"Make sure it's an agent before using your gift," Kell reminds her, and she nods.

We get closer, but it's too difficult to make anyone out unless we're as close together as the three of us are. She reaches her arm into the mist, half of it disappearing until all we can see is the dim red glow of her gift. Raegan drags it closer, then shrieks when the zombie she's holding snaps his teeth and pounces.

Her gift activates instantly, but Kellan doesn't wait for her to finish before he dismembers it. He grunts when a zombie flies at him, its mouth wide over his arm as it tries to bite down but skates over hard scales instead. And then another hits him. And another. They fly at Raegan too, like we've run into a fucking nest of them as they climb over them both and start reaching for me.

"Aaaangh!" Raegan yells, the weight of them pushing her down while her gift doesn't work fast enough to drop them.

Kellan's equally buried as they cling to him like spiders.

One of them grabs my hair, and another, my elbow. "Ahh, fuckers!" I shove and try to knock them down, but they keep coming.

"Dammit! Dane, run! Find and kill that fucking fog person so we can see." Kellan is brought to the floor, and he takes a final gasp on his way down. The zombies might not get him, but the gas could.

Raegan throws herself over the zombies on Kellan, her gift eating away at the ones between them and on her back. "Go! We've got this. And don't you fucking dare let them get you, Dane," she adds.

I dash through the fog, grabbing my gun and running blindly. I know the bar where we'd been, so I can picture the room in my mind, guessing where I am and where I can reach the perimeter of the room where I'm hoping the fog isn't. I think the zombies are just as blind as we are. As long as I don't make a loud noise or run into them, I'm able to pass right by. The ones I do knock into, I spin and dodge out of the way, then keep going.

The fog thins, and I gasp when I can see the job boards and hallway. Someone is crouched there, their hand on the ground and fog pumping steadily from it.

Found you.

Staying within the edge of the fog, I aim and fire. The agent falls.

The fog doesn't immediately dissipate as I'd hoped.

Glass shattering draws my attention to the ceiling, where Jackson's just broken one of the hexagonal windows overhead on the far side of the hall. His arm beckons the fog to him, pulling it out the opening when he's suddenly knocked down, disappearing into the fog.

Thorne dives in after him.

Fuck. Zombies, Vera, sleeping gas, *and* Thorne? Can it get much worse?

The fog continues to filter out of the hole Jack created, and it spreads more evenly across the room now that its user isn't controlling it, making it thin enough that I can see the others again. Raegan and Kellan are almost done taking care of the mass of zombies we'd had, and Aiden's applying metal on one side of the room to a vent. Thorne is throwing his attacks at Jack as if there's no one else in the room, furniture flying and sharp winds hitting others in their path. Jackson tries to deflect them where there are no Guild members or at agents and zombies instead.

Tinsley is speeding around the perimeter, knocking agents off their feet, while Reid appears behind them to take them out. Evie and Silas are still fighting, but Fabian, Gabe, and Zedd are lying on the ground.

"Everyone...*stop*," a droll voice declares, and cold fingers trail down my spine.

I've been listening to that voice through the computer, but hearing it in person is a different experience that makes my skin crawl.

The terrifying thing is...everyone in the room goes still except for agents, who continue firing darts at Guild members who don't even try to dodge or counterattack. The darts hit them while they do nothing, and then they drop...breathing in the gas-filled air along the floor.

Jackson crashes to the ground, his body frozen mid-motion in whatever attack he'd been about to create. Aiden's stiff by the vent he thankfully finished covering. And Raegan and Kellan...the zombies around them are down, but more are heading their way.

But me...I can move.

Royce.

My eyes find Vera's. She mouths something to me that I can't make out. This is it, isn't it? Whatever she'd stuck me with, it worked.

I can take down Royce.

The necromancer surveys the room, and my muscles lock on instinct. I barely breathe, too scared he'll somehow notice I'm not under his control and take me out before I can do anything. But he passes right by me without noticing me at all, then pauses near Jackson. "Ah, I remember you. You'll do well." He raises a hand, and Jackson stands, his movements stilted.

Fuck. I need to get to Royce without being seen. The fog is still around, still obscuring the view through the room slightly, but is it enough?

Sliding my foot to the side, I creep toward the bar while Royce is focused on Jack, and the agents are busy going after the members in the middle of the room. Once I'm close enough, I dive behind it, my heart jackhammering so loud I'm waiting for a zombie or agent to hear it and give me up.

Shit. Shit. Shit.

The others don't have time for me to sit here and get my shit together. It looked like Royce turned everyone's gifts off, including Rae and Kell who are now vulnerable to the zombies or darts. And Aiden's closer to the ground. Has the gas risen at all, or is he close enough that it might get in his lungs?

Peeking around the bar, I quickly calculate my route. There are plenty of overturned tables, benches, and chairs I can use for cover with the help of the remaining fog. I just have to get close enough to take the shot where I know I won't miss.

Deep breath.

Go!

Keeping myself hunched and low, I race to the first table. Then the next. Another one. Fuck, this room never felt so big before as it does now. I make it to the next one, then freeze when a zombie catches me, moaning and stumbling in my direction. A quick glance around the table tells me I'm not close enough yet.

At least the thing moves slowly, but how long until someone notices it's following someone?

Gritting my teeth, I push on to the next two. The first zombie picks up a following of others staggering toward me. When I check on Royce, he's frowning at them.

I can't sit here and wait for him to discover me, but if I move, I'm sure he'll notice me. My palms are sweaty, even as cold as I fucking feel, and I take turns wiping them on my jeans as I catch my breath, chest tight. After several gasping breaths, I dart to the next table then stumble when Royce looks directly at me. His brows pinch with confusion.

Fuck, it's now or never.

I'm not as close as I'd hoped to be, but I can already see Thorne and Jackson flying toward me in my periphery. It strikes me as I raise my gun that I might kill my sister with this, and I hesitate. Fuck. I knew we were going to take down Royce. I've known all this time, but now that the moment is here and it's up to me, I don't know if I can pull the trigger.

Get it together. They're all counting on you. Rae *is counting on you.*

The zombies were getting closer to her and Kellan. I would never forgive myself if she got hurt again because of me. I swore to protect her from now on.

I'm sorry, Vera.

I take a deep breath. Then fire twice on my exhale, the gun clicking empty on the third trigger.

Royce somehow dodges my headshot, but the second bullet catches his shoulder. He grabs at it with a scream and drops to his knees.

Jackson immediately attacks Thorne, interrupting his strike on me. Thank fuck. The zombies all trip and falter, and the Guild members start fighting the GE agents. Vera lowers her gun, her expression pleading as she looks at me. No...*past* me.

I follow her gaze to Raegan, whose hand is already planted on the floor. Red cracks split the hardwood. But it's not the zombies around her that she's aiming for. She sends it past them across the length of the main hall. I track it to Royce, and realize I have seconds to make it to Vera.

I race to her. Vera smiles, and this time, I'm close enough to read her lips. *"Goodbye."*

"Wait!" I shout, my heart pounding in my chest.

Royce screams.

Vera shudders, her eyes closing and face tight as if she's in pain. Her knees bend, and I dive to catch her.

"Vera! I've got you. I'm here." I pull her onto my lap, fear shaking my hands and voice.

"Dane." Her eyes slowly open. She reaches for my cheek, and I grab her hand, pressing it to my face. "I'm sorry I wasn't a better sister to you."

"It's not your fault," I rush out, squeezing her hand. "I should've protected you on the island. I should have noticed—should have been there for you more—" My throat clogs, all the words I want to say choking me until I can hardly breathe.

Vera shudders again, her face pinching, and I whip my gaze to Royce. He's still screaming on his knees, his skin split and bleeding as he clutches his body. The zombies are all twitching on the floor. And Thorne...Jackson's taking care of Thorne no matter how this ends.

"Don't cry," Vera whispers, and I realize my face is soaked. "You're always so emotional," she chastises, her voice weakening. "This is what I want. Don't make a big deal out of it."

I hold her to my chest as thick tears fall uninhibited. *This* is my sister. The one I'd been fighting to find. Did she break through only for us to kill her?

She grips my shirt as I hold her. As I sob over her. My body shakes as I gasp for air, my lungs squeezed in an angry fist. "I'm sorry I wasn't able to save you. I'm so fucking sorry." Her hand slumps between us. "*No!*" I choke, rocking her in my arms. "Vera!"

I bury my face into her and let the tears fall as all the memories of the first time she'd died come rushing back in a flood. That same hole in my chest aches and burns. It knocks the air from my lungs as the world spins around me.

I couldn't save her.

I failed.

"What have we here?" Charles casually inquires, and what breath was left in me expires.

I force myself to look up, to lift my heavy head to confirm what I don't want to believe is true. That Charles Whitmore, the president of GE, is here.

He smiles at Royce's defeated form on the ground. "Good things never last, do they?"

Remembering the last time when he'd snatched me out of nowhere, I activate my gift, keeping myself carefully still and hoping he doesn't notice where I am. I'm a fucking wreck right now, my body still trembling and weak, and my heart crushed in a vise. I can't win against him if he tries to take me, but I'll still fight as hard as I fucking can.

Kellan steps in front of Rae, and Jackson drops to her other side. Aiden shifts between them and Charles protectively. "What do you want, Charles? Your men were no match for the Guild. I think it's clear we won this one."

Charles cants his head, eyebrow raised. "Did you, now?" He disappears.

And reappears behind me.

Fuck.

He reaches for me, but I grab his arm first, smothering his gifts with mine before he snatches my hair. He wrenches my head back, and I grunt at the shooting pain in my scalp. Charles laughs when he sees my face. "I'd call this a win for me, if I do say so myself."

"Dane!"

I can't look at Rae or the others with his death grip, and I refuse to release my hold on him to let him take me away. I can hear them running, hear them getting closer. I just have to not let go.

He yanks on my wrist, then knocks his fist at the crook of my arm to break my grip. "Kill him! Now!" I yell at the others. I've got his gifts contained. Kellan's gift. He can die right now.

Charles tuts, jerking me between him and the others as a shield. He drags me away, and Vera's body thuds to the floor. I inhale sharply, anger surging in my chest. I dig my heels in, fighting his grip, his movements, but he's inhumanely strong. Even as Jackson throws knives at him, finding their marks in his face, his arms, Charles keeps moving to the nearest portal while he can't teleport.

And then we're gone.

Chapter Thirty-Eight

RAEGAN

"Dane!" I scream again, charging forward as the portal swallows him and Charles, then fades. "Reid!" Whirling around, the others are already surrounding me when Reid appears where the portal was. He gives me his hand, and once I'm sure the others are all attached too, I nod sharply that we're ready.

The beach is empty when we arrive.

No. No. No!

"That was the portal we went through. It should have brought them right here," Reid remarks, almost defensively.

Did he manage to break Dane's hold on him and teleport them?

My heart gallops, nerves tingling with adrenaline and fear as I try to think of where he could be. He's not getting away with Dane.

Jackson cocks his head as if listening to something only he can hear. Immediately, I lock on to him. "I hear him." His gaze swings upward to the top of the cliff. "Up there."

Reid sticks his hand out again. "Everyone, hold on."

The world tilts again, my tolerance of these jumps thinning after so many in one day, and then we're in front of the beach house.

Dane chucks a handful of rocky sand at Charles—the knives gone from his face and Kell's gift active where they'd been—but the sand and Dane bounce back as if something repelled them. Reid vanishes again just as a woman struts from the beach house, and Dane stands.

Reid teleports next to Dane and grabs him.

"Not so fast," the female sings. Vibrant red nails sharpened to a point on slender fingers wrap the side of Reid's neck and dig in.

Reid's jaw tenses, the only indication of pain, before his eyes widen. And then, nothing. His surprised expression doesn't clear. His body rigidly holds its position even as Dane struggles in his grip.

The woman laughs behind the back of her hand, then wraps her arm around Dane. "Looks like I caught two for one."

I drop to my knees, slapping my hand down, and snarl, "Hands off!" My gift shoots into the ground. It cracks and splinters in a jagged line toward her.

She dodges to the side, then shrieks when it follows her.

Gunfire pops like fireworks behind us.

I whip my head to look over my shoulder. Countless bullets slow their trajectory toward Aiden, Jack, and Kell. Six...eight—no, ten goons are spread out behind us as if they'd been waiting, their guns aimed at the guys.

Jackson tosses his hand at them, and the bullets fly back to the group.

Charles laughs. "I knew you wouldn't be far behind. I'm glad you've joined us. We can end this little game of back and forth once and for all."

"Split them up! And don't waste your bullets on those two!" one of the goons orders, jabbing a finger at Jack and Kellan.

The GE president looks to the woman with sharp nails. "Bring Dane and my son inside until this business is finished."

Kellan lets out a roar, running to the other side in seconds and distracting them long enough that he barrels into Dane, grabbing him, and then jumping onto the collapsed cliff. He works his way down the rockslide, adding distance between us until we can get Reid back.

"After them!" the agent who spoke up last time demands. Four of the goons race to follow, but Aiden and Jackson stop two of them.

Charles takes a call, turning sideways to focus on it even as fighting breaks out. The nail lady and another agent grab Reid, dragging him toward the beach house.

"Jack! Get Reid." Aiden slashes his arm in a diagonal, and his whip sword catches in a viscous substance.

"Go after the other two," the guy fighting Aiden tells the rest, and they run toward the rockslide.

"Hey!" I shout, pressing both hands to the sand and releasing my gift at them. One of them jumps in front of the others and stomps a boot to the ground. The earth caves in a perfect circle, taking my gift with it. They're after Kellan and Dane before I can send another attack.

Dane!

I shove back to my feet and leap over the hole.

"Raegan!"

I hear Aiden calling for me, but I can't let them get away to go after Dane. Seeing the guy who'd disrupted my gift the last time, I run and jump at him. He'll ruin any chance I have at getting the others from a distance, so he's the first to go.

He dodges to the side, but I'm used to chasing Kellan around a training room and pivoting as soon as I land to try again. The agent stamps his boot again. The ground quakes, then breaks inward to form another hole.

Right where I'm about to land.

I fall through the gap, and my chest and head hit the rocky terrain. Pain rings in my ears as I gasp for breath. I claw at the rough sand, my fingers sliding and offering me nothing to help me pull myself out of this pit. Screams fill the air, and I jerk my head up, wincing at the resounding throb when I do it.

Aiden's fighting the others back in front of me. I use the time he's given me to army crawl my way out with an exhausting heave of energy. Aiden slashes across the group once more, then spins to me. He brushes hair from my temple, inspecting something there with lips turned down. "Don't leave my side again."

"I'm fine. We can't let them get Dane."

He picks a clump of—is it wax?—off his sword and tosses it. "You can take the three on the left, and I'll get the three on the right. Let's push them in the other direction to add some distance. But if they try to go around us to get down there, don't chase after them without me. We'll go together."

Nodding, I fill my body with my gift. "Got it." I take off to the three I've been tasked with, using my gift in the ground to chase and herd them away from the sunken cliff as Aiden instructed. I keep my attention on the guy who can deflect my ground-based attacks, jumping over or dodging his pits and sending a new burst of my gift at them, forcing him to run as well when he can't keep up.

He turns down the headland, the long and narrow stretch of land that cuts into the sea. Is he trying to corner himself? The goon stamps his foot, then jumps into his own pit.

What the—

I'm kicked forward, and I stumble toward the pit as someone screams behind me. My balance and the ocean breeze fuck with me, not helping in the least as I drop to my knees at the edge, my upper half still falling. I grab the edge of the hole, digging my nails into the unforgiving earth and gritting my teeth. Whoever was behind me is still screaming. That's what they get for touching me while my gift is active.

The dirt disintegrates a little beneath my hands.

Fuck. Focus.

I use my grip to push myself back, throwing my weight in the other direction until I fall away from it.

Too fucking close.

The same guy is clutching his foot, his boot already gone. My heart's pounding a mile a minute as I catch my breath from almost falling into his pit. But he's in reach. I grab his arm and light him up with my gift, finishing the kill in seconds.

A gunshot fires. It's so loud, so close, that I think I go deaf from its echo in my ears.

I look up and find Aiden standing in front of me, blocking my view of where the gunfire came from.

"Aiden, what—"

Another shot rings in my ears.

Aiden's body jerks.

Once.

Twice.

Three times.

Four.

He falls.

I dive to catch him, my arm slipping beneath him at the last second before he hits the ground.

His eyes are closed.

No.

I shake him. "Aiden. *Aiden.*" My chest constricts tight enough to hurt. To make breathing sharp and cutting.

No, no, no!

This isn't real. This isn't happening.

He was just here. Ordering me around.

Pulling my hand free, I stare at the crimson color staining it. My world narrows to that vibrant, glistening shade.

"I promise, we'll be old and gray one day."

He can't be gone that fast. He wouldn't give up. He wouldn't lose.

"I've never seen anything, anyone, and felt even a sliver of what I feel when I look at you, Raegan."

I reach for his face with a shaking hand, spreading his blood on his cheek as I try to tell myself he's only been knocked unconscious. He isn't *gone.*

"I'll give you whatever you want, whatever you need, if it means you'll stay."

"Aiden. Wake up. I...I need your help." My voice cracks, and tears swim in my vision, distorting his face until all I see is red from the blood soaking his shirt. I angrily blink them away, pushing them free to track down my face. Anything, so long as I can see the moment his eyes finally open. "Get up!"

"No matter what happens, the five of us will prevail. I swear this to you, Raegan, on Gordon's corpse."

"You swore we'd all make it through this! You *swore* it!"

I smack his chest. Shove him. I don't care if it hurts him if it means it'll wake him up.

"Because for as long as we've known one another, I've wanted you. I've loved you."

The world spins around me, pressure weighing on my chest the longer he doesn't move. The more blood stains his shirt.

"You are my everything."

"Please!" I beg, tears choking me as I grip his shirt with all of my strength, refusing to let him go. "I love you, Aiden. I need you. The Guild needs you. We all need you so much. So, *please*...wake up." I sob into his chest, and the smell of copper rather than cinnamon fills my lungs.

A scuffing noise snaps my head up. Charles smiles. "I think I've had my fill of your pain. It was exceptional."

There's a gun in his hand.

"You. *You* did this?!" I demand, my grief twisting to something dark and ugly.

"Come, now. Don't look at me like that. Casualties are inevitable in war. You killed my ally, and I've killed yours. It's fair, don't you think?" The bastard pauses as if I might actually respond to that, then continues when I don't, "In any case, you shouldn't let your emotions get the better of you. We're still in the middle of a fight. Here."

Aiden's ripped from my arms.

I gasp, and Charles flicks his wrist just as quickly. Aiden is thrown past the cliff, out to sea so far that he's barely a black speck before Charles releases him to the ocean.

"Now you can focus again. Let's end this, shall we?"

My mind blanks. Checks out.

Even if there'd still been a chance...

If I'd had any inkling of hope before...

My blood boils, seething through my veins as I release a scream of violence and pain.

Of death and destruction.

My gift surges through me, lighting my veins in fire until there's nothing left but it and the wrath that feeds it.

I launch myself at him, throwing my body into him and knocking us both down as I scream and rage and lose myself.

I let my gift explode through me. To use my body as a vessel as it unleashes itself unchecked.

I want to reduce him to ash. To nothing.

It feels like lava's flowing through me, filling me up with scorching heat, but I don't feel pain from it.

It's nothing compared to the agony in my chest.

The headland is dust when Charles's body hits it, my gift skating over his burnt scales and to the ground beneath him. We fall to the sea, but I don't care about any of it. Charles is laughing, his arms wide as he doesn't even try to stop me.

The ground rushes toward us, and we crash into it, but still, my gift burns and disintegrates. The water's not there, held back by some invisible force as the ground craters underneath with us at its epicenter. I throw everything I have at him.

My gift.

My soul.

My fury.

My screams.

My tears.

All of it.

I've passed my limit, but none of that matters.

Aiden's dead.

"Is this all you have?" Charles shouts. "It's a beautiful display, but not enough to beat me, I'm afraid." He grabs my wrists. "I'm going to take Dane now and kill the rest of your friends. You should thank me for a poetic ending. I'll let you die in the same watery grave as your lover."

No. No. Beat him! I have to win!

He palms my face. "Sleep."

My gift dies, and I hear the sound of rushing water just before darkness claims me.

To Be Continued in Raegan of Ruin Book 5

Thank you for reading Remnants.
Please consider leaving your review.

Want access to bonus content?

Flip ahead to the Newsletter page to sign up!

Want to receive a bonus scene?

Or maybe stay up to date on the newest releases?

How about early access to ARC or giveaway opportunities?

Sign up for A. L. Rook's newsletter to stay in the know of all things Rook's books.

Scan or click the QR code below, or go to the website to sign up

@

www.alrookauthor.com

Join the A. L. Rook Reader Group on Facebook

The Rookery

@

www.facebook.com/groups/rookery

Or scan the QR code below

STALKING LINKS

amazon.com/stores/author/B0CYQJ2GWL

facebook.com/groups/rookery

instagram.com/alrookauthor

tiktok.com/@alrookauthor

WEBSITE: https://www.alrookauthor.com

NEWSLETTER: https://subscribepage.io/rooknewsletter

SPOTIFY: https://open.spotify.com/user/31g47djeh3oqclz7y
yaag2hwvtom?si=ca7e308dc7ec4b2c

FB PAGE: https://www.facebook.com/61557109453545/

ABOUT THE AUTHOR

A.L. Rook is an avid reader and has been dreaming of becoming an author since the first grade. She's been thinking up and writing stories ever since. Her favorite stories are dark contemporary or fantasy romance with strong characters that leave a lasting impression. When not drinking exorbitant amounts of coffee while writing, she can be found reading, binge-watching various shows, or traveling.

If you want to stay up to date on release dates, news, or for a chance at extra teasers and giveaways, follow Rook on her socials and join her newsletter.